# MINE

MMF BISEXUAL MENAGE ROMANCE

CHLOE LYNN ELLIS

**Mine**

1

CATE

*I'm here. I'm back.* It's all I can think as I look out the window and take in the Boston cityscape. The cab driver has been chatting wildly this whole time, and I'm doing my best to keep up with him and be polite, but there's just so much to take in. The hustle, the noise, the oddly winding streets. There's no place like it in the world. I can't help but roll down my window and bask in it a little.

The cab driver deftly navigates the Chinatown and Theater District streets, surrounded by impossibly tall buildings and thick with the morning smell of cars, commuters, and all that coffee. The breeze is still chilly for April, and it kisses my skin in a way that brings a smile to my face. It's all so overwhelming at first, but it only takes a moment for me to realize that my smile has turned into a full-on, ear-to-ear grin.

We finally emerge onto the Boston Common, and it feels like the one place where the entire city opens itself wide. Whereas everywhere else in Boston is almost fortress-like with its tall buildings, the Common is just a huge expanse of green. Paths snake through the gentle hills and valleys of the park, full of people walking their pets, heading to work, or just enjoying the sights as they sit on the green.

The scene is hypnotic to all my senses. I've been here a hundred times, a *thousand* times, but it has never felt quite as alive as it does now.

"All set, doll," the cabbie tells me as he slides into a narrow spot on the shoulder. I can't help but beam at him as I pull the fare out of my purse, along with a generous tip. *I'm here,* I think again. *I'm back.*

I step out of the cab and stretch my legs for the first time since boarding the train in New York. The vigor continues to course through every part of me, furious and uncontrollable. This is what it feels like to be free.

It's the first time I've felt like this in my entire life.

I spend another moment just enjoying the scene, then I grab my bag from the trunk and find myself casually slipping in with the rest of the pedestrians filing dutifully along to their jobs. Moments later, I spot Aw, Beans!, my favorite local coffee shop. It isn't long before I'm holding my first cup of hot Boston coffee, sinking into a well-loved leather armchair while the aroma winds around me like a promise. I close my eyes for what feels like the first time in forever and gradually let my heartbeat slow down.

In the last couple of weeks, I had dealt with losing my client, losing my boyfriend, and losing my grandfather. The client, a staple of the culinary reality show circuit, is a very exacting man with no tolerance for failure. Even knowing his reputation, though, I hadn't been afraid of working with him. In fact, he'd been so completely open about who he was and what he wanted that I'd developed an extremely good idea of what he'd love to see in his new penthouse. I had spent countless hours working up the designs, specifications, color swatches, motifs—the works. It had been exciting to try and match his wants with my designs, and I'd known deep in my bones that I was on the right track.

Of course, all of it went right out the window the moment my mother, Julianne MacMillan, got her hands on it.

My mother carries herself like a queen around everyone in her life, and most especially anyone working at MacMillan Design, her own personal Queendom. It didn't matter that I was her daughter; that day—the day scheduled for my final presentation to the client—I was just another employee to her. I'd watched with a sick, resigned feeling in my gut as she'd almost gleefully torn apart all of my work and replaced it with her own ideas.

A feeling that was all too familiar after a lifetime of being Julianne MacMillan's daughter.

Mother takes pride in her forceful personality, and there's no denying that it has won her many clients in the past, all of whom are utterly convinced that she's God's gift to the apartments of the New York elite. This time, though—between my mother and the client, two huge personalities who were both equally adamant that their opinion was the right one—I'd known that trying to steamroll him was a bad call for her to make.

I hadn't been able to stop her from making it, though.

The fallout had been spectacular. We'd lost him, of course, and according to her, I was to blame; had I just gotten it right the first time and sold the client on her vision, neither the blow to MacMillan Design's bottom line nor to its reputation would ever have happened. I'd taken the scolding like I took everything else in my life: eyes down, head nodding.

Always easier than standing up for myself.

That same night, I had asked my boyfriend if we could cancel our fancy dinner reservations and just have a night in. An hour later, I was still listening to him drone on and on about his needs and how I wasn't meeting them.

Again, I took it with my eyes down and head nodding as he finished listing all my shortcomings as a girlfriend and walked out the door. And while I was still crying over yet another relationship failure, the day's losses became a hat trick.

I got the phone call telling me that Hendricks "Sully" Sullivan, my grandfather—my rock—had finally passed.

Everything after that had gone by in a blur. The wake, the funeral, everything. I'd come to Boston to say my goodbyes and pay my respects, but hadn't stuck around for the reading of his will. Yes, Grandpa Sully's life had ensured that the Sullivan name meant money, but that didn't interest me. Much to my mother's bewilderment, it never had.

The only thing I'd wanted was my grandfather back, and since none of the provisions of his will could have given me that, I just wasn't interested. I'd gone back to New York and gone on with my life, numb and a little worse for wear, but what else was I supposed to do?

Mother hadn't understood, of course.

Yesterday, my day had been spent dealing with her nitpicking from dawn to dusk—just like every other day before it—and by the time it was over, all I'd wanted to do was relax with a glass of wine and have a little time without my heels on. I was soaking my feet in my (well, my *mother's*, according to the deed) New York apartment when I'd gotten the call. I admit, after another day of dealing with her relentlessly overbearing treatment, I'd been stewing a little bit about that when the phone rang. I suppose I should be grateful for the fact that my apartment was rent-free, but at the time, all I'd been able to think about was how it served my mother as yet another way to keep me in her pocket.

Just like my job at her firm.

Just like my entire life in New York, under her thumb.

I'd just started to relax, but wasn't all that surprised when the phone interrupted. After all, nothing else in my life felt like it was truly mine; why shouldn't my one sliver of time alone be interrupted? I seriously considered just letting it go to voicemail, but I finally picked it up right before it could.

Ignoring it would be rude, and don't I always do what I should?

"Ms. MacMillan?" the voice on the other end of the line had asked placidly.

A quick glance at caller ID confirmed why it sounded familiar. Gary Davidson, the family lawyer.

"Gary," I'd started, a smile tugging at my lips despite the exhaustion and numbness I hadn't been able to shake. "We've known each other for years. You know you can call me Cate now, right?"

"Of course, Ms. MacMillan."

I'd shaken my head at his predictability, stifling a laugh. But then I'd sighed, the moment of humor replaced by the realization of what the reason for his call must be. It wasn't that I didn't want to think of Grandpa Sully—remembering him was important, and he'd always be a part of me—but I had no interest in talking about the aftermath of his passing.

I wanted to remember him in life, not face the fact that he was really gone.

That there was no one in my life who really *got* me anymore.

That, despite my extensive social circle, his loss left me adrift.

Alone.

"What is it, Gary?" I'd asked, swallowing past the lump in my throat. "Because if you're calling about Sully's will, I already told you I don't want anything. None of it will bring him back, so if he's left anything to me, please give it all to a charity that you trust. It's what he would have done, and it's the best possible way I can think of to send him off."

"With all due respect, Ms. MacMillan, if that's what he would have done, he would have done it. And he certainly wouldn't have offered you the townhouse."

"Of course he wouldn't offer me the..." I'd paused, trying to process the words. "Gary, did you say the townhouse?"

"Yes."

Everything around me had gone still, and something that might have been excitement had started to bubble up inside me.

"Grandpa Sully left me the townhouse?" I'd repeated, needing to make sure I'd understood.

Gary's answer had come after an affectionate laugh. "Well, yes, in a manner of speaking. There are some details that we'll have to work out. You know your grandfather; he always did things differently from everyone else."

Gary had continued talking—something about notarized details and meeting in person—but my elation at hearing "yes" had made it hard to follow whatever else he'd been trying to tell me.

I'd been wrong when I'd said I didn't want anything. I wanted *this*. It didn't bring Sully back, but yes, yes, *yes*. It was something of his that he'd wanted to be mine, and the thought of it—of being back in the one place I'd always felt so safe—felt like a blessing. Like safety. Like a warm hug from the man I knew I'd miss forever.

"If you're serious about relinquishing your rights to the townhouse, Ms. MacMillan, I can send you the paperwork necessary to authorize preparations for a sale."

"I'm sorry, Gary," I'd interrupted, still swimming at the possibility of living permanently in Grandpa Sully's townhouse but definitely feeling like I'd missed something.

Sell my dream? The one place I had ever been happy?

"Sale?" I'd prompted. "What sort of preparations are you talking about?"

"I'd assumed your mother would have talked to you about it after the reading of the will," Gary had begun, an added note of restraint in his voice. "After the reading of the will, she made it clear that, given your life in New York, you'd be relinquishing your portion and that I should begin preparations to sell. With all due respect, I informed her that the decision was not hers to make and that I'd need to hear it from you directly."

I'd blinked back the hot sting of tears.

My mother... interfering in my life *again*. She'd stayed in

Boston for the reading of the will, of course, but no, she hadn't bothered to mention this to me. She had, in fact, steamrolled right over any thought of what *I* might want and assumed she could dictate my decisions here as she had in every other part of my life.

No.

In that moment, it had felt as though a dam had burst inside me. All the hopes, dreams, happiness—everything I had been keeping locked inside for my entire life—had flooded through me like a palpable force. I'd taken a deep breath, squaring my shoulders as a warm resolve settled over me.

Sully's arms around me? That was too fanciful, but it still felt true.

"Gary, are you free to meet me tomorrow morning?"

"Of course," Gary had responded instantly, a bit startled. "You're in New York right now, though, are you not?"

I'd smiled. Yes, but I didn't *want* to be. Not now.

"Not for long, no," I'd told him, my grin stretching even wider. "Can you meet me at the townhouse tomorrow at ten?"

There'd been a long pause. Gary knew me well, and he must have been just as stunned as I should have been feeling. This wasn't like me, but somehow, this uncharacteristically spontaneous decision had felt right. For once, I hadn't been racked by doubts. In fact, I'd felt more like myself than I ever had before in my life.

"Okay, Cate, er, Ms. MacMillan, I mean," Gary had answered cautiously. I'd known the man for years, and it was the first time I'd ever heard him stumble or call me by my first name. "Ten tomorrow morning, at the townhouse. I'll see you there?"

I'd almost laughed out loud as I'd agreed and ended the call. I'd felt slightly giddy. *Free.*

I hadn't even bothered letting my mother know. Why should I? After all, she hadn't bothered to let *me* know that the townhouse was in my name. Not giving myself time to second-guess the decision, I'd written a quick letter of resignation and printed it out, leaving it on the table by the door where I knew she'd find it when she inevitably came by the apartment looking for me. With that done, I'd packed a bag as quickly as I could manage, booked a seat on the early train, and left from Grand Central in New York to South Station in Boston while the sun was barely starting to glow beneath the horizon.

*And now I'm here,* I think to myself. And even though I've technically lived in New York my entire life: *I'm home.*

I look at my watch. Ten o'clock is rapidly approaching, so I finish my coffee and head out into the light chill once again, walking up to the east edge of the Common where the opposite side of the street is lined with homes. I know it intimately, could walk it with my eyes closed.

*Home.*

It really is.

And when I finally find myself standing in front of Sully's townhouse, it's almost more than I can handle. It's beautiful. Three stories of classic brownstone with a prime view over the Common, all wonderfully kept up over the decades with love and care.

I feel the hot tears of happiness and relief start to well up in my eyes, and I do my best to push them back. *Don't let 'em see you sweat, Wildcat,* he'd always told me. I walk up the steps and take a deep breath as I slip my old key into the door, and find myself relieved that the locks haven't been changed.

*This is it,* I think to myself, a frisson of excitement moving through me.

I turn the key, grab the handle, and walk inside. The first thing I notice is the smell of old books, the result of years upon years of Grandpa Sully collecting legal volumes and filling his bookshelves. He was a sharp man who had always prided himself on staying current. He'd known his way around the internet surprisingly well for a man of his years, but he'd still insisted on keeping physical books around.

I'd always thought it must have been for the nostalgia value, or maybe just that he didn't like getting rid of anything, but as I stand here now, I'm pretty sure it must have been that lovely smell.

The furniture is all just as I remember it, too. Sully had been a wood and leather man all the way, and he'd kept his house furnished accordingly, chock-full of polished tables and well-worn couches. As far as I could tell, not a thing had been moved.

I round the staircase and slide into the kitchen, the wheels of my bag rolling gently on the hardwood floors. Opening the huge stainless steel fridge, I can't help but smile from ear to ear. It's fully stocked and ready to go, and I can even see a package of my favorite strawberry yogurt.

He must have known I'd come, and he'd made provisions to prepare accordingly.

"Oh, Grandpa," I say with a sigh, closing the refrigerator door and walking over to the massive oak dining room table. I set my bag against the wall, pull out a chair and take a seat. Surrounded by the smell of books and wood polish—with just the faintest lingering hint of the cigars he'd always loved so much—I set my arms on the table and flop forward, letting my head rest inside them. My eyes close, and I exhale slowly, more at ease than I can remember being in a long time.

A moment later, I hear the front door open.

"Ms. MacMillan?"

"In here, Gary," I call out, my voice muffled by my arms around my face.

Another chair scrapes against the floor, and I lift my head to see Gary's kind face, weathered gently by time and marred only by the sadness of our business today.

"First," Gary starts, clearing his throat and setting his briefcase on the table as he removes his long black coat, "Let me just say that I am so profoundly sorry for your loss."

"Our loss," I remind him, touched by his sincerity.

"Yes," he concedes, the echo of a smile flickering on his lips. "I honestly can't say that I've ever known another man quite like Hendricks Sullivan."

"Come on, Gary, you know better," I tease, even though I know it's a losing battle. "I prefer Cate, and he wanted you to call him Sully."

Gary casts his eyes down for just a moment, but not before I catch a glimpse of the smile that finally landed on his face. He knows I'm right.

"I wouldn't feel as though I'd earned Hendricks' business, or his friendship, if I handled his affairs with anything less than the utmost professionalism," he admits, pinching the bridge of his nose for just one moment as his brow furrows. "But I do wish that he and I could have shared one more scotch together. I could listen to him talk for hours and hours."

"He could have read the phone book aloud and made it compelling," I agree, the wave of loss hitting me again... less painfully here, though, surrounded by everything that feels like him.

"I'm going to miss that man very, very much," Gary finally says.

Same old Gary, as sensitive as I remember. An absolute shark in the courtroom, but a kind soul. I reach out and place my hand on his forearm, squeezing gently. "We all are. And if he's still out there somewhere, I'm sure he misses you, too."

We sit there like that, in silence, lost in our own respective memories of Grandpa until it's broken by the ringing of my cell phone. I fish it out of my coat pocket and sigh. Of course. Mother.

"Gary, I'm sorry, I have to take this."

He smiles and nods, and I head out of the kitchen and toward Grandpa's study. I shut the paned-glass door before answering the call. For the first time in a very long time, I have no idea what I'm about to say to my mother.

"Yes?" I answer.

"Yes?" she repeats sharply. "That's all you have to say to me, dear?"

I have to hand it to her; she's doing an excellent job keeping her temper hidden behind her phony upscale accent.

I resist the urge to sigh. I don't want to do this, but when has that ever stopped her?

"What else can I say? You read my note, right?"

"Your note, your *note*, of course I read that silly little thing. I've already instructed your grandfather's attorney to begin sale preparations for the townhouse, so your trip to Boston is not only pointless, but poorly timed. Given the train schedule, we'll have to write off today, but I'll expect you back at work tomorrow and I'll warn you now, expect to stay late to make up for the bind you're putting me in with this little fit of temper."

Her dismissal of my choices isn't a surprise, but the reminder that she wants me to sell this house, *Grandpa's* house, fills me up with rage. I start to open my mouth to speak, but by habit, I pull back, pushing the emotion deep down into my stomach where it always goes.

I don't do rage. I stay calm. I work things out. And I always figure out a way to keep my mother happy.

What would Grandpa think about me selling his house?

*No, Wildcat. Not* my *house. Not anymore.*

I can hear his warm, deep voice, as clear as day. Not his house. *My* house. My inheritance. *Mine.*

And just like that, the knot of rage loosens up and gives way to the feeling of bubbles filling up my chest, threatening to float me right up to the ceiling.

"Caitlin! Are you listening to a word I'm saying?"

I look around the study, the sharp demand in my mother's voice failing to sting. I love this room. It's full of all the furniture I know and love, all heavy woods and comfortable leathers. It's Sully's room... but for the first time, I start to look at it with a different eye.

It's my room now.

I start to smile. Maybe a touch of the modern wouldn't hurt. My ideas. My vision. My house.

"Mom," I say, cutting off something else I wasn't listening to. "You had no right speaking to Gary. This house is mine. In fact, I'm meeting with him right now about the details."

There's a pause, and even though my tone was mild, I have no doubt that she's as shocked as she would have been if I'd slapped her in the face.

She recovers quickly, of course. "It's far too late for that now, dear. I've already prepared a design team to come in and tear that filthy old place apart. Gary knows better than to stand in the way of a MacMillan, I assure you."

I almost laugh. Is she forgetting that I'm a MacMillan, too? But of course, the name has never meant the same thing to me as it does to her. I look around again, my surroundings still buffering me from her harsh tone. I find myself unable to stop thinking about the changes I want to make here. Perhaps that old fireplace could use a new marble façade, something bright. Champagne drapes to go with those gorgeous high windows. A few glass tables, maybe?

"Unless you're sending your design team up to help me redecorate, Mom, I don't think I'll have much use for them running around here."

Another moment of shocked silence, and then: "Caitlin, I am so completely and utterly disappointed in you. One minute you're fine, you're working! You have a boyfriend, who, by the way, couldn't be any further out of your league! You have a beautiful apartment that I take care of for you! You have a future! And now you've decided to throw it all away, for what? For a dirty old park brownstone?"

That's enough to snap me out of my reverie, briefly. Her words cut deep, digging right into all my insecurities. What *am* I thinking? The townhouse is wonderful, but it's not everything. If I stay,

I'll need a job, some way to pay for the upkeep of this place, some way to keep myself alive.

I can feel that knot inside me beginning to tie itself up again, but this time, I squeeze my eyes shut and force myself through. I'm not going to back down. Not this time.

"Mom?"

"What?"

"Don't speak to me that way," I say, matter-of-factly. I don't have the answers, but Sully believed in me. I can do this.

"I beg your pardon?"

"You heard me, Mother. You do not get to speak to me that way."

She pauses for a moment, then jumps right back in with her assault.

"If this is what you're choosing to do, then you can consider yourself cut off from this family. You will not see a single dime from me, nor from your father. You might as well change your name from MacMillan to Sullivan if this is the road you want to go down. Honestly, I have no idea what you will do with yourself out there. Monetize your little hobbies? Teach kickboxing to public schoolers? Yoga seminars for the homeless? At *your* weight?"

"Maybe!" I blurt out passionately, suddenly self-conscious of my curves. I see Gary look up from the kitchen, and I avert my eyes. I calm myself down and add, "Maybe I *will* teach kickboxing, maybe I'll teach yoga, but that's my decision to make. It's my life to live, and I have to start sometime."

"You're impossible, Caitlin. Completely and utterly impossible. I don't have time for you right now."

And just like that, she's gone. I exhale, long and hard, exhausted by the call. For the first time since I arrived, I feel drained; the vibrant, effervescent energy I've been filled with all morning dissipating like smoke.

A light tap on the door pane brings me back to my senses. It's Gary, holding two empty wine glasses.

"Wine," I sigh. "Yes, please." I open the door, and we walk together into the den. He has a bottle of red set out on one of the tables, right next to the neatly-flagged paperwork.

Gary is a saint.

"Would another time be better, for the details of the estate?" he asks, pouring a glass for me and a much smaller serving for himself.

I nod, hoping I haven't inconvenienced him. A little recovery time from my mother would be appreciated, though.

"Would you mind, Gary?"

He smiles, shaking his head as he hands my glass over and nods toward the open bottle. "Only if you promise me that *that* won't go to waste."

"Gary, it's ten in the morning," I tease, smiling. I could use it, though.

"I think we both know what Hendricks would have said," Gary replies, smiling back. "I cannot think of a more apt toast. So," he lifts his glass. "Five o'clock somewhere?"

I can't help but giggle, remembering Grandpa Sully's silly, clichéd sayings. He'd had a million of them, and had never been shy about using them. I take my wine glass and gently clink it against Gary's. "Five o'clock somewhere."

We both drink, and we both swallow more than appropriate for a bottle of wine this old, and then—graciously refraining from commenting on the call we both know he overheard—he takes his leave with the promise to set up another time to discuss the terms of Sully's will. Once the door closes behind him, I close my eyes, letting all the good memories of the townhouse swirl around me and buoy my spirits up.

After a minute, I open my eyes, my gaze landing on the wine and my lips lifting with the memory of the promise I'd just made to Gary. I won't let it go to waste. I'm free, and I'm *home*, and for once in my life, I'm going to do exactly what I want.

———

"CHEERS TO ME," I repeat softly to myself as I hold up my wine glass to catch the light streaming in from the bathroom window. The morning sun turns the red wine into a cup of sparkling rubies, and I let myself take a moment to appreciate it as I sink back deeper into the bubble-filled tub. This was my bathroom, *my* room whenever I'd visited Grandpa Sully, and it just feels right to come back here.

Wine in the tub. So indulgent. Or, as my mother would say, so *cliché* and pathetic.

But she's said quite enough for today. I flick a clump of bubbles with my fingernails. Telling me what to do with *my* town-house, telling me what to do with *my* life. How have I put up with it for so long? It's probably just the wine, but right now, Bathtub Cate is full of certainty that she'll never put up with that kind of nonsense again. Bathtub Cate knows what's up.

I like Bathtub Cate.

"Threw it all away for a dirty old park brownstone," I sing-song, then giggle at how totally on-point I know my impression of my mother is, even if I never dared do it where someone else could hear it.

But that's not quite true, is it?

I *used* to do the voice, sometimes. *Here.* Way back when, in the kitchen... with Dylan. And Jack, too, of course, whenever he deigned to hang out with us.

Back when things made sense, as much as anything ever does.

Of course, it's not like my mother wasn't riding me about every little thing back then, too: "Stand up straight, don't wear that, don't be so loud. You'll never get married looking like *that*, boys don't like girls like *that*."

The litany of her constant criticism pops into my head unbidden, but I ruthlessly shove it away. I'm Bathtub Cate, and *that* soundtrack is not what I want to accompany this glass of wine.

Besides, why should I trust her opinion about my love life? She thought my ex-boyfriend was *perfect.*

I can't help but snort softly to myself at the thought. A perfect boyfriend, who, according to her, couldn't be "further out of my league."

I have to admit, I do like the idea that I was in the wrong dating league, though. It would at least explain why every guy I've dated had felt so poorly matched with me. I'd never been able to relax around any of them. Mother had approved of every one, of course, and why wouldn't she? They'd all been so perfectly society-ready, polished and put together and brittle. I'd spent all my time so worried that I might slip up—ruin things with the wrong word or the wrong action—that I'd never been able to just be myself around any of them.

What would being myself with a man I care about even be *like*?

What would it be like to just... let go, to stop worrying?

I've never done that, never put things down and just lived in the moment.

Not even in bed.

*Especially* not in bed, my God. You try having a good time with someone when there's a never-ending loop of anxiety in your brain; worry about whether you're doing things right, if this time will be the one when the guy you're with finally tells you that you're too much of a disappointment to bother with. I just can't risk being anything less than the perfect woman they expect.

So, in the bedroom, I... well, I perform. I copy what I've seen in porn, ecstatic moaning and fingers clutching the sheets at just the right moment, writhing in just the right way.

I've gotten very good at making sure my perfect boyfriends get to keep thinking they're perfect.

Do I hate myself for that? Of *course.* But there's so much that I hate myself for; sparing male feelings at the expense of my own pleasure barely makes the list.

I take a sip of my wine, letting it ease the lump forming in my throat. This is way too sad for Bathtub Cate. Bubble baths are meant to help you relax, bubble baths are soothing. They're happy places, not for brooding over your crappy love life and how you've never had an orgasm from anyone's touch but your own.

I snort, the wine starting to get to me a bit. But, oh my *God*, that really does sound pathetic.

Sadly, though, I have to admit it's true.

And with everything that's been happening lately, with all the stress and all the grief, I haven't even been doing much of that, either. I've been too exhausted and too sad, but now, here in the townhouse, ensconced in bubbles and on my second glass of wine, I can feel the fatigue and sorrow fading a little.

Everything that's been in the way of my libido starts to drain away into the hot water, the aches and pains replaced by one very noticeable need.

I blush, even though I'm all alone. I was a teenager in this house, so it's not like I've never taken care of myself in this bathtub, but... I'm already being so self-indulgent. I should get out of the tub. I should do work, or something productive, not lounge my day away.

But who am I trying to impress? The question comes from Bathtub Cate, and I smile. There's nobody here but me, in my own house, and as I sink back into the warm water I take a look at what *I* need for the first time in what feels like forever.

No faking this. My newfound freedom is allowing my body to wake up again.

My hand is moving before I've made the conscious decision, sliding slowly down the length of my body as my instincts take over. I let my head loll back against the cool porcelain, my eyes easing shut as I slip farther into the bubbles, and it's nice not to think. After all, my fingers have had a lot of practice and they know exactly what to do. A vibrator might make noise and wake up a sleeping boyfriend and give the whole game away, force me to admit that I wasn't perfectly satisfied.

But my own hand? I can get away with that anywhere, anytime.

I didn't realize how badly I needed this until I started, but the speed with which my body is responding to my own gentle touch almost shocks me.

I force myself not to think about all the mundane things my brain normally spins around and around, willing myself to slip into fantasy. My mind conjures up a figure, someone with a toned, strong body and confident, skilled hands who could tease me just the way I need. A man who would actually pay attention, who would make me relax enough to feel all the things I so desperately want to feel.

Who could stroke and massage and tantalize in all the ways I've never experienced with a partner.

I suck in a breath as I find myself settling into the rhythm I crave, losing myself in imagining my faceless fantasy lover. Faceless, because I can never make myself see a particular face, not when I touch myself. If I give my longing a face, it hurts too much to accept afterward that I'll never get to feel this way with a real live man.

To accept that I'll always be boxed into simply pretending, to make my lover happy.

I don't know how to do anything else.

I shove the twinge of sadness away and focus back on my daydream, my fingers speeding up as I start to lose myself in it again. I can feel myself spiraling up fast, the intensity almost brutal, but I can't stop. I don't even want to.

I need more, I need it so much that I could explode.

I groan in mingled frustration and pleasure, bracing one foot on the edge of the tub for better leverage as hot, tingling waves move through me, centering on my core. I'm so close, my fantasy lover doing things to me in my mind that make me buck and writhe in the soapy water. God, I want this.

I *want* this.

I can hear my own breath starting to come in short, sharp moans, loud and shameless, and I bite my lip hard, a whimper of pure, aching need escaping anyway.

I'm almost there, I'm almost *right there*, and I'm trembling so hard that I can hear the water slosh around me. A hot, sweet sensation runs through my entire body, lighting up all my nerves, and I feel like I'm balancing on the edge of a cliff, about to tip over into ecstasy.

I moan as I grind against my fingers, wanton and needy and putting the fake-porn soundtrack I've used with past boyfriends to shame.

Just a little... bit... *more...*

There's a soft sound, an unmistakably *male* sound, and my eyes fly open as shock jolts through my body.

A man is standing in the doorway of the bathroom—an incredibly handsome man; tall, built, piercing blue eyes and a short, dark beard straight out of my fantasies—and on his gorgeous face is an unmistakable expression of raw, unabashed desire.

Desire for *me.*

I should be mortified. I *am.* But *God,* the look on his face—

Pleasure rockets through me, and even though a distant part of my mind is screaming to cover up and hide, my body is in control, responding to the heat in the stranger's gaze despite the alarm and humiliation flooding my brain. The shame and horror and shock of having someone catch me pleasuring myself crash through me, and the erotic surprise sends me over the edge in an overwhelming, hot rush that I couldn't have stopped if I'd tried.

A throbbing cry rips from my throat, and my whole body goes taut.

I'm coming.

I'm *coming.*

My eyes are locked onto the man's face, his greedy eyes eating up every trembling ounce of my ecstasy, and I'm so wrecked by it, that—at least while the orgasm rolls through me in endless, bone-melting waves—I can't bring myself to feel anything but sensually, shamelessly satisfied.

I've never come so hard in my life.

2

## JACK

*I*t's already been a hell of a morning for me. I had to drag my ass to South Station and hit the commuter rail up to Worcester for a deposition at six a.m. Uncooperative witness, and garbage coffee in that conference room. It was so bad that the commuter rail back into Boston was pure heaven in comparison. Once it was all over and I finally got back into Boston, I still had a little time before my next appointment, so I decided to hit Sully's.

Best case: I might bump into Dylan before he leaves for the day. Worst case: at least there'd be good coffee.

I cross the park and I'm almost to the outside steps when I notice a familiar car just starting to pull away. Looks like Gary's. I wonder what he's doing here; we don't meet until tomorrow, at least as far as I can remember. Maybe he was talking to Dylan?

Whatever, not important. Coffee. Coffee's what's important right now.

I slide my key into the door and open it wide, and man do I love that old leather and polish smell. I could live here for a million years and never get sick of it.

I overdressed for the deposition, went with the full nine.

21

Tasteful deep chocolate, pinstripes, and my favorite suspenders. I slide my coat off and hang it delicately on the stand near the door, along with my tie. I treat them carefully, and I smile as Sully pops into my head.

I had nothing when I met that man. Was just about to have a hundred bucks from him, though, judging by what his money clip felt like while I was trying to fish it out of his pocket. I thought I was real slick back then, just this townie kid who knew the streets. I remember being shocked as hell when he busted me before I could even get my hand out of his pocket.

When Sully offered to pay me for being his errand boy, I remember thinking that he might have been slick, but he wasn't too bright. It was easy money, though: drop some milk and potatoes off in the morning, come by to sweep up the walk after school and do my homework at one of the smaller desks in his study.

I thought about robbing him blind every single day. And somehow, every single day, I didn't. I just kept showing up, more and more.

Sully was with me when I bought my first suit, back when I started interning for him. He showed me the ropes, taught me how to tie the perfect Windsor knot, all the stuff my own old man should have been teaching me how to do.

Too busy at Suffolk Downs, I guess, throwing his paycheck away on the racehorses.

It didn't take me too long to realize that Sully wasn't old money. Rather, he was one of those hardworking, earned-every-dime types. It meant that he didn't let me slack. He always demanded that I hold up my end of the bargain, but more importantly, it also meant that I could drop my guard with him over time.

He taught me everything I needed to know about how to take the backdoor into upper society. *Snow 'em,* he told me while we looked in the mirror at that first suit of mine. It fit perfectly, like a glove, and I can't remember a time where I'd felt safer than I did at that moment.

*Snow 'em, and don't take their guff, Ditto. We work for what we have, and we deserve every bit of it.*

Ever since that first suit, I treat every single one of them like it's my only suit, and I respect them accordingly.

I make sure that my coat and tie are set, and I reach up to the doorframe, running my finger over a particularly worn spot in the wood. Sully used to tease me about being so tall, kept telling me that one day I'd knock my block off by forgetting to duck through the door. I rub that spot for luck every single time I'm here. Luck, and a reminder to duck my head.

I hear a splash, and find myself snapped out of my little trip down memory lane. What the hell could that be? Dylan, maybe?

Nope. His bike isn't up against the wall where he always keeps it. No Dylan.

There's another splash, and I immediately feel my adrenaline begin to surge. At this point, there's no way I can't investigate what this is, so I roll up my sleeves over my forearm tattoos and unbutton a couple of my collar buttons. Always best to be as free and loose as you can in a fight.

I was always more of the roguish type, and got real good at sneaking around when I was a kid. I don't need to kick my shoes off to be quiet. I slowly make my way to the stairs and carefully step up without making a sound.

That splashing is still happening, faint but definitely there by the time I get to the top landing. Now, though, I can hear the moaning, too.

Sexy, gentle moaning.

My eyes fall to the floor, and I spot the trail of clothes leading to the bedroom, starting with a tasteful rose blouse. Is this my lucky day? I can feel myself getting hard at the sound, and the adrenaline sure isn't helping with that.

So, I follow the clothes into one of the bedrooms. Heels by the door, pants just inside, then a lacy ivory bra that's creamy in a way that reminds me of French vanilla ice cream. Matching panties on the floor, at the opening of the bathroom. The moaning is louder now, more frantic, and my heart feels like it's about to rip through my chest.

It's not the only thing that feels like it's gonna tear itself out of my clothes, either.

Do I walk in? Of course I do. No turning back now.

When I see her, I can hardly believe my eyes. It's a woman. A gorgeous woman, to boot. Her long, silky brown hair is draped over the side of the tub, leaving her face fully exposed. And her face... her face is *beautiful*, especially flooded with pleasure like it is now. One long, gorgeous leg is braced against the edge of the tub, and there is absolutely no mistaking what she's doing.

It's all I can do to not reach inside my pants right now, but I suppress the urge as best I can, trying to remain silent. But then she gets frantic and arches her back. I see the tops of her perfect breasts, lightly covered in soap bubbles, as she comes, and before I can stop myself, I suck in a sharp breath.

So much for remaining silent.

Her eyes fly open—an intoxicating caramel color that reminds me of good whiskey—and I can tell she's equal parts panicked and aroused, stuck in the throes of her orgasm.

It's the hottest fucking thing I've ever seen.

"What?!" she screams, immediately moving to cover up. She darts her head back and forth, like she's looking for a hiding spot. A moment later, I watch as she dunks herself under the water a little too fast. Her legs fly into the air as she slips around in the tub, and she fights to regain her balance before clutching at the lip of the tub and climbing to her feet.

It's so hot, and so ridiculous, that I can't help but laugh.

"What the fuck?" I say with a grin on my face. I'm sorry, but real things just don't happen like this.

"Who the fuck are *you*?! Don't laugh at me!" she screams, her eyes darting between me and the towel nearby, just out of easy reach. She settles for throwing one arm across her incredibly tantalizing breasts, and one hand down to cover the enticing dark curls between those perfect, creamy thighs.

I think I might be in love.

I follow the line of her cleavage up, and notice a small necklace closer to her throat. I know that necklace. I used to see it every summer when we were kids.

*Holy shit,* it's *Cate.*

Sully called her Wildcat. I always called her Duchess. It seemed appropriate for such a completely spoiled little brat. We were just kids, but I'll never get over the way she treated me, leaving the room every time I'd walk in, or staring at me like I was an oil stain on the carpet whenever she thought I couldn't see her.

She'd made it clear that she never wanted to be caught dead in the same room with me, let alone talk to me. I thought she was cute as hell back when I was 17... until I realized she was just 13. Doesn't mean I didn't try to talk to her at first, try to make friends with her. Eventually, though, I figured out that she thought I was nothing more than trash from across the tracks.

I'll never forgive her for treating me that way.

How utterly, deliciously ironic that here she is now, naked and exposed before me. I can't help but take a moment to fully absorb how much she's changed. Before, she was cute and curvy, and all the things I loved. Now, though, she's smoking hot with a show-stopper face and a killer body. She definitely added plenty of danger to those curves, that's for sure. Not a little girl anymore, as far as I'm concerned.

I must be lingering for way too long, because she gets agitated and shouts at me. "Do you mind?!" she yells, staring me down.

I reach for the towel nearby. "Not at all, Duchess," I say, unable to resist the old nickname. I certainly haven't seen any reason to think it doesn't still apply.

I throw the towel to her. I don't put as much force into the throw as I should, and it lands on the floor just out of reach.

Oops.

She bends down quickly to pick up the towel, and I get an eyeful of her sumptuous cleavage and a long view down her back, just enough to lay my eyes on the start of a plush, perfect ass.

"Jack!" she shouts as she pops back up, throwing the towel around herself. "I can't believe—" She scowls and cuts herself off mid-sentence. Now that she's covered, she starts to step out of the tub. "You're such an asshole!" she yells.

I feel my face get hot. With her, the cut was bound to happen eventually, but it's been so long since anyone has talked down to me like this. She always had an uncanny ability to jab her icepick right into my heart, though.

Before I can let it show on my face, I recover and smirk. "Hey now, language, Duchess," I tease, with a bit of a cruel edge in my voice. The way she used to treat me? It broke my heart; I don't feel too bad about taking a little revenge. "After all, we can't have you sounding like you're a townie like me."

"Oh my God, I can't believe this is happening," Cate says, shaking her head. "What are you even doing here, Jack? What the hell?"

"Me?" I say angrily, furrowing my brow. "Why wouldn't I be here? I work for Sully, you know. I have every right to be here. More importantly, why the hell are *you* here? Grandpa's little Wildcat feeling guilty about running away right after the funeral?"

She scowls at me, and I probably deserve that, but I don't care right now. All I can feel are the memories of being treated like a dog, all flooding back in.

"Excuse me, please," she says as she steps toward me. For a moment, her chest rubs against mine, and I can feel her breasts between her towel and my shirt. Just as I feel like I couldn't be any harder, my cock betrays me and tightens even more.

If I weren't so aggravated by her, I'd be doing my damnedest to

26

talk her into the bed a few feet away.

Then I look down and notice that there's a big, soapy wet streak on my shirt.

"Hey, pay attention to what you're doin' with all that mess!" I shout, reaching for a dry washcloth and pat-drying myself down.

"This is so completely, insanely inappropriate," she says tightly, picking up her bra and panties and turning to face me. "Please leave, Jack. I need to get dressed, and I can't have you staring at me like this."

"Yeah, right," I say, continuing to pat-dry my shirt. "It ain't any fun when *you're* the one being stared at, eh?"

She recoils as though I slapped her. "What the hell are you talking about?"

"Don't act like you don't remember the way you treated me," I shout, unable to keep my cool anymore. "Just a piece of trash, a little stoop-sweep for Sully who didn't deserve the time of day. You thought I never saw the way you looked at me? I remember all of it, Duchess."

"The way I looked at you?" she repeats, a flicker of confusion crossing her face.

Maybe she can't remember that far back, or maybe mean people just forget how many people they were jerks to.

"Jack..." Her voice is slightly softer, and it weakens my resolve to hold onto my anger just a bit. "I have no idea what you're talking about."

Well, not that much. What, I wasn't even important enough for her to remember?

"Yeah, not enough room in your life for the townie. I get it."

"No, Jack, I mean..." She lets the words trail off again, sighing and shaking her head. "Look, I need to get dressed, and I'm so beyond caring right now, so." She lets the towel drop and holds out her arms. "Here I am. Here's all of me, every last bit. You happy now, jerk? Seen everything you want? I can't believe you, Ditto."

Now it's my turn to feel slapped. Ditto was the name Sully had given me back when I was just a dumb teen. *Because I have to tell you everything twice before it sticks,* he would say back then. I'm genuinely shocked that she remembered that.

I have nothing to say back to her, but this seems like a good moment for it, as I watch her put on her panties. I can't help but follow the fabric as it caresses the tender flesh of her legs, covering up that delicious mound in such an appealing package.

Just as I'm feeling like I'm suddenly the vulnerable one, I catch it. That look, as she tilts up her head while standing up from her bent position. There's no mistaking where her eyes are; I can practically feel them running over my body, undressing me in her mind, focusing on my cock—so obviously pressed hard against the fabric of my slacks.

Her eyes slide up my body, over the tattoos on my forearms, over the damp patch on my chest. All the way up to my eyes.

For a moment, I can feel it.

There's a spark, a mutual hunger, burning bright between us.

A perfect moment of balance before the scales fall either way.

"You left so damn fast after Sully's funeral," I say, cutting through the silence.

"I was tied up," she says, still standing tall and open before me, bra in hand. "I couldn't get away."

Those breasts.

*Damn.*

"He missed you, you know," I say, pulling my mind away from where it won't do either of us a bit of good to go.

"Excuse me?"

Yeah, that's right. Her voice is sharper now.

"He missed you," I repeat, thinking about Sully's kind face. "You were only ever here for the summers. I was here year-round, and he missed you for the other three seasons. He was good about keeping it under his hat, but I knew. I might not have cared what you thought of me, but I cared what he thought about you." I drop the washcloth to the ground. It's done as much as it can, and I can only hope my shirt will be presentable by the time I get to my next appointment.

My words sting, I can tell. Cate's face has always been so damn easy to read. Best to finish it.

"He deserved better than being run out on by a part-time grandkid," I say, because it's true. And also, yeah, to kill the other thing that felt like it might have been happening for a second between us. "Especially at his funeral."

The moment is over, and we both know it. Any spark that was there has disappeared without even a puff of smoke to leave behind.

"Jack," she starts, the impatience and anger back in her voice as she throws her bra on and covers up those delicious breasts.

No, not just covers them. Puts them on display. Her underwear is a temptation.

I jerk my eyes back up to her face.

"I don't care," she says, clasping the bra shut with jerky motions and reaching for her pants. "I'm hungry, and I'm exhausted, and you don't belong here. You need to get the fuck out of my house."

The words hit me like a ton of bricks.

*You don't belong here.*

I don't even see her killer body anymore; I only see the memories of how she treated me when I was a kid.

I grit my teeth together, my stomach churning.

"You're mistaken," I say, as calmly and coldly as I can manage. "This house is *mine*, Duchess."

She sucks in a sharp breath, eyes widening. I've surprised her. What, Gary didn't tell her?

Well... good. Fuck her. Rich grandkid or not, it's a sweet moment to turn the tables.

And I'll be damned if she gets what's mine.

# 3

## DYLAN

$\mathcal{I}$'m so excited to get home and start the meal for tonight. I'm planning on beef stew. It used to be Sully's favorite, but it can take forever to make, so I figure I'll get an early start.

I'm not normally what you'd call a morning person; my culinary classes are mostly in the afternoon on weekdays, and that usually gives me plenty of time to sleep in and get up at my own pace. Today, though; today's definitely different.

Jack's coming over.

Jack, the childhood best friend that I hadn't spoken to in years, until Sully's death brought him back into my life.

It's been so long since I've cooked for Jack. Probably not since we were kids, back when the three of us would spend our summers together. Cate was the only one missing from this happy reunion, but I knew her adult life always kept her busy. At least, her minimal involvement with social media seemed to make it pretty clear that she didn't have much time for anything but work.

I'm so happy for her success, though, and I hope it treats her well. I'll get to see her soon enough, anyway; after all, we still have

31

to talk about what we're going to do with the townhouse. Another bittersweet blessing to come from losing Sully.

I finish loading up my backpack. Fresh leafy greens are poking out of the top, but the real prize is the bundle of short ribs at the bottom, wrapped up nice and neat in butcher paper. It's all going to smell so nice once I get it all in the Crock-Pot. I also picked up some breakfast sausage and some croissants, because I forgot to grab a bite before leaving the house and my stomach did the shopping for me.

It should all be perfect by the time Jack shows up later. I'm trying my best to not push too hard, but I can barely contain how excited I am to have him back in my life again. Our relationship hadn't been the best up until recently.

We'd had a falling out years ago over something very, very silly.

My first kiss.

It had been such a perfect night. I'd met this guy, Connor, in home ec back in high school, and he asked me out one day. I didn't know him super well, but I was flattered all the same. He was damn cute, so of course I said yes.

Connor was a perfect gentleman; we saw an awful movie and had some diner food, and just spent a lot of time laughing and smiling all around. At the end of it, while he was walking me home across the Common, he stopped me and we kissed.

Maybe it wasn't perfect, but it was mine, and you never forget your first.

Then, next thing I knew, Jack was there, screaming at me.

Connor, of course, took off right away and left me holding the bag. So much for the perfect gentleman. I hadn't understood why Jack was so upset at first, not until he started going on and on about how angry and disgusted he was. How he could never look at me the same way again. He never outright said it, but he didn't have to; it was because Connor was another guy.

Knowing how Jack had grown up, and in what neighborhood,

I should hardly have been surprised at an Irish Catholic Boston native taking offense at the idea of a man with another man, but he was my best friend, and I never saw it coming. We had talked about girls in the past, of course, amongst all the typical stuff that young teenage boys talked about. I liked them, too. A lot.

I remember enjoying many of those moments, just staring at Jack's lean body whenever I thought he wasn't looking. So many summers, so many stolen glances.

Honestly, I hadn't thought I'd been all that subtle about it.

I don't know whether Jack had actually been spying on me, or if it was just a stupid coincidence of timing, but I couldn't believe how outright nasty he was being to me.

Even later, when I tried to understand where it had been coming from, it had still hurt.

Jack and I had more or less spent our most important years together in Sully's townhouse, and I'd thought we were best friends. I'd thought we were *solid*.

Turned out that I was dead wrong about that. Nothing I said got Jack to talk to me again.

At least, not back then.

I was really pissed at him for a long time, but he mattered to me. I admit it. I always hoped for a reconciliation. All those years of silence between us? I didn't ignore him by choice, but every one of my attempts to have it out with him was roadblocked or ignored, so I eventually gave up.

It took me completely by surprise when he came over to me at the funeral.

Time had been kind to him; all of those sharp edges had smoothed out and refined themselves. He'd gotten hot as hell, quite frankly, but given our history, I've been doing my best to keep that opinion to myself. We just started talking again, and I'm trying my best to keep it grounded in the present. I don't need him running off again. If we can just keep things nice and chill, we should be totally fine.

Maybe even end up friends again.

Speaking of fine, I can already feel the breeze picking up just a bit, caressing my face as I hop on my bike and start to pedal off. Today I'll cook for Jack, and maybe in the next couple of weeks I'll get to cook for all three of us, if Cate shows up in town like I expect she'll have to at some point.

I'd always been sort of the middleman for those two—I loved them both. They didn't seem to get along very well together back when we were kids, but everything was more or less okay when I was in the middle of it all.

My childhood in that townhouse was as good as I could have ever hoped for. Back in those days, I wasn't Dylan, I was "Tater." Sully had taken to calling me that back when I refused to eat anything but tater tots. The memory makes me grin, even now. I was such a picky kid back then. My mother cooked for Sully for years, so I'd spend most of my days after school just hanging around, doing my homework or talking to Jack. And Cate, too, of course, during the summers.

Sully always seemed larger than life to me. His way with words and his sheer presence are both things that I still strive to emulate.

In a way, Sully was the reason I discovered how much I enjoy cooking. The moment I got started, I never once looked back. It gives me energy, makes me feel alive.

I've always been a quiet guy, very chill, even back then, but something about crafting a meal just awoke a spark inside me. Sometimes I wonder if he guessed it would happen like that.

He must have known how much I looked up to him.

Sully was sly as hell; would trick me into trying new things just because I saw how much he enjoyed eating them. You couldn't get me to so much as look at a carrot until he started talking about how delicious they were with a little cinnamon glaze on them. Before I knew it, he and my mother had unlocked my palate, and I was helping out in the kitchen in no time. And later? Sully got me into culinary school when I couldn't afford the first year.

*They'll see it in you, Tater,* he said, trusting that I'd be good enough to pick up second-year scholarships and making me believe it, too. Now, I cover the remainder on my own and I do pretty okay for myself, especially since Sully let me live in the townhouse. Having no rent to pay, especially in Boston, has been a huge load off of both my mind and my budget.

Hopefully, Jack and Cate and I will be able to work something out with the townhouse. If I can just stay there long enough to graduate this year, I can get myself a job and look for another place to live. And sure, it kills me to think of leaving the one place I feel so right in, but I'm not going to dwell on that when I could be appreciating the time I've got there now.

Besides, I'm sure it'll all work out, as long as I keep my nose to the grindstone.

I'm home before I know it, and I hop off my bike and lift it up the small stoop. I take just a quick moment to pop my earbuds in and start my jazz playlist so I can get myself in the proper cooking headspace, then I open the door and walk in.

The first thing I notice is Jack's coat hanging from the rack. I smile. He's early; what an unexpected surprise! Good thing I picked up enough sausage and croissants for two.

I practically skip into the kitchen, sliding my backpack down my arm, ready to greet Jack. I genuinely believed that our friendship had been irreparably shattered until he reached out to me at the funeral. The townhouse seems to have a way of repairing things, though—putting people at ease—and it's the only place I can think of where I would want to cook for Jack.

I spent years missing his friendship, and maybe it will never go back to the way it was, but for now, I'm just going to enjoy the fact that he's back in my life.

I arrive in the kitchen, but there's no Jack. Weird. I shrug;

maybe he's upstairs on the phone, or in the bathroom. No matter, there's no time to waste if I'm going to get this stew done up right.

I turn the volume up on my music and unbutton my sleeves, rolling them up tightly above my forearms. A moment later, I have my favorite dishtowel over my shoulder, and I'm unpacking my groceries. First things first: all the veggies go into the colander. I can already feel the energy coursing through me as I start the rinse, and all I can think about is how good all of this is going to smell.

Very, very soon.

Once that step is done, I grab a couple of plates and set them out for croissants and sausage, then I reach for the skillet and kick the fire on the stove. I unwrap the breakfast sausage as I wait for the skillet to heat up. The butcher did an amazing job; I don't know what I'd do without fresh cuts of meat.

A couple of minutes later, I've got the sausages on the skillet in front of me, and the first smells of the morning start to fill the air. I can't help but smile from ear to ear as I cook, making sure to keep the sausages moving so they don't burn on any one side. Sausage is quick, thankfully, because I can already feel my tummy rumbling. I hope Jack's hungry, too.

I flip the sausages onto the plates and slice open the croissants with a bread knife. I love mine with just a little bit of strawberry jam; a little sweet, a little tart, and a wonderful complement to the rest of the savory meal.

I undo a couple of buttons on my shirt collar, and bring it down so the air hits my chest. I dab a tiny bit of sweat away from my forehead with the dishtowel, and sling it back over my shoulder as I take my knife and get ready to start dicing the meat and veggies for the stew. Before I can get started on that, though, Jack finally pops into the kitchen and I feel my heart leap.

"*Jack*," I say excitedly, putting my knife down and popping the earbuds out. "I didn't expect to see you in so early. How're you doing?"

Some of my enthusiasm dims at the look on his face, though. I can tell he's upset about something, but before he can open his mouth to tell me what's wrong, someone else bounds in.

Someone with killer curves, wearing just a bra and a pair of *very* well-fitted slacks.

My eyes quickly roll over her body from bottom to top, until I realize who it is.

"Cate?!" I shout, opening my arms wide and walking over to pull her into a huge hug. I've always been a hugger, and other than a brief squeeze at Sully's funeral, it's been far too long since I've had my arms around her.

And... wow. She's never fit in them like *this* before.

Cate looks shocked for a second. I can feel the tension in her body, but before I can second-guess my impulsive embrace, it starts to melt away. She softens up and falls into my arms, and before I know it, I can feel my shirt start to soak through on my shoulder.

Is she crying? Laughing? Both?

I can't quite tell what's going on, but I gently stroke her hair as she presses into me, looking toward Jack in the hope of some answers.

"I'm lost here," I say. "What's going on? Are you two okay? What happened?"

At first, I wonder if Jack's even going to answer. He turns away from me... almost as though he's in disgust.

I can't imagine why.

"We're done here for today," he grunts.

"Done?" I repeat, still feeling a little lost about the whole situation. "We're still doing dinner tonight, aren't we?"

"Sorry, I have plans," he says, and I can feel my happiness start to fade a bit at his dismissive tone.

This had to happen eventually, I guess. Did I really think he'd changed his opinion of me? I don't know what I expected.

I do know what I'd hoped, though.

Silly me.

I swallow my disappointment. "Jack, we still need to talk about the—"

"The contract, Dylan, I know," he snaps back, cutting me off. "The faster we can decide what happens to the house, the happier I'll be to wash my hands of this place."

With that, Jack turns and grabs his coat, storming out the front door and leaving it with a hard slam.

I wince. Rude. I wish Cate hadn't seen any of that. I still don't know what happened between the two of them, but it clearly hadn't been anything good.

I continue to console her, and she continues to laugh-sob against me.

"Shh, hey," I start, working my fingers into a gentle massage, running over her neck and shoulders.

It's hitting me that she's half-naked, but I do my best to push that thought away. Things were never like that between us, and I just want to be whatever she needs right now.

"Dylan? It's really you?" she asks.

"In the flesh," I respond, smiling. It's been far too long since I've seen her, too, but thankfully, that's just been due to both of us growing up—life and distance—unlike my estrangement from Jack.

Cate seems to be calming down a bit. Her hair is damp, so I'm guessing her undressed state had to do with a bath or shower.

I didn't think I'd been gone from the house for all that long, but apparently it had been long enough to miss all of the action.

"I don't know what the hell Jack's problem is," Cate mumbles against my neck. "He's being such a jerk right now, and he says *he* owns the house. I have no idea what's going on, Dylan. I left New York because Gary said it was *mine*."

I lean back against the counter and she straightens up a bit. Her in only a bra, hair still damp, and Jack irritated? I can piece a fair amount of this scene together.

"It's Sully's will," I reply, giving her shoulders a gentle squeeze before letting my arms drop.

She swipes at her wet cheeks.

"Here," I say, pulling my dishtowel down and holding it out to her.

"Thanks," she says, taking it and gently dabbing at her face to clean up. "What about the will?" she asks, sniffing away the rest of her tears. "Gary told me I inherited the house."

Poor thing, I think. Gary's usually so thorough, but Sully's death hit us all hard.

"Cate, from what I understand, you did... sort of. Sully left the house to all three of us."

"All three of us?"

"Yep. You, me, and Jack. Equal shares, with some kind of Sully-type stipulations in there that I'm a little unclear on. Jack and I were supposed to go over the contract tonight over dinner. He says it's not his area of law, but he seems pretty confident he'll be able to make some sense of it. Honestly, I don't think he's looked at it too closely yet, either." I frown, glancing toward the door Jack had stormed out of. "I guess that's not happening now, though."

Cate looks puzzled, then sighs and shakes her head.

"Gary was going to go over it with me earlier, too, but then Mom called."

She grimaces, and I withhold my eye roll. I know what Cate's mother is like. All too well, in fact. She used to tell Cate not to hang out with "the help."

I have no idea how someone as beautiful inside as Cate could have possibly come from someone so ice-cold.

"Mom was mad at me for leaving so quickly, but I had to come," Cate says, a little hitch in her breath. "I wasn't going to miss the chance to be here again for the world."

"Well," I start, smiling and offering my arms. "*I'm* glad you came. Come here."

Cate smiles back, letting me turn her around so her back is

toward me. She sinks into my chest and I wrap her up tight, one arm around her waist and the other arm just below her collarbone.

Cate reaches up and holds onto my forearm with her hands, squeezing it as she lets her head fall back against me with a sigh. I can feel the tension ease out of her, and my smile gets a little wider.

This feels right. I've missed her.

"I can't believe it's you," she says again, practically melting against me.

We'd seen each other at the funeral in passing, but she'd looked lost, swept up in the wake of that force of nature known as her mother, and I'd been dealing with my own grief.

"I can't believe it either," I say, glad to have this second chance. "Before the funeral, what had it been? Seven years? Almost a decade now?"

"Oh God, I don't know," she says. "I lost count. The years just started rolling into each other, one into the next."

"Still feels like yesterday, though," I say, and I can feel her squeeze me just a bit tighter. "Sorry you had to see Jack like that. I don't know what got into him."

"He's *always* hated me," she says, her voice more confused than bitter.

"Oh, I doubt that," I say, shaking my head as I bite back another smile. Sure, there had always been some tension between them, but I definitely remember it differently. "I think Jack just has trouble expressing himself. You know how he gets. Or at least, how he used to get, back in the day. I can't say I'm an expert on who he is now, I guess."

Cate laughs. "Remember the first time you cooked for us?"

"Oh God," I say, grinning. "French toast."

"The perfect French toast," she replies. "Jack had never had it before. It took Grandpa so long to convince him to just try a little bit."

"Yeah, that didn't last long. Jack had that first bite and he was hooked."

"Until the sugar," she says. It's quiet for just a moment, then we both start laughing.

"I totally forgot about the powdered sugar," I say as it starts flooding back into my brain. "I don't think he'd ever seen it before. He didn't know that it clumps up and you can't just pour it out."

"Yeah!" Cate says. I can feel her body shake as she laughs. "He almost dumped the whole bag onto the table, remember? It got everywhere."

"Oh man, he was so angry about that," I say, grinning at the memory. "We offered to help him clean up, but he didn't want anything to do with it."

"Such a stubborn, stubborn boy," she says, shaking her head.

She's right. He always has been.

We stay like that, her in my arms, back against my chest, just enjoying the moment while our laughter cools off.

"I missed you, Dylan," she finally says, snuggling back against me with a happy sigh.

I suddenly become acutely aware of the fact that I'm holding on to the most beautiful woman I've ever seen in my life. I can feel the slope of her magnificent breasts beneath my forearm and her ass pressing into me like it had been custom-made to fit.

My whole body flushes as she moves against me, and when my cock starts to harden, I know there's no way that Cate's not going to notice. I'm frozen for a second, torn between not wanting to mess things up with someone I've always considered one of my best friends—time and distance notwithstanding—and a whole different kind of wanting.

Before I can panic, she presses back against me harder, her ass firmly against my cock, cradled between her cheeks.

Okay, then. She noticed, and her body is telling me exactly what she needs.

"I missed you, too," I say quietly, sliding my hands down to wrap around her hips.

I pull her against me more firmly, and she moans softly—the single sexiest sound I've ever heard—and raises a hand to my head, cupping the side of my face as she cranes her neck back to look up at me.

Any hesitation I had is gone when I see the naked desire in her eyes. Cate wants this as much as I do. I can read her as well as I always could. She *needs* it.

And I'm *always* going to do my best to give Cate exactly what she needs.

4

CATE

The air in the kitchen turns electric as my lips meet Dylan's, a charge passing through us as if a circuit finally connected. His hands are huge and heavy on my hips, almost burningly hot, and they feel incredible.

I wonder if my touch on his cheek feels as searing to him.

His tongue grazes my lips, then withdraws, and I bite back a moan at the denial as I fight to get some of my sanity back. He makes me feel safe, and I'm acting on pure instinct right now.

I never do that.

"Dylan," I whisper. My mouth is dry, and I lick my lips. What am I going to say? I have no idea, but my body seems to have a will of its own, and it knows exactly what it wants.

My hips press back against him, feeling the thick hardness of him against my bottom, the comforting wall of his muscular body at my back and a thrill goes through me, wild and new, intertwined with a thread of apprehension. I've never been this bold with anyone, never skipped past the careful three-date rule, never been the one to make the first move toward getting physical.

Never felt *wanton*.

I can feel Dylan tense up when I say his name. His hands tighten on my hips, and I know his mind must be warring with his body, just like mine is.

This is shameless.

This is so... not me. So totally beyond anything I've ever dreamed about doing, even when I imagine myself as a better and stronger and more confident version of me. I hadn't known he'd be downstairs when I'd stormed after Jack, I'd just been so mad that I'd barely been able to see straight... which is also not like me.

I don't rock the boat or make waves.

I'm definitely not the type to flounce around in lingerie and seduce a guy at the drop of a hat.

I'm definitely not the type to get so turned on that it's an effort to think straight. Hell, usually, thinking too much is one of my biggest problems in bed.

A naughty thrill goes through me. There's no bed in sight, and this isn't just any guy, either. This is Dylan, my very best friend growing up and the one guy I've always felt safe with. The one person my age that I've always been able to relax with, even at my most insecure. Even now, half-naked in the kitchen and feeling bolder than I ever have in my life.

"We don't have to," Dylan says, even though I can feel how much a certain part of him wants to. Wants *me.* "This is fast, I know... I'm sorry, I won't push if you don't want."

His voice is rough, ragged with desire, but there's concern in it, too. That concern makes me smile, makes the last bit of worry unknot from around my heart.

If I had any doubts, Dylan has made it crystal clear that I'm the one in the driver's seat. It's the last piece of the puzzle, confirmation that the kind, gentle boy I remember has transformed into this incredibly sexy, considerate man.

Dylan won't hurt me. Dylan would never hurt me.

I look up into his eyes—a warm hazel that I could get lost in—

and the expression in his gaze fills me with both an intoxicating sweetness and a wild hunger, all at the same time.

"I want this, Dylan," I murmur, even now amazed at what I'm about to do. I gently guide one of his hands up my body, covering my breast. "I want *you*."

Honestly, I'm a little shocked by just how true it is. Just saying it out loud sends a hot, damp rush between my legs, and I moan— not the practiced, deliberate version I've used with other men, but one that slips out of me unbidden.

I *want* him.

The effect is immediate, like I've unleashed him. Dylan takes charge of my body, spinning me to face him and leaning down to capture my mouth with his. The kiss is both gentle and ravenous.

It's exactly what I need.

I can't help but moan against his mouth again—aching at the taste of him and desperate for more—and when the sound makes his cock jerk against me, I feel powerful. *Hot.* Wanted.

Dylan's hands roam my body like he wants to touch every bit of me at once, and every place he caresses feels like just the right spot, driving me wild. I'm panting, my heart racing out of control as he teases me with his fingertips, testing and pausing to see how I react.

For the first time in my life, I'm getting what I've always fantasized about: a man who takes the time to get to know my body instead of just using it for his own brief pleasure. Despite the throbbing length of his erection pressed against me, Dylan is taking the time to learn my body—discovering me—and I feel like I'm going to go out of my mind with how intense it feels to be touched with such desire and care.

I don't know if it's a few seconds or endless, delicious minutes. I only know that his mouth is on my throat... on my shoulder... that I'm leaning into his touch and making desperate little noises and *aching*, trembling for more. My whole body feels like someone struck a tuning fork and now all of me is vibrating with the need for this man.

He slides his thigh between my legs, strong with muscle, and I grind myself against him shamelessly. I'm probably soaking through my slacks right now, dripping wet with need for him, and I don't even care. There's no space in me for shame or self-consciousness with Dylan, there's only this growing, greedy hunger beating a rhythm through my blood that I couldn't deny even if I wanted to.

And God, I *don't*.

I can feel the hardness of him through our clothes, and even that brief contact is almost too much for me to take. It makes me crazy. It's not enough. I tug at his shirt a little desperately, fumbling at the buttons with fingers that feel like they belong to someone else.

"Off, *off*," I beg him, my voice raw with how badly I need him.

Far, far in the back of my mind, there's a part of me that wants to blush at my own audacity, but that part is quickly overruled as the cotton of Dylan's button-down finally slides away to reveal the strong, smooth, cut chest I had just now felt against me. My mouth literally waters as he draws me close against him again, pulling me into another hungry kiss as his hands seek the clasp of my bra.

There's a split second of cold air on my breasts before the heat of Dylan's touch envelops them, his thumbs teasing my tight nipples in a way that makes me whimper against his mouth, that makes more heat shoot down to my core, pushing between my legs as I cling to him and rock against his hard thigh.

I need more, I need *everything*, and I need it now.

I reach for Dylan's belt, but he catches my hands, pulling away from the kiss and grinning down at me. I catch my breath for a second. That look, it's so sexy I want to bottle it. It makes me want to melt. Or beg. But I don't have to do either.

This is Dylan. He *knows* me.

46

He gently holds my wrists and my knees go weak at the strength I can feel in his hands. It grounds me. Frees me. I *want* to be in his hands. I trust him.

And oh God, I'm *so* turned on by him right now.

"Please," I say, nodding down toward the belt he stopped me from opening. I don't want to wait.

"You first," Dylan says, humor and wicked desire sparkling in his eyes. He pops open the button of my slacks and tugs them off my hips with quick, deft motions of his fingers, the soft wool slipping deliciously down my bare legs in a way that makes me shiver. My whole body is sensitized; everything feels erotic.

Dylan moves his hands up to my sides, gently caressing my curves as he kisses a line down my chest, over my stomach, his mouth like a brand against my skin.

"You're so gorgeous, Cate," he rumbles, and butterflies of pleasure and delight flutter through me. For once—from *him*—I believe the words. The desire and worship in his voice are unmistakable.

My hips tilt forward on their own as Dylan hooks his big thumbs under the creamy lace of my panties, every atom of me eager to help him, eager to be closer to him. His hands slide slowly downward—his touch both firm and delicate as he frees me from my lingerie—then he rocks back on his heels and looks up at me from the kitchen floor.

Dylan is enormous, even kneeling in front of me, and his height and strength make me feel delicate. *Cherished.* Especially with him staring up at me like I'm some kind of goddess.

"You're perfect, Cate," he says, his voice rough and low.

The sexy sound sends a full-body shiver through me, and I reach out my hands to him, too full of feeling and need to form any words of my own.

I don't need them. Not with him.

Dylan gives me a slow, hot smile, then rises to his feet so fast it makes me dizzy. Before I know what hits me, he's scooped me up like I weigh nothing at all and set me down on the kitchen counter. My legs open wide in an instinctive invitation, and he traces his fingers over my skin, trailing them down my chest and stomach to graze the tops of my thighs. A low, needy sound comes out of my mouth without any thought, and I arch into his touch, trying to get the most sensation out of each feather-light, unbearable caress.

When his fingertips finally make their way to the cleft between my thighs, I practically sob with relief.

The cool air of the kitchen is sharp on my wet skin, and every inch of me is buzzing with a kind of arousal I didn't even know was possible. I'm wetter than I think I've ever been in my entire life. My indulgence in the bath already feels a million years away. Did it prime me for this?

I don't know.

I can't think.

I'm sure, though, that I'd be soaking wet for Dylan—for this gorgeous, perfect man—no matter what the circumstances. I've never felt this way before. Not like *this*.

Dylan's eyes lock onto mine as his fingers stroke my entrance, easing into me confidently. Smooth and slow and exactly like I like it, as if he really *does* know my body, even though this is the first time for us.

I can't contain a whimper of pleasure; I'm a slave to the way he's making me feel, to the incredible intensity racing through me, threatening to overwhelm me entirely.

"Do you know how sexy that sounds?" he whispers, using his free hand to push my thighs open even wider.

I whimper again, trembling as it turns into a long, drawn-out moan of pleasure. I'm shameless. If he keeps teasing me like this, I'm going to go completely insane.

I reach up with both hands, cupping Dylan's face and yanking him toward me for a kiss that tastes like heaven. I twine my legs around his hips, and I can feel the power coiled in his body. It makes me tremble, every nerve in me screaming to get as close to him as humanly possible.

*Now.*

I try to tug him forward, digging my heels into the small of his back like spurs, desperate to make him feel the same primal urgency that's overwriting my reason. How can he be so patient?

"Dylan, please," I groan. No... I beg. *"Please."*

My breath hitches as his fingers move deeper inside me, stroking that perfect spot while his thumb grazes over my clit in slow arcs that make me feel like I'm going to come undone. The idea of him stopping is almost physically painful, but I need more.

"I need you, Dylan," I pant desperately. His pupils are blown wide with desire, the heat in his eyes almost enough to send me over the edge right then and there. "I need all of you, Dylan. *Please.*"

His eyes squeeze shut for a moment, his throat working, before he looks at me and nods sharply.

"One second." It comes out as a low growl, at odds with his carefully controlled movements as he withdraws his hand—making me whimper again at the feeling of loss, the void inside me a torturous ache—and then unhooks my legs from around his hips. He gently settles them against the counter, taking a step back, and I start to tremble.

Does he... does he not want me?

Dylan rubs a hand over his jaw, his eyes raking over my body with unmistakable longing, and the heat in his eyes reassures me.

I stare at the bulge in his jeans. Why did he stop?

"I'll... *fuck,* Cate, you're gorgeous." He swallows hard, tries again. "I'll be right back."

*"Dylan,"* I protest, pressing a hand against my mound. I don't want my own touch again, though. I want *him.* Inside me.

He stares at me hungrily for a second, then groans and sprints out of the room. I hear him rummaging around in the bathroom and some muffled swearing, and then he's back, holding a gold foil packet between forefinger and thumb.

"I'm so sorry," he says, capturing my mouth in a quick, hot kiss that tells me he really is feeling everything I am before pulling back with another one of those sexy, slow smiles. "I got carried away, Cate. Almost forgot to take care of you."

I stare at him, uncomprehending, and then my heart seems to skip a beat with mingled horror and relief. I've spent my whole life following the rules, being so careful, and Dylan's got me so worked up that I was going to throw that all out the window.

I completely forgot protection. I wasn't thinking at all, just feeling.

*Needing.*

"I'm, uh, I'm on the pill," I manage to stammer out as Dylan carefully opens the little packet. I know that's not enough, though. Normally, I'm almost religious about safety.

Dylan really is taking care of me.

I give him a smile that feels sheepish and weak... but it's still all I can do not to grab him.

"Thank you. For keeping a clear head."

Dylan laughs, setting the condom down on the counter beside me and pulling me in for another kiss.

"Barely," he admits. "Just... I want to do everything right by you, Cate. Always."

My cheeks are warm and a lovely, soft heat is springing to life in my heart; a counterpoint to the throbbing inferno still raging inside me.

Dylan steps back between my thighs, nudging them wide with his hips. He looks at me for a long moment, and his hands return to settle on my hips.

"Look at you," he says softly, then groans as I let my fingers splay over his broad chest. "Cate, my God. You're perfect— completely perfect."

I thought I was past blushing, but the praise hits me somewhere deep and I feel heat radiating out through my skin. It mingles with the dizzying burn of my own lust, amplifying something I thought couldn't get any more intense and making me moan. I can't form the words—I'm too overwhelmed by need—and I press my nails into Dylan's skin, pulling him forward with my legs.

This time, mercifully, he grants my unspoken wish; his hands go to his belt, undoing it and letting his jeans fall to the kitchen floor. His cock springs free, finally allowing me a look at the steel-hard thickness I've been feeling against me, and I almost gasp. The size of him, the way it twitches as he looks at me, the drop of pre-cum glistening at the fat head of him...

*Mine.*

The thought comes unbidden, and my mouth waters as I watch him wrap himself up.

Dylan looks up and meets my gaze, and his smile nearly destroys me. He leans in and kisses me, his huge hands sinking into my hair and pulling me in tight in a way that sends a jolt of delight sparking through me. He plunders my mouth with his tongue, and still it's not enough. I'm trembling, the taste of him making my blood sing. I wrap my arms around his neck and draw him closer, and Dylan reaches between our bodies, his cock pressing against my slick entrance.

*Finally.*

I gasp as he presses into me slowly, and even as drenched and ready as I am, my eyes go wide. There's just so much of him, impossibly hard and searing hot inside of me, and the feeling of my body stretching around him is so profound that I cry out and clutch at his neck.

I've never felt so full in my life, never felt so completely connected to someone as I do right now with Dylan finally inside me and his strong arms cradling me and his sweet, worshipful words filling my ears.

His hands clutch at my hips as he waits for me to adjust to his size, and I can feel him quivering with the effort of holding himself back.

I breathe out. Breathe in. *Throb* for him.

"Please," I whisper, more breath than word.

Dylan groans, and begins to move.

My head lolls back as he pulls back and thrusts into me again, my eyes fluttering closed from the sheer overload of pleasure. I can feel my body already beginning to tighten around him with his first few strokes, the ache in me twisting like hot wire wound taut almost to breaking. My heart is pounding so hard in my chest that I feel like I'm going to explode, and I know when I do, it's going to undo me.

Dylan is still panting hot, sweet, soft things into my ears, but I'm up in the clouds, up in the stars, far away from anywhere where words have meaning. I'm made entirely out of pure sensation, all nerves and energy and sweet, sharp impact, rocking together with this man in waves that have me feeling like I'm flying. It's unbearable, it's divine, it's everything I've ever needed and been unable to ask for.

And for the first time, for the first time ever, it's perfect.

I'm shaking in Dylan's arms, my bucking hips meeting his every driving thrust; it's too much, he's too much, but at the same time I can't get enough.

I moan, clutching him even tighter as it hits me: I'll *never* have enough of what Dylan's doing to me, of what he's making me feel.

My nails are clawing into his back as I desperately try to hold on, but I might as well try and stop the tide with my hands. There's no withstanding this, even if I wanted to. And oh God, I *don't*. As good as it is, as much as I want it to last forever, I need a release.

I need to let go.

I need exactly what he's giving me.

"*Cate,*" he groans, everything in his voice.

I cry out, a wordless sound of pure bliss as it pushes me over the edge. My nerves explode in a riot of fireworks, pleasure blindingly intense, and I feel like I'm shattering into a billion glittering fragments. I seem to come forever, my body quaking around him, over and over until there's nothing left of me but slick, aching muscles and the echo of that wailing scream I can barely believe came from me.

Perfect ecstasy.

"Cate," Dylan says again, raw and desperate. His hips snap forward, driving into me with hard, fast strokes that send aftershocks rolling through my body.

It's so good.

So... *good.*

His movements grow wild, his breath ragged, and then his arms tighten around me like a vise. I feel him go tense, his muscles flexing against me as his entire body shudders. He groans my name again through gritted teeth as he comes, and then—finally—he presses a kiss to my hair, his arms loosening a bit without letting me go.

I lean against his chest, listening to the beat of his heart as it starts to slow. I don't want to think yet. I just want this.

I feel perfect.

Dylan rests his head on top of mine. "Cate..." he says after a minute, his huge hands stroking lightly up and down my back.

*Heaven.*

I feel him swallow hard, and I smile against the warm skin of his hard chest, realizing it's the only word I've heard from him in a while.

"Cate," he repeats, and my name sounds like an answer to something he's been asking for a long time.

Maybe to something I have, too.

Dylan holds me like this for a while—gentle and close—and our racing heartbeats seem to mingle together as we float back down to Earth.

I feel liquid, boneless, truly satisfied for the first time in my life. I've never come twice in one day, didn't even know that it was physically possible for me, let alone that I could orgasm back-to-back like this. And so... intensely.

My lips curve up.

First, from the erotic shock of Jack walking in on me, and now, from what has been hands-down the most incredible, mind-blowingly perfect sex I've ever had in my life.

Warm drowsiness spreads through my aching muscles, and my mind feels pleasantly foggy. This must be what it feels like to have no stress, I realize. All the tension, all the worry has been utterly wiped away.

Wow.

Dylan's saying something—I more feel the rumble of his voice through his chest than hear it—and I force myself out of my hazy reverie.

"What?" I ask, yawning.

Not moving ever again would be a nice option.

He laughs softly. "I said, it seems like you really needed that." He kisses me gently, adding, "... as badly as I did."

Dylan steps away and my eyes drift shut. I hear the rustle of latex being shed, tied off, then the lid of the garbage opening and closing. There's the soft noise of him putting his jeans back on, of the kitchen faucet, and then Dylan is back.

"Mm." I smile up at him, my eyelids heavy. "Did I ever." He grins as he gently runs a warm, wet towel along my dripping thighs, between them, cleaning me up with delicate care. "And now I need—" I yawn again, interrupting myself.

"Naptime?" Dylan teases as he tucks the towel into his belt loop, and I nod. "Got you covered, gorgeous."

He effortlessly gathers me up into his arms, and I'm nearly purring. It all feels a bit surreal—this isn't my life—but for once, all the anxieties in my head are quiet, and I'm more than happy to go with it.

Dylan carries me gently up the stairs, nestled against the hard planes of his chest, and I must doze, because the next thing I feel is the sense of floating downward as he places me gently onto a soft surface.

I open my eyes to see I'm in Grandpa Sully's old room, resting on the massive, burled walnut bed with its towering carved posts. The sheets are new—a soft cotton, like t-shirt material—and I can't resist nuzzling against the pillow. I reach for one of the thick, plush blankets, but instead Dylan catches my hand, running his thumb lightly over my knuckles before placing my hand back down on the pillow.

To my delighted surprise, he proceeds to tuck me in, folding me into the kind of blanket burrow I always loved as a kid growing up. Still do. The layers of blankets are a comforting weight, a safe haven, and of course Dylan would remember that.

He's almost too good to be true, but I'm too satisfied and dreamy right now for even my legendary anxiety to gain even the slightest foothold.

I smile at him sleepily, my heart almost overflowing with peace and contentment. I've always despised it when someone takes charge of my life, making decisions for me without a single care for what I actually want. But this is different. It's not anything like that, not by a long shot.

Dylan isn't taking over, deciding what's best for me without consulting me. He's paying attention, listening to all my needs, and truly—the echo of pleasure rolls through me—*fulfilling* them.

"How are you real?" I murmur, my eyelids heavy.

Dylan leans down, brushing my hair from my face before placing a gentle, warm kiss on my lips. It's a sweet kiss, a satisfied kiss that still somehow carries the promise of a world of pleasure in the future. I groan, languid as a cat in a sunbeam, and Dylan laughs softly.

"You get some rest, Wildcat," he says. The warmth and desire in his eyes makes me feel safe.

*Cherished.*

I let myself float off into sleep, content not to worry about any of the events of this dizzying day, despite the fact that I haven't been acting like myself... at all.

There will be time to sort everything out tomorrow, and besides, I think I like this Cate.

I really, really do.

# 5

## JACK

$\mathcal{I}$ shove a hand through my hair, glancing around my well-furnished office as I take a breather from the pile of work that was waiting for me. Truth is, though, I'm relieved to have it. Never thought I'd be thinking anything like that, but can't deny it. Helps take the focus off... other shit.

Yesterday had been a flat-out nightmare, both at the town-house and everything after. I don't know why I'd thought getting friendly with Dylan again would work out. If I'd been smart, I really should have just buried myself in a hole first thing in the morning, the temptation of Dylan's dinner invitation notwithstanding, and waited for today to dig back out.

First off, what had all of that garbage with Cate been about? I can't even think about the crazy hot scene I'd walked in on when I'm still so steamed about what came after. How dare she talk to me like I'm still some sort of townie street trash? It had been one thing when we were kids—none of us knew any better back then, and sure, maybe I'd still been a little rough around the edges but I've had plenty of time to buff it out since. We're grown-ass adults now, and I know I present one hell of a package these days.

Her sheer lack of regard, all of that entitlement, it just blows my mind. Not that Cate and I were ever really *friends*, but Sully's dead and I think I deserve just a little bit more courtesy.

I lost him, too, and I swallow hard, staring blindly at the file open on my desk as I try not to think too hard about that.

After I'd gotten out of the townhouse yesterday, the train ride home had been a nightmare. I got nothing against kids for the most part, and maybe I'd even like to be a daddy one day myself, but I'm definitely going to be the kind of daddy who makes sure his kid's hands are clean so they won't get a stranger's very expensive slacks all sticky when they grab hold and rub their grubby, sticky mess into them.

The hits had just kept on coming, too.

Got off the train and ran smack into some fridge-sized Bruins fan. He body-checked me without looking, which ended up with his fresh, hot coffee landing all over my shirt. Worst part? He looks at me like *I'm* the asshole.

I can't believe this city sometimes.

Tried to drop by the market after that, and of course nothing I wanted was in stock. Insult to injury after giving up on whatever slice of heaven I could have had in Dylan's kitchen. I don't know what kind of crazy shopping bug had hit the city, but for whatever reason, the shelves had been just about bare. I couldn't even pick up a loaf of decent bread, and they were out of my favorite coffee beans, too.

Fucking ridiculous.

And the best part, of course, was when I got home. I tried to fix myself some early dinner and ended up dropping a chicken bone down the garbage disposal. Went ahead and rolled up my sleeves to take care of it myself, but at that point I was just sweaty, exhausted, and more than ready for bed. I ended up skipping a decent meal and just chowing down on two-day-old takeout.

The hell that was yesterday should have been over after that, and good riddance, but of course, the moment I'd started drifting off, Ma calls me up. Nothing new, no emergencies other than her entire life. She went on and on about the bills, and I had to sit there and "uh-huh" and "oh, really," both of us pretending I couldn't hear Pop in the background, whispering for her to ask me for money.

My old man always went on about the family name this, family name that, like he was doing such a bang-up job at bringing us any pride. I always get an earful from him about how I'm not living up to the Kelly name... right up until he gets someone to ask me for a handout. Guess that must mean I've done something right, huh?

Don't get me wrong, I've always tried to do right by my family even when they never did anything right by me, but it wears on a guy, you know? And no, not that I'd say it to my old man, I don't give two shits about being a Kelly. Doesn't seem to me that it's a hell of a lot to live up to, if you want the truth.

Sometimes, no matter what name I carry, it feels like Sully was the only *real* family I ever had. Of course, my people couldn't stand him, but it was his standards that pulled me up. Him that I wanted to make proud.

I swallow, glancing at the clock. Sully's dying is like a hole, and even being *here*—smack-dab in the middle of the good life he helped me make for myself—doesn't really help. And sure, today is still a wet dream in comparison to yesterday's crapfest, but gotta admit, some days, it feels like maybe I should have just gone and worked construction with my brother. It would have been a hell of a lot easier than being a high-octane criminal lawyer in the city, and even with the perks of the "better life," it's not always all it's cracked up to be. Nicer clothes, some spending cash, but even if my digs are better, they're still empty when I go home and get stuck eating takeout by myself with no one to unload about the day to.

I look at the clock again. It's already creeping into the early afternoon and I'm not making much headway here. Every time I dive in, I keep finding my thoughts drifting to Cate and Dylan and this mess the three of us are tangled up in with the townhouse.

Screw this. Can't focus, not doing any good here. Maybe it's time for a real break. The kind I actually leave my desk for.

I stand up and grab my suit coat, pulling it on as I stride for the office doors.

"Hey, Jack." It's Tom, the second attorney on one of my cases. "You okay, bud?"

Guess it is a little early for a break. Not to mention it's not really like me. Work is kind of all I've got, and just like Sully taught me, I give it my all.

"Yeah," I reply, doing my best to push my jumble of screwed-up feelings out of the way and put my business voice on as I offer Tom a smile. "All's well, I'm just a little claustrophobic today, know what I mean?"

"Ha, I can guess why," he says, grinning back. "Saw that stack on your desk."

"Yeah," I agree absently, even though that had been more of a saving grace than a burden—today, at least. "Listen, mind covering for me for a bit? I ain't all here today, got some family business to take care of."

I'll shoot some money over to Ma, so that it doesn't turn into a lie. I take care of the finances for my parents, not that I'll ever hear a thank you.

"Hey bud, no worries," Tom says, and I sigh inwardly, relieved. "You owe me one, though."

"I'll catch you on the flip," I say, then turn and get the hell out of there as inconspicuously as possible. No guilt, though, since it's not like I don't put in the hours and then some.

There's a real nice brewpub down the road called Hamilton's Wake; I go there every once in a while after work, real nice spot. Never been in before 6 p.m., though. When I head over, it's chock-full of tourists and a bunch of other folks I don't know.

I grab a stool at the bar. I know it's early, but I don't drink much as it is, so why not treat myself?

"You're here early, sugar," the bartender says. She's a sassy little thing, a little bit punk, dyed hair, amazing breasts.

"Yeah, Tina, what can I say?" I rub my forehead for just a second. "Had a rough day."

And fine, the rough shit was *yesterday*, but still holds true.

She smirks and cocks her head. "Want a drink to put those flames out?"

"Yes, please," I say, finally feeling like I can exhale a little. "Macallan 18?"

"You got it, sugar," Tina says, and flounces off with that fantastic ass of hers.

I set my hands on the bartop and let my head drop on top of them. Finally, some peace.

My mind drifts, and I start getting a mishmash of feelings and thoughts as I let myself process. Dylan, and how excited he'd looked when I'd stormed into the kitchen after Cate's little show. I yank my thoughts offa *that*, but even focusing on Dylan... something hot stirs low in my gut.

Damn, but his smile always kills me.

I jerk my head up, making sure to ogle Tina's rack as she gets my drink, getting my head back where it needs to be before I can think too hard about any weird feelings about Dylan. Still, just looking at a nicely put together woman makes my thoughts go straight back to Cate. How delicious her skin looked, all beaded up with water droplets over her spectacular breasts.

Nope.

Shouldn't go there, either.

But... damn, even keeping my mind off all that, my mouth is still watering. Those sausages I missed out on. They smelled effing *amazing*.

I'm still staring at Tina, but I'm kind of out of it, too. Truth is, even though I'm still upset with Cate and Dylan, thinking about all the fun they must be having without me there to ruin the party, I have to admit that for a split second, even with all the bullshit, just being there in the kitchen with the two of them felt a little like family again.

The real kind; Sully's kind, not the fucked-up version with my own people.

"If you don't take this, I'm going to drink it for you," Tina says, her voice snapping me out of my reverie. "Too beautiful a scotch to let it go to waste."

She winks, and I laugh, but apparently it doesn't hide shit, 'cause I see a look in her eyes that I can read like a book. Kind of the way it looks like she's reading *me*.

Tina's always been perceptive, but I guess all bartenders are. It's like a job requirement.

"Thank you, Tina, you're a lifesaver," I say, picking up the glass and taking a sip as I wonder if she's going to push or let my inner turmoil slide.

The lovely, smooth burn of the scotch goes down my throat, and even though I'm not a big drinker, I could get used to that. It's a good alternative to wallowing, at least.

Tina bites her lip and smiles at me. Not really flirty, just... nice.

"Listen, I'm actually off work as of a few minutes ago. I swapped out with Bobby for the afternoon shift. You wanna buy me a drink, tell me what's all over that face of yours?"

She's sweet. And sure, maybe it'd be nice to vent a little.

"Pour yourself whatever you like," I say, not worried about what she'll choose. I can afford it, and the truth is, I'm not averse to the company or the offer of an ear.

Classic Tina, though. Offered an open slate, she goes right for a beer.

She pops open an IPA and leans over the bar. "Hit me," she offers, smiling as she downs the first sip.

I turn the glass around in my hand, realizing I'm not really up to whining. But still, yesterday sucked.

"A friend of mine is in a real bad spot right now," I start. Still feels good to say it, even if I'm not gonna admit how shitty my good life feels, some days.

"Oh yeah?" Tina responds, lips twitching like she can see right through me.

*My friend*, my ass.

"Yeah," I say, forging ahead with the story like I don't know she knows what—*who*—I'm really talking about. I take one more small sip, savoring the richness as it does that slow slide down my throat again. Fucking delicious. "My friend, uh, his mentor died recently, and a couple of people came back into his life that he hadn't really seen in years. People that used to kinda mean something, well, one did, and one who also meant something, but was also kinda a pain in the ass—"

"Hey, sugar," Tina cuts in, reaching out to give my hand a quick squeeze. "I know I'm a bartender, but we can cut the crap. I heard that Sully died."

I blink. "How?"

I'd never even mentioned Sully to her, had I? Maybe I'd mentioned where I worked, and she knew it was Sully's firm? Had she known him?

I must have asked that last one out loud.

"Of course I did," Tina says, laughing. "You have no clue, do you? He bailed the boss out a couple of times, got him out of some nasty scrapes and helped him on a few cases. Boss gave him a little office upstairs that Sully could use when he needed to get away from everything. Huge tipper, that guy. Talked about you three a lot. You're talking about Dylan and Cate, right?"

Now it's my turn to laugh, in disbelief. You think you know a guy... I smile and shake my head. Actually, yeah. I *did* know Sully. Not sure why I'm surprised by Tina's revelation, since he was always bailing people out. Helping without any need for recognition.

"There's no end to the tricks up that man's sleeves, even now that he's gone, huh?"

"There definitely ain't," Tina replies, tipping back her beer again before waving a hand at me and adding, "But go on, I'm listening."

"Alright, fair enough. Dylan and me, we were close when we were kids, you know?"

She nods. Guess Sully really did talk about us. *Close* is... the word ain't enough. Doesn't really do what we were justice. I'd never had a friend like Dylan before. He *got* me. Still does, even with all the shit between us, and the years.

And even though I don't always get *him*.

I clear my throat, suddenly needing to explain it to her. Just needing to *say* it. "Close, like, never saw one of us without the other too far behind, thick as thieves, the whole nine. I don't know if we were just friends, or something more..." I trail off, my stomach tightening that I'd actually said that last bit out loud. But Tina's still just looking at me, so I power on. "It was ages ago, you remember what it was like. That... stuff didn't really fly."

"Oh, I remember," Tina says, nodding. I know her people are like mine. She gets me. After a minute, she asks, "So what happened with the closeness?"

"Dylan ruined it," I say flatly, not wanting to remember that part. "All of it. I just always assumed he was my friend, and was always gonna be there for me, and then..."

I pause, my voice trailing off as that visual of him kissing another guy pops right up in front of me. A guy. A guy who wasn't me, not that I would've, but... *fuck*. I can still feel that sick-scared-mad feeling churning in my gut.

"He ruined it, Tina," I repeat. "Dylan ruined our bond. I went off to college and didn't speak to him for years."

And fuck me if that hadn't sucked.

"Up until the funeral?" she asks after a minute.

"Yeah, that was the first time I'd seen him or talked to him in a long time." I'd been looking for him. Figured he'd be there, but still felt a little blindsided when I'd actually seen him. I smile despite myself. "Seeing him felt... good. It felt different, you know?"

I figure "different" isn't going to make sense to her, since it doesn't really make sense to me... until Tina nails it on the head.

"Not so lonely anymore?" she asks.

Yeah, that might be it. The word definitely strikes a chord in me. *Loneliness*. I hadn't even thought about it that way, not once, but for all that I'd clawed my way up to a higher place in the world, it had been my companion. I didn't fit with my people anymore, and I hadn't found anyone to replace them. Not since pushing Dylan away.

"I had a really rough day yesterday," I say, knowing I wasn't answering her but my mind already skipping two steps ahead. Or back, maybe. "Just mistake after mistake all day long, and it started with a big fight."

"You and Dylan?"

I grimace. "No, the other blast from my past." Cate, I silently think. "When we were kids, she treated me like I was just another punk from the street, y'know?"

Tina cocks her head to the side, giving me an assessing look. "That doesn't sound right to me."

"I know, right?" I snap back, my indignation rising hot and fast again.

"No," Tina says, holding up a hand like she can see me getting pissed. "I mean, that doesn't sound like the girl Sully always talked about. This is his granddaughter, Cate, right?"

I nod, but I don't get it. Or maybe I do. It wasn't like Sully was going to speak poorly of his own flesh and blood. He'd thought the sun rose and set on that girl, and it had been a harsh wake-up call when I'd started to get to know her back when we were kids and realized how much she looked down on me.

Not gonna call Sully on that now, though, but Tina's still giving me that quizzical look.

"Sully talked about Cate, huh?" I say, half curious, half just to be polite.

Okay, maybe that's a lie. I'm pretty curious. Hell, as pissed as I am, Cate in that bathtub isn't a sight that's gonna leave me anytime soon.

Tina shrugs, running the bottle rim lightly against her lower lip before answering. "I don't know," she finally says, clearly trying to put her thoughts in order. "Sully just made her sound like she was shy. I always got the feeling she had some things she was struggling with, but he was never specific."

"Entitled," I mutter, but Tina shakes her head.

"You know how Sully felt about his position in the world," she says. "Everyone was his equal, no matter the money or name or status. I can't imagine he'd let his granddaughter grow up thinking like all the other rich assholes do, or that she'd treat you like that under his roof."

This kind of catches me off-guard, but honestly, it's too much to process at the moment. I know how things were. Not just then, but fucking *yesterday*.

I shake my head, not buying it.

Tina shrugs and takes a drink, not pushing it.

I'm pretty sure she'll leave it alone completely if I want, but my mouth opens all on its own, and I end up spilling out more of my guts.

"Anyway," I say, pausing after the word to clear my throat. Muster my courage. Whatever. I've never been big on talking about shit like this. *Feelings.* Tina's just waiting on me, though, so I go on, "Her and Dylan were always close back when we were kids."

I hadn't resented it.

Well, yeah, okay, I had. Truth is, I always had to work at my relationships, just too prickly for most people, I guess. And I never, *ever*, had it as easy as those two seemed to.

Tina's just staring at me, so I add, "It's like they fell in a rhythm and didn't even think about it. Like they just *fit*."

"Oh, so she stole him away from you?" Tina asks, her lips twitching in what might have been a smile if she hadn't hidden it behind her beer.

"No, nothing like that," I say. And really, it hadn't been. Cate had never taken Dylan away, it had just always bugged me that I wasn't part of what they had, too. It was me and Dylan, or it was her and Dylan. But we couldn't ever manage to make it more than that. To make it all of us. But whatever. I look down at my drink, mumbling, "The two of them, they just always made it look easy."

Nothing in *my* life had ever come easy.

"I know the feeling," Tina says, smiling. "I think both you and I come from a place of loneliness in our lives. You're a big fancy lawyer in the city now, but I know that look in your eyes. I have it; everyone I like the most has it. Always an arms-length kind of thing. Hard to let people in when it might hurt to lose them."

I scowl. Losing Sully still hurt. Losing Dylan back in the day had hurt like a bitch, under all my anger. Anger was easier, though. And Cate... I'd never had her to lose her, but there'd been a time when I'd thought we were all part of Sully's makeshift family. When I'd thought we'd be... something.

"So, what?" I ask Tina, starting to get a little pissed off again. Always easier than feeling other shit, right? "This is my fault? For not making it easy on people who want to be close?"

"Hell, no," Tina answers with a laugh, showing that the black cloud I'm sitting under doesn't get to her. "It just takes a while for people like us, that's all. It doesn't come naturally, so we've got to work to let people in, to trust that maybe it will be okay if we do. Maybe practice assuming the best instead of looking for the worst, yeah? It gets easier the more you do it."

"Yeah," I snort, raising my glass to my lips to finish off the scotch. "I wish."

But there's something inside me that wonders if she's right. And another part that's scared to hope for it.

I can feel the pit in my chest growing. Loneliness is right.

"Give it a shot," Tina says, smiling. "Always sounded to me like Sully thought the world of all three of you, and seemed like he knew a thing or two about people. And he also…"

She doesn't finish that, letting her words trail away behind another long pull of beer.

"He also what?" I push, because she's right. Sully knew people. What else had he said about the three of us?

Tina shrugs. "I don't know. I'm actually surprised to hear you guys are fighting, I guess. Seemed like Sully always thought you three were close. Family. And now… here you are. All three back in each other's lives."

I snort, mulling this over for a moment. Back in each other's lives because of *Sully*.

I came into the pub feeling one way, but after Tina's words, I'm confused. Am I still having a shitty day? Because nothing's changed, but maybe I feel a little lighter. Doesn't make sense, but I'll take it.

I finish off the scotch, take my money clip out, and slide some twenties across the bar.

"Keep the change," I say, winking. "You earned it, listening to my garbage."

"Yeah, yeah," she says, feigning irritation. She can't hide the fact that she's smiling back, though. "Get outta here, big shot."

"Thanks again," I say, throwing my suit coat on and cracking my neck. A few moments later, I'm back out on the street and lost in thought, walking the sidewalks and mulling over everything we talked about.

I'm not paying attention to my surroundings, and I just about knock myself over running directly into Gary. Shouldn't surprise me, given that we both work for the same firm and have good taste in drinks. I always liked Gary.

"Mr. Kelly!" he exclaims, grabbing onto my arm to keep me from falling.

I swear, that man is built like a brick house. He could have had a great career playing for the Patriots.

"Gary, hey, I meant to give you a call earlier," I say, remembering for the first time. He'd reminded me a couple of times, but I kept putting it off.

The truth is, I still couldn't fully wrap my head around Sully putting me in his will. He'd already given me so much. Not gonna lie, though, the thing with the townhouse was a bit of a twist that I didn't fully understand. I couldn't say I'd minded it bringing Dylan back into my life, though.

Or Cate.

Maybe.

The jury is still out on that one, but even being pissed at her... damn. No denying she's always got to me, and that was even *before* I saw her coming undone like some kind of sex goddess yesterday in the bath.

I discreetly adjust myself, glad I'm carrying a briefcase.

"Nothing to worry about, Mr. Kelly, no harm done," Gary's saying, smiling at me and thankfully not seeming to notice my moment of distraction. "I was going to suggest that we set up a time to discuss the remaining provisions of the will. I also need to ensure that Mr. Smith and Ms. MacMillan are brought fully up to speed."

Dylan had been surprised when I'd admitted to him that I didn't get the thing with the will at first. *You're an attorney too, right?* he'd asked. I'd just snorted. Ask me anything about criminal law or stick me in a courtroom and I'll tear it up. Estate law? Yawn. Still, I knew once Gary walked me through it I'd follow along just fine.

And maybe the truth was I'd avoided going through the paperwork too closely because Sully's loss still stung.

I was grateful for the consideration, him putting me in the will, but I also hated it. Hated that he was gone, I mean. Clouded my judgment, maybe, when it came to clearing up what shoulda been a simple thing to deal with in regard to the townhouse.

Can't say I wasn't great at avoiding what was hard to deal with, right?

"Sure," I say to Gary though, knowing he cared about Sully, too. Well, that and he needs to do his job. The thing he said about bringing Cate and Dylan up to speed, though... suddenly I'm swamped with some kind of sense memory, all those delicious smells from the kitchen yesterday. Dylan had been cooking for *me* on Friday. I clear my throat. "About that, Gary. How about you let me talk with the two of them first? I'm going over there this evening anyway."

I am? I guess I am now. Thanks, mouth, for running away without my consent. Saying it has got me grinning, though, and fuck if I coulda seen *that* coming after the perma-scowl I'd been sporting for the last twenty-four hours or so.

"Are you quite certain, Mr. Kelly?" Gary asks, sounding a little unsure. "Have you had a chance to review the provisions of the will enough to explain it to them?"

I shake my head, my smile slipping as my throat suddenly goes tight, and Gary's eyes soften.

"It's not a responsibility that you have to take on alone," he says compassionately. "I'd be happy to take care of it. And... there's the deadline to think about, of course."

"No, it's okay, Gary," I say. "I'm headed there tonight. I can make sure we go over the gist of it, then get with you later to talk about the particulars, 'kay?"

Gary smiles and nods. "Of course, Mr. Kelly. In that case, I must thank you for freeing up my afternoon. I need to see to one more piece of business, and then I believe I'll go home and catch up on my programs."

"Still watching *Hearts & Kisses*, Gary?" I tease, remembering Sully doing the same to him. Who would have thought a man like Gary would have a soap opera obsession?

He laughs out of that huge barrel of a chest. "Yes, well, the quality of the writing is amazing," he says, winking. "You find the things you love, and you stick with them. I've never seen any shame in that."

That catches me a bit. "Funny how that works," I mumble, for some reason flashing back to that scene I've never been able to wipe from my mind.

*Dylan.* I'd never even guessed he was gay before catching him in the act. Ruined our friendship, but even though he'd been the one to do something my parents would have been quick to label deviant, *I'd* been the one who'd felt ashamed.

Never quite got how that worked, but just as unfair as the rest of life, I guess.

I frown, but Gary pulls me out of the bad memories with a non sequitur.

"Mr. Kelly, do you remember the Monopoly game?"

The moment he says the words, I'm grinning again as the memory floods back to me. It was all of us, the five of us together. Me, Dylan, Cate, Sully, and Gary, all sitting around the coffee table.

"Yeah, I do," I say, laughing. "God, Gary, that was ages ago."

That day had really been something, though. A lot of good humor, smiles, and laughter. I remember Cate actually being totally okay that day, after a little bit of warming up. Dylan was doing an excellent job facilitating between the two of us, making sure he was guiding our jokes and conversations with a gentle, deft hand. Gary and Sully might have been the glue that held the entire house together, but Dylan was always the glue that held the three of us kids together.

Because the truth is, even with Cate's bad attitude, it had felt like we were together. That we were something.

Maybe family, like Tina had talked about.

"I haven't thought of that in years," I add, missing it. Well, not Monopoly. Fuck if that game didn't take forever. But that *feeling*. That was really something.

"Yes," Gary says, cocking his head to the side and smiling at me. "It's funny how we forget moments like that until much later on in life."

He takes his leave, and I head back to the office, mentally rearranging the rest of my day with this added responsibility that I'd just taken on. My nerves almost get the best of me. What was I thinking? Sitting the two of them down to talk about the townhouse after everything that happened would be a nightmare.

I don't even know if they'll want me to come over.

Then I grin. Even without estate business to talk about, that's a lie. Dylan always makes me feel welcome, even when he's pissed, and Cate... well, she always makes me feel *something*, at least. So fine, whatever I have to say to make it happen, tonight we'll talk. Maybe over dinner. One of Dylan's fantastic dinners. And who knows, maybe it'll go fine.

Maybe—unlike yesterday—it'll go *well*, even.

After all, Sully wouldn't have set it up so we had to deal with each other if he hadn't figured it would work out, right?

6

DYLAN

*B*y the time I open my eyes, it's already almost noon. I can't believe how well I slept. I can't believe how well *everything* has gone so far, I guess. I look to my side and see Cate, snuggled up in her blankets, out like a lamp. Poor thing; it has almost definitely been a rough couple of days for her with everything happening so far.

I get up and stretch out, looking out of the window and enjoying the goings-on below. This city really moves like no other in the world, and I can't believe how lucky I am to be here right now. I take another glance at the clock to see how much time I have. Maybe a couple of hours? Good. Plenty of time for brunch.

A few minutes later, I'm freshly showered and downstairs in the kitchen, wearing my comfiest sweatpants. I love the way they sling low on my hips, and the material is so, *so* soft. I neglect to put my shirt back on; the temperature is just so perfect inside right now, and if we're being completely honest, I never much liked wearing clothes anyway.

*Let's try that breakfast one more time,* I think as I quickly prep the bagels, then get the eggs and bacon out of the fridge. A moment later and the telltale sizzle of bacon fills the room, along with

73

those delicious smells. I look down and pat my stomach; my abs would prevent anyone from accusing me of avoiding the gym, though I don't quite have the washboard six-pack that Jack does.

*Did*, at least. It's been years since I've seen him shirtless.

My thoughts wander off for a bit, imagining his body. I used to see it often, glistening with sweat when we would work out in Sully's basement gym together. I remember stealing glances all the time. I just couldn't help myself. Maybe that's why I was so shocked when Jack blew up at me for kissing another boy. I just figured that I was being so obvious about it all that he must have known from the beginning.

Serves me right for being so trusting, I guess. Or naïve?

I'm snapped out of my reverie by the sounds of floorboards gently creaking. Cate must be up. A smile spreads over my face as I put the bacon on a napkin to let some of the excess grease soak up. I start prepping the eggs, whisking in just a little bit of cream to keep them thick and rich. Scrambled, just like she liked when we were kids.

I'm so, so happy for Cate. Granted, we've spent way more time in bed than in conversation, so I only have a small part of the picture of her life, but it seems like she's done very well for herself. A woman as impressive as that, and with such killer curves on top of it?

I can hardly believe she's single.

I reach down to adjust myself, grinning. Can't say I'm not happy about how that's worked out for *me* so far, though.

Even over the din of the stove, I can hear the stairs slowly creaking, footsteps making their way gingerly down. My ears are finely attuned to every sound that this house makes. I think all of ours are. This house was every bit as important to our lives together as we were to each other. I know for a fact that, for me, it felt more like home than my own. Not that my real home was difficult—not like Cate's and Jack's were, in their own very different ways—but still, between all the time I spent here at

Sully's and how much like family he made us all feel, when I think of home, it's always been here.

I slide the eggs onto the plate next to a toasted sliced bagel and a healthy serving of bacon, just in time to watch Cate slink into the kitchen.

"Hey, you," I say, beaming.

Damn, she's gorgeous.

"Hey, you," she says back, and I can hear the tentative edge to her voice.

She isn't quite dressed yet, but she does have my robe wrapped tightly around her like a blanket of armor. She's always had that. Armor. Can't blame her, the way her mother was, but I hope it doesn't take her long to figure out she doesn't need it around *me*.

I turn off the burners and quickly move everything to the sink for cleanup later.

"I'm glad you slept in," I say, giving her a reassuring smile. "You clearly needed it."

"I think I did," she says with a self-conscious laugh, as if for some reason she thinks she should have been Superwoman instead. Able to deal with all the emotional hits Sully's death dealt us, plus the upheaval of her life, without flinching. It makes me want to wrap her up in my arms and not let go.

I must be staring, because her cheeks go pink, and the hint of a matching smile appears at the corner of her lips.

Kind of makes me want to have a taste, and I grin even wider, still loving the fact that I finally *have*.

She's delicious.

"I must have been tired," she says, looking away. "After everything that happened yesterday, I don't think I could have kept my eyes open even if I'd wanted to."

I wash my hands, quickly dry off, and sling the dishtowel over my shoulder. I can feel her eyes gliding over my body, starting from my chest and dropping down to the cut of my hips. I smile and reach one hand out, using my curled index finger to gently raise her chin, guessing that she's not nearly as comfortable with the sex now as she had been while it was happening.

"It's all okay, you know," I say, and I can tell immediately that she knows what I'm talking about.

"Is it?" she asks, eyes darting up to mine. Her voice starts steady, but then starts to quietly unravel. "Honestly, I don't know how I feel about what happened yesterday. I was just so tired, and everything moved so quickly and... *God*, Dylan. The smells and the sights and all of the sounds, it brought so many memories back, and you and Jack..."

I take a step forward, closing the gap between us, and wrap my arms around her shoulders. I delicately take the back of her head in the palm of my hand, her silky hair running through my fingers. She stops talking, seeming grateful not to have to say more, and rests her head on my chest.

Feels pretty much perfect.

"It's all okay," I repeat. "You're home, you're safe, and you're with someone that you can trust."

"Promise?" she says, picking her head up for just a moment.

"Promise," I say without missing a beat, and I can tell right away that—unexpected or not—it's just as right as everything else has always been between us. Cate and me, we've always fit. Time apart and years between us hasn't changed that a bit.

I smile, and the little hitch in her breath when she smiles back has me leaning in. I gently catch her soft lips in mine, and the minute I do, both of us exhale and melt into each other, like we've just let go of all the stress in the world. I like that. I like to take care of people, and I want to do that for her, especially. She's always mattered to me.

My fingers trace a delicate line along the side of her face and neck, and I give her lower lip a gentle nibble as we break apart.

Her eyes flutter, and she draws in a deep breath. "That... oh, that's so nice," she says on an exhale. Then she takes a deep breath, and sort of squares her shoulders. It's kind of adorable. "But we can't complicate things, Dylan," she says, sounding like she's not sure whether she wants me to agree or talk her out of that statement.

I shrug and smile. It doesn't seem that complicated to me, but I've always been pretty comfortable in my own skin, and Lord knows I'm a fan of the pleasures in life. If sex is stressing her out, though, we can table it for now in favor of other things.

"So then, let's not complicate it," I say agreeably, noting how my answer makes the last little bit of tension leave her shoulders. I grin, nodding my head over toward her full plate of brunch. "Hungry?"

Her eyes go wide, then narrow as she looks at me. "How many calories in that feast, pal?"

I laugh and shake my head, then take her plate in my hand, moving over to the table.

"That's the wrong question. Sit, yeah? Relax a second?"

I set the plate down and draw her chair out.

She sits and settles in, and I take the chair right next to her, spearing a bit of both bacon and eggs and bringing the fork up to her delectable mouth.

"You're gonna love this," I say confidently. I know Cate, and I know food. I've got no doubt at all that I'm right.

She opens her mouth hesitantly, and once she tastes it—just like I thought—she lets loose with a sexy moan that reminds me of the other things we've done here in the kitchen, and her eyes positively glitter.

"Oh hell, Dylan," she says, grinning at me while chewing. "Pardon my manners, but you're right. Nothing beats a classic."

"Coffee or orange juice?" I say, pleased with her reaction as I set the fork on the plate.

"Coffee." She waits a beat, then smiles and tears a piece of bagel off. "No. Orange juice. I love orange juice."

"Coming up," I say, and leave her to her meal, walking toward the fridge and pulling a pair of glasses down to pour our drinks. Cold brew for me, orange juice for her.

"So," Cate starts between bites. "What's the deal with the townhouse, Dylan? I just need someone to be straight with me. Did Sully really leave it to all three of us?"

My thoughts blink over to Jack for a moment, putting just the smallest damper on an otherwise wonderful morning. He mattered to me, too, but he'd always been so quick to anger. It's a side of him I'd thought he was working to get rid of, but Sully's death had hit him hard and anger had always been what he was most comfortable with when he felt anything too strongly. In his blood, as he'd often said, and I know he figured it was just part of who he was.

It doesn't have to be, though. At least I hope not, for his sake.

Cate is still waiting for my answer about the townhouse, not that I know much.

"Yeah?" I say, pouring the drinks. Her eyebrows go up at the uncertainty of my answer, and I shrug. "Far as I know, all three of us own it together. I don't know all the ins and outs, though. Haven't been able to match up my schedule with Gary's yet to go over it, but I know he needs us to sign some paperwork or something."

Cate nods. "Is that why Jack was coming over yesterday?" she asks.

"We were going to talk about the townhouse, yeah," I say. "I'm not sure that he has all the details either, though, but at the least we were going to talk about practical things."

Her eyebrows go up. "He's still a lawyer though, right? Hasn't he gone over the will?"

"Jack? Sure. But I guess this kind of law isn't his area of specialty."

And honestly, the way he'd shied away from discussing the will when we'd talked, I'm pretty sure it brought up more of those emotions he wasn't that well equipped to deal with. I don't mind waiting for us all to sort it out, though. Honestly, just having the two of them back in my life is more important to me than a real estate transaction.

"I just can't believe how angry he was yesterday," Cate says, frowning. "I barely get into town and he just explodes. I know he always disliked me, but I just can't for the life of me understand why."

I put the pitcher in the fridge and walk the glasses back to the kitchen table. "Sometimes there's no getting inside that man's head," I say as I put the orange juice down in front of her.

"Yum," she says, her mood brightening. I'd like to always do that for her. "Thank you so much, all of this is so wonderful."

She picks up the glass and takes a tentative sip, smiles conspiratorially, then takes a nice long gulp.

"Anytime. So yeah, I thought Jack and I were going to talk about the townhouse over dinner yesterday, but you saw what happened. I'll need to give him a call and figure out when he wants to reschedule."

"Gary has to be the one to make anything official though, right?" she asks.

"Yeah, I think so. Maybe I'll give him a call and see if he can reach out to Jack; maybe that'll go over more smoothly than me reaching out directly."

Cate frowns. "I wish Sully were here," she says. "He'd be able to fix this."

"Probably," I say, smiling. No probably about it. Sully always brought us all together. "I know you weren't there long, but remember the funeral, Cate? How packed it was?"

Her lips curl into a fond smile. "Yeah. Everyone really loved that man."

"They did," I say. "I bet he solved a lot of problems in his time."

"Jack," she says, closing her eyes on a frustrated sigh. "If only Sully could solve one more for us, yeah?"

I just smile. We'll work things out with Jack. I'm not sure how, but a part of me trusts that it's true.

Cate shakes her head, then looks at me again, smiling. "Sully called me Wildcat to piss off my mother, and he knew it would make me feel powerful. Maybe not at home in New York, but for sure in this townhouse. She was never the boss here. *He* was."

I laugh. "That he was. He helped me start on the path to realize my dream of being a chef. All I needed was a place to stay and an office to work in, and he gave me both." I smile, but feel a damp note take hold, remembering one of the details Gary had shared during the reading of the will. "I really hope I'm able to find another place close by, once we settle the house business."

Cate does a double take. "Dylan, why wouldn't you just keep on living here? Sully wouldn't have wanted you out there, anyway; you know he was fond of you in his kitchen and in his office. I don't quite get how the three of us are supposed to share owner-ship, but I, for one, would never want you to leave."

"Thanks," I say, reaching out to squeeze her hand. "The contract has a deadline, though. Didn't Gary tell you?"

"A *deadline?*"

I'm going to take that as a "no" about Gary. Understandable, maybe, from what Cate had told me about how the day before had gone down for her.

"Yeah," I say, wishing I understood more of it so I could explain it to her. "Right now, the house is technically owned by the estate, but there's a deadline for the three of us to decide how to handle it and formally transfer ownership."

She looks stricken, and I hate that I'm springing something on her she wasn't prepared for.

"By when, Dylan?"

"Sometime in the summer," I say. "A few months away, not entirely sure. We'll have to get the date from Gary."

By now, Cate is ignoring the rest of her breakfast, turning

MINE

toward me and staring intently. This is her business face, I think, and I can see why she got as far as she did in her line of work.

"Dylan, all of the best memories in my life are here."

"Mine too," I say, smiling. "This place changed my life. You all changed my life. I'd be working fast food right now if it weren't for all of this, and I'm so grateful for it every single day of my life. Still, even if you and I worked something out, I just can't afford to buy Jack out on what I make now, especially with tuition. From the hints he's dropped, I'm pretty sure he just wants us all to agree to sell and split the profits."

Her eyes harden at that, and she presses her lips together tightly.

I shrug, not liking it any better than she does. "I still need Gary to spell it out for us, but I'm pretty sure that whatever we do, we have to all three agree to," I tell her. "I don't graduate until late June. I think it's before the deadline, but there's no way I can line up a job or the savings in time if Jack isn't on board with keeping the place." I flick my eyes over to hers. "What about you?"

Cate frowns, shaking her head. "I have savings; I was planning on staying here when I thought the townhouse was left to only me. But I can't live on that forever, and it's nowhere near enough to buy either of you out. *Damn* it. How can Jack want to sell it?"

"Yeah, I don't know," I say, not able to wrap my own head around it, either. Jack's always pushed good things away, though. I clear my throat. "I could use the money, obviously, I'm sure we all could, but how much is that worth to lose this place?"

"Absolutely not," she says, shaking her head. She stands up and takes her plate to the sink, running the disposal and clearing the small scraps left. "We're not going to let that happen."

I'd like to agree, but it depends on Jack... who stormed out.

Last time he'd walked away from me, it had taken too many years and the death of a man we both loved to bring him back into my life. I'd like to be more hopeful that things will be different

81

this time, and honestly, I'd be willing to do a lot to make it happen, but it wouldn't work if it was all one-sided.

I cut a glance at Cate. She's wonderful, but she's always had her own issues with Jack. Another thing I'd love to help ease, regardless of the townhouse. She's got her back to me, cleaning up, and I sigh and fold my hands on the table, resting my head on them, facedown. I know every creak, every smell, every nail of this house. Sully never treated me like anything but family, and always made sure I knew that I was home here.

I can't help but go over and over the current situation in my head. He was always bringing people together, smoothing things over. This is so unlike him. Sully wasn't a stupid man; he knew about the division between the three of us—mostly centered on Jack—and I can't imagine he didn't see any of this coming. I just don't understand, and I've racked my brain over it until I've exhausted myself. I need more information.

I need Jack and Cate.

"Jack's being a vulture, just like my mother," Cate says bitterly from the sink, finishing a quick scrub of the dishes and the frying pan, setting everything on the drying rack. "I can't believe either of them."

I look up. "Your mother?"

"Yeah. She was horrified at how Grandpa's estate was handed out to almost everyone he ever met. Every dollar found its way into the pocket of someone he'd touched along the way in his life. That's why the funeral was so crowded. Sully knew how to treat people." Cate turns the water off and dries her hands, frustration apparent in every jerky, abrupt motion. "Mother is such a snob. *Nobodies*, that's what she called them. A pile of nobodies with their hands in Grandpa's pocket."

"Nobody was a nobody," I say, not offended, even though I have no doubt Cate's mother included me in that category. She was a *MacMillan*. I'm just a Smith. I snort, shaking my head. "That's not how Sully operated," I say to Cate. "Not ever."

Cate finally turns to look at me, smiling again at the reminder. She takes a deep breath, letting it out slowly.

"He also didn't give up on anyone, right?"

"Right," I say, reminded of how much like him she can be under her armor and insecurities.

"We'll figure this out together," she says decisively.

"With Jack."

She presses her lips together, but then laughs. "With Jack. Fine. I guess Sully must have had a reason for that."

"He always did," I remind her, gaining confidence from that fact. The three of us would figure out something that worked, and maybe—if I was lucky—I'd end up with the two people who mattered most back in my life.

7

CATE

*B*reakfast was amazing, both the food, and the way Dylan was just so... attentive. I've missed him so much and hadn't even realized it until I'd gotten here. All of those years cooped up in that New York tower selling my soul for the sake of the MacMillan name had really cut me off from all the wonderful things in my life.

After we'd cleaned up the kitchen and Dylan left for his culinary class, I started unpacking, thinking that the task would take long enough to fill up the rest of the night until he got back. Finishing in only 20 minutes instead made me realize just how quickly I had left the condo. I hadn't even bothered arranging for any of my things to be shipped over; I was too caught up in the momentum of running away from that life I hadn't wanted. Or maybe running toward this one, even if I still don't know what my life will end up looking like here.

I already like it better, though.

The townhouse is *home*, and having Dylan back in my life is heaven. The food... the sex. I stop myself there, still not sure how I feel about how wanton I was with him.

Even if it did rock my world in a way that I'd honestly thought I just wasn't built for.

I squeeze my thighs together, the memory almost making me decide to go for another round of self-pleasure, but the memory of Jack walking in on me... I just can't. Not yet. I let out a slow breath, refocusing on settling in. At this point, retrieving the rest of my things from my former apartment would have to involve my mother, and I just don't know if I can deal with that selfish, nasty woman right now.

Not here, not in this lovely place.

No, I decide, pushing the thought away.

I find myself smiling—not something that usually happens while thinking of my mother, but I'm really enjoying how comfortable I am right now. Earlier, after Dylan left, I stripped down to my panties and one of Dylan's undershirts. More freedom... plus that intoxicating scent of his. Sexy, but safe, too. Comfortable. I'd never felt that way in any of the homes I'd lived in before, never allowed myself the decadent pleasure of walking around in just my underwear during the middle of the day. I was always too frightened that someone would catch me. Always so worried about what others would think that I'd never let myself just be *me*, under any circumstance.

Now, I just don't care.

Even weighed down as I am with all of the townhouse talk, I'm still free of so much stress now that I've shrugged off my old life. It has only been two days, but it might as well be a million years for as light as I feel now. I don't ever want to go back, and letting loose with Dylan—letting myself go and just enjoy what I wanted without feeling bad about it—that's part of it, too.

I'd told him I didn't want to complicate things, but really, I'm the only complication. I want to be the version of myself that's free enough to have kitchen sex again. To act on an attraction that, honestly, has probably been brewing for years.

Jack watching me springs to mind again, and I shove the

thought away sharply, doing my best to ignore the surge of heat that almost has me touching myself again. I just slept with Dylan, and yes, my reaction to Jack is a complication.

Doesn't matter, though. Like I told Dylan, Jack has never liked me.

I push the thought away, and inhale Dylan's scent again, hugging my arms around myself as I hold his shirt close to my body. He's so big, so muscular compared to me, that this under-shirt is just a tad loose, even at the chest. The boy definitely knows how to shop for comfort, though. This material is so soft and cool, smooth to the touch. It's got none of the roughness that I'm used to when wearing men's shirts, but that shouldn't surprise me.

Dylan loves the pleasures in life, and has never been ashamed of it.

I grin. I'm totally on board with adopting that attitude.

I take a step forward and feel the fabric run lightly against my nipples, sending another spark of pleasant electricity down my chest to pool in my core. I walk over to the four-poster bed, savoring the feeling with every step and deciding I don't need to ignore it completely. Haven't I just decided that I, too, can enjoy the pleasures in life?

I lean in to rub my cheek against the well-polished wood of the bed frame, cool and refreshing to the touch, and let my eyes start to drift closed so I can focus on more sensual pleasures. I exhale slowly, bringing my hand down to the front of my panties and then extending my fingers, applying just a hint of pressure. Not enough, but I've got all the time in the world.

I can enjoy this.

Before I can really start in, though, I'm snapped out of my reverie by the doorbell. A jolt of shock goes through me, and my eyes snap to the clock. It's early yet. Work for most people isn't over yet, and Dylan would have told me if he was expecting someone.

I quell my body's disappointment at being denied, laughing at myself a little when I consider the fact that the day before, I'd just had the two greatest orgasms of my life. Greedy, much? I can wait a minute, though, so I head for the stairs.

No way am I going to let anyone in right now, but I can at least look through the peephole and see if it's a package delivery or something.

"It's the Wildcat again," Jack's voice calls out as I take my first steps down the stairs, and I want to groan. Let himself in again, did he? What the hell is he doing here right now? His timing is too much, two days in a row, and I squeeze my thighs together again, telling myself that even if my talk with Dylan earlier had softened my outlook on Jack a bit, I'm still outraged by his behavior yesterday.

I'm definitely *not* remembering how it felt to have him watch me, no matter how my traitorous body might be reacting.

"Jack, you might own part of this house, but it's still customary to wait for someone to answer the door when you knock, right?" I snap, putting an extra sting in my voice in self-defense.

"Yeah, well," Jack says, coming into view as he rounds the bend in the stairway and pauses on the landing. And he's making no effort to hide the fact that he's raking his eyes over me. *Again.* He smirks, adding, "I don't stand much on ceremony, you know that."

I try to keep myself calm, but all I can think about is how much of a repeat this is... and how much it's *not*. The man had seen more of me yesterday in thirty seconds than he'd seen over multiple summers, and even if my body was very okay with that—very, *very* okay with it—my mind can't seem to make peace with it. I immediately regret not grabbing a robe, but I'm determined not to cower.

"Repeat performance?" he asks with a sly twinkle in his eyes, still ogling me.

"You're such an asshole."

Being brazen and unashamed with Dylan was one thing—I

trust him—but Jack is a whole different animal. I give in to my insecurities and cross my arms over my breasts. I can't do a whole lot about my legs, but I can at least keep his probing, intense eyes off of my nipples—hard nubs that betray my body's reaction to him as they press against the fabric of Dylan's shirt.

Jack's eyes heat up, and I'm sure he's just staring to torture me; I know how unattractive he's always found me, which just makes how I reacted to having his eyes on me in the bath all the harder to bear. When we were teens, he always avoided me or poked and prodded at my emotions, like some sort of neglected toy. Not to mention how many times he swung by Sully's with a perfect girl in tow; thin ones who looked like models and looked down their noses at too-curvy me.

Exactly the kind of girl my mother had always pushed me to be... all the while assuring me I'd never manage it, of course.

"Back off, Duchess," Jack says, his face darkening at my *asshole* comment. "I just came over to talk about the townhouse."

He takes a step toward me, but then he pauses, remaining on the landing. *Shit.* Could he see that I'm nervous? Not *scared*—Jack has always pissed me off. Hurt my feelings, if I'm honest, with his dismissive, sneering attitude lighting up every one of my insecurities—but somehow, for as rough as he'd always been, I'd always known Sully was right about him. Dylan, too, with his staunch support of Jack.

Jack had a good heart under it all... not that he'd ever wanted to share that with *me*, of course.

I swallow, telling myself to give him the benefit of the doubt, but Jack's eyes rake over me again, and I realize nothing's changed between us.

"I come into a house *I* own, and you get all high and mighty on me? Seriously?" he says, and now he's stalking up the stairs toward me again. "You really wanna pick a fight, Cate? *Now*? After everything that happened yesterday?"

His tone had started out belligerent, but that last bit... it had dropped low and deep and done something to my insides.

"Do *not* remind me of that," I snap. Self-defense. "I was there and I remember it just fine, thanks. And I *wasn't* picking a fight—"

"Yeah?" he interrupts. "Couldn't tell, what with the way you led with 'asshole' for a greeting, eh? Next time feel free to try, I don't know, maybe 'hello' for once in your stuck-up life?"

He's pushing me so close to the edge right now, and I don't know if I can keep myself from rising to the occasion. At least my nerves are gone. As is all the ingrained self-restraint I've cloaked myself with all my life. I've *had* it with him.

"What the fuck is your problem right now, Jack?" I ask, getting right up in his face. I'm done with retreating. "What exactly has your problem been with me for all these years? Am I that ugly to you?"

"The way you treat people is ugly," he says, tossing his brief-case down. It tumbles back onto the landing, smacking the floor loudly and making me wince.

Or maybe it was his words that made me wince. They're untrue, and unfair. *God*, are they unfair. I've always gone out of my way to stifle what I really think from showing, to present the world with a more acceptable version of me than the real one. And he says I treat people poorly? Oh, hell no. If anything, I've held back from speaking my mind so many times I could choke with it.

"Years, Jack. *Years* of this," I grit out, dropping my hands to my sides and balling them into tight fists. I can feel my voice starting to rise with every word, but I can't seem to stop it. It's like I've been uncorked. "One second you close yourself off to everything, the next you're picking a fight. I'm *done* with that in my life, I'm done with people like *you* in my life!"

"There it is!" he yells sarcastically, raising his hands and taking another step forward, putting him just one step below me. Eye to eye.

Is that supposed to intimidate me? He leans in, getting so close I can feel the heat of his body on my breasts, but it's not going to work. I'm not backing off.

I hold my ground, staring into his steely eyes.

"I knew it wouldn't take you long," he sneers. "Once a spoiled brat, always a spoiled brat. You're such a piece of work, Duchess." He sticks a finger in my face, and I swear to God, I almost bite it. "You treat me like I'm trash, Cate? I'm not the one who's trash in this house right now, sweetheart."

I smack his hand away, so worked up I swear I'm going to explode.

"Don't you *ever* put your fingers in my face ever again if you want to keep them on that hand, you son of a bitch!"

He looks shocked for one split second before grabbing my wrists tightly in his hands. "Don't talk to me like I'm nothing. I built myself from the ground up, I left that neighborhood behind, and I'm *somebody* now. You remember that, or else."

I feel like we're having two different conversations, but even now—even as I struggle in his grip—I can't make myself feel scared of him. Pissed off? Oh, yeah. Hurt? Still that, too.

More turned on than I can ever remember being? I'm dying a little inside, because even if I try to lie to myself, I can't.

Definitely turned on, too.

"Yeah?" I ask, wishing I didn't like the feeling of his hand on me so much. I'm going for a haughty, dismissive tone, but instead my voice ends up coming out raw and husky. Even to my own ears, I sound like sex when I add, "Or else... what?"

I swallow as I watch the moment his eyes shift from one kind of heat to another. Oh, yeah. He definitely heard me. A second later, I'm in his arms. His lips claim mine in a fierce, passionate kiss that shoots through me like lightning. All that anger that he stoked as he stalked toward me up the stairs explodes out of the center of my chest, spreading throughout my entire body like fireworks as it changes into something totally different.

CHLOE LYNN ELLIS

I can't let myself think, or else I'll have a million reasons to pull away, and oh God.

Oh... *God*.

I don't want to pull away. I'm more turned on than I've ever been in my life. I don't even know who I am right now, and I wind my arms around his neck and pull him tighter against me, moaning into his mouth as all my softness presses against the hard heat of his body.

His hands slide up my back and caress my shoulders... my throat... then he takes hold of my face—hands strong and sure, coarse but yielding in all the right ways—and I lean in deeper, letting my tongue slip into his mouth and interlock with his. Moaning again when he takes it and makes it his own.

This is so completely unlike what I felt with Dylan.

Not better; Dylan was perfect. But so is this... in a completely different way. Despite our hateful words only seconds ago, this feels so right, like another piece of what I'd been missing. Another version of what I didn't think was possible for me, but which feels inevitable now that I'm getting a taste.

I can't help but let myself fall into it with everything I have, and my mind goes quiet as my body responds.

I'm lost in him.

We don't break away from each other until we need to come up for air, both of us heaving breathlessly. His eyes scorch into me, and just from that, I moan again, clenching my thighs together when the sound makes the hunger in his eyes flare up, hot and primal and all for me.

He's mine. Jack is *mine*.

I'm soaking wet, panting, and for now, I'm not worried about complications, or right and wrong, or a single blessed thing other than what needs to happen between us. What's *going* to happen.

Jack's going to fuck me—he *has* to—and oh God, I'm so ready.

A sound. A scuff down by the front door, bursting the bubble that had contained just the two of us. Just *this*, with no history

92

between us and no need—no *ability*—to think beyond the moment.

Jack turns first, but the footsteps on the stair already tell me what I'll see. And… yes. Oh my God. Dylan's standing there, paused on the landing next to Jack's briefcase, watching us.

"Dylan," I say, forcing the word out from my suddenly dry mouth. A mix of horrified shame and hot lust spikes through me, and it's exactly the same as when I'd opened my eyes to find Jack watching me come in the bathtub. *Making* me come. But now? That feeling is mixed with something that makes my stomach hurt.

I'd just slept with Dylan *yesterday*. I would never want to hurt him. What was I *thinking*?

I let out a shuddering breath. The answer is… I wasn't.

I pull back from Jack, putting some space between us even as he jumps away from me, too. Taking two stairs down with one step, then pausing, caught between Dylan on the landing and me up above. He grips the rail, and I see his knuckles go white.

"Dylan, what the hell, man?" he says, his face going red. "Where did you come from?"

"This isn't what it looks like," I blurt out impulsively, although… *God*, isn't it?

Dylan grins, and over the hammering of my heart, I start to realize that he's the only one of the three of us who's not freaking out.

"Mm-hmm," Dylan says, arching an eyebrow. "Sure it's not."

He winks at me, then lets his gaze travel over both of us. It's not a look of censure, though. He looks like he's enjoying the sight, and for a moment, I almost preen, filled with the same heat I'd felt when he'd made love to me in the kitchen.

What is *wrong* with me?

"Why aren't you at class?" I ask, wondering if I can get away with ignoring the elephant in the room. I clear my throat and try to smooth out the undershirt, suddenly self-conscious. I must look decadent. I'm so wet I wouldn't be surprised if my thighs are slick, and I'm wearing his shirt. *Dylan's* shirt... while kissing Jack. My nipples are hard pebbles, jutting out through the sinfully soft material, and even now, mortified as I stand exposed to these two men, every breath makes the cotton rub against me in the most erotic way imaginable.

I tug the bottom of the shirt just a little lower, as though I can hide from both of them, but the movement only serves to draw Dylan's eyes.

And Jack's.

God, who *am* I that having them both look at me turns me on even more?

"The chef no-showed today," Dylan finally replies, bringing his eyes back up to my face slowly. He grins again, then cuts a glance between me and Jack, adding a teasing, "So, you two talking about the contract for the townhouse? Deep... conversation?"

"Um, Jack was..." I start, looking between Jack and Dylan but then letting my voice drift into silence. I'm not really sure how to end that sentence.

Jack isn't any help at all; he just stares at me, looking like a deer caught in the headlights. His erection is still straining against the tight confines of his pants, and I'm suddenly flooded with guilt again. I *just* slept with Dylan, he's gone out of his way to make me feel comfortable and at home, and here I am, starting in with another man.

One I don't even like.

One who doesn't like me.

I look back at Dylan, biting my lip as my eyes well with tears. He means so much to me. "I'm so sorry, Dylan, I wasn't planning on any of... this."

"It's okay," Dylan says calmly, smiling.

That rattles me more than anything. I *know* Dylan, and I know he doesn't lie. He doesn't have a dishonest bone in his body. How can he not think I'm horrible right now?

"I don't even *like* Jack!" I shout, driven by the need to make my point despite the fact that Dylan isn't asking.

My outburst snaps Jack out of his silence, and his expression immediately darkens.

It twists something up inside me to see, and now I feel bad for a whole new set of reasons. God, I was about to go to bed with him.

Not that we would have made it as far as the bedroom.

I draw a shuddering breath, quelling the surge of heat that the thought sends through me, even now. Jack, pushing me up against the wall. Pulling off my panties and balancing my ass on the railing while he...

I blink. No. *God.* Jack's face is like a storm cloud, and here I am, imagining things that can never happen between us, no matter how ready I was to have him take me exactly like that a few minutes ago.

I owe him an apology, even if what I'd just said was true. Well, sort of true... but clearly, it isn't the *whole* truth.

"Jack, I didn't mean..." I trail off as he turns hard eyes on me, his expression totally closed off again. I try again, "It's not that I... *Shit.*" I give up. Jack isn't giving me an inch, and I don't know what to say, anyway. I wanted him. I wanted Dylan, too. And I'm so fucking tired of feeling bad about what I want. I throw my hands up in the air, exasperated. "I just didn't want this to be complicated!"

Jack's lips tighten into a thin line, but Dylan laughs.

"I mean, it doesn't seem all that complicated to me," Dylan says, smiling at me warmly before his eyes move over to Jack. Dylan looks him over slowly, and even watching it, his gaze feels like molten honey to me, lingering on that mouthwatering erection that—despite Jack's angry scowl and closed-off expression— is still at full mast.

God, Jack wears suits like nobody's business, and this one looks particularly sexy against that strong, lean body.

I have no doubt that my own expression matches Dylan's at this point, but I only realize it when Jack looks back and forth between the two of us, swallowing hard as his scowl turns to a sexy brand of confusion.

"What?" he manages, crossing his arms as if he can shield himself from both of us.

It's almost cute—not a word I've ever associated with Jack— and a part of me wants to laugh. *This* is the man who'd just taken my mouth like he owned it?

Dylan looks over at me, the same warm heat I'd seen in the kitchen flaring in his eyes.

"Not complicated from where I'm standing, Wildcat," he says. "I mean, hell. Jack's hot. I'd probably kiss him, too, if I got the chance."

I suck in a sharp breath as his words do something wicked to me. These two men... I bite my lip, stifling a moan. *So hot.*

Jack makes a small sound, and my eyes snap to his. His confusion has turned into something close to terror.

He shakes his head, holding up his hands in front of him. "Jesus fuck, Dylan!" he shouts. "Why would you think that's an okay thing to say about me?"

Dylan's open expression suddenly goes dark. It might be the first time in my life I've ever seen him looking anything other than easygoing and relaxed.

"Jack, I've never hidden my feelings. If you can't handle it, get over it, but I'm an adult now, and I don't have time for that kind of bullshit anymore."

Jack takes the last few steps down to the landing, his body hugging the wall as if he really *is* scared of what Dylan's saying, and he almost trips over his own briefcase as his eyes dart toward the front door. Toward escape. He's obviously embarrassed and upset, and when he snatches his briefcase up from the floor, he makes a break for it. He doesn't say another word to either of us, just storms past Dylan and clatters down the stairs to let himself out.

The front door slams hard after him, and I wince at the sound.

"Guess we aren't talking about the house tonight, eh?" Dylan says, joking lightly as he looks at me with concern. "Are you okay, Cate?"

I draw in a shuddering breath, trying to will my body to ramp it down and my mind to kick into gear. I want to talk to Dylan about... all of it. But complications? Yeah, here they are. In spades.

I just nod, and Dylan—perfect, perfect man that he is—lets me get away with it, not pushing for more.

I'm grateful.

For now.

But oh Lord, as I turn and head back up the stairs, trying to focus on other things—like figuring out what I'm going to do for work out here, how to get my belongings from New York, how on earth the three of us are supposed to sort out the details with the townhouse on top of everything brewing between us—I know that not talking about what happened with Jack... what was said between Jack and Dylan... what happened with Dylan and me...

That reprieve isn't going to last long.

And, if I'm being honest, I'm not sure I want it to.

## 8

JACK

*W*hat a fucking bust. I throw my house keys on the counter, kicking my apartment door shut with my foot. I must have put more of my frustration into that kick than I expected, because the heavy wood slams hard enough to make it rattle in the frame. I scrub my hands over my face and through my hair.

*Shit.*

Dinner with a pretty woman shouldn't make you feel like you've got a piece of tinfoil stuck in your teeth, but my last two hours felt more like being at the DMV than on a date. Office has had this temp paralegal, Mindy, for the past couple of weeks— cute, bouncy curves, and does she ever know it. She's been batting her eyes at me since she started, and today she made her move when I came to get my mail from her at reception. Dinner, drinks, very heavily implied post-drink fun.

I said yes, because God knows I needed the distraction. All week, I've been fighting to not think about Cate, about Dylan, about the whole mess, and it's taken every bit of willpower I have. I threw myself into work like I was bucking for a promotion, and then as soon as I got off work I was hitting the gym to punish my body into exhaustion so I wouldn't get stuck in my own spinning thoughts. So by the time Mindy got to me, yeah, I was kinda desperate for anything that might keep my mind off all of it.

Turns out, though, going out with Mindy was the exact wrong move to make.

Every time she giggled I thought about how it wasn't *Cate's* laugh; every time Mindy leaned forward to push her breasts up in her low-cut dress I thought about *Cate's* gorgeous body, dripping with soapsuds... pressed against mine... and fucking Christ, those *moans*.

Basically, I spent the whole damn date arguing with myself inwardly, trying to deny that I was thinking about Cate at all and berating myself for doing so at the same time. Complete and utter torture. I couldn't even make it through dessert without bouncing my leg, I was that eager to get away. Mindy had looked almost shocked when I pleaded an early morning and bundled her into a cab I paid for, just to get some breathing space, but I had to, right?

She wasn't what I needed.

I almost growl as I take my shoes off at the mat, and the sound is loud in my empty apartment. Tonight is no different than the rest of the week: I can barely focus, can't seem to enjoy *anything*— the fuck is wrong with me?

I sigh, some of the steam going out of me. I know the answer. *Cate* is what's wrong with me.

Big surprise, she's throwing a wrench into my life again. Stuck-up, self-righteous Duchess, taunting me with how hot she is before yanking it all away. Not that I can blame her for pulling back when Dylan showed up.

My cock twitches, and I frown, not willing to let my mind go there. Instead—

*That doesn't sound like the girl Sully always talked about.* The memory of what Tina, the bartender, had said cuts through my familiar internal ranting. *Sully made her sound like she was shy... had some things she was struggling with.*

I snort. Phrased a hell of a lot nicer than the shit Cate screamed at me, but bartender-style tact or not, same sentiment.

This is part of why I tried so damn hard not to think about her all week. Not just the massive case of blue balls she'd left me with, but also the confusion of maybe starting to see her in a different light. Cate's hot, yeah, but she's also maybe... not what I'd always thought. Honestly, if I think too hard about what she'd yelled at me on those stairs—especially in light of Tina's words—I end up feeling not just confused, but maybe a little ashamed, too. The last thing I want to do is have to re-evaluate my whole opinion of her, maybe admit I'd been wrong, but now, alone in my apartment with no work left to do, I think I'm not gonna have a choice.

Fuck it. Not without a drink, though.

I carefully hang up my suit jacket and tie in the closet and toss the pants and dress shirt into the hamper to go to the dry cleaners. I still feel constricted, my undershirt too tight, so I shuck that, too. Feels a little better to be down to skivvies, to stretch and get some cool conditioned air on skin that's way too overheated.

I head back into the kitchen for a scotch at the counter, just a small one. I'm never gonna let myself drink like a "real Kelly"— like my old man—but now and then, a little helps put me in the right mindset to mull shit over. I know I've got a hot temper, but for a lot of reasons, I'm going to try to keep a lid on it and think this through a different way. For one thing, like it or not, Sully has put me in a position where I'm gonna *have* to deal with Cate, at least until we come to an agreement on what to do with the townhouse.

But it's not just that.

*Christ.*

The way she'd felt in my arms, the way my cock had felt like it needed to be inside her... not just horny. Hell, I'd never had trouble finding a girl to take care of that when I needed it. But with Cate, for a minute there, the idea of fucking her had felt like coming home.

I adjust myself and drag my thoughts out of her panties with an effort. I've gotta try to look at my history with her in the same way I'd look at a case file. Really look at the *facts*. Be objective, instead of letting teenage hurt and horniness color my memories.

I exhale hard through my nose. So, what new info do I have? I tick it off on my fingers. Weigh it. Analyze it.

I've got Tina's word about what Sully said, and yeah, I put a lot of weight behind that man's opinion, even posthumously.

I've got Dylan's tight friendship with her, which, not gonna lie, speaks volumes. Dylan knows people, and the man is... well, to be honest, after Sully, he's the best man I know.

And back to Sully: I've got my own knowledge of what he was like. What traits he valued. How he always put his money where his mouth was and treated people like *people*, regardless of their net worth. And even without Tina's extra insight, guess I'd always known that Sully thought the world of Cate. I snort again. I know damn well that Sully's high opinion of her wasn't just because she was family. He didn't roll like that; the proof was in his relationship with his daughter, Cate's mother.

That woman was a piece of work.

Imagine Cate, growing up under her thumb. I'd always figured Cate was a chip off the old block... but if I'm truly being objective, if this were a *case*, I'd have to say that when I discard all my old filters, the answer is pretty fucking obvious.

Cate wasn't a snobby, too-good-for-me rich girl, looking down that cute nose at me. She was shy. And maybe a little screwed up by the pressures on her, too. Different pressures than being a Kelly, but—with her mother's attitude about being a MacMillan—probably just as intense.

I shake my head, annoyed now that it took me this long. I'm usually so fast on the uptake, pride myself on it, but this is a years-long blind spot. Don't know how ready I am to say it to anyone else, but right now, I can at least admit it to myself. I got it wrong. I got it so fucking wrong.

*Jesus, Jack—who's the asshole now?*

Any way I slice it, looks like the answer is me. Me now, cynical and confrontational, picking any fight I can because I don't want to go back to feeling like a scorned teenager. Still always running away from something I left behind a long time ago. Me back then as a dumb, angry kid, always snapping at Cate when she didn't treat me the way I wanted, the way—maybe in retrospect—she wasn't confident enough to. Hating her then for what I thought was snobbery. Never giving her a chance or looking any deeper, despite my best friend at the time—Dylan—always telling me I should, showing me by example.

Truth is, I suspect I've been a dick to Dylan, too, but that's still too much for me to look at yet.

I throw back a little more scotch, letting myself go back and think about the other day with this new point of view. I'd thought that maybe Cate was trying to prove something, that she could make me want her—at least, up until I couldn't think at all because of how damn good she felt against me—but now I'm really thinking about what she'd said. *Ugly?* Jesus H. Christ. The woman was a goddess. How the hell could she have ever thought I considered her to be plain, accusing me of always overlooking her, when I spent every single summer practically drooling over her?

Shit, I know damn well that the stuff going on in your head isn't always logical, but Cate thinking she's anything other than gorgeous is just so unbelievable. Even when I was a teenager and I thought I hated her, that didn't stop me from rubbing one out to the thought of her every chance I got. My cock stirs again at the memory, and it hits me that maybe that's the problem right here and now. I've been forcing myself not to think about Cate so damn hard that I haven't taken care of myself at all.

All guys do it, and yeah, maybe me more than most—just something I do to keep my head clear more than anything else— but ever since I'd walked in on her in the bathtub, a part of me has known I wouldn't be able to even touch my cock without her springing to mind. My balls are so blue right now they've practically got real estate in the Hamptons. Being that pent-up would make anyone get a little crazy.

I grin. Maybe finally letting myself think of her can be a relief in more ways than one.

I down the last bit of my scotch and head to my bedroom, then settle in on top of my covers with an arm behind my head. My dick starts to perk up the second I really let myself picture Cate's face. Fucking gorgeous. No doubt. I've dated some beautiful women, but Cate... Cate takes the cake. Maybe it's because I met her so young, always had so many emotions wrapped up in our relationship, but can't deny that she's always been the standard for my perfect woman.

Physically, up until now. But now, maybe more than just physically.

I push a hand under my boxer briefs, covering my cock while it pulses like it knows I'm about to make it happy. Or Cate is. Fucking-A, she had it really fucking happy there on the stairs, even if that didn't end the way I'd sort of started thinking it might. For a minute there, none of my anger was in the way of wanting her.

And, huh. Guess it isn't now, either. In fact, without that protective barrier to hide behind, I can't keep myself from picturing all the things that make me so damned attracted to her. Don't even want to. It's almost insane how much hotter she is now, as a grown woman. She's got so much more personality, she's so much stronger and more confident.

I tighten my fist around my shaft, so hard I'm practically throbbing, but I hold on and wait. Kinda tempting to just go for it, fast and furious, but damn, it's been this long, I'm going to let myself enjoy it.

I close my eyes and let my mind drift over my picture of Cate, working myself a little, but not enough to get things moving too fast yet. Her strong, fit body with all those delicious curves felt unbelievable pressed up against me. And Christ, those lush curves of hers would feel so much better in my hands. All too easy to picture those long legs hooked over my shoulders.

I groan, feeling my balls start to tighten a bit even though I'm really not doing much for my cock yet.

Cate is, though.

The memory of her, at least. Of that *kiss*. All the hotter because she was being so fierce, driving me wild with the fight I'd never gotten to see in her before. Might have been shy once, but little Cate had definitely grown out of that, huh?

I liked it.

Liked *her*.

Got off on how she'd stood up to me, hell, how she'd threatened me. That fragile *Duchess* image I've always had of her definitely doesn't mesh with that ferocious, sexy woman calling me a son of a bitch. I can't help but grin, but it turns into a grunt as hunger curls through me, and I start stroking for real.

I kind of have to, the way the memory is affecting me.

Cate would never be boring in bed, I can tell that much. *Wildcat*. Not a joke anymore, just fact. *Here, kitty kitty.*

I hiss through my teeth, remembering the scent of her. She'd been beyond turned on. I'd felt her heat through those thin panties, smelled how wet she was, pressed my cock against it... I groan again, my eyes snapping open as I shove my underwear all the way off so I can do this the justice it deserves. My body's responding so fast and hard that my take-it-slow-and-enjoy-it intentions are shot to hell. Well, not the enjoy-it part, but fucking Christ, this is gonna end hot and fast if the need shooting through me like a lightning storm is any indication.

Where could that kiss have gone?

Was she still pissed at me?

Would she have given in to it?

Seemed like she had been. Maybe. At the time I'd been sure.

There'd been a passionate hunger in her, a brutally hot, strong pull between us—was I right? I'd been a little lost in her, to be honest. What would have happened if Dylan hadn't come home and interrupted?

Or... if we hadn't noticed, hadn't jumped away from each other?

My hand stills, even though my throbbing cock doesn't like that. Dylan again, interrupting my fantasy the way he'd interrupted me and Cate. I mean, I had to stop when he walked in, right? What Cate and I were doing, that's not a show you put on for someone else.

But—my hips thrust up without me meaning for them to, driving my cock through my tight fist, and I groan again—honestly, before I'd come to my senses, seeing him there, it hadn't made me want to stop.

Not at all.

I start working my hand faster, needing to refocus. Dylan isn't part of this fantasy. This is all Cate.

If we'd kept going, would she have pulled that loose shirt over her head, or would I have torn it off of her? I like the idea of her naked, but call me a caveman, I like it even better when I'm the one to do it. Let her know how badly I want her. How irresistible I find her.

Yeah, tearing is good.

Those panties, though... after having seen her in the bath, I don't think I'd have the patience for her to get out of them, tearing or not. I'd want to just shove them to the side and get to the good stuff right away. Touch her. Feel how wet she was for me. I'd seen it, and my breath hitches as I imagine how good it would feel to let my fingers explore that wet spot I'd seen at the front of her panties when we broke apart.

And damn, the fire that had been in her eyes...

Heat pools in my stomach, liquid *want* making me lightheaded as my balls pull up even tighter.

I'm really fucking into my fist now, but can't help it. All too easy to imagine sinking my fingers into that blissful wet heat, teasing her clit until she's gasping and squirming and making hot, sharp moans against my shoulder. Those same ones that escaped when we were kissing, that made me so damn hot I lost all reason.

The look in her eyes when we were fighting was crazy hot, the crackling anger interlacing with raw, animal hunger. I want to see her look at me that way again.

Shit, I want that look again and again and *again.*

I could fuck her endlessly and never get enough. Just that one taste, and I already know it. And speaking of tasting... *Christ.* I almost come, and I snap my eyes open again, buying a little time. The vision is too good to let it end yet, not after I've waited this long to let myself go here.

Eyes wide open, though, I can still see her.

I want to taste her so fucking bad my mouth waters.

Want to find out everything about her, claim every part of her, hear her beg for me.

No, not beg. Not my Wildcat. I want her to *demand* that I give her what she needs. That'd be a sweet final nail in the coffin of my old insecurity about her not wanting me, and fuck if that fire in her didn't do it for me.

Throbbing hunger pulses through me as I think about tormenting Cate in the sweetest ways, about working her up to a fever pitch before letting her have what she needs, what we both need. I swear softly, my hand getting frantic again as that liquid heat pulls behind my balls, getting tighter and tighter as I prepare to unload. *Fuck,* I want to take everything Cate's got, and then... I hiss as my thumb brushes over the head of my cock and sends a jolt of pleasure through my nerves that almost undoes me.

I want to give *her* everything I have.

I can't help but buck into my own hand, the images racing through my brain too hot for any human being to withstand. Would we have made it to the couch in the living room before I couldn't stand not being inside her anymore, or would we have been so damn keyed up that we'd have been unable to resist going at it on the floor of the landing? Or up against the wall. Yeah, fuck. That's how I'd take her.

I groan as the hot, twisting need inside me ratchets up another notch, like a goddamn roller coaster about to plunge over for the part of the ride that leaves you screaming.

Cate, tearing at my clothes.

Cate, those sexy-as-fuck moans.

*I want you, Jack, I need it.*

She's never said it, but I can hear it anyway. She sounds like an angel. Like torment. Like the kind of hot promise I'd never let go of.

I swallow hard on a suddenly dry throat, and my fantasy changes in a flash. I'm not pounding her into the wall, she's shoving me down, desperate for me. Mounting me like she was made to do it, sinking down onto my full length in one burning movement, fitting around my cock like we're a matched set.

I shudder, my body aching to feel it, to feel *her*.

The Wildcat I'd had in my arms on those stairs would be riding me at a gallop, those perfect breasts bouncing and her face the picture of ecstasy as she uses me, takes everything she needs, shows me that she's been desperate for it for way too long and I'm the only one who can give it to her right.

I crack my eyes open, my abs flexing as I curl up to work myself even harder. Faster. My breath's coming in hard little pants now, fast and ragged, and my hand's practically a blur around my cock, but I'm only half-aware of being here on my bed. All I know is those long, hot thighs of hers flexing and shaking around me, my hands gripping her sweet, full ass as she impales herself on me, fucking me at a merciless, punishing pace, just like the one I'm using now.

*Yeah, Cate, that's it, baby. That's so fuckin good, so good, Wildcat.*

I'm so close to exploding I can barely stand it, my balls pulled tight now and every nerve of my body molten with lust.

And then—

My brain does something it's never done before.

Something I thought I'd had some solid, industrial-strength protection set up against.

It tosses me a picture of Dylan.

And not just a flicker of a thought, either, like when you suddenly think about a bill you gotta pay. This is a full color, surround-sound broadcast that makes me freeze into a statue, my fist around my dripping cock and my ass tightened up mid-thrust.

Dylan interrupts us, just the way he did the other day, but now —even when I squeeze my eyes closed tight and try to get my mind back on Cate riding me, all I can see is his face. Not instead of hers. Christ, I'm a dirty fuck, aren't I? Dylan's there, *too*. Grinning down at me as Cate loses it, behind her, twining a hand in her hair so he can pull her head to the side and get at her throat. Kiss along her jaw and swallow her moans. And I'm not... not mad. Not screaming *"mine"* like I probably should be.

I'm so fucking hard I hurt.

I'm still not moving, not even an inch, but it still feels like I'm about to come just from that.

Cate on top of me, moaning into Dylan's mouth, his hands covering her breasts as her body tightens around my cock like a vise. She's squeezing me, sending me reeling, overloading me.

*Holy shit.*

I'm not holding still anymore. I'm fucking my fist so hard I'm gonna be raw. The thought may be wrong—everything I've grown up with tells me it is—but the reaction from my body is immediate, harsh, and unequivocal.

I want this.

I fucking *need* this.

*Jack's hot. I'd probably kiss him if I had the chance, too.*

A bolt of sensation rips through me, so strong it makes me

groan through gritted teeth. Fuck if hearing him say that hadn't stopped me in my tracks. Hadn't sent something hot and wild tearing through me that I'd known for sure was not okay. I mean, you know a guy's gay, and maybe it's a shock, but you'd think it'd occur to you that maybe he's looked at you that way before.

But somehow, I hadn't let myself go there.

Hadn't ever thought Dylan noticed me... like that.

Oh fuck. Oh *fuck*. I'm going to come, though. I can't stop thinking it *now*. Can't stop hearing him say it. Can't help but wonder—I shouldn't shouldn't *shouldn't*, but—how would Dylan taste?

He's got stubble. He's not soft. Not curvy. He's a *man*, and I shouldn't be sharing fantasy-Cate with him, much less wondering shit about not just sharing but... indulging. But I can't stop. My cock jumps in my hand like it's got a life of its own, and even if the brain in my skull doesn't know what to do with thoughts of Dylan in the middle of getting myself off, the brain in my pants sure as shit does.

I'm barely breathing now. Breathing too hard. I don't know what the fuck I'm doing. I just know I'm tipping over that edge where nothing I do is gonna matter, I'm going to shoot hard and fast and I can already tell it's going to be better than what I've had in a long time. And yeah, sometimes when you're getting off your dick likes something your brain doesn't, like when a chick in porn uses a weird word that normally would make you go *lady what the fuck*, but this, *this*—

*Jesus H. fucking Christ!* My cock is slick with all the precum dripping out of me, pouring out, I'm hot and thick and letting loose with sounds that are too much. Too raw. Too fucking needy to really be from me. My cock is painful now, straining as I pound into my strokes desperately, picturing all three of us together.

This isn't some kinda porny fluke, this is something different altogether.

This is weird and fucked and new and *intense*. So goddamn intense I feel like I can't breathe.

God help me, I'm beyond trying to clean up my thoughts. I lean into it. Let my imagination have the reins. Tell myself that I'm just along for this ride, can't help it, can't stop it.

Can't care right now about how twisted or kinky or flat-out wrong it might be.

My eyes roll back and my mouth falls open and for now, at least, I'm past giving a shit. Living in the moment. Ready to shoot right into the unbearably perfect heat of Cate. And then... and then... oh Christ. Oh, fuck. How tight would she be with *both* of us inside her, me and Dylan, both giving her everything we've got?

How much would she love that, love all that attention and friction of the three of us all connected?

Fuck, I bet she'd go off like a goddamn Fourth of July rocket.

*Scream for us, Duchess.*

And that's it. It's over. Heat explodes through my body and my brain blanks out, my thoughts all seared away by the white-hot pleasure racking my body. Cate's ecstatic face, Dylan's, both of them, *oh Jesus fuck —!*

I cry out as I shoot all over my stomach, halfway up my goddamn chest, scalding spurts of relief that seem to go on and on and fucking *on*.

God*damn*.

I can't think about it.

Can't... think.

But fucking-A, even after I come down, not letting myself think about it can't stop me from *wanting*.

## 9

## DYLAN

*I*t's been a lovely Saturday afternoon so far. No drama, no nothing. I remember how terrified Cate looked when I walked in on her and Jack earlier in the week, and so I've tried my best to keep things nice and relaxing, friendly, low-key and low-commitment. It's been wonderful, despite the fact that I want her every time I lay eyes on her.

Speaking of which, I'm watching her now, her lovely curves moving with purpose as she unhitches and folds old drapes.

"I loved these drapes as a kid, but they have to go," Cate says, continuing her work.

I laugh. "Yeah, Sully's taste was always a bit Old Spice, wasn't it?"

"That's definitely one way to put it," she replies teasingly. "I think we can do a lot to brighten this old house up."

"Yeah, I agree," I say, standing on a small stepladder and helping with the next set of drapes. "The ones you picked out are astounding. Very chic, very welcoming. You're amazing at this."

"Thanks, I try," she says, smiling.

We still haven't talked about the townhouse. I feel like time is starting to run out, but there hasn't been much that I could do about it for the past few days. Jack isn't taking my calls, and Cate has been determined to move on as much as humanly possible. She's a tough cookie, that one, but I'm caught in the middle of these two again. I'm starting to feel like that might be my place in their lives, which isn't the worst thought in the world, but it'd be nice if we could get things settled.

Even nicer if we could get things *good*.

"All of those interior decorating skills are going to come in handy if it comes to preparing the house for sale," I say, wincing the minute the words are out of my mouth.

Sure enough, Cate stops for a moment and shoots me a glare. Kind of cute, if I'm being honest, even though I hate to have upset her. Still, it might as well be an air-kiss for how non-threatening it is.

The two of us have been falling into a playful rapport, and I'm glad to see that it can stand up to a discussion like this. We won't make it far if it doesn't, and regardless of what happens with the townhouse, now that Cate's back in my life, I don't want to let her go again.

"I don't want to let this house go, Dylan," she says, blowing a stray lock of hair out of her face as she all but parrots my thoughts with her words.

Well, so she's talking about the house, but the connection between us? Even with our current lack of sex, I can tell she feels it, too.

"I don't care what we have to do, but we're going to figure this out together," she goes on firmly. "We're not leaving this house to anyone else. It's our *home*."

I want to agree. Instead, I say, "The only problem is, we're not the ones who can make that decision. Not just the two of us, anyway."

Jack's always on my mind.

"Just say it, Dylan," Cate says, throwing me a playful look.

I haven't brought Jack up since he stopped by, knowing she's not nearly as okay with her attraction to him as I am, and it's good to see her teasing me about it instead of looking like she might combust.

She finishes with the drape in her arms and throws it onto the stack on the floor, adding, "This has been so nice with the two of us, it really has, but I know the... the situation with the town-house—" *with Jack* "—has been hanging over our heads like a guillotine all week."

"Okay," I say, and motion with my head for her to join me in the kitchen. "Let's talk about it over some lemonade, yeah?"

A moment later, we're both sitting on the couch with our fresh glasses of lemonade. It's not that hot outside yet, still a little too early in the year, but we've been working hard all day and the sweet, cold liquid comes as a welcome relief.

"Everything you touch turns to gold," Cate says, resting her head back into the cushions contentedly. "You're going to be an amazing professional chef. They ought to just give you that certificate right now."

I laugh, pleased, settling in and enjoying the moment. "Yeah, well, there's still a lot I don't know. Catching up quick, though."

"Speaking of catching up," she says, spearing me with a look.

Cate's always been magnificent, but like this? Shedding the shyness and reserve she's worn like armor ever since I've known her, a little bit more every day?

Sexy doesn't even begin to describe her.

I take another drink of my lemonade, ignoring the surge of heat and refocusing on Jack.

Well, that brings *another* surge of heat, but I ignore that, too.

"The sooner we talk to Jack, the better," I say. "If I have to be out of here this summer, I don't have a lot of time to get my life together for a big move into a new place, and I know you've got to figure out what you're doing, too."

Cate winces, frowning. "Dylan, I'm so sorry. I know I've been selfish this week, and you've been so, so perfect about making things lovely for me."

I smile, and by the flush in her cheeks, I realize I haven't been able to keep all the heat out of it. Not that I want to hide it from her, but I also don't want to push her until she makes her peace with what she called "complications."

"It's been my pleasure," I say, and yeah, Cate hears the innuendo.

She clears her throat, glancing away. "But you're right," she continues after a second, finally looking back at me. "Dragging our feet on this isn't fair to you any more than it is to me."

"It's not fair to Jack, either," I point out.

Cate bites her lip, and I wish for the millionth time she felt comfortable talking about her feelings for Jack with me. He's the hottest man I've ever known, and if she thinks I blame her for wanting him, she really doesn't know me as well as she might think. And if she thinks I'd judge her for that? Well, I'm not going to say I'd love sharing her with someone else. Would probably back off if that's what she wanted. But Jack is... Jack. All I felt seeing them together was happy.

Well, happy, plus turned on, but I'd been able to tell that if I'd let on to that—at least, any more than I had with my comment about wanting to kiss him—it would have freaked both of them out even more than they already were.

"Jack has money and his own home," Cate's saying now, pulling my thoughts out of some of my hotter fantasies and back to the reason we're talking about Jack right now. "No matter what we end up doing, he'll be fine at the end of this."

Jack's money and position don't necessarily equal "fine" in my head, but I'm not going to push that conversation with her.

Cate gives me a quizzical look, and something about the little flare of heat in her eyes makes everything inside me perk up.

"So, hey, personal question," she says.

I laugh. Her tone is cautious, but I'm an open book. Like I'd said to Jack, I don't hide who I am, and certainly don't have any interest doing that with *Cate*.

"Shoot," I prompt her when she doesn't go on right away.

"Okay," she says, her cheeks pinking up again. "Did you mean it?"

I'm at a loss.

"Mean what?" I ask.

She flushes even more, and her breath picks up a little. It's sexy as hell, and even before she tells me, that reaction finally gives me an idea about the subject she's fishing around so carefully.

"When you... when you said you'd kiss Jack too, did you mean that? Were you just trying to scare him off? What's the deal there?"

I grin, raising my eyebrows. I'm trying to remember if we'd talked about anyone I was interested in back when we were kids. Anyone I'd dated. I think not. Certainly not Jack, because there was always that tension between the two of them, and not anyone else, because... well, honestly, because in the summers, when Cate was there, between her and Jack, I didn't really pay much attention to anyone else.

"You don't have to tell me," Cate says, holding up her hands and looking mortified. "If it's personal, it's okay, I totally understand."

I laugh again, but a part of me feels the tiniest bit sad. I mean, she's been raised with such a narrow idea of right and wrong. Just as harsh, in its own way, as the way Jack grew up.

"Cate, it's okay," I say, grabbing those hands and squeezing them. "I'm bisexual. I'm open about it. It's who I am. Jack is gorgeous, attitude notwithstanding, and the answer is *hell yes*. I'd totally take a piece of that, if he'd let me."

A myriad of emotions flit across her face, almost too fast for me to read. None, however, is disgust. I see everything from curiosity to lust, and I wait it out, wondering where she wants to go with this conversation.

Finally, she smiles, and it looks a little fragile. Self-conscious. "So, when we slept together, would you have rather it have been…"

"No," I say, and see the instant relief on her face. "Wanting Jack doesn't mean I don't want you, too. And seeing the two of you together?"

She goes even redder, squirming. I can tell part of it is embarrassment—those damn voices of "right" and "wrong" playing in her head—but another part of it… another part of it is something hotter.

I sit up and put my lemonade down on the coffee table, then take hers from her and do the same.

"Cate… come here."

She bites her lip, and I can tell she's surprised. I'm a pretty mellow guy, and I know she knows I'd never push her, but I can't handle those doubts on her face, and that—combined with how much I've wanted her all week—makes my words come out a little more forcefully.

She stares back at me for a second, then stands and—when I grab her hand—lets me pull her down on my lap.

I kiss her.

For a second, she freezes up, and I wonder if she's thinking of Jack's lips… Jack's mouth… Jack's tongue inside her. And then, oh fuck, *I'm* thinking of those things, and my hands are tangled in her hair and I'm getting hard. Swelling under her curvy ass.

"You don't mind?" she gasps, tilting her head back as I lick my way down the smooth column of her throat. "*Really* don't mind? That I was with Jack?"

"I'm thinking of it, too, Cate," I say, rolling my hips to let her know exactly what that does to me.

She moans, then laughs, and for once, she sounds free. *Happy.*

And then I'm laughing too, because whatever happens here, with the two of us—the three of us—it's right. I know it. Everything about being in this house has *always* been right. Has always been exactly what each of us has needed.

"So, you don't just not mind," she says, pulling back a little and giving me an impish grin. "You like Jack, too, right?"

"Oh yeah," I say. True, on so many levels. I grin at her. "Dude's hot, what can I say? You've seen his suits, right?"

"Ugh," Cate says, flushing as she laughs some more. She nods, though, even though she adds an obligatory, "He's such a jerk."

"Oh yeah," I agree, nodding solemnly. "He looked like he was being horrible, kissing you like that the other day."

"Shut *up*," Cate says, still laughing as she leans against me and pouts playfully. "He *is* a jerk. But... maybe he's a jerk with a spectacular ass."

"Maybe?" I tease.

We look at each other for a moment, then both burst out laughing. It's the most laughter I've heard fill this townhouse in a long, long time, probably years, and even though I haven't been pining away for anything in particular, it suddenly occurs to me that having her here... having Jack in my life... they fill in pieces that I hadn't really realized were missing.

Sully would be so happy. He loved us. All of us.

"Jack's not a jerk," I say, smoothing a hand down her back. Cate snorts, and I laugh again. "Okay, maybe he *is* a jerk, but that's not all he is. He's funny, and he's quick-witted, and—"

"Sexy," she whispers, then makes a little "eep" sound that's adorable, as if the word had slipped out without her meaning it to.

I grin. "Yeah, that. And I know he can be abrasive and judgmental, but remember where he grew up."

"You're right," Cate says, sighing. "Poor guy. I think I met his parents one time. It was one of the very few times they ever showed up at the townhouse to pick him up. They were brash, obnoxious, real class acts."

I remember the time she's talking about. It had surprised me, since most of the time, it had seemed like Jack's parents didn't

give him much thought. Let him run wild, do his own thing. I
don't even think they even knew Sully was a part of Jack's life for
the first few years... but once they'd found out, well, let's just say
that they definitely cared about Jack rubbing shoulders
with money.

"He was so embarrassed," I remind her, my heart hurting a
little for him, even after all these years. "The two of us were
upstairs when his parents showed up, and I could hear his mom
screaming for him to get his ass downstairs or he was gonna
get it."

"Jesus, yeah. He was already eighteen at that point, too, wasn't
he?" Cate asks, shaking her head. "Definitely way too old to deal
with that sort of talk from his parents."

"They still... reach out to him." I grimace. Can't help it.
Normally, I like to look for the best in people, but either there
really isn't a lot of good to see in the Kelly family, or I just care too
much about Jack to be generous.

"Really?" Cate asks, looking curious.

"Yeah, he mentioned it at dinner not too long ago. It's just
them looking for money, always looking for money. They try to
guilt trip him with the family name, and how he's not living up to
it. I don't know, it sounded like a bunch of crap."

Even worse had been the look in Jack's eyes. He deserved
better. A family who loved him for him.

"Well," Cate says, frowning. "I can certainly understand the
family name pressure. Being a MacMillan is not a walk in the
park, and I can't count all the times I've dealt with my mother
yelling at me for it. If Jack was too old at eighteen to be yelled at
by his mom, I'm *definitely* too old at twenty-four to be yelled at
by mine."

"Agreed," I say, glad that was never an issue for me. I'm "just" a
Smith, but mostly I'm just... me. My mother never pulled that
kind of bullshit, and it's not in me or anyone close to me to care.

I'm still hard, but when her stomach rumbles, the part of me that wants to take care of her in other ways, too, wakes up.

"Dinner?" I ask, standing us both up.

For a minute, she looks embarrassed again, but she gets over it and nods. Seriously, the number her mother pulled on her... I shake my head. Cate's perfect just the way she is, and hopefully once I cook for her enough, she'll get over worrying about what she eats and just give in and enjoy it.

"We should ask Jack to dinner," she says, following me into the kitchen.

I can tell it took some effort to say it, but I agree. Plus, I *want* to.

"How about tomorrow night?" I ask, grinning. "You and I can have one more evening to ourselves, then we could try it out again with Jack. See if we can keep everything civil over a meal, talk about the townhouse, and maybe..."

I shrug, smiling without finishing the sentence. I'm not sure what exactly I'm hoping for between all of us, but I don't want to give up on working something out with our joint ownership of the townhouse, any more than I want to give up on either of them. Sully wouldn't have. And maybe... maybe... the way things are going with each of us, maybe we can take the connection that's always existed and turn it into something more.

*Maybe.*

# 10

## CATE

$\mathcal{T}$he chains rattle hard against the heavy bag as I kick it, over and over again, against the backdrop of the blasting music keeping me motivated. Every single time, I let out a fierce yell, and every single time I'm thankful that Grandpa Sully soundproofed the basement. Dylan is upstairs, cooking up a storm. I offered to be his sous chef, but to no avail. Secretly, I'm glad; this is the first time I've had an opportunity to really get a lot of the lingering stress out of my body.

Not to mention the frustration.

Yesterday, when Dylan finally kissed me again, I thought it would lead to some more of what we'd had in the kitchen. We got off track, though, talking about Jack, and even though we flirted the rest of the evening, I ended up in bed alone. That puts it at a week since I slept with Dylan, and just about a week since Jack almost made me come from a kiss alone. Compared to how unfulfilling my sex life was before coming back to Boston, that's practically a miracle... but I'm greedy. My body is aching for more where that came from, and until I get the nerve to go for it on my own—or one of them steps up and offers—I've gotta keep my libido in check somehow.

Kickboxing helps.

A little.

Other than decoration, most of my hobbies didn't revolve around the typical expected skillset of a *society woman*, as mother would say. I kickbox, I lift weights; I enjoy the feeling of my body working at its peak. It may have started because of endless ridicule and scrutiny from my mother—exercising has always been easier for me than dieting when it comes to maintaining my weight—but over the years, I've really made it my own thing.

I feel good when I use my body like this.

I feel *strong*.

The thought gives me pause, and I bounce on my toes for a minute, watching the bag swing. Mother had made her comment about me teaching classes in that snide, condescending tone that's like nails on chalkboard for me, but you know what? Maybe I *will* do this more. I love decorating, but finding clients and setting up a business like that in a new city isn't something I can hope to support myself with right off the bat... maybe teaching kick-boxing or yoga is exactly what I should be doing out here.

At least for now.

I'm actually certified, believe it or not, even if I've never tried to earn a living doing it. I've done my fair share of impromptu or short-notice sessions for clients of MacMillan Design, though, and always got glowing reviews. Now might be just the time to hang out a shingle and become a professional instructor. Or, who knows, maybe even a personal trainer.

I grin. The possibilities feel endless right now, and I put a little more energy into my next few kicks, snapping the bag back hard, again and again, until the music stops. I drop to the ground as soon as it does, stretching out on my back and enjoying the cool polished concrete beneath me as I go through a yoga-pose cool down.

I stare up at the ceiling, and suddenly find myself blinking back tears. How can I give any of this up, ever?

I feel free here.

Dylan's cooking spoils me. The house comforts me. Even Jack... *God*. That man has driven me crazy, one way or another, for as long as I've known him, but the idea of how he might drive me crazy in the future is just as tempting as the rest of this life I'm starting to carve out in Boston.

I want it.

Want him.

Want *all* of it.

He's coming over in a bit—Dylan set it up—and I know we're supposed to talk about the townhouse tonight, but... God, I hope it's just fear and not intuition. I have a feeling that it's not going to go my way. It's just too hard to imagine Jack making it easy on me —on me *and* Dylan—when he doesn't need this place like we do.

Doesn't love it.

At least... I don't think he does. I guess there's a lot I may not know about Jack, though. A lot I might have been blinded to. What I *do* know is that I'm positively in love with this place, and no matter what it takes, I want to keep it.

It's *mine*... and somehow, the fact that it's theirs, too, doesn't take away from that at all.

I just don't know if I'll ever be able to let go.

I take a deep breath, letting it out slowly, and try to convince myself it might work out. A glance at the clock confirms that Jack will be here any moment, so I do a few more stretches—really making sure that my body is lean and loose in all the right spots— then hop up to my feet. About 15 minutes later, I'm freshly show- ered and have some basic makeup on. Nothing fancy, certainly not for Jack, but I can't have either of them seeing me completely undone.

I guess sometimes, there are just some things you can't shed from society living.

I open the closet and pull out one of my favorite dresses; a simple, red skater dress. I've always loved this dress and how it swishes around my hips and thighs. I lay it carefully out on the bed, and reach inside one of the drawers to grab my bra and a pair of panties.

The bra is easy to find. The panties, not so much.

*Shit.*

I shove the drawer closed in frustration. I completely forgot to do my own laundry. Dylan has utterly spoiled me this week, taking care of me, feeding me... I've been so relaxed that I guess I just spaced out on every single bit of responsibility. I bite my lip, not even remotely comfortable with going bare under the short dress but not really coming up with any other immediate solutions—I *want* to wear it. I feel confident and sexy in it. And then the doorbell rings.

Of course.

Why wouldn't Jack arrive at the perfectly worst time?

I frown, the old voices in my head ready to blame him for everything, but as I throw my bra on quickly and then slip into the skater dress, I have to admit that I'm feeling something else, too. It's the memory of having his lips on me. His cock pressed against me. I squeeze my thighs together, closing my eyes for a minute to remind myself that we're talking about the *townhouse* tonight, not... the rest. But the minute my eyes are closed? I get another rush of heat, remembering the feel of Dylan's erection pressing against my ass yesterday, when he pulled me down on his lap.

God, I'm shameless.

I want them both.

I sigh, opening my eyes, and try to find the balance between the exhilarating sense of freedom I've had ever since walking away from my life in New York and, well, reality. Sure, it was fun—and hot, if I'm being honest—to talk about Jack with Dylan yesterday. Doubly hot to picture the two of *them*... but as wanton as I've been since I got here, I know that sort of thing isn't the way real relationships work. And no matter what goes down tonight about the townhouse, I don't want to let my relationships with those two—that's right, even with Jack—go back to where they've been.

Meaning: to not having one.

I hold my head up and leave my room, the movement of air under my dress as it swishes against my thighs making me feel bold and a little excited, like I've got a secret. And it *is* my secret. I'll stay focused tonight—if we've got a deadline to sort out what we're doing with this place, that's important to me—but it's still nice to have this little something that's mine.

This little bit of naughtiness.

As long as I keep my legs tastefully crossed, no one has to know, and I give myself a sly smile as I pass the mirror in the hallway, surprised at how confident and, well, *sexy* I look.

Maybe that's just what confidence does.

When I get downstairs, Jack's seated at the kitchen table, his briefcase on the chair next to him. Dylan and I decided not to do the formal dining room, it's not exactly stuffy, but it's also not as comfortable as just eating in the kitchen. And comfortable will help right now, I hope.

Jack glances up at me as I enter the room, something flaring in his eyes too fast for me to make sense of it before he shutters them, his face impossible to read. Before, I might have rolled my eyes or made a snide comment or just silently seethed at what I interpreted as his dismissal of me, but now?

I can't help another one of those rushes of heat between my legs.

My eyes dance over his shoulders and neck... the freshly cut hairline at the nape of his neck... the shape of his jaw. That sexy, light beard of his that felt soft against my face, but also just rough enough to drive me wild.

My whole body flushes, and I jerk my eyes over to Dylan.

It doesn't help.

Although, I guess that depends what kind of help I'm looking for.

The two of them couldn't look more different right now, but both make my mouth water. One of them buttoned-up and sitting at the table looking like professional eye candy, the other with his shirt sleeves rolled up and his shirt collar undone enough to show off the tops of his pecs as he works on plating. I have another quick flashback to my conversation with Dylan—to the idea of the two of them, *together*—but like I said, sometimes I'm greedy. Before I can control the direction of my thoughts, the image has me in it, too.

All of us.

Together.

A little sound tries to escape my throat as my whole body flushes, and I regret not figuring out a solution to the panty situation. I'm wet and throbbing, and I bite my lip hard, hoping that neither man is paying attention. That neither can read me as easily as I think they can.

"Everything okay, Duchess?" Jack asks, smirking at me.

I narrow my eyes, my hackles rising from long habit. Does he *know* that I've just fantasized about the two of them at once? He can't.

"Perfect," I say brightly. "Glad you could make it, Jack."

That seems to fluster him, and he grabs his glass of wine and takes a deep drink.

I grin, feeling like I've won something, even though I'm not sure what.

"Hey, you," Dylan says, smiling at me and letting his gaze move over my body in a slow, gentle slide.

I want to moan again. Does he know what he's doing to me?

"You look beautiful," he says before turning back to the food. "I'm just about done here. Pour yourself a glass of wine, settle in, and I'll be right there with the first course."

I do it, and Jack jerks his smartphone out of a pocket and immediately lowers his eyes to it.

That's interesting.

I've taken the seat on the opposite side of the table from him, and where once I would have made up a story in my head about him not wanting to look at me because he couldn't stand the sight, now—after the way he devoured me the week before on the stairs —I wonder if it's something else.

Hope it is, if I'm being honest.

Jack glances up, then his eyes dart to the empty chair. Probably smart to keep Dylan in the middle. If things go south, he's the perfect one to make sure Jack and I don't go for each other's throats. And if we're going to get any of the serious business we're here to discuss handled, he can also act as a buffer between our lips.

I press mine together tightly, stifling a giggle. God, who *am* I? Being this shameless—even in the privacy of my own mind—isn't like me. I need to stop this. We *do* have serious business to discuss, and it's why Jack came. Not for a repeat of the week before.

At least... I don't think so.

He glances up again, and I clear my throat, flipping my hair behind me and pouring myself a generous glass of wine.

"Week was that good, huh?" Jack asks, his lips quirking up on one side as he nods toward my glass.

"It's not an escape," I tell him. "It's an indulgence."

"A celebration, maybe?" Dylan offers from across the kitchen, winking at the two of us.

I grin, nodding, and bring the glass of wine up to my nose. Swirling it, taking in the aroma, I remind myself of what Dylan has taught me. It's okay to enjoy the pleasures in life.

"My week was very relaxing, actually," I tell Jack, pretending I didn't hear the hint of sarcasm in his earlier question. "Very low-key. Dylan and I got a lot of work around the house taken care of. It was... nice."

"I see that," Jack says, looking away from me and glancing around. He frowns, though, instead of smiling. "It's pretty bright now, isn't it? You lose that feeling of comfort when things are tampered with."

Really?

Is he *trying* to be an asshole?

I can't say my libido minds, if I'm honest, but I still find myself getting a little ticked. I'd hoped the two of us had turned over a new leaf, but he's treating me the way he always has. I don't know if I can bear it... but I also know I'm not going to just roll over and take it.

He doesn't want to explore new territory? Fine. I take a deep breath in and prepare to fence with him.

"Sometimes you need to let a little light in to breathe. You know, disinfect. Get all the old air out, and bring some fresh air in." I smile tightly, taking a drink from my glass.

I didn't want it to be this way.

I take another drink in the silence—a little deeper than I should—but at least I'm not the only one. Jack does the same.

"You can never dig all of it out," he says, setting down both his glass and his phone and spearing me with his eyes. It's unexpected and intense.

*Hot.*

"You must be an excellent lawyer with that insight," I respond, shifting in my seat as all that intensity starts to rev me up again.

"I am," he says, matter-of-factly. "No matter how expensive my suits get, I'll never get the grit out. It's who I am."

He says it belligerently, as if he thinks it's something he has to defend.

It reminds me of Grandpa Sully. Not that Sully was as rough as Jack, but just like Jack, he was unapologetic about who he was and staying true to it... no matter how successful he got.

Jack's staring me down as if he's waiting for me to fight him on it, and I bite back a smile, arching one eyebrow as I go for a cool look, just to see more of his "grit" come out. Okay, fine, I'm goading him. For once, though, I'm enjoying it, not feeling torn up inside about it.

"Is that so?" I ask him, taking another casual sip of my wine. "Proud of your... grit?"

"Yeah, that *is* so," he snaps back, right on cue. "Wouldn't want it any other way. Some of us like to remember our roots, Duchess."

I clench my jaw at that. My roots are Sully, as far as I'm concerned, and Jack should know me well enough to know that. This isn't fun anymore if he's trying to tell me I've lost touch with that. He *doesn't* know me. Not the real me.

"Some of us recognize that we can shape our destiny without changing the core," I say tightly.

"Yeah," he says, raking me over with a look that's *not* complimentary. "I always figured you for one of those onward-and-upward types."

"What are you doing, Jack?" Dylan asks softly, pausing behind Jack's chair with three plates expertly balanced in his incredibly strong, incredibly dexterous fingers.

Jack starts, then flushes.

Interesting.

He goes for more wine instead of answering Dylan or throwing any more verbal jabs at me, and as Dylan arranges the food and takes his seat, I'm staring at his hands again. I press my thighs together, vividly aware of how bare I am as I remember exactly *how* dexterous those hands are.

God, I'm a hot mess tonight. Horny one second, insecure the next. Confident, then angry. Getting my feathers ruffled when what I *really* want is—

"I hope you two are hungry," Dylan says, grinning as he looks between the two of us. Unlike Jack, he's all smiles... but I can read the steel underneath that exterior. Dylan is nice... *kind*... but never a pushover.

Jack mumbles something under his breath, and I stiffen at the tone, even though I couldn't make out the words.

"We're not doing this tonight, you two," Dylan says simply, proving my point. "You know Sully's rule."

Jack smirks, but softens just a hint. I can see it in the corners of his eyes. *"Not at the dinner table,"* he says, quoting Grandpa.

"Never at the dinner table," I say, my own lips tipping up at the corners.

Jack and I lock eyes again for a moment. Now, without an argument growing between us, the look on his face is still fierce... but it's cut with a little bit of softness, too. And—no, I'm not mistaken—underneath it, that hot, melting desire I experienced firsthand the week before.

Desire for *me*.

I'm suddenly keenly aware of my body again... my dress... the fact that I've been intimate with both of these men at the table. Oh hell, "intimate" sounds so mild compared to what we've done.

Both of them have made me explode.

"That's right," Dylan says, the words sending a hot flush through me before I realize he's not responding to my actual thoughts. He's just agreeing that we've both remembered Sully's rule, and—by his tone—he's planning on enforcing it.

This townhouse may belong to all of us, but the kitchen is Dylan's.

I'm okay with that.

*Very* okay with that.

It's actually a relief to know that he's going to be in charge, no matter how gently he wants to couch his control over the situation.

"Thank you," Dylan says, his lips twitching with humor as he looks between the two of us again. "Now, Jack, you pour me a glass, and don't be shy with it. Cate, you're gonna try my meatballs, and you're gonna love them."

Bossy Dylan. I bite back another smile, trying and failing not to get turned on. What, a few mind-blowing orgasms and now I can't even last a week without my libido going into the red zone?

I guess this is the real me.

The free me.

"No argument on the meatballs," I say, grinning as I eye the plate he prepared for me and *not* thinking about calories.

Not in Dylan's kitchen.

"Agreed," Jack says, taking the wine bottle and filling Dylan's glass, as directed. He tops off his own glass, too, then looks at mine. "Fast worker, Duchess?"

He's smirking again, and I look down. *Shit.* I honestly hadn't realized I'd finished it off. Guess I needed it, and... no. Nope. I am *not* going to go back to letting him get to me.

As if Dylan would even allow it.

I square my shoulders and feel another rush of confidence. Huh. Confidence really makes me feel sexy, and I look Jack directly in the eye with my own special brand of fire, and smile at him with every bit of what we'd done on the stairs together showing on my face.

"Jack, shut up and get me drunk."

He jerks as if I'd slapped him, and his face is a gorgeous mix of surprise, reassessment, and... yes. He's thinking of it, too. Of *me*.

"I can do that," he says, his voice dropping low and sexy as he freshens up my glass. His eyes stay locked on mine, and ohhhhhhh —delicious, delicious heat. It moves through me again, and again, I find myself squirming in my chair.

"Mmmm," Dylan says, smiling as he looks between us.

He has to see it. He really doesn't mind? He'd said so, but... I guess I'm surprised.

Definitely in a good way.

"Tonight, we're going to eat a little, drink a little, and get the contract business out of the way so we can stop thinking about it so much," Dylan says, laying it out for us. He leaves it at that, and we dutifully start in on the eating and drinking, but I can't help thinking that something in his tone conveyed that that's not *all* we'd be doing.

The meatballs *are* delicious, and accompanied by thin slices of lemon and a bit of white wine, I finally get my mind onto something other than the low hum of desire these men inspire in me and enjoy the heaven Dylan's whipped up for us.

After we've all relaxed a bit, there's pasta primavera. My eyes meet Jack's when Dylan places it in front of us, and I know we both remember that it's one of the first dishes Dylan's mother taught him to make as a kid.

Dylan is so sweet, I almost can't believe it.

By the time we finish up with our plates, we're all sitting way more comfortably in our chairs than when we started. Jack's loosened up enough to regale us with oddball legal stories for most of the night, and Dylan's chimed in with a series of memories of our childhood that the other two of us had somehow forgotten. My libido has finally calmed down, sated by the fantastic food and, yeah, the fantastic company, too, and despite my earlier fears, the whole evening has somehow turned out to be really, really pleasant.

*This* is what Grandpa Sully would have wanted under his roof after he died. Had he really known the three of us could achieve it?

"Christ," Jack says, laughing as he uncorks a fresh bottle. "I can't believe we've already killed two of these."

"There's plenty more where that came from," Dylan says, winking. "Cate did ask you to get her drunk, yeah? And the cellar is so chock-full of that stuff, I'm convinced Sully must have bought the whole damn vineyard."

"He would, too," I say, giggling. That's right. I'm a bit of a lightweight. "Even if the wine wasn't any good, he'd do it to help out some poor bastard who'd just lost his kid's tuition at the horse track or something."

"Yep, that was Sully," Jack agrees, smiling as he pours fresh glasses for all of us. "It's like he specialized in that. He had a nose for people with a lot to offer, who just needed a little bit of help."

"I wouldn't be even a little surprised," Dylan starts, reaching for his wine glass, "if one day, a truck backs up to our door with crates of the stuff."

I laugh. "See? We *can't* sell this house. Who knows what surprises are going to show up on the doorstep for the rest of our lives? We shouldn't want to miss out, right?"

Jack grins, throwing me a sexy wink. "Trying to get us back into business talk again, is that right, Duchess?"

The name doesn't sting. Not in that tone.

"It *is* why you came, isn't it, Jack?" I remind him, mesmerized by the play of the light on my wine as I swirl it in my glass. I look up, catching that heat in his eyes that does things to me, and give an unladylike snort. "It's not *my* fault you keep refilling my glass and trying to distract me with all... *that*."

I wave my hand at him, indicating his... everything. Body. Face. Strength. Passion. Damn, the man is sexy.

Jack's eyebrows shoot up and Dylan hoots with laughter, and I flush hotly—no doubt turning as red as my dress. I can't take it back, though. Not just because it's true, but because... well, I don't want to say I've thrown down a gauntlet, exactly, but I've definitely opened the door to see where we stand.

Jack's frozen—deer in the headlights—but then he grins. A wicked, wicked one that makes me clench my thighs again. He darts a glance at Dylan, but I guess Jack's had enough wine that he's comfortable flirting in front of Dylan, unlike the week before.

Although, sure, we'd been doing more than *flirting* in front of Dylan, that time.

"All of *this*?" Jack asks, loosening his tie and unbuttoning his collar. He raises an eyebrow at me in challenge, then looks at Dylan and backs down with a self-conscious laugh. "I think I fed the Duchess too much wine. She's talking crazy."

Dylan just grins, shaking his head. "She's talking like you two need a room."

One of those telltale moans escapes me before I can bite it back, and Dylan's smile grows even wider. He leans back in his chair a little—like he might want to watch the show, or maybe he's giving me his tacit blessing, I don't know. What I *do* know is that I'm mortified again, because that sound gave me away.

I'm not just flirting. Not teasing. I want him. The blush that still hasn't left my face spreads. I can feel the warmth traveling down my body, beneath my chest, through my belly, coursing between my legs.

"I wouldn't mind a room," Jack says, his voice rough again as his eyes bore into me. He looks at Dylan again, uncertainty flashing across his face for a second, then forges ahead. "I would've done that last week, if, you know, someone hadn't interrupted us."

If he's waiting for Dylan to get uncomfortable, or chastise him, or pretend it's all a joke, he's going to be disappointed. I can tell. I *know* it. Dylan body is still relaxed, but his face is starting to flush, too. His pupils are dilating. Breath coming faster.

I had this man inside me. I recognize his signs. And I remember... *God.* I remember what he said. About me. About Jack. This erotic tease is turning him on as much as it is Jack and me.

"Can't apologize for that," Dylan says to Jack, letting his own brand of heat flare in his eyes. "I wish you two hadn't stopped."

Something crackles in the air between the two of them, some deep current of energy that makes my mouth go dry, and Jack's mouth opens and closes without anything coming out.

Dylan leans back in his chair, his eyes hooded as he holds Jack's gaze. "I would have loved to watch."

Jack sucks in a sharp breath. Or maybe it's me. Jack starts turning red, and when he jerks his eyes away from Dylan, his gaze landing on his wine glass, I *know* he's about to blame this whole conversation on too much alcohol.

Dylan doesn't let him, though.

Dylan's kitchen, Dylan's rules.

"What are you doing?" Jack asks when Dylan stands abruptly and starts clearing the table.

Dylan gives him a smile that's pure sex, and Jack mutters a sharp oath under his breath.

"I still would," Dylan answers, and it takes me just as long as Jack to figure that one out.

He still would... still would... still would love to watch.

*Us.*

Together.

Oh my God. A decadent, curling heat unfurls inside me as I get it, and when Jack turns his head and looks directly at me, I almost gasp at the heat in his gaze. He heard Dylan, too. Loud and clear.

"Cate?"

I'm not sure which one of them said my name, but it doesn't matter. I nod. Yes. Yes. *Yes.*

I want this.

*God*, do I ever.

# 11

## JACK

*D*ear Penthouse — *I never thought it would happen to me...* The night's taken a sudden turn for the surreal. Came over for dinner, prepared for a fight despite my recent realization about Cate, and for a while there, it looked like I was going to get one. Then Dylan stepped in, and the wine started flowing, and things got... well, "good" doesn't even begin to describe it.

These two.

Fuck.

They're... they mean something to me.

Maybe everything.

And *this*? What's about to happen?

I honestly don't know how the fuck we got *here*—does Dylan actually know me well enough to read my mind?—but this moment is too much of a good thing for me to jinx it by looking too hard at the *why* or the *how*... or even the *whether I should*.

I *am*. I'm doing this. Oh, *fuck* yeah, I am.

"She wants you, Jack."

Dylan's voice rips through me like pure sex, jolting me out of my panting incredulity and into action.

He's really okay with this? But... again, not gonna jinx it. Plus, can't even question it, really. Not when Dylan sounds like *that*.

Not gonna lie, other than rubbing one out the other night, I've never let myself go there about guys, but that voice? *His* voice? Like *that*?

I'm just about wound up enough that that alone might be enough to get me off.

For once, the thought doesn't shut me down. Like I said, I'm too fucking wound up. Energy crackles between us—between all three of us, just like in my own private fantasy—and it's a raw, sexual hunger that makes me feel like my blood's been replaced with liquid fire.

I don't remember moving, but I'm out of my seat, Cate looking at me like I'm water in the desert. Dylan whispers something else, but I don't hear what it is even though my body shudders at the tone.

Can't look away from Cate, though.

Not now.

Her sexy lips are parted, just a little, and their plump, wet invitation has got my cock straining at my slacks.

She's not looking at me, though.

"Dylan," she says, sounding sort of broken.

Not... not bad broken. Raw. *Hungry.* And you know what? I'm about to fuck her, and she said another guy's name, and I'm okay with that.

No. Not okay. I'm turned *on* by that.

Who would have thought?

But Dylan... *fuck.* I kinda get why she's looking at him. Don't get me wrong, I know how to fuck, and I sure as hell don't need his permission. But that's not what this is. It's not his blessing, either. He said "watch," but damn if it doesn't feel like he's just as much a part of this as the two of us are.

Hottest thing I've ever felt, and all three of us are still fully clothed.

Not even touching yet.

"Look at that dress, Jack."

I grunt, my cock jerking in the tight confines of my slacks. I can't *not* look at that dress, but I know what Dylan's really saying. *Get the fuck over there and do something about it, Jack.*

I nod, or maybe I say something. I don't fucking know. He's right, though. I can't take the chance that this little slice of unreal heaven might evaporate, just because I took too long to seize a golden opportunity.

My whole world narrows down to Cate; Cate and that *insanely* hot little red dress that's been torturing me all damn night. That's apparently been torturing *both* Dylan and me, based on the way I can hear his breath quickening as he keeps saying dirty things to me, goading me on to go get her. The way that it swishes around her thighs, fluttering like water and giving me little glimpses of her gorgeous, smooth skin has had me wanting to shove her skirt up around her hips all night...

I bet she's already dripping wet.

Hell, I know she is. She has that look, the same one she had on the stairway last week, and it's sexy as hell.

I shove my chair aside, and it clatters to the floor. Cate jumps, her perfect tits bouncing deliciously, but her eyes are locked on mine as I stalk toward her.

She's panting.

I grab her as soon as she's within reach, twine my hands into her long, dark hair, and pull her up out of her chair into my arms. She moans, and I can't get enough of it. She makes the hottest sounds I've ever heard, and then—

*Finally,* I'm tasting her again.

Tasting the wine on her lips and the deeper richness that's all Cate. Dylan's the guy who knows how to put together a million amazing flavors, but right now I think I'd be happy if the only thing I ever tasted again was her. And when her lips part for me, her tongue darting out to graze mine?

I fucking *growl* at the sensation.

She's *mine*.

Cate presses against my chest, the heat of her body more torture, and when we come up for breath, her mouth is swollen and red and I groan, needing it again. Needing it *always*.

"You have too many clothes on, Jack," Dylan says, and I laugh, because fuck yeah, I do. I also look over at him, that husky tone of his voice pulling my eyes like a magnet, and fuck if he isn't in the middle of pulling his shirt off, like he was talking to me, but talking to himself, too.

His body.

I guess it shouldn't turn me on. At least... that's what everything I've ever been taught tells me. But dammmmmmmmmmmn. I can't... can't deal with that. I rip my eyes away and struggle with my tie, finally managing to get it off and then working on the rest.

"You're so sexy, Jack," Cate says, her voice trembling like she means it as she reaches to help me. "I used to look at you..."

Her eyes dart up to mine, and a flush of embarrassment colors her already pink cheeks. Her pupils are blown and her wet, sweet lips are parted like they need me again, and something in me—some primal thing—roars to life.

She wants me.

*Has* wanted me.

"Me, too," Dylan says, and hearing it straight out like that—that he used to look at me, too—drags my eyes back to him again.

If I'd thought too hard about it, I guess I'd have thought he'd be jealous. Any guy would, watching me and Cate, right? I woulda maybe expected to have to deal with fallout later, but Dylan—shit, he's *into* this. Into watching us. If I'd had any doubts, and really, I hadn't, not the way he'd pushed us together, the massive tent he's pitching right now makes that abundantly clear.

The sight should freak me out, but instead it's like gasoline poured on a fire, sending a wave of raw lust through me so brutally hot that I have to lock my knees to keep them from buckling. This should be weird to me, make me feel uncomfortable, *something*, but the idea of having him here... all I can think about is how I came my fucking brains out when I jerked off to the three of us together like this.

Hell, *closer* than this.

And having him here in reality? Having Cate here, her hands on me, her trembling thighs shaking against mine?

It's a million times hotter than any fantasy.

"Show me what she's got under that dress, Jack," Dylan says, his eyes locked on Cate.

I turn back to her, happy to oblige. I'd ask her if it was okay, but no. I don't need to. I think this is a little out of the box for both of us, and having Dylan there... watching... guiding... I can tell it's working for her just as much as it's working for me.

I settle my hands on her hips and put her on the edge of the table. Help her scoot back a little. Spread those luscious legs apart.

"Jack," she gasps, a hot-as-hell hitch in her breath as she clutches at my shoulder.

"Yeah," I say, sliding my hands under the skirt of her dress like I've been aching to do all night.

Slowly.

Inch by torturous inch, all the way up her thighs while I keep my eyes locked on hers.

"Please," she says, panting gently as she spreads her legs even wider. Her eyelids are heavy and she's biting her lip and *goddamn*, she looks incredible.

Feels even better than that, if such a thing is possible.

I run my hands over her hips, seeking the band of her panties, eager to get them out of the way as fast as I can, but all I touch is Cate, warm and trembling and bare.

*No panties.*

It takes a second for the thought to register, and then it's like a lightning bolt of desire, straight to my dick. I suck in a breath, ragged and raw.

"Oh, *Duchess*," I groan, meeting her flashing eyes. "You..." I swallow hard, shaking my head slightly. "You really are a fuckin' wildcat."

Dylan groans as I squeeze Cate's hips. She makes this little *ah* sound of enjoyment, and it's amazing how such a tiny noise has such a huge effect on me. Dylan was right about me having too many clothes on. My cock is throbbing. Ready to burst right out of my slacks. Straining against the zipper to get to her, but I can't be bothered yet.

Can't take my hands off her.

Can't *wait*. I have to see her again, see *all* of her, in the flesh instead of in my dreams.

I reach for the hem of her dress and she's just as hot to go as I am. She grabs it before I do, pulling it up over her head and messing up her hair so it looks all tousled and sexy like an old-school pinup, and now I'm the one groaning. This is, without a doubt, the sexiest woman I've ever seen.

She always has been.

"Her breasts drive me crazy," Dylan whispers from off to the side, and all I can do is nod.

She's wearing a bra, and as much as I need to feel them in my hands, I've gotta admit, it's sexy as fuck. It's a foamy, crimson little bit of nothing. Delicate and insubstantial, like the bubbles on the surface of freshly-poured wine.

"You two are driving *me* crazy," she says, laughing in a low, sexy way that has my cock doing the throb-and-jerk-and-try-to-get-to-her dance again.

She palms her own breasts, rubbing her hands over that hot little number barely covering them, and I take the hint, snapping the clasp open and drawing it down her arms. Finally getting to see those gorgeous breasts I haven't been able to stop thinking about. My eyes burn down her body, my hands tracing down her sides, and even though I know what to expect, the sight of those sweet, dark curls between her thighs hits me so hard I almost can't breathe.

A part of me wants to skip the rest and just pound into her. Get inside and make her scream my name and fuck her until neither one of us can think.

But a part of me can't bear the thought of this ever ending.

Wants to enjoy the journey.

Wants...

"Cate," I almost whisper, looking back up into her eyes. I lick my lips, words totally deserting me. That's what I want. *Cate.*

I'm kissing her again. Inhaling her. And her hands are on me, working on that getting-me-naked suggestion Dylan made. I let her take care of it, my own hands too busy—too full of her—to help. But when those lush breasts finally touch my bare chest?

It's an electric jolt that's got *me* groaning.

"Damn, you two look hot together," Dylan says, groaning right along with me.

I look over at him, my hands sliding down Cate's back to cup her curvy ass, and groan again. He's got the heel of his hand over his groin, pressing and rocking slowly against the hardness there, drawing it out.

And... *fuck.* Can't deny it. Don't even want to. That's hot.

Dylan meets my eyes, another electric jolt. Then he smiles, Dylan-sweet but with a hot, wicked undertone that's got me groaning again.

"Try light strokes with your fingertips," he says, gesturing to Cate with his free hand. His breath is starting to come faster, and I see his hips pressing up—little thrust after little thrust—as he works against the bulge in his pants. "Cate likes that. Torture her a little. Really make her wait for it."

Cate hisses. "Oh, you're the *worst*, Dylan," she says, but her voice is breathy and excited, and I can see how much it's turning her on to have him be a part of this, too.

I start doing what he says, and oh yeah... Cate's panting again.

*Hard*. Writhing against me and driving me crazy. It takes me a minute for the meaning to kick in, though... Dylan *knows* this? Knows how to touch her?

They've been together, then.

And again... no jealousy. Just, *damn*. Just heat. I squeeze my eyes closed, my cock about to burst. Wish I could have seen it, honestly, and I groan in spite of myself, realizing that that's what *this* is—me and Cate—for Dylan, right now.

Maybe he and I have even more in common than I'd ever realized.

"Lower," Dylan says, and my hands obey him without me needing to think about it, my cock jerking at... at... I don't know. At all of it. The feel of Cate. The weight of Dylan's gaze. The sounds she's making. The way I can picture *exactly* how his cock is feeling right now, under his own hand... the way *mine* is feeling, Cate grinding against it, her thighs wrapped around my hips with my fuckin' slacks still between us.

I never thought I was the kind of guy to like having someone else help me up my game, but not gonna lie, it's crazy how hot it is. Kinda feels like both Dylan and I are with her at the same time, just like I wanted, and it's got me going so hard I suddenly have to stop for a second to avoid things ending too soon.

"Duch... Duchess," I manage, surprising myself with how raw my throat feels. How dry my mouth is. "I need a second."

"And *I* need you inside me," she throws back, which does *not* help.

I laugh, wrapping my arms around her tight while I desperately think about baseball for a second.

"I need to see you fuck her, Jack," Dylan says, the slow drawl like warm syrup. Warm syrup with a holy-fucking-hell kick.

I groan, running a hand down Cate's chest. I can feel her heartbeat racing under my palm, and she arches into my touch, urging me lower. I've got myself under control, though. Or maybe I'm

146

just selfish. Because fuck yeah, I want to be inside her, but not before I get another indulgence out of the way.

"How does she taste, Dylan?" I ask, catching her wrists with one hand and holding them out of the way as I finally dip my fingers into her dark curls with the other.

"*Jack*," she gasps, arching into my touch with a needy whimper.

"You'll have to tell me how she tastes," Dylan says, and I hear his zipper go down, but can't look away from Cate to see him take out his cock.

I want to, though.

Can't help it. Can't deny it.

But right now?

Can't focus on it.

My fingers are deep in her honeypot, warm and slick and tight as I dip inside, and Cate... holy fuck. Her *sounds*.

"Ask for it, Duchess," I say, my voice a low growl. "You're a grown woman, tell me what *you want*."

What we both want. All of us do. But I want to hear her say it. Need to, suddenly.

The look she gives me is pure fucking fire. For a second, I think it's all our old fights. That she's going to be stubborn and deny me this, even though all three of us know she's dying for it. Just like I am. But I underestimate her. Cate doesn't hold back, once she decides she's all in.

"Jack," she pants, licking her lips. "I want you to—to go down on me. I want your mouth on my clit. I want to feel your tongue—"

I thumb her nub and kiss her, *hard*, cutting her off even though I could have listened to those dirty words drip out of her mouth all day. Can't help it, though. She's wrecking me with those words, all that brazen want. All those little sounds. Those desperate, grinding little movements she's making against my body.

"Anything you want, Wildcat," I tell her, dropping to my knees and pushing hers apart even farther.

Cate leans back on her hands, and for a moment the sight of her—bare and wet for me, for *us*—takes my breath away. I yank her hips toward me, my mouth already watering. I don't have the patience for slow anymore, and I don't think she's got it, either.

"Taste her," Dylan groans, and the sound is backed by the slick slide of his hand. I don't have to look to know he's fisting himself. Watching us. Going slow... but I think it's like me. Wanting to draw it out. To savor it. Not because his body isn't screaming just like mine, to *fuck*. To go faster. To go hard and deep and take what Cate's offering us.

*Fuck*, her thighs are amazing, soft and smooth and quivering with muscle as I draw my tongue along her skin, heading for the apex of her legs. The smell of her, the taste of her, it floods my senses and turns me into something almost inhuman, something made only of instinct and desire and *need*.

My cock is a painful, raging bar of fire, harder than I've ever been, and I fumble with my belt and undo my fly. I *have* to.

"Oh, fuck," Dylan whispers as soon as I free my cock. "*Yeah,* Jack."

It slaps up against my stomach, and I don't know what feels better, getting out of those pants, or the surge of heat from his voice.

But then it's all Cate. She twists and squirms as I savor her, and a sexy litany falls from her mouth, a cascade of "please" and "yes" and "more" and my name. My fucking name, dripping from her lips along with bossy demands and desperate begging. Music to my ears.

A live wire to my cock.

I hold her hips tight, not letting her move as I lick and suck and lose myself in her hot, slick folds. I'm not sure who I'm torturing more, her or me—or, fuck, from the sound of it, *Dylan*— but I can feel how close she is already. The way her thighs tremble, the tiny shudders moving through her, those sexy-as-fuck sounds.

Her heat.

I speed up, my own hips humping at the air in a desperate bid for some relief as I slip two fingers inside her. Stroking. Thrusting. My tongue working her clit as she starts to lose it, as she gets louder and hotter, and those gorgeous thighs, gripping my head as her hands tangle in my hair... so fucking *hot*.

I grin, my lips spreading wide against the delicious treat between her legs, and then I make that beckoning motion with my fingertips...

Works like a charm.

Cate's hips buck forward, driving her hard against my mouth, and she digs her fingers into my scalp, shuddering and keening like a banshee.

"Oh, God," Dylan moans. "Oh, yeah. So hot. So... *gorgeous.*"

Her orgasm lights my nerves up like fire down a fuse, and the minute she goes limp—gasping and sated and fucking incredible—I'm on my feet with my cock at her entrance, raring to go.

"*Jack,*" Dylan says, grabbing my attention. I look up and he tosses me something shiny that I catch in one hand without thinking.

Fuck.

Right.

Condom.

Dylan's a fucking star.

Before I can even think about suiting up, Cate's plucked it out of my hands and has the package open and ready. She rolls it down my throbbing cock herself, and *Jesus*, safe sex has never been so fucking hot as it is right now, with the look she's giving me.

The raw hunger in her eyes.

The hunger for *me*.

It's intoxicating, and everything that's come between us in the past, it's gone. *This*, right here, right now? I'd do anything to keep her looking at me like that. I *will* do anything.

She wraps her legs around my hips with a wicked smile, and the tight hold of her plush thighs is like a drug. My fingers dig into her hips, caress her amazing ass, run down the crease behind and then circle around to anchor myself at the base of her thighs.

I need to touch all of her, all at once, every way I can.

Cate's looking at me like I'm some kind of sex god. Like I'm ten feet tall. Like she needs all the same things I do, and she needs them *now.*

"Fuck me, Jack," she whispers, wrapping her arms around my neck and pulling herself flush with my body. Those amazing breasts flatten against my chest and her legs tighten around me and her heat, her core, that sweet, sweet pussy I can taste on my own lips, connects at the perfect angle...

"Oh, *fuuuuuuuuuck,* Cate," I groan, pushing inside her, going deep into her tight, wet heat as I crush my mouth against hers, swallowing more of those delicious sounds she's been giving me all night.

And... *holy fucking shit.* I'm balls deep, and she feels amazing. Feels like heaven. Feels better than I could ever describe. I'm done with slow. Just can't anymore, and she doesn't want it. I pull back and thrust in hard, and then I do it again. And then *again.* We're moving together, immediately in sync, and it's exactly like my fantasy, but a billion times better.

It's fucking *perfect.*

"You two look so good," Dylan pants. "Look at Cate, Jack, look how amazing you're making her feel, look how much she fucking *loves* your cock."

My balls start to tighten up as I listen to him. *Christ,* where did he learn to talk like that? And when I look over—oh fucking God —his eyes are hooded and his face flushed and his hand jerking hard and fast over a cock that... that...

Fucking-*A.*

Dylan is hung. He's fucking gorgeous.

I groan, watching him fuck himself into his fist as I drive into Cate, hard and fast, in the same rhythm.

"Yeah," he says, one hand drifting up to his chest. Rubbing across his pecs. His nipples. "*Yeah*, Jack. *Cate*. That's it."

"Oh God, *Dylan*," Cate moans, her heels spurring me on, digging into my ass. "You... you... like this?"

"You're incredible, Cate," he grits out. "So fucking sexy. Jack looks so good, buried inside you. How does it feel?"

Her nails score my back, and her incredible body starts to tighten all around me. She moans, and I know she can't answer him. I can't, either. But oh please, oh fucking please, I want to hear it. Want to hear him urging us on. Getting off on it. And Dylan... *Dylan*. He doesn't let me down.

"She's about to come," he pants, making me groan. "Her thighs are shaking, Jack. *God*, your ass. Pound her. She's loving it. You're loving it, Cate, aren't you? Jack, fuck... fuck... do it. Come for me. *Cate*."

Neither one of us have wanted to say no to him, not all night. Not when he's the one that's giving us all what we need. Telling us it's okay to want what we want.

This is no different.

Cate cries out, a stuttering, shuddering wail that strokes every fucking cell in my body. She's tipping over the edge. She's *gone*. She clenches around me, squeezing my cock hard as I thrust deep one more time. And then another. And then I'm gone, too. The orgasm Dylan asked me for ripping through me and leaving me in tatters. Shooting out in hot spurts that have me shouting, slamming into Cate, again and again, as she comes undone around me. As I lose track of where she ends and I begin.

And Dylan's still giving me what I wanted.

His voice, his low, deep moans, vibrating through my whole body as my knees shake with the force of my release. I don't want to move. But damn, I want to see.

Want to *watch*.

Dylan bucks up into his hand as my eyes meet his. "Oh, fuck, Cate, *Jack,*" he cries, the slick, fast sound of his action almost overriding his voice. "Fuck, you two are so gorgeous, you're so *hot,* I'm—"

His voice chokes off, turning into a throaty, guttural shout as I watch him explode, jets of white arcing through the air to land all over his hand, the cut ridges of his abs, the hard curves of his chest.

Oh, yeah.

Oh, *hell* yeah.

That was hot as fuck.

And for a minute—one blessed, perfect minute—that's all that exists. Me and Cate and Dylan, basking in the afterglow.

Damn, I wish this could last.

# 12

## DYLAN

*I*'ve always admired how compact and oddly small Boston actually is, but when you're in the thick of these behemoths, it's easy to lose track. Jack's office is in a huge building in the Financial District, amongst a nest of other massive glass towers, and I pedal up to the building and lock my bike to a nearby rack, then make my way through the revolving door and across the long polished floor. A moment later, I'm zipping up one of the many elevators, and the doors open up onto a long hallway leading up to the main reception desk. The hallway is lined with couches, and they're just about chock-full of lawyers and their clients. The whole feel of the place is hectic, at odds with how tastefully decorated it is—a classy mix of modern design combined with old strong wood.

These are details I would never have noted before, but Cate must be rubbing off on me. The woman really knows her stuff, and it has been delightfully easy to pick up the things she says.

I walk up to the receptionist and smile as she hangs up her phone.

"Dylan Smith in for a lunch appointment with Jack Kelly."

"No problem," she says, picking her phone up again. "Just a second."

I nod and smile, and turn to the side to admire the art on the wall. Nothing that I'd recognize, of course, but I do know what I like when I see it. Speaking of which... my smile gets even wider as, from behind me, I hear Jack say my name. I *definitely* like him.

"Hey, you," I say, turning to greet him. I try to tone down my grin when a warm flush goes over his face at my regard. Love seeing that I affect him, though.

"Hey, yourself," he answers, sounding a little stiff... but welcoming.

I'm going to take that as a good sign.

My grin grows at the confusion on his face, and when he nods in the direction I've just come from and says, "Walk with me. The front desk told me we have a lunch appointment?" I have to laugh.

Jack's never been great with surprises, but he's rolling with it.

"We sure do," I wink at him, loving the way it catches him off guard. He let himself go last night. Gave himself permission to have what he wanted, even though I know him well enough to guess that there were some this-isn't-right voices he had to fight off to get there.

Worth it, though.

I hope.

God, he and Cate were hot together.

"Did we, uh... I mean, I don't remember..."

I laugh again at his stumbling attempt to figure out what I'm doing here, and put him out of his misery.

"Just because you didn't know about our lunch date, doesn't mean we didn't have one in the works."

Jack's eyes widen, then he barks out a laugh, loosening up a bit. "I swear," he says, grinning at me and just about making my heart stop. The man is *gorgeous*. "It's always about food when it comes to you, isn't it?"

"Who doesn't like food?" I ask rhetorically. "We start and stop wars over it. The least I can do is respect it. We're very lucky, you and I."

Don't get me wrong, I love food, but it's not what I want to talk about right now. Still, I'm happy to do what I can to put Jack at ease.

I don't want to lose him again.

"No," Jack says, glancing at me and then darting his eyes away fast. "*You're* the lucky one, Dylan. Look at your body. Nobody I know eats the way you do and looks like that."

There's definitely admiration in his voice, and I eat it up. I'd seen him looking at me last night. I'd been able to read him as clear as day, and it had made everything even better for me, but now... in the light of day and without his mind clouded by sex, I can sense that he hadn't really meant to say it.

He flushes, looking away and obviously uncomfortable, but I decide to power through.

"Is that a compliment, Jack?" I ask, winking again.

"*No,*" Jack sputters, tripping on the carpet. He darts his eyes toward me again, going red. "I mean, yeah, but..." He shakes his head, laughing at himself. Another good sign. "It's been a long day already, Dylan, sorry. I don't know what I'm saying right now. I probably would have forgotten to eat entirely if you hadn't shown up."

Hearing that makes me even more happy that I'd decided to stop by instead of just calling or texting. He follows me out of the building without any further complaint, and the farther we get from his office building, the more I can see the tension draining out of him.

Clearly he's overworked, and I wonder what he has in his life for stress relief. Our new stab at friendship hasn't really gotten far enough to talk about those things yet.

We spend most of the walk in silence, and I lead him to Wilkes' Steakhouse. It's not one of the more high-end establishments in this city, but it's definitely a hidden gem. It only takes us a couple of blocks to get there, so we're inside in no time at all. The interior is dark, and the decor is all classic, rich wood. A very comfortable place that reminds me of Sully in more ways than one, so I figure it's pretty much perfect for taking Jack out to lunch.

"Tell me why you like this place again?" Jack asks once we're at the table. He removes his suit coat and folds it neatly, draping it over the chair beside him as he glances around.

Okay then, we'll stick with talk of food for a little bit longer.

"Whoever buys the meat here does a fantastic job," I tell him, inhaling deeply. "Smell that," I say, and wait to see Jack's chest rise and fall slowly.

Jack nods. "Nice, that's real nice," he says.

He's dodging my eyes, though, and now I'm starting to worry a little bit. Last night, he all but sprinted out of the townhouse after everything was done. Doesn't surprise me that he's not entirely comfortable, but I didn't figure he'd be this worked up. He'd wanted to be a part of "dessert" just as much as Cate and I had, and as far as I'm concerned, he's got *nothing* to be ashamed about.

"Are you... okay, Jack?" I ask, as gently as I can manage. What I really want to do is shake him. Or kiss him. Drag him home and feed him there and then, oh yeah. *Then* do other decadent things with his body.

But I'm a patient man.

I know this is hard for him.

He blinks at me, looking a little scared that I'd actually dared to ask him outright... even though I'd made the question as circumspect as I could.

"Yeah, Dylan," he says after a moment. "I'm okay. Feel fine. Let's just order, okay?"

He picks up a menu and begins flipping through it without giving me a chance to push, and I'm wondering if it's a good idea or a bad idea to call him out directly. To let him know that it really *is* okay.

To see if he's brave enough to come back for more.

"Sure," I finally say, once it becomes clear he's mastered the art of not meeting my eyes. "No problem."

I just got Jack back into my life. The last thing I need is to have him run off again.

He nods, but still doesn't look up.

Doesn't speak.

"What are you thinking about having?" I ask, my lips twitching. Sure, I hate that he's uncomfortable, but Jack's actually kind of cute when he's flustered.

"I don't know," he answers me tersely, still staring hard at the menu. "Probably just steak. Well-done. Nice and simple. Maybe some mashed potatoes? I don't know, I'm probably gonna box most of it anyway, my appetite isn't huge right now."

I sigh and smile, shaking my head. Well-done. Not today. I'm going to baby him out of his funk, give him something he'll like, if he'll let me.

And we'll start with food.

"Jack, may I make a suggestion? You don't have to take it, but I think you'll really enjoy it if you just trust me on this one."

Jack finally looks up at me, and I can see that the longer our eyes meet, the harder it is for him to hold onto this self-protective distance he's putting between us.

There's heat there, but he's not okay with showing it.

Not to me.

Not yet.

"Okay," he finally relents, exhaling as some of the tension leaves his shoulders.

*Good.* It's a start.

"Alright," I say, unrolling my silverware and folding the cloth napkin to set on my thigh. "Today, you want to order a steak, but make it medium rare. A little blood isn't going to hurt you, and you won't regret how juicy and flavorful a proper steak is, I promise."

"Just a steak, then? No sides?" Jack grabs onto my suggestion like a lifeline, and I can see how relieved he is that we're talking about food instead of how much he liked what happened at the townhouse last night.

"Of course there are sides," I reassure him, smiling. "Get your mashed potatoes, but ask for them to sit atop a small serving of asparagus. Then, let's see if the waiter will do you a favor and arrange to have freshly sliced strawberries to surround and complement the steak."

Jack's brows crinkle in confusion. "A... fruit steak?"

God, he's adorable sometimes.

"No, of course not a fruit steak," I answer, making sure he can hear that the laughter in my voice is *with* him, not at him. "Just a properly prepared steak with a complementary side, and a little bit of sweetness to offset all of the savory tastes you'll be experiencing. Trust me, yeah? Have I steered you wrong yet?"

Another flare of heat in his eyes at my subtle reminder of last night. I grin, and he looks away again... but not before I see his lips twitch in what might have been the start of a smile. After a minute, he looks back and nods.

"Good," I say, closing my menu decisively and then plucking his out of his hands, too. Perfect timing, as our waiter shows up to take our orders and, a few minutes later, brings us a couple of gin and tonics to ease the conversation a little.

Jack takes a few sips of his drink, then puts it down and meets my eyes. No more running.

"So," he says. "Why are we doing this right now, Dylan?"

Direct. I've always loved that about Jack. No matter what, he eventually just asks the damn question.

I grin, sipping my own drink once more before answering. Savoring.

"Cate and I decided to invite you over last night to talk about the townhouse and get that all resolved," I remind him. "Thought it would be nice if we could all get a good night's sleep over it. You know, be nice not to have the whole matter hovering over us, waiting in the wings like it has been for the last week or so."

Jack snorts, and I laugh. Okay, so maybe I'm easing into it a little too slowly. After all, he'd gotten over his reluctance and addressed it head-on.

And before I can go on, he does it again.

"But..." he says, raising an eyebrow and inviting me to finish that sentence.

"*But.* Yeah." I grin. "Things got a little... off track, didn't they?"

I run my finger lightly around the rim of my drink, and I see Jack smile in spite of himself. It's like his regular smile but somehow different, somehow *more*.

Sexy.

Is this what he looks like when he's turned on in public? I'll bet it is, one hundred percent. And when he shifts in his seat, his eyes getting back some of that heat that had me throbbing last night?

Yeah, I'm right.

Better than that, I'm *lucky*. He's not running away from it. Not yet.

Hopefully, not ever again.

There's still some of those doubts clouding his eyes, though, and I remind myself again how bigoted the environment he grew up in was. Baby steps.

"What happened last night wasn't wrong, you know, Jack," I say, lowering my voice in the hope that I won't spook him. "It wasn't a bad thing. We're all consenting adults here, we all wanted what happened. All three of us, together."

Jack gives a jerky nod, but still... not running away. I wait him out, and after a minute, he adds a reluctant, "I guess so. Just not—" a self-conscious laugh as he looks away for a second, "—not really what I'm used to, you know?"

He's wrestling with the idea, learning how to be okay with it. It's written all over his face.

Sometimes, I really feel bad for him, growing up in the neighborhood he came from. It can't be easy to live most of your formative years in that sort of closed-minded environment, and I can see why he would struggle with the concept. I'm here for him, in every sense of the word.

I got this.

I'm never going to give up on him.

"I mean it, Jack," I say firmly, stopping myself from reaching across and taking his hand. Might be too much for him right now, out here in public. We'll get there, though. "You did nothing wrong. *We* did nothing wrong."

I can tell my stern tone surprises him, but I don't want him to have any room for doubt that I mean what I say.

His knee is bouncing under the table, I can tell, and after a minute, he blurts out, "So... what? You're *into* that kinky shit?"

That startles a laugh out of me. "What kinky shit?"

"You know." He shifts, looking away from me. Cute. *Sexy.* "Watching."

My lips twitch. "Well, of course I enjoyed it, Jack. Two of the most attractive people on this planet, two people who mean everything to me, and they're eating my food? Enjoying each other on my table?"

Oh, I'm getting to him. The knee has gone still and his color is rising. His breath, too. Damn, but I'd like to feel those hot little gusts on my skin.

"How could I not love watching that?" I ask, softer now. "How could *anyone* not love that?"

Jack's eyes flick back to mine. "I guess. I mean, yeah. It was hot. I just don't know if I should have done that. Should have let you... should have... wanted... "

His voice trails off and I watch his Adam's apple bob in his throat as he swallows hard. I can practically hear the Irish Catholic in his voice, but I'll be damned if I let him feel guilty over something so beautiful.

"Listen, Jack," I say, leaning forward and willing him to meet my eyes. He does. God love the man. "I *loved* watching you and Cate together, but if we're being completely honest here, I would have enjoyed participating, too."

"You would?" Jack asks, sitting up straighter. There's an unmistakable undercurrent to his voice now. Excitement. *Want.*

"Oh, yeah," I tell him, letting him hear it in my voice. How much I'd love that. *"Definitely."*

He hadn't been ready for it last night, though. And it's not like watching had been a chore. *Hell* no. It had been beyond hot. And then there's the fact that Cate and Jack... well, they need to resolve the tension between them.

I grin, hiding it behind another sip. Yeah, I'm pretty sure that had been accomplished.

Jack's looking at me like he's trying to sort out a puzzle, rubbing the back of his neck. One of his tells.

"The way you were talking about Cate," he starts. Then stops. Then starts again. "You and her... you got together?"

I nod. No hiding. Not with the three of us. *Ever.*

"I thought you were, you know, into guys," he finally says. *"Gay."*

I suppress the urge to reach out and punch him in the shoulder like we did when we were kids and he was being an ass. "Jack, I'm not gay."

He looks at me, confused. How can he be so damn smart and still struggle to wrap his head around this? We used to talk about girls all the time when we were younger.

"You're not?" he finally asks.

And I have to smile again, because *yes*, there was some disappointment in his voice. Totally unnecessary, though. He's blind if he hasn't caught onto how attracted I am to him.

"Not gay," I say again. "I'm bisexual."

"Oh." And then, after a moment, "So, you *do* like guys?"

He looks at me, and the mixture of conflict and attraction in his eyes is as clear as day. That, plus just a tinge of hopefulness.

I feel like cheering—finally, it got through to him! I almost laugh, out of kindness of course, but I manage to bite it back. It would destroy him right now, and I need to remember that this is all very new for him. Whatever I do, I need to make it very clear where he stands with me.

He matters too much to mess it up.

I look back at him, meeting his conflicted gaze directly. Slow and easy, baby steps.

"Yes, Jack, I like women, and I like men. A *lot*."

The shadow of relief washes over his face for just a moment, but before I can celebrate it, like a soap bubble popping, it's gone. He clamps down hard, just as the food arrives.

"Actually, I've gotta get back to the office," he says to the waiter, avoiding my eyes again. "Would you mind boxing that up for me? Appreciate it much."

"Sir?" the waiter says, looking at me.

"No, I'm going to stay, thank you," I say without looking away from Jack. The waiter leaves quickly, and I continue. "Jack, stay. We can have a nice lunch. I'm sure the office won't miss you for another twenty minutes."

"Sorry, Dylan," he says, pushing out of his seat and standing up. "It's kinda crazy back there right now, and I need to get it all sorted out."

I don't bother getting out of my seat, and it takes a lot not to sigh. I felt like we were starting to make progress. But that's okay, I remind myself. It took me time, too. I need to make sure he knows that I'm committed, solid, a rock. I need him to know that I'm here when he's ready.

"If you change your mind, I'll be here finishing my lunch. Otherwise, we still need to talk about the townhouse and what we want to do about it."

"Yeah, well, I don't care," he says harshly.

Oh, Jack. Self-defense, I get it… but you don't have to defend yourself from me *or* Cate. You can have it all. But I can't say that yet, not when he's like this. Running scared from who he *wants* to be and who he mistakenly thinks he *should* be.

"I don't need the place," he's saying, brusque and distant but not fooling me for a minute. "I just wanna get my share and move on with my life. If you two need to stay, fine, no skin off my back, just buy me out and we can close this down altogether."

I can tell that he's having to wrestle with every single word. I recognize the cold exterior that he puts on like armor, the repression taking hold again. I feel frustrated, disappointed, but more than anything, I just feel so damn bad for him. Hell of a way to feel like you have to live, especially when there's really no need.

"We have so many memories in that house, Jack," I remind him. "All of us. You and me. If those walls could talk, they'd be telling a hell of a happy story."

I smile up at him, trying to draw him back into happier territory.

Doesn't work.

"If you want the damn house so bad," he snaps, "why don't you get your new rich girlfriend to buy it for you?"

And that's it. That's all I can take right now. After having spent a week with Cate, learning about everything that led her to run away from New York, I just can't let this slide. I like to think I'm an easygoing guy, but even I have limits. All the patience in the world when it comes to getting what I want, but if he *still* can't see past his own messed-up ideas about Cate?

I get up slowly from my seat, taking a moment to hit my full height before leaning over the table with my hands pressed flat against it. He pushed too far, and now I can't help but get in his face and push back a little.

"You're wrong about her, Jack," I say, and my voice comes out rough and harsh. "She's not *any* of that. She's *never* been any of that, and she's not going to turn into that just because, way the fuck back when, you decided you knew her without ever getting to *know* her."

People are looking at us now, and I can feel Jack starting to radiate embarrassment, but I don't care. I've coddled him a lot today, done my best to make him see the good right in front of him, but he needs to hear this right now. I tried the kid gloves, but now it's time for some old-school tough love.

"You remember her mother? Remember how we used to joke about putting coal in her ass, 'cause she'd turn it into a diamond overnight? Cate left all that behind, Jack. It's gone. Cut off. Nothing. Everything she has, everything she *ever* had, all came from Sully. Sully, and her own hard work, and nothing else." Normally I wouldn't point, but I'm *pissed*—I level a finger at his chest and hold his gaze. "Just. Like. *You.*"

Jack does his best to put on a fake lawyer smile, clearly burning with embarrassment from the not-so-subtle stares from the diners around us.

"You two just... figure it out between you. Let me know what you decide," he says, and his voice is strained with false professionalism. "I've gotta get back."

He reaches down, picks up his glass, and drains the gin and tonic.

His hand is shaking.

The sight douses my anger. God. Jack matters, too. If only he'd just let me in. Either of us. *Both* of us.

"Okay," I say, my suddenly calm tone of voice clearly startling him. "We'll do that. And then, we'll... invite you over for dinner."

Jack slams the glass down onto the table with a hard smack, and a few diners gasp lightly in the background. His eyes flare up, and there's an edge to them, something else mixed in with the anger he's trying so hard to hold onto like a shield. And that something else? It looks a heck of a lot like that old current of excitement, the mix of rage and hunger I saw on his face when I caught him and Cate on the stairs. It's hot as hell.

"Why?" Jack spits at me, clearly at war with himself. "You want to get off on *watching* us again?"

I grin, and I can tell that just pushes his buttons even more.

"*I* was talking about having you over to talk about the house, Jack," I say, arching an eyebrow as I hold his gaze. "But if watching is on the menu again..." I push in my chair and walk around the table, slowly enough that he could leave if he wanted.

He doesn't, and we end up face to face, close enough that those hot, hard little breaths I was wondering about tremble over my skin.

Oh God, I want this man.

"I can't speak for Cate," I tell him, letting him see everything I've got. "But I'd *love* to do that again. Or, like I said before, to be a part of it next time. An *active* part."

We stare at each other for a long, tense moment, a moment where I'm *almost positive* he's about to reach out and grab me by the shirt and yank me in for a blistering kiss.

God, *yes*.

Please.

I can see him struggling, trying to fight past his own fear, his own limitations, a lifetime of being told what he feels is fucked-up and wrong. And he comes so close, so heartbreakingly close that I'm almost reaching out, leaning into a kiss I'm sure is coming. My heart lifts, and I think finally, *finally*.

I've been hoping for this for years.

But he's not brave enough. Not yet. I see the moment it all floods back in, a tidal wave of conditioned bullshit and self-doubt, and I've got a front-row seat to watch as the panic blazes back into his eyes. Jack whips around, grabbing his suit coat and sprinting out of the restaurant.

He doesn't even wait for his boxed food.

Not that I thought he would, but... damn. The disappointment almost crushes me.

## 13

## CATE

"Cate! Hello, darling!" the voice hollers pleasantly over the other end of the line. I take a quick glance at my phone clock. Saturday at seven o'clock in the morning? Who the hell is so chipper at this time of day? The number was unlisted.

"Good morning," I say back. "I'm so sorry, but may I ask who's calling?"

"It's Margaret, dear, you remember."

I most sincerely don't, but I've spent the entire week putting out feelers for anyone in the area who might be interested in personal training, so I suppose this could be anyone. I *did*, after all, ask everyone to tell their friends about me.

"Of course, Margaret," I lie, slipping into my pleasantly professional tone. "It feels like it's been ages. When's the last time we spoke?"

"Oh, my," Margaret responds. High-class, society woman, older. I rack my brains.

"I know, dear," I respond, matching the tone and timbre of her voice. The wealthy are suckers for kinship, fake or otherwise. "The days move so quickly now, don't they?"

"You're so right, you're *so* right," Margaret responds. There's a beat of silence, and I think maybe I'm going to be found out. "Oh," she exclaims, and I exhale in relief. "I think it may have been the MacMillan charity event last year, you remember."

Oh. *That* Margaret. Now I remember. Margaret St. John, the Manhattan socialite. She's the rail-thin, overly cloying woman who is just chock-full of nitpicky opinions about how she finds the modern design movement to be utterly gauche. The last time I saw her, she was six champagnes deep and comparing the charity event's design work to a common beach brothel. Where the hell had she seen a beach brothel before? What does that even mean?

I pinch the bridge of my nose, thankful this isn't a video call. It's *absolutely* too early for this.

"Right. Of course," I say, doing my best to not sound as grumpy as I am. "It was Designs on the Dock if I'm not mistaken. I'm so sorry that you had such a negative experience."

"Oh, darling, don't dwell on it," she responds with thick, chipper venom. "There's a learning curve for everyone, is there not?"

"You're absolutely right," I say through gritted teeth. "I view all criticism as stepping stones on the path of perfection. Is there anything I can do to help you this morning, Ms. St. John?

"Yes, actually," she started. "I don't know if you're aware, but I summer in Cape Cod these days. I understand you've recently made a grand return to Boston, is that right?"

"That's right," I respond. "About two weeks ago now, I think? The days have gone by so fast, it's hard to tell."

"Well, that's just positively lovely. I always say that a young woman should travel while they still have their looks, and those years do start to dwindle fast, don't they?"

*Fuck you*, I scream inside my head. *Fuck you and the whole army of horses you rode in on.*

"They certainly do," I reply, biting back that other voice. "For-

168

give me for cutting to the chase, but I assume someone let you know that I'm now offering personalized fitness sessions?"

"Yes, they did."

Finally. A bite. I force a smile, hoping it will improve my attitude about the prospect. Truth is, I need this. After shopping for necessities, my savings have started to dwindle a lot faster than I anticipated they would. Not that last week's dinner table fling wasn't ten different types of lovely, but I do *not* plan on getting caught without panties again.

"That's wonderful," I say, and my forced smile must have worked, because even I can hear that my voice sounds a bit more cheerful.

Of course, that could also be due to memories of dinner with Jack and Dylan.

I yank my thoughts back to Margaret. This isn't the time to get distracted, and she's the sort of person who thinks milk at the grocery store costs fifty dollars. I can probably get away with a very generous rate for my troubles, and the thought cheers me up even more. Maybe this move to Boston really *will* work out.

"If you'd like to discuss the types of services I offer, I can give you a free consultation," I tell Margaret, and now the pleasure in my voice is genuine. Things are looking up all around. "There are many options that I specialize in."

"Oh, darling," Margaret says, cutting me off. "No, I'm sorry, I'm afraid I may have gotten your hopes up. Unfortunately, I will not be availing myself of your services this summer."

And just as fast as my mood had risen, it now free falls right into the toilet. What the hell is she calling for? And at 7am?

"You… won't be using my services?"

"No," she says flatly. "I had considered it, of course, but imagine my luck when I was presented with a more sensible alternative, someone who is the picture of fitness. I was calling merely to express my sympathy about your late grandfather, and to encourage you to keep at your new little business. It's always so difficult to transition between two completely different fields, isn't it?"

I'm honestly surprised that I can even form words right now. I'm seeing blood-red. What a *bitch*.

"Yes, it certainly is," I grit out, politeness too ingrained for me to say what I really think. "Well, if that's all, I'm afraid I have an appointment to get to."

Okay, maybe that last line slipped over the edge into rude, but I have no regrets. As bad as this conversation is making me feel, it doesn't even feel like a lie: I'd say I'm totally justified in making myself an appointment to bury myself back under the covers and never come out.

Either that, or setting one up with a hitman who specializes in wealthy socialites.

"Of course, I don't want to keep you," Margaret replies, saccharine sweet. "Perhaps I can provide a recommendation. A sort of train-the-trainer arrangement? I hear that the *professional* I'll be working with is amazing at getting all of those hard-to-reach spots."

That settles it. Hitman it is.

I pinch the bridge of my nose again, willing myself not to get a stress headache, and I'm suddenly very thankful that I have the house to myself for most of the day. Dylan took an overnight event job with a catering company up in New Hampshire, and said he won't be back until much later today.

"I'll keep it in mind, Ms. St. John. Goodbye," I manage.

"Yes, we'll be in tou—"

I hang up. I can't help it. I've been awake for not even ten minutes, and I've already hit my limit for the day. I swing my legs out of bed and take a moment to enjoy the cool hardwood on my soles, then I walk over to the dresser and remove my oldest set of underwear: a white bralette and a pair of faded yellow boyshorts.

No wires, no lace, all comfort.

Since I get the whole day alone, I'm going to enjoy it.

I head toward the bedroom door, then stop. So far, every time Jack has shown up unannounced, he's caught me in my underwear. My body reacts to the thought immediately, but that's silly. There's no reason to think he'd show up *today*. Dylan told me about Jack pushing him away when they'd gone out to lunch, and neither one of us has heard from him since.

It's been more than a week.

I've tried not to be hurt by that—not only had the sex been amazing, but I'd really felt connected to him. And... yeah. I'd had to fight my own sense of having gone too far after it was all over, but honestly, it hadn't taken me long to shut down those voices. Maybe some might have called it kinky, and I know for sure *some* would call it wrong. All I know is it was the hottest sex I'd ever had, an orgasm that had nearly wrecked me, and that—with Dylan there, and even Jack, for all our history—I'd never felt more okay with anything in my life.

Obviously we'd have to hear from Jack at some point. Grandpa Sully had made sure of that when he'd tied us all together with this townhouse, but when that would happen? With Jack, I had no idea.

Still, for today, I turn back to my room and grab my comfortable plush white robe. I'm not in the mood for more surprises. Margaret St. John was more than enough of one for today, thank you very much.

I walk downstairs and fill the coffeepot, pouring the water into the reservoir and setting it down on the warmer. I flip the switch and spend the entire time it brews marveling at the nerve of Margaret to call me up like that.

Was this a morning ritual for her? Bump a little cocaine, flip through the Rolodex, pick out the poorest people she knows, then ridicule them in order to get through her day?

I scowl, staring blindly at the coffeepot. I hope she chokes on her overpriced cereal.

I get a little lost in my revenge-fantasy reverie, so it takes me a little too long to notice that I forgot to put coffee grounds in the filter.

"*Shit,*" I mutter aloud, staring at the half-full pot of water. It looks like seawater, light brown and unappealing. I shake my head and flip off the switch, then grab the coffeepot and turn for the sink. So much for salvaging the morning.

I grab the coffeepot to try again, but I spin too fast, splashing incredibly hot water all over my robe.

"*No,* goddammit," I wail, reflexively dropping the coffeepot.

It falls into the sink, shattering, but I barely have time to notice that as I tear my robe off and brush frantically at my chest. Just red, thankfully, versus the harsher burns it *felt* like I'd just given myself. Still hurts like a bitch, though. I can feel hot, angry tears starting to well up in my eyes, and I blink them back as hard as I can.

"Not today," I say out loud to nobody. "I refuse to spend my day like this."

I take a deep breath, trying to calm myself as I pick up my robe and examine it. Perfect fluffy fabric everywhere except a big patch of damp, brown discoloration from the coffee water. I sigh and drop my head, then trudge off to the laundry room. I need to get a load going anyway, and this is as good a reason as any to avoid putting it off, I guess.

I can't deny I'm starting to feel like I should have gone with the pull-the-covers-back-over-my-head option. I'm not usually a negative person, but while I don't regret my spontaneous decision to uproot my life, I have to admit that it's come with a lot of uncertainty. If I'm honest, it's been eating me up inside, slowly but surely, and it's also come with more of an emotional rollercoaster than I'd counted on.

I wonder if it's more than I can handle.

A few minutes later, everything is in the wash and churning along, and I exhale, feeling my emotions start to ebb a little. I can do this. I *can.*

One step at a time. And next? There's still a mess in the sink that I have to deal with.

"Might as well do it now," I say, my mood starting to lighten as I wonder when I started talking to myself. Had I done that back in New York? I don't think so. Maybe it's living with someone for the first time.

I adore sharing the house with Dylan, and I guess I've gotten used to having someone there to hear me when I need to get something off my chest.

I start to head back to the kitchen when my phone begins to ring.

Please, not Margaret with her *professional* trainer recommendation. I look at my phone and groan. The way this morning has gone so far, it only makes sense. Not Margaret... it's even worse.

My mother.

I take a quick second to debate whether or not I want to throw the phone in the wash as well, but it's too important to my future livelihood. I indulge in one more sigh, then answer.

"Good morning, Mother."

"Is that all you have to say to me, Caitlin?" she snaps, forgoing a greeting or any pretense of maternal affection.

"What are you talking about?" I ask, rolling my eyes. Really, it could be anything. Or, more precisely, everything.

Has she *ever* approved of anything I've done?

"It's been two weeks since you went off on this little tantrum of yours," she says, her tone clipped. The words sting; she *always* knows how to make them sting. "And now I have to hear about how rude you were to Margaret St. John this morning? What on earth is your problem, young lady?"

I didn't think the day could get any worse, but I'm rapidly being proven wrong. I wedge the phone between my shoulder and ear, crossing my arms over my reddened breasts. I should get ice, but right now, I just want to get this call over with.

"Mother, that woman called up specifically to make jokes

about my business and my weight," I tell her, my patience running thin. "But despite that, I was perfectly civil."

"If you consider hanging up on her to be civil, then yes, you did *such* a lovely job," she says, sarcasm set to high. "It's time for this nonsense to end, Caitlin. I'm sure your savings have to be nearly gone by now, and I know you haven't gotten a job yet."

My blood starts to boil at that. It's all too easy to hear the smug satisfaction in her tone. What kind of mother *wants* her daughter to fail?

"All of this personal training business is cute," she goes on. "But you need to face reality, dear. No one is going to hire a chubby girl to train them. Especially one who overcompensates for the deficiencies in her appearance by being a smartass with her own flesh and blood."

And suddenly, I'm done. I've been brought to the highest of highs in the past two weeks, and now I'm at the lowest of lows. I feel the tears coming to my eyes, and I don't make any effort to stop them this time.

"Julianne MacMillan," I say sharply, refusing to call her anything motherly right now. "Did *you* put Margaret up to that call? Are you that cruel?"

She sucks in a sharp breath, but of course her response isn't an apology.

"You will address me as *Mother*, you little brat," she snaps. "And of course I told Margaret what you were up to. I never really thought she'd hire you; we both know how ridiculous that idea is, so I didn't bother sugarcoating the facts when I explained your situation."

"You're so, *so* mean," is all I can manage to say, choked up, tears streaking down my cheeks. I sniffle, but she talks right over me, not acknowledging my words any more than she does my feelings.

"You will end this nonsense *now*, Caitlin, and come back home immediately," she says sharply. "I need you to work on our new summer seasonal presentation, and it's too late to hire anyone else for the job."

"I'm not coming back to New York, Mother," I say raggedly. "I *am* home."

Before she can respond, I hang up the phone and shut it off completely.

Fuck this.

Fuck *all* of this.

My entire body is racked with sobs as I struggle to fathom how anyone could be so cruel, or how any one day could turn so awful, so quickly. Forget coffee, forget cleanup, forget doing anything productive today. The only thing I want now is ice cream and pie, and I don't give a shit about anything else.

Dylan, my best friend, my sweetheart, he'll know what to do when he gets home. All I have to do is hold out until then. He'll fix it, or at least he'll listen to me vent it all out.

I head to the kitchen, on a comfort mission now. It's all I have the capacity for anymore. I'm done with this day already, and it's barely gotten started. I'm so wrapped up in my own thoughts that I don't immediately realize that I've stepped on the tiniest piece of broken glass from the shattered coffeepot.

When I do, the pain hits me way harder than it should.

"*Fuck!*" I scream. "*Why? Motherfuck!*"

I start crying all over again, and I can't help myself even a little bit. I gingerly remove the tiny piece of glass, crying openly and loudly while I do so, and toss it in the sink. I don't deserve this. I don't deserve *any* of this. And sure, it's a pity party, but right now? I really can't find it in me to hold it together.

"Grandpa, just fix it, please," I find myself wailing crazily. "Just fix it and take it away. I can't anymore. I can't right now."

I get no answer... of course. My Grandpa Sully is dead, and there's nothing I can do to change that.

Still crying, I move to the freezer and dig out the container of cookie dough ice cream, then pull the leftover strawberry pie out of the fridge. Dylan made it from scratch, and it tasted like heaven.

I put the ice cream and the pie platter on the counter, dig out a spoon from the drawer, rip off the ice cream lid, and dig in for a bite. The sweet vanilla mixed with the bit of cookie dough hits me like the hardest drug I've ever done in my life, and my sobs intensify for just a second longer before subsiding.

Oh my *God*. I've never tasted *anything* this good in my life before.

Not a single thing.

With the spoon still in my mouth, I pick up the container in one hand and the pie platter in the other, and limp tenderly toward the kitchen table.

And of course, there he is.

Completely unannounced and big as life, Jack stands in the kitchen doorway. Staring at me without my robe on, no makeup, face blotchy from crying, in my ratty underpants, my tear-and-coffee-stained bralette, giant tub of ice cream in one hand, big plate of strawberry pie in the other, and a spoon dangling from my mouth.

Fucking *perfect*.

Everything snaps. I'm flooded with emotions, all at once. Rage, desire, humiliation, regret. I can't help it anymore. I'm done. Really, truly done. I spit the spoon out of my mouth and it clatters unceremoniously on the floor.

"What the *fuck* is *wrong* with you, Jack?!" I scream, lobbing the pie awkwardly in his direction.

Jack jumps, avoiding the crash of the pie and the splatter of the filling, though it still manages to get all over the bottom of his slacks.

"Jesus, Cate," he starts, building up his own rage-filled voice. "What the hell's a-matter with you?"

"You! It's always *you*!" I shriek, slamming the ice cream container down to the floor with a gigantic splat. It gets all over my ankles, and I'm so beyond caring. "The last two weeks, it's just you throwing your dick around, you barging in unannounced, you refusing to work with us on the townhouse, you turning your back on this *family*."

Jack's eyes widen. "Cate, I don't know—"

"This is the *one* thing that anyone who's ever mattered to you has asked you for!" I yell over him, cutting him off with my hands balled into hard fists at my sides. I lean into it. In for a penny, in for a pound. "This *one* thing! You don't need the money from selling the townhouse! Why the fuck are you stonewalling us at every turn?" I start sobbing into my shrieks. "Why the fuck haven't you called? How dare you come in here and fuck me that way, then leave without another word? How *could* you? What kind of *monster* are you?"

I start to feel my legs go weak, and I realize that the only thing I've eaten today is a single spoonful of ice cream. Sobbing, I pull a chair out from the table and sit down, burying my head in my hands.

Even so, I still find reasons to yell at him through my fingers. There's too much inside me. It has to come out.

"You can't treat people like this, Jack! You can't just walk into my life like this and use me all up, then drop me the second you get scared! You *know* how hot I think you are; how hot you've *always* been to me! But I'm not that shy little girl anymore, and I'm not afraid to tell you exactly what I think of you! I don't care *how* ugly you always thought I was. You bastard, you fucking asshole!"

I continue to sob, but I'm coming down from the peak now. The righteous fury drains from my body, and all that's left is sadness and hurt.

"I'm so tired of always doing my best, and getting nothing in return," I weep. "I'm so exhausted by all of it. I'm done. I'm just done."

I drop my head on the table and get the rest of the tears out, a heaviness coming over me.

CHLOE LYNN ELLIS

I'm too tired to cry; I'm too tired for anything. I just want to sleep and make it all go away. I know Jack is going to start raging at me any second now, and I'm going to feel even more like trash than I already did when he walked in on me.

So I wait for it.

And wait.

And... wait some more.

But Jack's rage never comes. What does come is a warm hand on my bare shoulder, and another sliding into my hair to gently cradle the side of my head.

"Hey, Duchess," Jack says softly, and it's the first time I've ever heard him sound genuinely kind and concerned. "It's okay. I'm sorry, I mean it. It's going to be okay."

My heart constricts in my chest, so hard I can't breathe for a moment. And then... warmth rushes through me. Not the hot *need* I've felt around Jack ever since returning to Boston, but something sweeter.

I love this man.

Him *and* Dylan.

I've loved them since the beginning, and it's overwhelming to be confronted with that realization, all at once. It's something I could never tell either of them, not in a million years, but it's... nice.

I pick up my head and look up at Jack. "I'm a hot mess right now. I'm so sorry."

He smiles. "It's okay, Duchess." It sounds like a genuine term of endearment, rather than the insult it always was in the past.

Jack's comforting me. *Soothing* me. And I... I want him. I want him more than anything right now. But I'm also tired. So, so tired. I turn toward him, feeling his arms come around me as I press my face into his hard stomach and let out a shuddering breath. A couple more sobs shake my body as I get the last of it out, but for once, I feel safe around him.

Relief.

Trust.

"I'm here, and it's okay," Jack says, over and over. "I'm here and it's all going to be okay."

And with that lovely warmth in my heart, the strength of his arms around me, I start to think that it really might be, after all.

# 14

## JACK

*W*hen Cate starts to unload on me, I almost can't help myself. My first reaction is always rage. It served me well when I was a kid in the slums, and it serves me well today. But this is beyond the pale. I don't know what's wrong with Cate, but I'm clearly not the first bad thing in her day.

That moment gives me pause, though.

*Am* I a bad thing in her day? Is that what I really want to be to her? And... goddamn, is that blood on her toe?

Seeing her hurt does something to me. And *tears...* fucking-A. They get me every time, too.

I know something is very wrong right now, and even if she's doing her best to rip me a new one, I can tell that whatever set her off is beyond just me.

I open my mouth to speak, but she cuts me off before I can.

"This is the *one* thing that anyone who's ever mattered to you has asked you for!" she shouts at me, and it hits me like a slap in the face. "This *one* thing! You don't need the money from selling the townhouse! Why the fuck are you stonewalling us at every turn?"

I start to open my mouth, but think better of it. It's not going to end well if I try to argue my position, not right now.

I think back to what Dylan told me at that lunch he'd caught me off-guard with, that she has nothing of her own and worked for every scrap. It's hard to believe, given that she's a MacMillan, but why would she be so upset about me not wanting to keep the townhouse if she had the money to just buy me out?

And it's not that I don't *want* to keep it...

"Why the fuck haven't you called? How dare you come in here and fuck me that way, then leave without another word? How *could* you? What kind of *monster* are you?"

She seems finished, and I watch her sink into her chair and cover her face. Her *gorgeous* face. It's something that I've kind of missed all these years.

"You can't treat people like this, Jack!"

Okay, so I guess she wasn't done. I can listen, though. She matters, and I can get past my knee-jerk reaction and do that for her.

I *want* to.

"You can't just walk into my life like this and use me all up, then drop me the second you get scared! You *know* how hot I think you are; how hot you've *always* been to me! But I'm not that shy little girl anymore, and I'm not afraid to tell you exactly what I think of you! I don't care *how* ugly you always thought I was. You bastard, you fucking asshole!"

Got to admit, that one sets me back a bit. Does she honestly think that I find her ugly? Impossible enough that, in the past, I've brushed it off as her just giving me shit. But now, based on the look on her face, I start to think maybe she *does* think that.

I'm dumbfounded, but I guess now isn't the time to try and have an actual conversation. It's not what she needs.

I can tell she's running out of steam, and I look down to the floor. It's an absolute mess, and these slacks of mine are probably ruined, but I find myself not really caring. Cate's right. I have the money. I can replace them. But I get the feeling that if I fuck this up with *her* right now, I'm not going to be able to replace *this*.

To be perfectly honest, I'm still conflicted about how I feel about Cate. No matter how good things were with her the other night, there are too many years of bad blood for me to easily say I *like* her, even in the privacy of my own mind.

Even if I'm pretty sure I *do*… once I get over myself.

And, regardless, I know that I like Dylan. It would kill him if I fucked this up yet again, and that's reason enough to keep biting my tongue. Keep shoving down the part of me that wants to lash back in self-defense. Keep listening. Trying to hear her. Take in what she's saying.

Listen with the part of me that really *does* care about how she's feeling.

The part that maybe even hurts a little bit at seeing it.

"I'm so tired of doing my best and getting nothing in return," she sobs. "I'm so exhausted by all of it. I'm done. I'm just done."

Is this a good time to comfort her? I'm conflicted, not sure if my presence here is doing more harm than good. I could just leave her be. I assume Dylan is out, but he could be back any minute, and Lord knows he's better at this shit than me.

What do *I* really have to offer? Dick, sure, but this other stuff… these feelings.

I swallow, the look on her face killing me. And what if Dylan's *not* coming back soon? Then she'd be alone here, just soaking in her own tears.

I step over the mess to avoid tracking pie and ice cream over the floor, going with my heart for once, even though it's scary as shit.

"Hey, Duchess," I say, setting my hands on her as gently as I can manage. "It's okay. I'm sorry, I mean it. It's going to be okay."

She looks up at me, and in that moment, I see her very clearly for who she is. Who she *really* is, not the version I've made up in my head all these years. Self-loathing, confusion, determination, they're all over her face.

I should know, I recognize them 'cause I see them in the mirror every day.

Right now, I can also see the high color in her cheeks, and how her perfect breasts heave with every single breath... fucking gorgeous.

I swallow, refocusing so I can be here for her the way she needs. This moment ain't about my dick, it's about her heart.

And maybe mine, too.

"I'm a hot mess right now," she says. "I'm so sorry."

"It's okay, Duchess," I say, rubbing her upper back in slow circles to help her calm down. "I'm here, and it's okay. I'm here and it's all going to be okay."

I'm repeating myself, but I don't even care. I don't know if it matters to her that *I'm* there, but right now, it's all I've got to offer.

And I *will* make it okay.

I don't know how, I just know that I *need* it to be okay for her. And after a while, she calms down. Once it feels like she's more herself, I stroke her cheek lightly with my thumb. "Hey, you. You got it all out?"

"I think so," she says in a high-pitched, heartbreakingly sad voice. "I made a big dumb mess, Jack."

I laugh a little, I can't help it; she's so damn cute right now, even tear-stained and sniffling.

"Yeah, Cate, you sure did, didn't you? How about we go to the couch. Come here."

She relents, and I carefully hoist her up in my arms. It's easy, and she feels warm against my body. My cock stiffens up in my slacks, can't help it, but I do my best to keep it suppressed. I would love nothing more than to take her to bed right now, kiss all the tears away and soothe her and then, yeah, fuck her deep enough to put her right to sleep. But behaving like teenagers is part of why our relationship, whatever it is, is *in* this tangled shit show.

I ignore my cock and carry her over to the big plush leather couch, setting her down gently.

"Can I get you anything?" I ask, draping a knitted blanket on top of her.

She curls into it, sniffles, and looks up at me. Oh... *shit.* I'm lost. This isn't just my cock that's swelling. She's gotten inside me, burrowed right into my heart.

Or maybe she was always there.

I watch her gnaw her lip and have what looks like an internal fight with herself, and I'd bet money she's telling herself some bullshit about how she's gonna look weak, but then she huffs out a little sigh and gives me a sheepish smile.

"I was hungry, and my day went to complete shit before I could do anything about that."

I grin. *Perfect.* For once, something practical that I can help her with. I've always done better when I can put my hands on a solution. Feeding her is simple. Straightforward. Hell of a lot easier than all these sudden *feelings* brewing up inside me.

I motion to the coffee table. It's where I'd set the paper takeout bag with my breakfast sandwich and my coffee from that local spot down the road when I'd come in.

She stares at the food, and the way her eyes widen, I feel fucking ten feet tall, even if it *is* just a five-buck meal.

"Can I?" she asks, practically drooling.

I almost laugh, but I'm not sure if she's there yet after that tsunami she unleashed in the kitchen.

"Yeah, Duchess, it's all yours." I hand her the sandwich bag and coffee cup so she doesn't have to move from her cozy little nest in that blanket I gave her, and yeah, call me caveman or whatever, but I'm getting off on this taking-care-of-and-providing thing right now.

Plus, I can still feel heat radiating off the bag, fantastic. I'm doing right by my woman.

Cate digs in, making little noises of enjoyment that I find both adorable and weirdly hot. She had to be starving, that kind of breakdown will take it out of anybody.

I sit with her in relative silence for a few minutes, letting her eat while I wait for her to recover the composure I usually take such pains to shatter. Finally, after popping the last bit of bacon from the sandwich into her mouth and taking a long, last pull from the paper coffee cup, she collapses back against the couch cushions. Her hair bounces around her face, and the look of satisfaction on her lips definitely doesn't help my valiant efforts not to think about getting her into the sack.

"I'm human again," she says, cutting me another sheepish look. "Thank God."

I snort softly, still not sure if it's cool for me to laugh with her yet. "That bad of a day?"

"Oh my *God*," she says, looking at me with incredulity in her eyes. This time, though, I can tell that it's not directed at me for once. She's got that don't-get-me-started look you give a buddy at the bar. "You wouldn't believe me if I told you."

"Tell me," I say, making that c'mon gesture with my hands. "Get it off your chest."

*Along with your bra—no, shit, goddammit Jack! Down, boy.*

"Okay," she says, smiling at me with this shy heat that fucking melts me.

A slow, shaky breath, and then she does. She unloads everything, every bit of it. The phone call. The coffee. The robe. Her mother. Her toe. The dessert-for-breakfast feast she was carrying when she finally noticed me standing there.

I sit there listening, and the more I hear, the more I'm right there with her—pissed and hurt and off-balance from all the shit thrown in her way. Not that it takes much for me to get a head of steam up against Julianne, the cruel old bitch. Even the little I saw of her interactions with Cate way back when was brutal, nasty as anything my family could dish out in the insult department.

Might not be the best time to lead with that, though, so I dial it back some.

"That sounds awful. That all sounds like the worst," I say. I wait a bit, and then I can't help but ask, "Was the food okay?"

And I mean, damn, but I'm still in that fix-it mode. Plus I want to know, you know, that I've taken care of her the way she needs. I shift in my seat, doing my best to ignore the way my cock wants to participate in the taking-care-of-her conversation.

"It was the best thing I've eaten, ever," Cate says, and she doesn't even sound sarcastic. Just... grateful. And, damn, maybe more than grateful. Maybe some of those other things I'm feeling inside, too.

I laugh at the comment, but can't deny that it lights up that *Jack Did Good* center in my brain.

"You've been living with Julia Fuckin' Child for the last two weeks, you sure about that statement?" I tease her, even though I'm eating up the way she's looking at me and don't really want to hear a "no," even though we both know what I gave her can't hold a candle to that magic Dylan does in the kitchen.

And... great. Now my cock *really* starts to swell, from the thought of Dylan in the kitchen.

Cate giggles. "Your breakfast was what I needed. It was everything I needed." She smiles, and yeah... it melts my whole heart to see it applied to me. Shit, it really does. "Thank you, Jack," she goes on. "I'm sorry for everything I said, I didn't mean it."

"Yeah," I say, shrugging, trying to play it off. I don't want her to feel bad, but I don't know if I can hack a talk that gets close to *my* feelings right now. They're maybe a bit too new. I clear my throat. "You did mean it, but that's okay. I haven't given you much reason to think otherwise, right?"

She casts her eyes down, but she's still smiling a little. I'll take it, it's not a retreat and it's not tears. Win.

But then—

"You've been a huge jerk lately, it's true. I have no idea what I was thinking when I slept with you last weekend."

She bites her lip and doesn't look at me, and I can feel the ground getting shaky.

I know I should have called or something but, fuck. What was I supposed to say? And especially after Dylan blindsided me with that lunch the day after?

She's clearly waiting for something from me now, and I chicken out a bit, going for an out.

"We were all drinking, so, you know..." I let it trail off, not sure if I'm trying to give her something she can hide behind if she thinks she needs to... or do that for myself.

But it hadn't been the wine.

*Hell*, no.

Not for me, and not for her, either. I know what I saw in her eyes, all of that raw hunger, and just thinking about it now, about the way we moved together, makes my mouth go dry. Does other things to me, too, but I'm still doing my best to be in ignore-the-little-head mode.

She hasn't jumped at the drinking excuse, but she's still looking conflicted, so I add, "Wasn't your fault."

"I don't even *like* you," she says through a watery laugh.

For a split second, it hurts, but... no. It's a lie, and all it takes is looking at her—remembering—and my ruffled feathers smooth right back down. I get it. She deserves to save a little face right now, especially after how embarrassed she was earlier. And I'm not gonna lie, in a weird way, having a joke between us, even just a small one, is kinda nice.

"Hey, I don't like you, either," I tease back, my attention caught by those delicious lips of hers when they curve up into an answering smile.

Cate's beautiful.

I've never quite seen her in this light before; I always thought she was gorgeous, but now, snugged away in her knitted blanket and kinda undone, not put together, *soft*...she's just perfect.

*Mine*, my oh-so-helpful brain offers. Well, one of them. Okay, both of them.

I don't want to fuck this up, I know how fragile this moment is, but God help me, the way she's looking at me... I can't stop myself. I lean in, and I reach for her.

She doesn't shy away. Fuck, that alone makes me go rock-hard. Makes all those feelings I'm having for her—the heart ones—swell up, too. Cate leans into me just a fraction, just enough, and her eyes start to flutter shut as her head tilts up to give me access.

To invite me.

Cate *wants* me.

She's soft and warm in my arms as I kiss her, and I can feel the muscle of her core and the tantalizing softness of her breasts pressed against my chest. All I can think of is how I want more of this moment. I'm almost painfully hard, but I'm still ignoring that.

"Cate," I say, moving my lips along her jaw, down to that silky throat. Sucking. I can hear the raggedness in my voice, and I guess she can, too, because she suddenly stiffens, as if coming back to herself.

Shit.

*Shit.*

Hadn't I been telling myself ever since I walked in that this wasn't what she needed from me right now?

She pulls back, and I really do think I've fucked it up, but even though she's biting that plump lip and looking embarrassed, she doesn't pull all the way away. I can tell she's still in feelings mode more than fuck-me-Jack mode, though.

"So, Mister Doesn't-Use-Doorbells," she says after a minute. "What are you doing here in the first place?"

Her wry smile takes the sting from the words, and I think about why I really came.

Am I seriously about to admit this?

I swallow, starting with a kind of truth. "Well, uh, Dylan kind of invited me over when we had lunch the other day."

I leave out the part where I was sleepless last night, and most of the week, lonely and worried about losing my friendship with Dylan again. And about... the rest.

I fought so hard to not break, to stay away from this place, but in the end, I couldn't keep up that struggle. I'd fucked up once when we were kids, and I'd fucked up a number of times since getting back in touch with him. I don't know how I feel about myself, or all these feelings I've got running around inside of me, the things I *want*, but I do know that I don't want to be without him again.

And now, maybe not without Cate, too.

She's just staring at me, waiting for me, and I chicken out.

"Maybe I shoulda called first." I shrug, playing it off like it's no big deal, even though it's just about the biggest deal of my entire fucking life. I go for my usual cocky. "But I do own a part of this house, you know. Kinda need to be able to get in here when the situation demands."

"We'll put in a dog door for you, I *guess*," Cate says, with an eye roll I'm pretty sure is just playful.

Her eyes flick to mine, and I can see worry there that she over-shot, pushed us back to fighting. Yeah, playful, all right. I shake my head and smile, putting my hands up as if to say *yeah, guilty*, and I see her relax.

"So," she asks, not content to leave it alone. And maybe... maybe I'm grateful. "Did you come over to talk about the town-house, then?" she presses. "Or did you want... something else?"

Her voice takes on a sultry tone, and I gotta admit, it throws me. I'd been holding back from her, seeing her as delicate, and yeah... maybe she has that side to her. Maybe she needed some non-sexual comfort there. Comfort that I'm pretty sure I did okay with. But now...

I grin. My Wildcat is back.

"We can talk about the townhouse," I say, psyching myself up to go where I never thought I would. Yeah. *Yeah.* I can do this. I can say it. *Do* it, hopefully.

Holy shit.

I'm really going in.

"But, I mean, if there's anything else on the menu, uh, Dylan *did* technically invite me over for... uh, for m-more."

Oh, Christ on the cross. Stuttering like a freaking virgin?

But I mean, I guess in one sense, there are still some things I'd qualify as that for.

Cate narrows her eyes and tilts her head to look at me appraisingly. "So he invited you over for... sex? That's what you're saying?"

I swallow. *Hard.* "Yeah."

Her fingers tighten on the back of the couch, and for a second I think she's about to launch herself at me.

"With me?" she finally asks, her voice turning sharp. "He, what, *volunteered* me? Are we talking about the same Dylan here, Jack?"

I laugh. Wrong response, but thank fuck for the tension reliever, right?

"No," I say, the idea of Dylan pimping her out just too... never happening. *Dylan?*

I get my laughter under control when I see she's totally not there with me, and clarify for her.

"Fuck no, Cate, of course not. No, he invited me over for, uh." I can do this. "For... himself."

My cheeks burn and I hate it, but at least I managed to get the goddamn words out.

Cate's staring at me, mouth agape. "He... You? *Him?*" she finally splutters.

She looks stunned, kinda like I felt when Dylan first brought up that he'd like to kiss me.

My cock jerks again.

Yeah, she looks *exactly* like that. Stunned... but turned the fuck on, too.

"Well, Dylan *is* bisexual," I say, managing to sound way more matter-of-fact than you'd think I could, given how hard it's been for me to wrap my mind around that. Not the concept, but... it being a real thing. And it being okay.

Cate looks at me for a long moment. "You aren't joking, are you?" she finally asks. "Jack, I swear to God, this is such an inappropriate joke, if that's what you're doing."

Shit, Cate's so damn good at putting me on the defensive, I feel like *she's* the one who went to law school. Gotta remember we're not enemies, though. And fuck, I've already admitted I want this, albeit in a roundabout way. Can't back out now. It wouldn't be fair to Dylan, and... I *do* want it.

Christ, wasn't I basically jerking myself raw to this fantasy just a couple of weeks ago? And after what happened in the kitchen with the two of them when I'd come over for dinner, seems like my fantasies have a pretty damn good chance of becoming reality here.

"I'm not joking," I reassure her, happy my voice comes out steady. "I wouldn't joke about Dylan that way. Never."

There's another long pause, then, "So...you want to have sex with Dylan, too?" Her fingers drum on the back of the couch. "Are *you* bisexual, Jack?"

I try to speak, but guess I don't need to. My cock tents my slacks as some vivid flashes of that being-with-both-of-them fantasy run through my head, my own mental porn. Here we are talking about it, like I never, *ever* thought I would, but suddenly having her see the proof of the deviant things I want—no, fuck. *Fuck.* That's just an old voice in my head, and it's not one I'm gonna give into.

It's okay to want Dylan.

Dylan *and* Cate.

But when her eyes flick down and a knowing smile curves her

gorgeous mouth at the sight of my erection, a flood of old shame hits me again—this popped up for another *man*—and I feel totally out of my depth and woefully fucking unprepared for this day.

I chicken out.

*Again.*

"Maybe I should leave, Cate. I'm sorry about barging in, really. I'll call next time." I start to get up, trying to adjust my pants, as if there's any possible way to disguise the rod there, but before I get very far—

"No, stay."

It's Dylan's voice, and my head snaps toward the sound as my cock jerks against my zipper, getting even happier.

And yeah, there he is, standing just inside the door.

I'm cornered.

Fuck. *Me.*

Dylan laughs, real and throaty and *pure*, somehow, and for a minute, I wonder if I said that last bit out loud. If he took it as an invitation. If he *wants* to...

"I'm glad you're back," he says to me, and the warmth and, shit, the *welcome* in his voice makes me painfully aware of my aching dick again. It's clear that I'm wanted here. I don't know how he does it, but Dylan's presence alone just makes everything better.

Always has.

All that chicken-shit stuff calms down, and when he adds, "Please, stay," I don't even hesitate.

There's nowhere else I want to be.

## 15

## DYLAN

*I* don't feel guilty about listening in on their conversation, not when I was standing right there in plain sight... and definitely not since I got to hear Jack admit that he'd come for sex.

Sex with *me*.

Still, he looks like a deer in the headlights. A ragingly horny, sexy-as-sin deer in the headlights, but still scared of what he wants, nonetheless. These two. God, they kill me. They're the two people I care about more than anything in the world, and I can read the uncertainty and need and desire on both their faces, clear as day.

I want nothing more than to take care of them. To make them mine.

*Both* of them.

I'm so damn proud of Jack for getting over the bullshit in his brain and coming here. Proud and, yeah, turned on. Kind of insanely so. I've wanted him forever, and then of course, there's Cate... I will want her *always*.

She's amazing, lounging on the couch like some kind of goddess.

We belong this way. All three of us, here, together. Now I just have to make them see it. Make their brains accept what their hearts already know, deep down.

Jack clears his throat, his eyes raking my body in a way I've only dreamed about. I can see his cock twitch under those refined slacks of his, and his color gets high as he gestures between us and asks, "So, uh, how do we…?"

God, he's hot when he's flustered.

I grin. Well, he's *always* hot. Literally, the sexiest man I know. I want him… but I also want to ease him into it. I know just being with both of us at once is pushing against his boundaries of acceptable pretty hard.

"This isn't about you and me, Jack," I say, crossing the room to the two of them. A flash of disappointment crosses his face, so I rush on. "And it's not about you and Cate, or Cate and me." I grab their hands and squeeze, and they both give me smiles back that are one part nervous, a million parts eager. "This is about *all* of us."

Cate makes a sexy little sound that makes my jeans suddenly feel far too tight. I was already getting hard earlier, just listening to Jack talk about coming here for sex, but now… I *need* them.

"Christ, Cate," Jack whispers, looking down at her while squeezing my hand. I can hear everything I'm feeling in his voice, and when he looks up and meets my eyes, I don't even think.

I kiss him.

And Jack… *Jack.* Holy hell. After a split second of frozen shock, he lets go of my hand and wraps his around my waist, yanking me against him.

Jack may have his hang-ups about liking men, but when he's decided he wants something, he's always been one to go balls-out and get it. I started the kiss, but he takes it over. *Owns* it. Hungry. Greedy. Claiming my mouth like he knows he has a right to.

It's the hottest kiss I've ever been a part of.

"Holy shit," Cate whispers from the couch, and I hear the same raw lust in her voice that's coursing through my veins and making my cock try to leap out of my jeans.

Her interruption knocks Jack off his game, though, and he lets go of me, taking a step back with a self-conscious laugh as he glances between the two of us, looking like he might bolt. It's funny, because in some ways, both Cate and Jack have far more forceful personalities than me, but with *us?*

They need me to push them, guide them. Take charge.

And I like it.

I take Jack's hand again, twining our fingers together, but turn my attention to Cate so that he can have a second to get comfortable with the fact that we're doing this.

And oh, yeah. We *are* doing this.

They need it just as much as I do. I just need to make sure they both realize it's okay.

More than okay.

*Necessary.*

"Here, or upstairs?" I ask Cate, holding out my other hand to her. She bites her lip, flushing as her eyes dart back to Jack. And that look? I bite back a moan. It's the same look she gave me when I spilled over my fist at the dinner table.

So sexy I almost can't stand it.

"Careful," Jack whispers, his voice husky and raw and shooting straight to my dick.

But... careful?

I look over at him, catching my breath at the heat in his eyes. His breath quickens as he holds my gaze, but then he clears his throat and—oh fucking God, adorable—he *blushes* as he looks away from me, back at Cate.

"She fucked up her foot earlier," he tells me. "If we're taking her up to the bedroom, gotta watch it."

Cate looks surprised, then touched. "You're pretty good at this caring thing, Jack," she says, giving him a smile that melts *my* heart.

These two.

God.

How do you explain to two people like Cate and Jack that your first crush as a kid was on *both* of them, that the torch you've been carrying since you were a teenager was for two people at the same time? Having them here together—*this*—it's a dream come true. And after a lifetime of seeing them hurt each other? What I see in Cate's eyes—Jack's, too, as he goes even pinker but doesn't look away from her—it kills me in the best possible way.

I love them.

I really do.

I clear my throat. I don't think either one is ready to hear that from me, but sex? Sex is a great way to *show* it. Hot, yeah, but with Cate and Jack, something more than just hot, too.

"Here works," I say, and as soon as the words leave my mouth, Jack grabs the edges of the blanket that's wrapped around her and yanks, almost tumbling her off the couch. I laugh—eager, much?—but then groan at the sight he's revealed.

Cate's laughing too, her hands fluttering over her delectable body as if she thinks she *should* cover herself... but much to my delight, she doesn't. Bold little Wildcat. Watching her come into her own is the sexiest thing I've ever seen.

Well, *one* of the sexiest things, at least. I glance at Jack, grinning with his face lit up like he's actually let go of his worries for once and decided it's okay to enjoy himself. Yeah, that would be the other.

Cate's wearing nothing but a pair of soft panties and a white camisole-looking top, and just seeing all that smooth skin and the heat in Jack's gaze as he stares down at her too, I'm suddenly reminded of how incredible she looked with Jack deep inside her.

Her top looks coffee stained, and her skin is flushed pink around it. I almost frown, wanting to make sure she's okay, but I can tell her attention isn't on that.... and the heat in her eyes? My cock jerks again, throbbing as it swells, and when I see Jack palm

MINE

himself through his slacks out of the corner of my eye, it jerks
even harder, making my jeans suddenly feel uncomfortably tight.

I want Jack's hand on me, too.

Hell, I want my hands on *him*. But we'll start with Cate today.
I'll take care of what looks like a light burn, but I'm not going to
let it slow this down since she doesn't seem worried about it. And
focusing on Cate? It will make it easier on Jack, I hope.

Less likelihood of another post-sex freak-out.

As if she's read my mind, Cate gives another one of those sexy
little moans and stops trying to cover herself. Instead, she arches
her back, lying herself out on the couch like a buffet. And her
face? Oh, sweet heaven. It's clear as day that she wants this as
badly as I do. She wants me, wants Jack, too.

Wants everything that the three of us could be.

*Should* be.

I squeeze Jack's hand one more time before letting go of it,
then scoop up those long, strong legs of Cate's and sit myself
down between them, settling them around me. I give Jack a look,
nodding toward the far end of the couch, and he gets my message
loud and clear, scrambling to position himself at her head.

Cate's eyes go wide as she realizes what's happening—that her
whole body is stretched out between me and Jack and that she's
the center of our combined attention. A beautiful blush creeps
across her face, spreads down her chest, colors the tops of those
luscious breasts a sweeter shade of pink than the coffee burn—
peeking out from that should-have-looked-innocent top that, on
her, is as hot as hell.

"Oh," she says, licking her lips as her lovely thighs tremble on
my lap. "Um. Hi, guys."

Jack's finally got himself back in the game. He leans down and
kisses her without any further prompting from me, holding her
wrists in one hand while he tangles the other in her hair. I watch
them, stroking myself through my jeans, until they break apart.

Cate stares up at him, her pupils blown.

199

Jack smirks, that sexy, cocky bad boy making an appearance. "Hi," he says... and the way it comes out, possessive and back in control, makes Cate shiver and my cock leap against my palm.

I lift Cate's ankle up to my lips, not taking my eyes off the two of them, and start kissing a line slowly up her long leg, finishing with a tiny bite at her thigh.

She gasps, her knees spreading apart and lifting her hips toward my mouth.

An invitation I will definitely take her up on... in a minute.

"Hi," I tease when she pouts at me stopping. My fingers trace up and down the inside of her bare thigh, and Jack laughs.

"You gonna give the lady what she wants, Dylan?"

He's still holding her wrists with one hand, but his other is stroking her face now... her throat... skimming over the tops of her breasts, careful of her pinked-up skin there as he teases her nipples through the thin material of her little top. Watching it is erotic as hell, and when he moves his hand back up to cup her jaw, she sucks his thumb into her mouth, moaning as she stares at me in entreaty.

Oh... *yeah*. I'm definitely going to give her what she wants. What we *all* want.

"Jesus fuck, Wildcat," Jack whispers, shifting in his seat.

His cock has got to be as rock-hard as mine, and I know that suction action she's treating his thumb to has got to be making it throb.

It's sure doing it to mine.

And Cate... Cate's hips are squirming something fierce. Those cute cotton panties she's got on look like they're soaked through— she gets so fucking wet it's insane—and all I can think about is how Jack made her ask for his mouth before he tasted her.

Cate needs to know she can have what she wants, what*ever* she wants... but she's going to have to let us know.

"Do you need something, Cate?" I tease, letting the fingers I'd been trailing over her thighs skim over her mound.

She gasps, arching up, and nods.

"Tell him, Wildcat," Jack growls, and he lets go of her wrists to rub his cock, pressing the rich material of his slacks over that hard length that I can't *wait* to get my hands on at some point.

Cate pulls Jack's thumb out of her mouth—a long, slow glide and a lick at the end that has us both groaning—and then murmurs, "Touch me, Dylan." She's gone pink, but she's holding my gaze. *"Please."*

I grin. "Hands?" I ask, pressing the heel of one hand against the soaked panties while I spread her thighs wider with my other. "Or mouth?"

"It's always about eating with you, Dylan," Jack teases, making me laugh as Cate moans.

"You read my mind," I tell him.

Cate swears softly, and Jack laughs, grabbing her wrists again. She squirms as we each hold her tightly, then gasps as I let up on the pressure from my hand and go back to tracing my fingers lightly over the top, circling her clit through the wet material.

I wink at her. "Sorry, Cate, didn't quite catch that, what'd you say?"

"I said, don't tease!" She pulls her hands free and grabs my shirt, yanking me down toward her, and Jack laughs.

The sound turns into more of a groan as Cate kisses me, and I hear his breath get shallower while he watches us. His hands reach down and slip under her top to cup her breasts again, teasing at her nipples, and Cate breaks our kiss with a little sound of delight, arching into Jack's touch.

"Please," she gasps. "Touching can come another time. I need... need one of you inside me."

I look at Jack, and his eyes go hot. For a minute, I think he's going to suggest something else entirely, but then a shudder goes through him, and he grins.

"You got to watch last time," he says, pulling her top off and setting those gorgeous breasts free. "I'd fucking *love* to see how you look inside her, Dylan. Watching you fuck would be... *damn*."

A muscle twitches in Jack's neck, and he gives me a wicked, wicked smile.

My throat goes dry. "See if you can keep each other occupied for a minute, yeah?"

I pull Cate's panties off as I stand, and as tempting as it is to stay and watch what they get up to, my dick is too hard to wait.

I head toward the bathroom, tossing over my shoulder, "We keep doing this, I'm going to start putting condoms all over the house."

"That's what cookie jars are for!" Cate calls after me, and I hear her and Jack laughing, a laugh that cuts off into muffled moans that are all the hotter since whatever they're doing to earn those sounds is left to my imagination.

I grab the box of condoms and head back as fast as I can, not wanting to miss the sight of them even for a moment.

Cate, naked, flushed, and needy on the couch, is a sight I could drink in every day. But Cate plus *Jack*? He made quick work of getting out of that suit, and his body makes my mouth water. The two of them are pressed together, his mouth locked on her throat and her hand wrapped around his cock. His hands overflow with those amazing breasts, and when he pinches her nipples, she practically comes off the couch.

"Oh, Lord, you two," I gasp, tossing the condoms down on the coffee table and shucking off my jeans and shirt as fast as I can. Jack's still up near Cate's head, and I nudge her thighs open to make room for me, suddenly overcome with an urgency that isn't at all like my usual patience and control in the bedroom.

God, can you blame me, though? With Cate, even something as simple as spreading her legs open is indescribably hot. Her eyes drift open, pupils so big that they're all I can see under her hooded lids as she stares at my cock. Her lips are parted, short, panting breaths escaping as Jack's mouth moves from her throat down to suck her breasts.

"Please," she whispers, and... *yes*.

Anything.

I'd do anything for her.

And him.

Jack sits back up, staring at me hungrily. "Fuck her, Dylan," he grits out, covering Cate's hand with his own as he starts to thrust into their fists. "I want to see you two. Want..."

I don't even think he realizes he's let his words drift off like that, his eyes are locked on my cock so hard. I suit up faster than I ever have, wanting to give them both what they're asking for, and knowing how wet she is, I don't even hesitate.

Pulling Cate's legs around my hips, I drive into her with one thrust.

She gasps, arching up to meet me, and her tight, wet heat—it *is* heaven. Fucking *heaven*.

I grab one of her thighs, pulling her more tightly against me as I drive into her again, and press my other hand against her clit.

"Dylan," she cries, her head falling back and mouth falling open in a soundless cry.

"Fuck, that's hot," Jack groans, and there's a gorgeous blush across his cheeks that I think he'd deny until his dying day if I pointed it out.

Or maybe not.

It looks like he's just as far gone as we are, beyond caring about the stupid shit that normally swamps our day-to-day lives. I hold his gaze as I sink deep into Cate's heat, the sensation of her around me wrenching a ragged groan from my throat, and when her hands start to flutter, looking for purchase, I give Jack a hot smile.

"She needs you, Jack."

"Yeah," he mutters, grabbing her wrists again. He reaches for her breasts again, and I know she loves that, but her eyes snap open and she shakes her head.

"No... *Jack*... Dylan..."

She's panting, forcing out her words in time with my thrusts. I'd meant to go slow, but she's already coming undone. Her thighs clenching around me and little tremors moving through her, tremors I can feel from the inside out, egging me on.

Making me crazy.

"I want to... see you," she says, using her captured hands to tug Jack in my direction. "See you two together."

Jack's pupils are wide with lust, his color high, and when he rises up on his knees and leans over her, I grab his shoulders, never slowing my rhythm, and pull him against me.

"Fucking *God*, Dylan," he says, one hand around the back of my head and the other on my ass. "I can feel you fucking her."

I laugh, but then he's kissing me, and Cate... Cate loses it. Letting us have the kind of hot, erotic sounds that no man on the planet could withstand. They're going to drive me over the edge. That, and her tight heat as I thrust into her, again and again, and Jack's *mouth*. His tongue, tangling with mine, claiming it, his hand in my hair.

This is everything.

This is what I need.

This is perfection.

And then Jack gasps, his body jerking, and when his mouth leaves mine I look down and see Cate—shy, self-conscious, beautiful Cate—with her mouth stuffed full of his cock.

"Oh Christ, Cate," Jack moans, staring down at her like he's just seen Jesus. "*Christ*, that's good."

He braces his hands on the back of the couch, and I can see by the tense set of his body how much effort it's taking him not to thrust into her mouth. To be respectful. To let her set the pace.

But she's a Wildcat, now. Writhing on my cock while she takes his deep into her throat. Her lips spread wide around his shaft as she stares up at him with that same greedy heat that's coursing through all of us. Her face is pure sex... but it's also full of a kind of joy that I recognize. It's *yes, we really can have this.*

Cate's pussy starts to tighten around me, and I groan, knowing she's close.

And me? I'm not going to last.

Not as good as she feels.

Not as hot as the two of them *look.*

Jack hisses. "Oh, Jesus, Cate, that feels so good," he groans, moving one hand off the couch to rest on her head. Not pushing her... but definitely guiding as he thrusts a littler deeper into her mouth. And his hand? It's trembling. The sight has my balls pulling tight as I imagine what he's feeling.

I make a sound and Jack looks up at me, giving me a hot smile, like we're sharing the best kind of secret. "You're both... so perfect," he says, panting. "Both so—ahhhhhh, *fuck.*"

His eyes squeeze shut as Cate makes this amazing moaning sound of satisfaction, tonguing his slit and then swallowing him down.

I can't look away.

My hips smack against Cate's thighs deliciously as I pound into her, and the way she bounces forward with each thrust and then slams herself back into me is about to push me over the edge. That, and those delicious noises she keeps making around Jack's cock as she blows him, sounds that are driving me as crazy as I know her tongue and lips are making him.

Her body grips me tight, and Jack and I are in a rhythm, his hips have started thrusting—just a little—driving his gorgeous cock into her throat, and Cate wants it.

Urges him on.

Takes *all* of him.

The three of us are moving together in perfect sync, wave after wave of incredible sensation rocking through me as I watch the two of them race toward their climaxes. As I feel my own, building so hot and fast that I can tell it's going to wreck me.

And then I see Jack's hand tighten on the back of Cate's head and his other one comes off the back of the couch, reaching for me. Yanking me to him. And he kisses me again, hot and fierce and sloppy with need, taking my mouth with a low, passionate growl.

"*Nnnnnnnnnnnngh,*" Cate moans around his cock.

It's so fucking sexy—*all* of it—that I know I'm done.

And then Cate comes. Every one of her muscles goes taut all at once and her body clamps down on me, shuddering with the force of her orgasm.

Jack groans into my mouth, and it hits me that we're both buried deep inside her. That we can *both* feel the waves of pleasure rippling through her body.

"Oh, *shit,* Cate," Jack says desperately, wrenching his mouth away from me as his hips buck wildly toward her face. "I'm going to come."

She moans again, still shaking, and clamps her lips around his cock.

Not stopping.

Not slowing down.

I have no idea who comes first, Jack or me, or if it's both of us at once; I just know that it's *over* for me. I slam into Cate's tight heat, and Jack grips Cate's head tightly with both hands, burying himself in her mouth with a long, low moan that rips my orgasm right out of me. I see him go tense, and my balls start to empty in heavy, hot spurts that almost blind me, shooting through me in wave after wave of a kind of bliss that's so much more than just sex.

It's so good that my vision whites out for a moment.

But I don't need to see. Jack and Cate surround me, and—as I grip Cate's hips and cry out with the tingling, mind-blowing pleasure—emptying myself inside her with Jack's hoarse shout ringing in my ears feels exactly like coming home.

Jack's hand wraps around the back of my neck and I open my eyes, still coming. It goes on, and on, and *on,* and once I'm finally emptied out, Cate pulls both Jack and me down on top of her, the three of us somehow managing to fit in a tangled, perfect mess on the couch together.

Sweaty.

Spent.

Satisfied.

*Perfect.*

God, I love these two. I really, really do... and someday soon, I'd like to tell them that.

16

CATE

"*A*gain!" I shout, and my students join me, kicking their heavy bags in unison and filling the gym with loud, satisfying thuds. "And three!" They kick again. This is always the best part, the final countdown. "Now two!" Another kick. "And one!" They kick their bags one last time with a little more power. "Good!" I exclaim, grabbing my water bottle. "That was excellent work, everyone. Same time on Friday, and remember to bring your club dues."

There are assorted cheers and groans, and conversation picks up as the students all start to clean their gear up and move on, some to home, others to another class.

After I found out that my mother poisoned the well for my personal training service, I ended up reaching out to an old friend from college to see if she had anything at all. Turns out, she's still a Boston local, and she owns this gym. Just like that, I'm an instructor with a class, and it's not even that far away from home. Just a nice brisk jog away.

Of course, I can't quite let go of that voice. The nagging, eternally critical voice of my mother, always popping into my head when I least expect it. I look down at the slight curve of my stomach, pinching at my clingy gym wear. I'm soaked with sweat, and I probably look as fat as a house in this getup. What a mess I am.

The first couple of days, I couldn't get it out of my head. I just kept thinking about how I shouldn't be teaching anyone when I'm not even happy with my own body. Today, though, it's Wednesday and I'm having a good day. I'm getting the hang of this. I'm not going to let Mother get the best of me, especially from hundreds of miles away. I love the work, and I'm good at it.

I repeat it in my head like a mantra every time she bubbles up.

I take a long, deep slug of my water, and dry my forehead and face with my towel, when I notice that Jack is standing just inside the room, holding a gift bag, watching me.

I wonder how long he's been there. It couldn't have been the whole class, but I can tell by the look on his face that he at least caught the tail end of it. I can feel the color flooding into my cheeks; it's a little embarrassing, having people watch you when you're in work mode. Then again, I've been doing high kicks all afternoon; maybe he got a bit of a show. I know he wants me. Maybe he didn't when we were kids, but he does now. It's hard to accept it fully, but he's made it pretty clear at this point.

Extremely clear, really. He starts to walk toward me, in that impeccable suit of his, and I mentally undress him. That lean, perfect body, his strong arms, the way he carried me from the kitchen to the couch. The feel of his lips against mine, and how his beard feels against my cheek. I have a short but intense memory of him deep inside of me, filling me up in the best of ways, and how I practically begged to get that cock in my mouth so I could suck him completely dry.

And seeing Jack and Dylan together?

I tighten my thighs a little, feeling arousal starting to throb inside of me, my desire whispering that I could drag him into one of the windowless studios and have my way with him; nobody would know.

I *far* prefer the voice of desire to the voice of my mother.

"Hey, stranger," I say, trying for a casual tone like I totally wasn't just imagining tearing his pants off.

"Hey yourself, Duchess," he says back with a grin, and I nearly melt.

*Keep your cool, Cate.*

"What brings you down to my little grinder?" I ask, winking. When Jack's around, I find myself using body language that I normally wouldn't dare to; moving my shoulders and hips around when I say things to him, leaning inward, inviting him to touch me wherever the hell he wants. I shift my weight from foot to foot, my hips swaying gently, as I wait to see why he's here.

"I actually came to give you this," he starts, and hands the gift bag out to me.

I smile, and feel practically giddy inside. A gift, for me? From *Jack*? What world am I living in now? "What is it?" I ask playfully.

"I felt real bad about everything that happened on Saturday, so."

I wince a little internally. "Everything?"

I can see him recoil a little, as he realizes what he's saying. "No, I mean, y'know. About the first ten minutes or so, let's say, yeah?"

I smile, and reach inside the gift bag, pulling out a box. I laugh. It's a coffeepot.

"You really shouldn't have," I say. "That happened way before you showed up."

"Yeah, well," he starts, shrugging. "I hated seeing you hurt. This one's all shatter-proof, or so it says on the box, anyway. In case you have another bad day, y'know?"

I can't help but beam at him, seriously touched. He cares. He *really* does care about me.

"This is very thoughtful of you. I can't tell you how much I appreciate it, Jack, really."

We stare at each other, but it's not awkward at all. It's just calm, content, happy. After the whirlwind of the first two weeks here, this third week has been surprisingly pleasant. I can get used to this.

We're interrupted by one of my students, a young girl named Sam with a deep brown ponytail. She's maybe nine years old? Ten? Just the cutest thing. I have a quick thought about having kids of my own one day. Maybe if everything works out here, and if we somehow manage to keep the townhouse? Who knows. For now, anything feels possible.

"Miss MacMillan?" she asks, looking shy with Jack standing there.

"What is it, love?"

She stares at Jack a little longer, and I look at him. To my amazement, he offers a perfectly comforting smile, and holds his hands palms-up.

"Don't worry about me, I'm not gonna get in the way of someone who kicks as hard as you two ladies do, believe me."

Sam giggles, and looks at me. "Is this your boyfriend, Miss MacMillan?"

Both Jack and I laugh together, and look at each other just a little bit awkwardly. "I, uh…" I start.

"Yeah, well," Jack continues. "I think we're still figuring that out, pumpkin pie."

Sam beams and looks at me, whispering conspiratorially, "He's nice. Keep him."

"Oh, I'll definitely think about it," I say back. "Need me to sign your participation form?"

"Yes, please." It only takes a second, and as soon as I sign it, she yells out a quick "Thank you!" and sprints for the door. She's gone in a split second. Jack and I look at each other, and share another loud laugh.

"She's a character, ain't she?" Jack says.

"I think she just has good taste," I reply. "So was this all you came down for? To shower me with gifts?"

"Nah, not entirely," he responds. "I thought maybe we could have dinner."

"Oh!" I say through a quick laugh, and blush a bit. All I can think of is that first dinner, and how sexy Jack sounded when he went in for the kill. Is he saying he wants to sleep together again? Is this our new code? I'm not completely sure how he's dealing with his newfound bisexuality, if at all; if we were anywhere else but work, I could be more explicit.

"Do you mean, like last time? With you, me, and Dylan?" I ask coyly, covering up my anxiety. What if he says no?

"Yeah, definitely," he says, and I let my breath slide out of me in relief. He sounds a little anxious, but I can see in his eyes that he means what he says. We've shared so much at this point that I can't imagine him doing anything he doesn't want to do with us. "I mean, if that's cool with you."

"So, at the house?" I ask, a little note of hopefulness in my voice.

"Well, y'know," he starts, and I suddenly feel a pang of anxiety. "I thought maybe we could do this in public."

"Public?" I ask.

"Yeah," he says, looking sheepish. "Y'know, to finally talk about the contract, without all the... distractions we keep running into?"

"Oh, right! Yeah, of course," I say, trying my best to sound cheerful and unbothered, but I don't know that I'm doing a great job of hiding my disappointment. I feel just a little ashamed and self-conscious; great sex, no, *phenomenal* sex has never been a part of my life before, and the more I get, the more I find I crave it. I've been so focused on the hot, amazing fun we've all been having that I almost completely spaced on the contract hovering above all of us. "That's probably a really good idea."

"But hey," Jack continues, with an edge of playfulness in his voice. "Maybe afterward, we can all have a nightcap? Back at the townhouse?"

"Oh, God yes!" I blurt out before I can stop myself. I cover my mouth and grin like a kid. I take a quick moment to compose myself. "Yes, of course. That'd be lovely."

Jack laughs. "Yeah, okay, Duchess. How's Friday night? Give you a couple days to think about what you wanna do before we get together and hash it all out?"

"That sounds perfect, Jack," I say.

"Good," he says, and I feel that flutter in my heart as he leans in. Is he going to kiss me here, in semi-public? The thought has barely occurred to me before he's pulling me in close, his hands gently cupping my face as his lips meet mine, and suddenly all thoughts melt away, replaced by sensation and fluttering delight. I sink into the kiss easily, and smile into it as it comes to an end.

"Good," I repeat, eyes half-lidded as I look up into his. God, he's tall. Both of them are. I love feeling small around them. Small and safe and *wanted*. "I'll see you then."

"Not if I see you first," Jack says with a wink, before turning and striding out of the practice studio. He gives me one last glance over his shoulder, and I wave like a dopey teenager. He laughs and pushes out the gym door onto the street.

I watch him go, every single step, until he's out of sight. I can feel I'm smiling, and I know I must look ridiculous and dreamy. How does he do this to me? How do both of them keep doing this to me? I've never felt this way with *anyone* before, and now I have it with *two* people. Two almost completely different people, who, when you put them together, make something so beautiful that I can barely comprehend it myself. It leaves me breathless, and aching for more.

I've known them forever, and yet I feel like I've only scratched the surface in some ways. I look down to the gift bag with the coffeepot in it, and beam all over again. This was the end result of me being myself, my whole ugly and beaten-down self. A gift, an apology, being taken care of. The world didn't end; it just opened up in ways I would never have imagined before.

I touch my fingertips to my lips, still tasting the ghost of Jack's kiss. I can't wait. Two days seems almost like forever, now.

# 17

## JACK

The rest of my work week goes by in an instant, like I sailed right through it, looking forward to this night. The three of us are at a round table, sitting around it like points on a triangle, in perfect view of each other. I can feel bubbles in my chest, and I'm not sure how to deal with it. This is all so damn new, so damn *different* than anything I've ever done before.

We get steaks. It's my own personal touch on an apology to Dylan for how I'd acted the last time we were at this restaurant. He, of course, takes the time to give the waiter special instructions, and Cate teases him about kicking the chef out of his own kitchen. Dylan shrugs, his hands spread. He knows his stuff, though; Cate and I have to admit that it's the best steak we've ever had in our lives. I trust Dylan, with food, and now I'm realizing, with everything else, too. I can only hope that they learn how to trust me; I haven't given them much reason so far.

We don't do much talking during dinner — we're too busy eating. But then the waiter clears the plates and brings us after-dinner drinks, and I realize talking's going to have to start.

"Hey, there we go," I say as the waiter sets the glasses down in front of us. "Go on, drink up," I say, smiling. "You might be the best chef, Dylan, but you're gonna find out that I'm the best bartender. You'll love it."

"What did you call them?" Dylan asks, picking his glass up and looking at the bubbles as they fly to the surface of the mostly clear drink.

"French 75s, right?" Cate answers for me, then takes a drink. She closes her eyes, and it looks like she's enjoying the bubbles all the way down. She gives me the girliest smile, all catlike satisfaction and indulgent glee. "It's perfect."

I watch Dylan as he takes another look at the drink, then over to the two of us, before raising the glass and taking a tentative sip. There's a brief moment of evaluation as I watch his chef's mind turn over the flavor profiles or some other shit. Who knows what someone with that kind of skill thinks about? Ultimately, though, he grins and takes a larger drink.

"This is delicious!" he exclaims, smiling at me. I feel the bubbles in my chest again, and I haven't even touched my drink yet.

"Perfect," I say, taking my own glass and having a sip. "So, not to kill the mood, but I think now's as good a time as any to jump into the townhouse talk, eh?"

Cate and Dylan glance at each other, and then nod together. I try not to feel a pang of envy at how obviously on the same wavelength they are; I'm not some asshole intruding, I'm part of this.

"I brought some paperwork that we can all sign together, once we're all on the same page about what we want to do," I say. "In the meantime, I'll fill you in on Sully's wishes."

"Is this something that Gary should be here for?" Cate asks. She looks a little uneasy. Such a sweetheart, worried about hurting the old guy's feelings.

"Oh, we're okay. I bumped into Gary a week or so back. He brought me up to speed on the basics, and he gave me his blessing to discuss it with you all here."

"Ultimately, Gary will probably have to approve the paper-work, right?" Dylan asks.

I nod. Truth is, I'd only listened with half an ear as Gary had walked me through the legalese, but nothing had jumped out at me as requiring my additional research. I'd been a little distracted by, well, by everything that had been going down between Cate, Dylan, and I, but it had all sounded pretty standard other than him splitting ownership among the three of us, and some provision about the requirements to ultimately transfer the title.

Still, no worries. I know Gary would review it all with us in full once we were finally on the same page. Right now, that's the hurdle we have to get over.

I look at the two of them, some of that warm feeling that's been growing in me over the last couple of weeks surging up again. They both matter so damn much to me, but I have to keep a clear head. I appreciate what Sully has done, bringing us back together, wanting to give us each something that mattered, but this shit has to be dealt with now so we can all move ahead.

"Ready to start?" I ask, looking at the two of them. They both nod, and I continue. "Sully knew that the house means different things to each of us. For me, it was a place to get away from the streets. Without him, I'd probably be dead or in jail by now."

"It was the place I learned to shape my identity," Dylan says. "To truly be the person I want to be."

"For me—" Cate pauses, takes a sip of her drink, then meets my eyes. "For me, it was an escape," she says. "From New York, from the MacMillan name, and from my mother most of all."

I nod. "But," I continue. "Sully also knew that things change, and life goes on. I think he was well aware, and very proud, of the people we all turned out to be. He touched our lives on such a fundamental level, and shaped who we would become. I know I wouldn't be a lawyer without his help, that's for damn sure."

Both of them nod, listening. Encouraged, I go on. "Sully told me that he wanted each of us to benefit from the townhouse in one way or another, to take whatever was meaningful from the house, and to sell off the rest. For the market value of that house right now, I think he knew that it would be life-changing money. Retirement money, in some ways, if that's what we want out of it."

"I think that assumes that Sully believed we all had our own lives," Cate says. "I mean, he had to have thought I'd live in New York for the rest of my life, and look at me now."

"Same," Dylan says. "He left me enough to cover my old student loans, so I could afford to go to culinary school, and I think he figured that I'd move on with life after that, maybe travel the world. Maybe he underestimated how attached I am to that house, I don't know."

"With the house sale..." I say, trying to nudge them toward the promise of money. Money is simple, money is easy to handle. Not like memory, not like feelings. I reach for my own drink, begin again. "With the house sale, we can all do whatever we want. We can start our own businesses, move wherever we'd like, do whatever, wherever and whenever. We can all start fresh, on our own terms." I try not to sound excited, but I'm more than a little exasperated at how difficult it's been to get this point across, and hell, who *doesn't* want a fresh start? "We can have it all."

"Except the changes I made to the decor," Cate chimes in. "All of that work I want to put into that house. Something to honor him while also modernizing the look, opening it up, making it even more cheerful than it already was for us."

"And I've always loved that study," Dylan says. "I get all of my best work done in there. And that kitchen, my God. I know my way around it like I know my own body. That's *my* kitchen, it's home, it's where I thrive. It's where I'm happy."

"Living with Dylan has been a complete breath of fresh air for me," Cate says. "It's night and day compared to the life I had before."

I feel a pang of jealousy strike me deep as I look between the two of them. They want to live together? Was I just some sort of unicorn to them? Someone they play around with, then dismiss when they want to *thrive*, whatever that means? Someone they can discard?

"Well, look," I say, shaking my head. "I mean, maybe there's a simpler solution to this. Maybe we just wait and see who you end up with, Cate." I look at Dylan. "If it's you, Dylan, then the two of you can buy me out and live your happily ever after." I realize that my voice is rising a little, but I can't help but feel a little stung over this. It's all the old bullshit again, all the feelings of worthlessness, of not being enough. "And if it's me, then maybe we can buy you out." It comes out sounding harsh and ugly, but I feel so raw right now.

"I don't want to fight you on this, Jack," Cate says. I look toward her, and I can see her eyes tearing up. "I just... I don't know, Jack, maybe it's just me, but things are just starting to work out for me here. My life is already becoming what I want it to be. I don't want to have to choose between the two of you, not ever, not in a million years."

The pleading look on her face hurts me inside, makes me feel ashamed for lashing out. I can see it in her eyes again, that part of myself that I saw in her the last time she cried in front of me. The self-loathing, the confusion, the determination. But there's something different this time, something I didn't see at all before. She cares about me. She truly, genuinely cares about me. It's not just the sex for her; I'm not someone she's using for whatever she can get out of me. This is a woman who accepts me for who I am, warts and all. I didn't know such a person could exist, and sure as hell not for me.

I start to reply, I'm already leaning forward and opening my mouth to speak, to tell Cate I'm sorry, but Dylan gets there before I can.

"Jack, I don't think it has to be this way, these black-and-white choices. There's always another way."

Having someone cut you off never feels good, but right now?

221

Right when I'm about to put down my defenses and cop to being scared? Right now it feels like Dylan just rubbed me the wrong way with a handful of fucking rock salt. I don't know if it's my emotions already running high, or seeing the way Cate looks at me, but I feel myself go into my defensive mode before I can stop it.

"Alright, then, if you've got all the answers, tell me how this plays out." Dylan pulls back, gives me a look, but I just keep on rolling. "Tell me your magical solution, huh? How about *you* keep the house and *I* get to keep Cate? That work for you?"

I don't even say the other one. The one that... *fuck*. A part of me wouldn't mind, but another part of me still shies away from.

Dylan could choose me. The two of us...

But fuck. *No.* I know I'd gone to him for... for sex. But a *life*... we're talking about who gets to settle down with whom. Building a life together. Even if I wanted that with him, why would he choose me over Cate?

Why would *either* of them choose me?

I scowl harder, and Dylan raises his hands up, his voice turning all soothing and gentle-like, as though he's trying to talk me down.

"Whoa there, cowboy," he starts, giving me a smile that does shit inside me that I'm not ready to deal with. Especially not *now*. "This isn't a competition."

"You're damn right it's not," Cate says. There's fire in her voice, and that look of love and care is gone, replaced with daggers that cut right to the deep parts. *Jack*, that look says, *you just fucked up but* good.

"I don't belong to *anyone*, Jack, don't talk about me like I'm—" she flutters her hands, casting about for the words. "Like I'm freaking *furniture!* I'm a person, Jack! You don't get to waltz in here and use me like I'm some sort of bargaining chip in your pissing contest!"

My embarrassment turns into anger. "So you choose Dylan

222

then, eh? I knew it from jump street; he's the nice guy, he's the home fire. How the hell was I ever gonna compete with that?"

Cate stares at me. "What are you even *talking* about, Jack? You're not making any sense!" Her voice comes out high and sharp.

She might as well have slapped me. Telling me I'm not making any sense when all I've done is try to be clear about things? Might as well tell me we're speaking different languages because we come from two different worlds. I can feel the old chip on my shoulder again, the one I thought I'd left behind. I start to speak, and Dylan cuts in again.

"Alright, you two," Dylan says. "This isn't helping any of us. We didn't come here for this, and no one is choosing anyone. Let's finish our drinks, calm down a little, and maybe we can get back on track. All right?"

"No," Cate says, shaking her head and sending her hair flying around her face. "No, fuck that. Jack wants to come in here and start making demands like he was Sully's one and only? Like we didn't lose him, too? God!" She turns to me, and the daggers plunge deep again. "What is it with you? Why do you always have to ruin a good thing? Why do you hurt every single thing that you touch?"

"Excuse me?" I say, my voice dropping low into a snarl. "I don't recall you saying that when I was making you come like a freight train. My touch was real nice back then, wasn't it?"

"That's enough, Jack," Dylan snaps.

"Fuck you, Dylan, you're not my dad. Stay in your lane, buddy."

"Why?" Cate demands. "Why is this so important to you, breaking all of us apart? Why the hell are you so desperate to sell? Do you need the money? Get yourself in a scrape like your old man used to, down at the racetrack?"

Nope. That's my limit, that's so far below the belt I can barely believe she went there. I'm not putting up with this shit anymore. I slug the last of my drink, then slam the glass down so hard it rocks and tips over. I don't care if this is the second time we make a scene in this restaurant; this time, it's on my terms.

Fuck them for making me feel like I'm nothing; I'm not nothing, I'm not that guy anymore.

"Do you have any clue," I start, standing up from my seat. "Even the faintest idea, how much I make for a living? Take a guess!" I shout.

"Sit *down*, Jack," Dylan growls at me, but I flip him off and keep going.

"I work from sunrise to sunset. I'm never not thinking about my work. You wouldn't believe me if I told you how much money I have. Do you see these suits?" I practically rip off my tie. My temperature is rising fast, and I'm feeling like I might suffocate. "Thousand dollars each. Easy. No big deal, got a bunch of 'em. My house? Top floor condo in Back Bay, no expense spared. You think I need the *money?*"

Cate looks mortified and hurt, tears threatening to fall any second now, and it hurts, but I'm just *done*. A waiter walks up to me.

"Sir," he starts. "I'm going to have to ask you to take this outside."

"Fuck. *Off*," I spit. It's enough for the waiter to turn around and stride quickly away. I turn my attention back to the two of them. "I haven't needed the money in a long time now, and I'm never going to need the money ever again. I've got more money than I know what to do with, and what fucking good does it do? What fucking good has it *ever* done?"

I can feel hot tears starting to hit the inside corners of my eyes — Jesus, I'm gonna cry in a fucking restaurant. I swipe my arm across my eyes, feeling like a little kid. I'm done being pushed around by these two.

"Nothing! It never did a single good thing! Money for what, for paying my parents off? To keep them the hell out of my life? To just keep enabling their shitty addictions, because I can't force myself to tell them what I really think about them and their goddamn family name? Ain't no Kelly ever been worth a *damn* in this town until me. The money doesn't get rid of them. I can't talk to it, I can't fuck it, I can't wake up next to it, and I certainly can't figure out a way to make it keep me company!"

They're both looking at me differently now. They've gotta think I'm insane. Maybe I am, I can't seem to shut up, can't seem to stop the flood of hurt and anger pouring out of me.

"I go home every night, alone. All by myself. There's nothing there waiting for me, no memories that I can look back on, nothing to make it a *home*. It's a fucking fancy box in a stupid expensive filing cabinet, and I keep filing myself away, hoping that one day it'll all just go away and I won't *feel* like this. My life is already in the toilet; I don't need that townhouse on top of it all. It hurts that it's still in my life. It hurts me every time I have to walk into that place. It's just a reminder of everything I lost years ago, and it's never coming back. None of it is."

I stop, the lump in my throat threatening to choke me if I don't catch my breath, my chest heaving. The back of my shirt feels wet, like I just ran a mile.

"Jack," Cate starts. Her voice sounds small, and part of me howls with guilt that I'm the one who made her sound so hurt and sad.

"No," I say, cutting her off flat. I don't want to hear it, after everything I just unloaded I think I *can't* hear it. I can't take her being soft, can't take her needing me to be a decent guy, not right now. Not when I just showed her who I really am.

There's a hand on my elbow suddenly, and I whirl around to see the waiter standing there behind a guy who's got to be the manager.

"Sir, I have to insist."

"Yeah, yeah, I'm making a scene, I'm scaring the nice people, I fuckin' know, pal!" I shout, practically tearing my money clip out of my pocket. I thumb through it quickly, then shrug and toss the whole damn thing on the table. "That oughta cover it, I'm outta here."

I grab my suit coat and storm out as quick as I can, before I can humiliate myself any more than I already have. If that's even *possible*.

Out on the sidewalk, the city continues to move around me like the world didn't just explode. Cars, taxis, people, all of them darting here and there, too much movement and too much hurt and just too fucking *much*. It'll die down soon enough, but not soon enough for me. I wish I could make it all go away right now. Maybe then I could get a little peace. *Peace.* I think of sitting with Cate on the couch that morning she threw the pie at me, and my guts twist. No such thing as peace.

I shrug my suit coat back on and reach inside my pocket to pull out a pack of cigarettes. I quit, mostly, except for emergencies, and this sure as shit qualifies. I flick the lighter and suck on the filter, drawing that smoke deep inside of me, and exhale a thick plume into the air.

I wait a bit longer, puffing on my smoke, until I can feel my heart rate start to come down. It's just enough clarity to show me how much of a rat bastard I just was.

Fuck.

*Fuck.*

I think I really did it in there.

I think I really fucked it up completely for all of us. What was I thinking? How could I be so stupid? How could I be so *cruel?* Jesus, talk about being a true Kelly son.

I exhale shakily, and draw in another deep breath of tobacco.

"Jack." Cate's voice.

"Hey, Jack," Dylan says right behind her. I look over. The two of them are walking toward me. This is it, I think. This is when they tell me to get out of their lives for good. And I deserve it. Every bit of it.

"I know," I say. Brace for impact.

"No," Dylan says. His tone is firm, no bullshit, but it's kind, too, much kinder than I deserve. "You don't know, Jack. But I do. I know what you're feeling right now."

"We both do," Cate adds softly. I notice she's holding the briefcase, and most of the contents of my money clip.

"I can't believe I did that," I say, holding back the emotions. Be a man. No crying in front of anyone, not ever. "Sully's gone. That house is a graveyard to me. Nothing grows there, and the memories hurt too much. They're all my happiest memories, and now I can't think of any of them without getting a lump in my goddamn throat. And I can't— I can't— *Fuck!*" I suck on the cigarette like it's an oxygen mask, but the goddamn thing's burnt out. I drop it and crush it out on the pavement, wishing I could crush out everything I'm feeling along with it.

"Shh, it's okay," Cate says, coming around to my left side. She touches my arm, and it's so gentle and sweet that it makes me want to scream with how much I don't deserve it.

"We can make new memories," Dylan says, to my right. "Happy ones. Memories that are just for us, the three of us."

"Together," Cate finishes. She gives my arm a little squeeze, and her cheeks color as she smiles tentatively. "We already have, Jack."

I look between the two of them, and I can't believe that they're smiling at me right now. I can't believe they're doing anything other than walking away or kicking me out of their lives.

"Those aren't new memories," I say, trying to remain hard inside. Christ, I'm already craving another cigarette, even if just for something to do with my shaking hands. I jam them into my pockets. "That was just sex."

Cate looks hurt, reeling back like I slapped her in the face.

I reach out for her, like I'm trying to pull the words back into my mouth.

"No, *shit*, that's not what I meant. I'm sorry," I say. "It's not that. It's just, those new memories aren't the ones I wanted." Fuck, that's almost worse. "I mean...they're not the same, right?" My voice sounds like I'm pleading, but they've gotta understand. "Sully gave me my entire life, practically laid out on a silver platter for me, and I'll never be able to honor or repay that, not in a million years. What he gave me was so huge, so massive. I don't know how to describe it."

"I do," Dylan says. "It's family."

The truth of it hits me like a sucker punch. My throat closes up. I'm going to cry again, I can feel it, if I don't get out of here right now. Dylan's absolutely right, but it's something I never should've had, can never have again.

"I gotta get outta here," I say, turning away.

"Don't," Cate pleads, but it's too late. I'm already into a brisk stride. I don't know how I can ever explain it to them, this feeling that I live with every single day, endlessly waiting for every good thing you've got to just *end*. Everything I have is transitory, it always has been. You learn not to make these attachments when you've lived my kind of life. You just expect that everything will go away eventually, and you move on with your life. One day, those two are gonna see right through me, if they don't already, and this happy little fantasy is going to collapse in on itself. I can't afford any of this in my life anymore.

It's a house of cards, and I don't want to be around when it falls down. Best to show myself out now, before they figure out the truth. Before they figure out that I don't belong. Never have, and never will.

No matter how much, for a while there, it had felt like it was the one place I *did*.

# 18

## DYLAN

"*A*re you sure you're going to be okay?" I ask Cate at the foot of the steps leading up to the townhouse's front door.

"I'll be okay, Dylan," she says, shivering and drawing her shawl around her shoulders a little tighter. "I need to go inside, I can't believe it's still chilly this time of the year." She turns to walk inside, stops, and turns back to me. "If you know where he is, promise me you'll find him and bring him back safely, okay?"

I nod. I know exactly where he is. It's where he always used to go when a joke went too far, or when his parents would show up to make a scene.

When he was hurting.

It was his hiding spot away from the world.

"I'll take care of him, Cate. I promise."

She smiles, cupping my face for a moment. "Take care of you too, yeah?"

"I promise," I say.

She nods and heads inside.

It's not far. Jack never strayed far from the townhouse.

I walk away from the steps, down the street a ways, until I

229

get to the alley the next building over. Just as I suspected, the fire escape ladder is down. It's been years since I've been back here, and I figured it would have fallen down or been torn out by now.

If it had, though, I have no doubt that Jack would've found another way to get to the roof.

I step over to the ladder, test my weight on it, then climb up. It's a good, solid climb for the first two stories, then steel steps that lead all the way up the side of the building in a zigzag pattern. I've got about five stories to go, and I take them as quickly as I can. By the time I reach the top, I'm more winded than I remember from when we used to do this. I keep myself in shape, but I guess I'm not a kid anymore.

I take the last short ladder to the top of the building and throw my leg over the ledge, landing on the fine grit of the rooftop gravel. God, it's been more than a decade since I've been up here, but yeah... I see Jack about fifteen feet away at the street-facing ledge, high enough that he doesn't have to bend to rest his arms on top of it.

Old dogs and their tricks.

My heart contracts a little. I hate that Jack's hurting. I wish I could just take it all away from him, but I know it's not a battle that I can fight on his behalf. I can still try to help, though, even if he's the one who will have to do the heavy lifting.

My foot scrapes against some loose gravel, and Jack calls out without looking.

"That you, Dylan?"

"Yeah," I say, smiling as I cross the distance to join him. He knows me as well as I know him, even after our years of estrangement. "It's me."

I rest my arms on the ledge next to him, and we both look over the side in silence. The stars are out and the breeze is crisp and refreshing—peaceful, but I can practically feel the coiled tension radiating off Jack at my side.

After a few minutes, I break the silence. "So, did you bring along a couple of 40's for us?"

Jack laughs at the reminder of our youth, some of the tension easing out of his body. When he answers, I can still hear it in his voice, though, like he's choking on his own emotions.

"Sure," he jokes. "Bribed Old Man Garretty to pick 'em up for us at the packie down the way."

I snort, shaking my head. I remember us leaning out here, watching the traffic, or the sunset, or the fireworks on the Fourth of July. Anything, really. It was our place, but I only ever came up here with Jack. I knew he had come up here at least as many times by himself to get away from the stress of his home life. He'd told me once that it felt like the only place he was ever able to truly breathe.

"I know I fucked up real bad tonight, Dylan," he says after a minute, his voice low. "I swear I didn't mean any of those things I said."

"I know," I say, and I do. I get him. I *love* him.

I put a hand on his back—comfort, support, connection—and I'm not sure how he'll react. He tenses up for a split second, but it doesn't last long before he lets that go. His muscles relax, and I rub slow, wide circles against the tightness there, hoping I can get through to him.

I'm right here with him. Right here *for* him. He's not as alone as he thinks he is.

I'm crazy about this man, and I think I may have always been.

"I can see you, Jack."

"I'm standing right here, of course you can see me," he says, going for a laugh. But even I can hear that it sounds more like a choked sob.

"You know what I mean," I say, not willing to let him get away with hiding from this. From *us*.

He sighs, then nods. "I do. I just... I don't deserve it, Dylan. And you don't deserve to waste your time on a wreck like me.

You're so close to getting your dream, and all I'm gonna do is shit all over it."

He's part of my dream, ridiculous man. "You'd never hurt me, Jack," I say, biting back a smile at his stubbornness. I *will* get through to him. "I know you. That rage, that sadness... none of it is who you really are."

"It's all I have left," he says quietly.

"It's not," I say firmly. He hasn't moved since I joined him here, and I slide my hand up to his shoulder, tugging gently. "Hey, look at me."

He sighs again, but does it. It takes him a moment to let his eyes lock onto mine, but once he does, I hold them firmly in my gaze, refusing to let go.

I let him walk away from me once, but that's never going to happen again.

"Jack, just let it go. We're up here where no one else can see. It's just you and me. Let it *go*."

I can see the dam start to buckle under the weight, and then —*finally*—it bursts. "I'm a fraud, Dylan. I've always felt like it. Known it. Everything I have is thanks to Sully. I meant that part. I'd have nothing if it weren't for him, and what'd I do to deserve it? Pick the man's pocket? He should have thrown me to the fucking wolves, just like anyone else would have."

"But he didn't."

"No." Jack shudders, and I don't even think he realizes he's leaning into my touch now. "He didn't. He took me in and gave me everything I was never gonna get from my own family. The Kelly clan's legacy is always going to be booze, bruises, and being broke. This life I'm living now? I wouldn't have gotten *any* of it without Sully. I cheated. I'm a fucking imposter."

"So... what? You're going to give it all back?" I ask, squeezing his shoulder. "Go back to the life you were born into?"

"*No.* God, no, not ever. You better believe the moment Sully came calling, I ran as fast as I could outta that place. Every single time. I never missed an appointment with him, never missed an opportunity to get away. That townhouse is my *home*, Dylan. It's not that I don't want it in my life, I just... I don't know how to deal with the pain of all that loss, now that he's gone. Now that I'll never have that again."

God, my heart hurts for him.

"Jack, I know. Both of us know, me and Cate. It feels like someone burned a hole clean through you, doesn't it?"

"Yeah," he says, and a shudder goes through him.

"It hurts in a way that'll never go away, right?"

He nods.

"Like someone took a limb away, and all you have left is the phantom pain."

*"Yes."* His face screws up with a parade of emotions, and then, with a choked sob, he lurches toward me, burying his face in my chest. Crying into me.

"I don't ever want to go back to that. To being a Kelly," he mumbles into my shirt, shaking. "I pay them off, again and again, but I can't get away. And I don't get a damn thing in return. *Ever.* No love, no thanks, nothing. Just a big fat pile of judgment, neglect, or whatever other garbage the Kelly family feels like dropping on their awful, ungrateful, sell-out of a son."

He continues to cry and I cradle him in my arms, holding onto his back with one hand and stroking his hair with my other. As awful as this is, as painful as this is, he needs to get it out. It's killing him inside, and it has to be purged. He'll never get around this. He needs to go *through* it.

And oh Lord, I'm so, so thankful he's letting me help him do that.

"You have us," I remind him, remembering how devastated he'd looked when he'd been shouting about how alone he was. "Me and Cate. You have *me.*"

He relaxes against me, and after a minute—clearing his throat—he lifts his head. It's the first time I've ever seen him cry, and it says more than anything that he was willing to do it in my arms.

"I know I have you guys," he says after a minute, not quite meeting my eyes. Still letting me hold him, though. "But that's... *you*. It's all I have, and I know..." He sighs, a sound of defeat. "I know that's not gonna last. I'll fuck it up, like I did when we were kids. I'm not, you know, all that great with relationships."

"Who have you had in your life, all these years?" I ask.

He snorts. "No one. Sully, I guess. You know me, Dylan. I don't know how to get close to people. I always push them away when shit gets too uncomfortable. Too *close*. I mean, sure, lots of girl-friends, lots of sex, but never a... a connection. Never anyone that I could feel..."

I tighten my arms a bit, a silent prompt for him to tell me.

He clears his throat, then mumbles, "You know, *intimate* with."

"No one?" I ask, tipping his face up so he has to look at me again. "Even now?"

He returns my stare, and I can see the corners of his lips start to raise into a small, sheepish smile. "Cate, maybe. Who'd have thought? But... yeah. I guess I felt that way with Cate."

He stops, wrestling with it, and I raise my eyebrows.

"And..." he pauses, clearing his throat again and taking a deep breath. "And you, Dylan. Guess maybe I've always felt that way with you."

"Remember that, yeah?" I wrap a hand around the back of his neck, tipping his head forward and resting our foreheads together. "You're not alone, Jack. You never have to be."

He'd come to the house the other day for sex. Reached for me. *Inhaled* me. Took what he wanted. But that was sex, and I know— as much as it scared the crap out of him to go there—it was easier, in a way, than this kind of intimacy. Than accepting *love*. So I don't mind that he hasn't reached for me now. That he's just accepted, but not initiated. Let me comfort him. Let me touch him. Hold him. And now, when I finally lean in and cross that last inch between us, let me kiss him.

I can taste the salt of his tears on his lips. The desperate need as he opens for me, invites me in. And then something tips inside him, and it's not just a comfort kiss anymore. A connection, but hotter.

*Need.*

His hands go around my waist and when he pulls me against him, the heavy weight of his erection bumps mine. He freezes.

"Is this… you think this is okay, Dylan?" he asks, his whole body radiating a totally different kind of tension than when I'd first come up to the roof and found him here. "Just you and me?"

"Oh, *hell* yeah." I grin, doing a hip roll to emphasize just how very okay I think this is.

He laughs, and even in the darkness I can tell he goes red. "I mean, what would Cate think?" he asks. "It's always been, you know, all of us."

I smile. Maybe he's getting it, after that outburst at the restaurant insisting we pair off. Stuck seeing the world in the narrow, narrow limits he grew up with. *All* of us. That's how it should be.

I step back, grabbing his hand. "How about we go ask her?"

## 19

## CATE

"I don't know how this—" I flutter my hands up and down, indicating both of them, all three of us. "I don't know how this is supposed to work; I never thought this would be my life."

I bite my lip, joy that the fact that this *is* my life sending sparkles through me, points of light that war with the darkness of my fear.

Dylan found Jack.

I don't know how or where; they wouldn't say. But it doesn't matter. He's safe now. My heart's finally beating at a regular speed again now that I know he's okay, that they're *both* okay. I made us all coffee and we listened to Jack apologize profusely about how he handled dinner.

I'm just glad that everyone's home.

*Everyone's home.* That's the crux of it, right? The idea of the three of us, together, all at once, making a home, making a life. It's so overwhelming, and yet... it feels *right*, more than any relationship I've ever known.

I continue, swallowing my fear and letting that joy continue to spread through my body. "But I *do* know that I want this to work, I want *us* to work. And I want—"

*Oh, God, I can't believe I'm going to do this.*

But the idea has been in my fantasies for so long—ever since I came back to Boston and saw Jack and Dylan in the flesh—and now it's actually possible.

I can't bear not to ask, even though I'm terrified they'll tell me no.

I need them to know what I dream of, what I think about when I touch myself in my moments alone.

I look at Jack, at Dylan, meeting their eyes as confidently as I can, and reach up to touch their faces.

"I want you both." I swallow hard. "I mean, obviously, you're both amazing in your own ways, awesome ways, I know you know I *want* you. You both make me feel like no man ever has, better than I even thought was possible, I mean I thought coming more than once just happened in the movies—"

I bite my tongue to stop the words babbling out of me, step back to get a little breathing space. The two of them are so damn hot, my body's response to them makes it hard to think.

This isn't coming out right.

"I mean, um. I want *both* of you," I try to explain. "Both at the same time. With me."

I know I'm blushing, can feel heat searing across my cheeks until I feel like I must be giving off steam. Jack and Dylan exchange a split-second look that I can't quite read before they look back at me, practically squirming from my own nerves.

Dylan's eyes seem to bore into me like searchlights, an intensity he doesn't normally give off. I squeeze my thighs together. I can't help it. It's *hot.*

Jack rubs a hand across his jaw, and his voice is careful, like he's picking his words one by one.

"You want... both of us. You mean, like before on the couch?"

He licks his lips, and I know he's imagining how I took him in my mouth while Dylan fucked me.

A shiver goes through me at the memory, the burning intensity of that night, but I shake my head.

"That was wonderful, that was… that's not what I mean," I manage to stammer out. "I mean—" I grumble, frustrated. "*Ugh*, let me just *show you.*"

My annoyance and hunger, my need, overtake my shyness as I pull Jack into me by his shirt, hard, his chest flush with mine.

"Damn, Duchess," he begins, heat flaring in his eyes, but I put up a finger to shush him.

I'm not done yet.

I turn to Dylan, reaching out the hand that isn't gripping Jack's collar, and yank him toward us. I pivot back to face Jack—which means Dylan's chest collides with my back, his hips hitting my bottom with a satisfying *smack* that sends a delicious shiver through me.

"Like *this*," I tell them.

And then the situation hits me—how I went from skittish about asking them to fuck me together to being flat-out bossy and manhandling them into position—and it's been such a long day, and it's just so *funny*. I start laughing, I can't help it, leaning back against Dylan's chest with Jack's shirt still balled in my fist.

"Is that clear enough for you two?" I ask, wiping tears of laughter off my cheeks.

Dylan's big hands settle on my hips and tug me tight against his body, and I realize with a jolt of lust that I can feel him, hard and hot, through his jeans. Lust curls tight in my belly and suddenly I don't feel so ridiculous anymore.

"Oh, I think we get the picture, Cate," he says in my ear, his breath hot on my skin. "You want us both inside you at once, you want us both kissing you—" yes, "—and fucking you—" *yes*, "—and making you feel amazing."

Oh, God. *Yes.* So very, very yes.

I shiver as Jack's hands come to rest on the curve of my waist, just above where Dylan is gripping my hips.

"Yeah, Wildcat, we get it," Jack says, and his eyes are blazing with the same need I feel coursing through my nerves. His thigh slides between my legs, pressing deliciously against my aching sex. "You wanna be as full as we can make you, coulda just told us that." His fingers tighten and I squeak softly without meaning to, earning me a wicked grin from him. "I think we can make that happen for you, beautiful."

Dylan chuckles. "Oh, we *definitely* can. I know *I've* been thinking about that particular... ah, combination," he says. "I just didn't want to bring it up before Cate did, didn't want her to feel pressured to do that particular thing if she wasn't into it."

Jack nods. "Same, bud, same. Not the kind of thing you just spring on a woman. But now that we know..." He looks down at me, then bends in and kisses me so deep and hot that I feel my knees go weak.

If it weren't for both of them holding me up, I'm sure I'd sink down on the floor.

"Well, now that we're all on the same page," I breathe, licking my lips, "you two need to take me to bed, right *now*. Because I don't think I can stand being teased any longer."

We practically race up the stairs to our bedroom—and God, how nice is it that we have an *our bedroom*—and we're tearing at each other's clothes before we even hit the first landing, shirts and belts and shoes discarded on the mad dash to new territory.

The thought makes me breathless.

This truly is new for me. Not just two at once—that's *definitely* new—but also, the fact that one of them is going to be entering me from behind. It's something I've never ever done in all the years since I started being sexually active. I've had boyfriends who wanted to do it, sure, but to be honest, I never trusted any of them enough to go there.

In the past, I've been scared that it would hurt.

Scared of what they'd think of me... especially if I liked it.

But the idea of Jack and Dylan both filling me up at the same time? Front and back? *God*, it makes me feel like my insides are molten gold. Twisting, liquid flame. It makes me crazy.

We get to the room, and Dylan pulls condoms and lube out of the nightstand drawer while Jack scoops me up and tosses me onto the bed. I can't help but giggle as I land on the mattress with a bounce. Sex with these two is *hot*... but it's also fun. Always.

They're my everything.

Jack kneels on the mattress next to me and Dylan sits on the bed on my other side, and suddenly I'm not giggling anymore. Trembling, maybe. So keyed up with anticipation that I feel like I might break apart at the slightest touch, sure.

But I'm definitely not giggling.

I reach out to them both and all three of us fall back onto the mattress, a wonderful mess of hands and kisses and soft, hungry noises.

"Shut your eyes, Duchess," Jack tells me, his voice a low, throaty growl that lights up my nerves like a neon sign.

I don't know how it is that I manage to obey him and still feel like I'm totally in control here, but somehow, I do—this is all for me. *They're* all for me.

I let my eyes flutter closed and just focus on the rush of sensation as Dylan and Jack worship me.

Hot, strong hands stroke and tickle and tease what feels like every inch of my body. Eager mouths lap at my throat... my breasts... my inner thighs. I squirm and twist, eager to feel everything, and every jolt of pleasure is made all the more intense by my willing blindness.

My breath catches in my throat as I feel a hard, male body lower itself between my legs, broad shoulders pressing into the softness of my spread thighs. I raise my head to look, to see which of my incredible men is kissing and lapping at me, making desire and pleasure shiver through my chest, but a big, hot hand

CHLOE LYNN ELLIS

gently lowers over my eyes and pushes my head back down on the pillow.

"Oh, *God*," I moan, and then after that I just do my best to hold on as whoever's between my thighs does his very best to destroy my grasp on reality.

That *mouth*. It's wrecking me. Ramping me up so hard and fast that I lose touch with everything but *this*.

My hands tangle in soft hair, my heels dig into the muscles of a broad back, but beyond that I give up entirely as pleasure spirals through me, erasing everything but sensation, and then—so fast it takes my breath away—light and color explode behind my eyes as I cry out, clamping my thighs hard around someone's head as I come in a hot, blissful rush that leaves me gasping.

"Beautiful."

I don't even know which one of them said it, the deep voice so soft and worshipful, but the word winds around my heart, working its way inside. These men, these amazing men, they really believe that.

As I come back to myself, shuddering under the gentle, soothing strokes of a pair of talented hands, I hear a soft *snick*.

The bottle of lube.

"Oh my God," I breathe out, nerves and excitement warring within me. I want this, I *do*. But... oh, *God*.

The bed moves under me as someone shifts position, and the man whose mouth just wrecked me in the best possible way moves over. I suck in a breath as slick fingers trace down over my dripping sex, skirting my still-throbbing clit and trailing lower, dipping underneath me, reaching back and then—

"Oooooohhhh," I gasp, a tremor coursing through me.

The fingers circling the tight, virgin ring of my ass are both gentle and insistent, and they feel like nothing I've ever experienced before. I'm trembling. How did I not know this spot was so sensitive? So... euphoric?

I whimper as the fingers start to probe gently, slow circular

242

motions that gradually spin deeper. My heartbeat is pounding in my chest, and the sensation is so totally new, so totally different, it feels like I could climax again, just from this.

My body is responding more intensely than I ever thought possible, and I can't help it—when a thick finger slides into my ass, smooth and slow and opening a part of me that is untried and untouched—I let out a long, low moan that sounds more like something a porn star would make.

Not refined Cate.

Not shy, self-conscious Cate.

"Oh, fuck, she's beautiful."

I moan again when insistent lips land on my throat. Hands on my breasts. And that *finger*. Oh, God, it's bliss.

I feel like I'm going to burn alive from the inside out.

I whimper, my thighs trembling, as it pumps in and out of me, stretching me, opening me up to share myself with my men the way I've dreamt of. And then suddenly I hiss out a breath as the stretch starts to burn. That must be a second finger, which I guess I need. Neither of my lovers are small men.

The burn doesn't last long, though, before it's back to bliss, and my head twists from side to side on my pillow, my breath starting to come in short, hard little pants when the burn comes back and they stretch me even more.

"Want you prepared for us, Duchess."

"You're amazing, Cate."

I'm shameless. Desperately thrashing with their hands on me, in me. It's the only way I know to withstand how incredibly *good* this feels, how new and strange and wonderful all at once.

"God, please," I gasp. It's good, but it's making me crazy. I want what I asked for. I want both of them.

"Ready for us now, Cate?" Dylan's voice, laced with heat and raw with lust, right in my ear.

I nod, or maybe I say yes. Whatever I manage, my men get the message. I can't imagine being any *more* ready than this, not without shattering into a billion pieces.

"Good," Jack growls, and I can hear the smile in his voice despite the animal hunger dripping off the word. "Then open your eyes, Duchess."

My eyes flutter slowly open, the light in the bedroom blessedly dim but still enough to clearly reveal the two exquisite men sharing my bed, *our* bed, both hard and ready for me, gazing at me like they're looking at a goddess instead of, well, *me*. I can't believe how insanely lucky I am, can barely believe this is happening as Jack surges forward and draws me into his strong arms. Our lips meet, sweetness tinged with desperate hunger, and he leans back on one arm, lying back flat on the bed with me astride his lap.

I grind myself against his thick, hard length, shameless and slick, and reach a hand between us to guide him into me. Despite how relaxed and soaked I am, despite the buzz of orgasm still tingling in my blood, his size still makes me gasp as I take him in, take all of him all the way down to the root.

I'll never get used to him, or Dylan, not fully, but this is part of what makes it so wonderful to be with them—being around them makes me feel safe... loved... *home*.

But the excitement? That never, ever ebbs.

My hips start to rock against him, riding him, almost on their own. I can't help myself from acting on my need, my wordless hunger for *more*, even if I wanted to. And I can't imagine a universe where I'd ever want to stop.

Jack groans beneath me, and it's one of the most amazing sounds I've ever heard, raw and throaty and all for me.

It's all the sweeter because of the pain he was in earlier tonight. I'm so glad he came back to us. I'm so glad Dylan found him. I'm so glad... we're... together.

"You feel so good, Wildcat," he says, his hands covering my breasts.

Oh fucking God. *Heaven*.

"Jack," I start, but then lose whatever I'd meant to say in a gasp as I feel Dylan move in close behind me. His broad chest presses against my back as he begins kissing across my shoulders, the steel-hard bar of his cock pressing deliciously against my bottom. And oh God, oh *yes*.

I want him there.

Jack inside me only sates part of my hunger, but stretching me earlier, those talented fingers thrusting in and out of me, it's made me need more. I need *him*.

Dylan's knees settle on either side of my legs so we're both astride Jack, Dylan's legs pinning me between my two wonderful men. *My* men, and the thought, the knowledge that it's the truth— they really *are* mine—sends a twisting curl of love and desire through me that seems to spin around the beautiful hot hardness of Jack inside me.

I hear a slick, erotic sound behind me—Dylan's hand on his cock, which makes me moan in anticipation and grind down harder on Jack—and then a sudden shock of coldness. It trails down between the cheeks of my ass, chased by the heat of Dylan's large hand. Lube. I blush, the heat of lust and pleasure and yes, also a little bit of fear, roaring through me as he works the lube inside me.

"Oh, fuck," Jack gasps. "Your fingers are inside her, aren't they, Dylan? I can... I can feel them."

Dylan groans. "*Jack*."

Oh, Mother of *God*, Jack's words... the lust in Dylan's voice... they send a surge of heat rocketing through me, and I become almost frantic, moving against them shamelessly. I want Jack deeper, and I want to press back against Dylan's fingers, taking them farther.

I want it *all*.

"I need to be inside you," Dylan whispers, his fingers thrusting in and out in a maddening rhythm that has this hot, burning, delicious, crazy-making need coiling inside me, tighter and tighter, with the promise of another orgasm that's going to take me apart.

"You love this, Duchess," Jack grits out, smiling up at me with fierce heat. "You were *made* for this. For us."

"*Yes*," I manage, rocking on top of him. Back against Dylan. Over and over.

"Hold her still," Dylan says to Jack, his voice at my shoulder ragged. Raw.

Jack's hands tighten on my hips, halting my movement, but even holding still, I can feel the pulsing heat of his cock inside me, throbbing. Micro-thrusts of his hips. The digging pressure of his fingers into my curves.

It's intoxicating.

Dylan's fingers pull out, and I whimper at the loss, turning to look at him over my shoulder.

The look on his face... oh *God*. It almost tips me over the edge into another climax, and Jack hisses below me, feeling the flutter of my inner muscles. Fire floods through my belly, washes away the last of my nerves at what we're about to do.

And then the fat head of his cock presses gently against my rear entrance.

It feels amazing.

Terrifying.

I'm hungry for it.

I swallow hard. *Oh, God—this is really happening!*

"Relax, beautiful," Jack says gently, his hands running up my thighs, fingertips grazing over the place where we connect so sweetly. "Relax, we've got you."

The look in his eyes captures me, steadies me, drives the lust inside me even higher. I see desire and care and the same golden feeling of perfection, of *belonging*, that I feel every time the three of us are together.

I let out a shaky breath and relax back into his hands, trusting him.

Dylan tugs back on my hips, then lets me rock away from him again. "I'll hold still for you, Cate," he growls softly. "You take as much of me as you want, this is all for you."

I moan at his words, pushing back slowly onto his massive, slick cock, impaling myself inch by perfect, agonizing inch. It burns, at first—*I* burn—but not like I expected.

Not like I feared, even as the idea excited me.

The delicious feeling of completion mounts higher and higher as I take him into me. I'm impossibly full, impossibly stretched with both of the men I love so, so much deep inside me.

I *love* them.

I love *this*.

It's exactly what I needed. What I've wanted for so long.

I feel like... I feel like... I just *feel*, feel everything. And it's spectacular; pleasure that makes my eyes go wide and then flutter closed as I let the sweet, dirty words they're both mumbling wash over me. Buoy me up. Carry me into this new experience.

My body's trying to savor every sensation, and my brain struggles for a moment, then shuts down. Sensory overload. This isn't about thinking. This is so right it transcends thinking.

And it's so... *good*.

"You feel amazing," Dylan whispers, his hands coming around to palm my breasts as he starts to thrust into my back entrance. I arch into his hands, letting him have me. Letting them both carry me where I need to go. I don't need to do anything right now but be here, accept it, ride it out to a kind of glorious climax that's building fast, already feeling more intense than anything I've ever experienced, even in my fantasies.

Dylan moves inside me—so different, but so familiar at the same time. All the sweet, perfect spots that his cock strokes inside me are the same places Jack's touching, but from a different angle. And *Jack*. He's got my hips secured, and rocks up into me, stroking inside me where I need it, pulling me against him so my clit is stimulated again... and again... and *again*.

CHLOE LYNN ELLIS

It's so much erotic sensation I almost think I can't stand it, but at the same time, I never want it to end. I'm trapped between them, I have no place I can turn to hide from the raging pleasure of feeling both of them inside me, and it's...

It's everything.

They both thrust into me at the same time, and my mouth falls open on a soundless scream of ecstasy.

*"Fuck,"* Dylan groans, his body bowing back from his hips like his entire being is distilled into the places where he and I connect.

Beneath me, Jack is softly swearing a blue streak of his own, filthy words mingling with endearments in the most exhilarating way.

"I can feel you *through* her, man," he grits out. And then, when I tighten my inner muscles: *"Jesus,* Cate."

He all but whimpers, and suddenly I'm not just letting them take me. Not just giving myself to them. I'm powerful. I'm *here.* I'm rocking their world just as much as they're doing to mine.

"You're perfect," Jack whispers. "Cate, you're..." He licks his lips as words fail him. "I've never felt anything like this."

The way he's looking up at me, it's so clearly, rawly the truth that I feel like I'm basking in the sunlight.

"Jack..." It's Dylan's voice, not mine, and I know he's looking down at Jack, too. And all the love, all the lust, all the... the *perfection* I feel at this joining, I hear it in Dylan's voice, too.

"Oh, Christ, Dylan," Jack says, and one of his hands leaves my hips. Reaches back.

I moan, knowing he's touching Dylan. Reaching for him. Wanting him, too.

Then Dylan begins to *move.* Faster. Deeper. Spurring us both on. And *my* breath comes out of me in a low, ragged groan as he withdraws, then thrusts in again, his thick cock pulsing across my G-spot as he fills me up. He pulls back, and Jack buries himself within me, hitting it again. And then it's Dylan... and Jack... back and forth, ramping me up so high I feel like I'm flying.

Like they're turning me inside out.

Delicious fire ripples out through my body in golden waves, and I bend down to Jack's chest, clutching at his skin with my nails. I feel like I'm barely holding on to my sanity, let alone coherence. Dylan bends with me, his chest close to my back, and I'm trapped between the two of them, between their strong, beautiful bodies and their kisses and the perfection of their cocks inside me.

My world narrows to the ecstatic, torturous rhythm the two of them set.

To the space that doesn't exist between our bodies anymore.

To the space that doesn't exist between our *hearts*.

And oh God, oh *yes*—to the pulsing, coiling, utterly *delicious* tension building inside me. Winding me up, tighter and tighter until I'm frantic with it. Until these two men inside me, *surrounding* me, are all that exists.

"So good."

I don't know who says it.

*"Fuck."*

"Yeah... oh, hell yeah."

"Oh, God. Oh... *oooooh*."

My body is quaking, every nerve alight with pleasure, trembling, and I know any second I'm going to shake apart. Jack is kissing my mouth, my throat, anywhere and everywhere he can reach, Dylan's hips are slamming into my ass with the most delicious impact, and I'm *so close*.

I just need... something.

Jack looks up at me, his eyes heavy-lidded with pleasure as his gaze seeks mine, then slides to Dylan's.

Both of us, all at once.

His gaze is hot, fierce, possessive and possessed, and I see it clearly—*finally*—there's no difference between the lust he feels for each of us.

"Kiss me," Jack begs. Demands. "Cate, *kiss* me."

His voice is strained, tight as he thrusts up into me, making me gasp. I want to. But oh, I want something else even more.

I shift—another gasp—so Jack can see Dylan more clearly.

"Kiss *him*."

Dylan makes a gorgeous, guttural noise in my ear, and I feel the pressure at my back increase as he leans in low. Jack pushes up on his elbows to reach him, and their mouths meet with such passion that I feel it radiating through me, a palpable wave of need and want and lust and love that makes me feel as if I were part of that kiss, too.

As if I *am*.

And then there are no more words. None of us can do it. Just hot, needy moans and the wet, slick sound of our bodies moving together and the heat of the gasping, panting breaths, and the rising pressure, higher and higher, driving us all to the brink.

My head lolls back to rest on Dylan's shoulder as they pump into me, in and out, a perfect rhythm, and my eyes stay locked on the gorgeous sight of the men I love kissing each other while they share me. That's what I needed. That's... *it*.

I'm lost.

Bliss lights me up, shooting through my nerves like fireworks, searing and sweet all at once, and my eyes squeeze shut as I begin to ride the bucking, punishing waves of orgasm, screaming out my climax.

"*Cate*."

"Oh, *Christ*."

Pulsing heat fills me inside, sending ripples of pleasure through me as they both come at once, crushing me between them and stretching out my own orgasm into an endless, mindless, perfect wave of ecstasy that consumes me.

I don't even know how we get from there to the tangled mass of sweaty, warm, sated bodies, and I don't care. My heart is as full as my body was—overflowing—and right here, right now, with both Dylan and Jack holding me, is the single most perfect moment of my life.

They're murmuring soft, sweet things to me, to each other, but words are beyond me right now. I'm full of starlight, full of warm, swirling clouds. Sure down to my bones that this is exactly where I need to be. To *stay*.

Always.

# 20

## JACK

*T*oday's been a good day so far. Hot as hell out, but still a damn good day.

It's been a couple of weeks since I started seeing both Cate and Dylan. I gotta admit, I'm still not really all that sure about what we're doing, but it's good.

I'll take good for now; it's better than I normally get.

The three of us have meals together every couple of days, depending on my work schedule, and it feels like Dylan's cooking just gets better and better with every class he goes to. I'm so proud of him, my best friend, getting everything he wants out of life. Good for him. I hope he keeps grabbing it by the horns.

Cate, too, my other best friend. It feels weird to say that, given that we all but hated each other back at the beginning of April. But now it's early May, and the chill has finally given way to the thaw. She's killing it at her fitness class, far as I know. It's amazing to see how much happier she gets every single day.

And me, well, I just dunked my biggest case to date. My closing argument was on point, and the jury came back in an hour. It's a partner-making case, I'll bet. Not trying to put the cart before the horse, but there were a lot of telling handshakes and pats on the

253

back at the courthouse today. It'll only be a matter of time before I'm sitting in that boardroom with all the rest of them, and none of them will ever know how I grew up or where I came from.

That's my little secret. Our little secret, I guess.

Anyway, it's too hot for the T; ain't no way I cram into a subway car when it's ninety degrees out, so I got myself a luxury taxi from one of those apps. Why not? Gotta learn how to live it up a little more if I want to fit in on the top floor.

Speaking of the taxi, here it is now. Big black SUV. Perfect. I hop in.

"Where ya headed, pop?" the driver asks me. I grin. He's practically a boy, gotta be his first job out of high school. Townie, too. Good for him, I hope he crushes it.

"Out to the Common," I say, thinking about the townhouse. "Northeast."

"You got it," he says, and we start to roll off.

The air conditioner is perfect, cool, crisp, feels wonderful on my face, but as we pass by the towering buildings of downtown, my smile slowly begins to fade.

What if I'm imposing, stopping by like this?

I was just there yesterday, and I didn't ask ahead of time to hop on over. Cate keeps telling me I don't need to ask permission anymore, but I still feel bad for the times I barged in on her in the past, and I don't want to fuck this up.

"Hey kid," I say, reaching into my suit coat and peeling a fifty-dollar bill out of my money clip. "Change of plans, sorry about that. Take me on over to Back Bay, I'll comp you the lost time."

"Damn, pop," he says, grabbing the bill. I can see him beaming in the rearview mirror. "Thanks! No prob, on the way."

Sure, my throat's a little tight with disappointment, but it's better this way. I don't want to push, or overstay my welcome. Cate and Dylan have been living in that place without any incidents together. Don't get me wrong, I've been really enjoying our thing, but I don't know if it's gonna last. I still can't break that habit of being ready for a thing to disappear from my life.

Once a townie, always a townie, I guess.

Things are good now, but the two of them are probably better off there without me right now. Honestly, there's no telling that either of them are as into this arrangement as I am. It's sex. Yeah, good, mind-blowing, *amazing* sex, but still... just sex.

Sex with friends.

Two very *close* friends.

But... there's a reason they call it the third wheel, right? And the last thing I need to do is get in the way of their feelings.

Then again, maybe I'm overthinking it?

I stifle a sigh, staring blindly out the window. I just don't know. I guess it's not *always* just sex. Like I said, the dinners are wonderful, and we've done a lot of talking about Cate's decor ideas for the townhouse. I'm still not quite convinced that keeping the townhouse is the best move, but we've all reached a sort of unspoken understanding for now. Keeps the boat steady. And anyway, Cate's design decisions are amazing; they've really started to grow on me. If we end up selling after all, the market value ought to go up like crazy based on her taste alone.

I'm so dug into these thoughts that I barely hear the kid asking me a question from the front seat.

"Say again, kid?"

"I said, that's a lotta smoke up the way, pop. Looks like someone fell asleep with a lit cigarette. My old man did that all the time, dunno how we managed to keep the house from burning down."

But I stopped listening about halfway through, rolling down the window on the passenger side and looking out. That looks *awfully* close to my building.

"Keep on goin', kid," I tell him, frowning.

"You got it," he says, but then I hear the sirens approaching behind us. The kid pulls the car to the shoulder, honking the horn at the folks in front of him to let him in.

I watch as the fire trucks start zooming past us, weaving through the tight spaces like they must have done a million times before.

"Kid, there's another fifty in it for you if you tail 'em," I say, starting to feel worried now.

Please don't be my building.

Please just be the shitty one next to it.

"Yep yep," the kid says, and swerves the car into traffic the moment the last fire truck gets an inch past us.

I'm thrown to the other side of the car, but I don't care, as long as he gets us there fast. And he does; kid's amazing, gotta admit. He stays hard on the tail of the last fire truck, aggressively blocking anyone from cutting him off. As we get closer and closer, passing rows of buildings and alleys, it's looking more and more likely that my wish isn't going to come true. My heart slowly sinks with every block that goes by.

It feels like a million years, but we finally get there. My gut clenches. It's my building, and it's bad.

A brigade of fire trucks is surrounding the place, and there are paramedics, cops, and firefighters everywhere, along with a healthy crowd of rubberneckers that keep getting pushed out of the way. Of all the fucking *luck*. But of course. Of fucking *course*. Hadn't I just been thinking how good things were going? Jinxed it.

Fuck.

*Fuck.*

Fucking *fuck.*

I swipe at my face, tearing a few bills out of my clip and throwing them up to the front seat.

He turns to face me. "You want—"

"I'm out here, kid," I say, and a second later, I fling the door open and hit the ground running, briefcase in one hand and my money clip in the other. I use my briefcase as a wedge, digging my way into the surrounding crowd until I can finally push through to the inner circle. "Hey!" I shout, running smack into an officer.

"Get *back*, pal," he shouts right back at me, looking at me like I'm the asshole interfering with him doing his job.

"That's my place," I grit out, brushing him aside. I only get a few yards before he grabs me again and holds me in place.

"Sir, you can't do that," he says, raising his voice to be heard, but without the underlying *asshole* in his tone now. He's got an arm firmly around my neck, and gestures with the other one. "It's full up with smoke!"

"It's my *place*!" I yell again, struggling to break free of his iron grip.

"I don't wanna have to hurt you," he yells back, tightening his grip. "But going in there *will* hurt you. You're acting crazy. Stay *back*."

Finally, I can't fight against it any longer; I'm getting nowhere. I fall still and hold my hands up.

"*Alright*. Fuck. I'm done," I say, and he lets me go.

I take only a single step forward, staring up at the building. The fire might not have started on my floor, but it was definitely on my floor now. I can see the flames licking out of the sides of where my windows once were.

"No," I mutter, dropping everything I'm carrying and bringing my hands up to my head, tearing at my hair. "It's everything."

"Sir, is anyone else in there?" the officer asks, looking concerned.

"It's everything!" I shout. "It's my life! My art, my files, my computer, all my pictures! My suits! My thousand-fucking-dollar suits!"

Everything that meant I'd made it. Everything I'd worked for. All I had.

"Loved ones, sir," he shouts, trying to be heard over the roar of the fire and the crazy scene around us.

I almost don't understand the question at first, staring up at the building. But a moment later I do, and my thoughts shift to Cate and Dylan, my heart freezing in my chest. No question: if either of them were in the building, I'd run in past a million officers.

I'd fight and die for either of them.

For both of them.

"Oh my God," I whisper, my hands dropping to my sides.

The officer looks at my expression, horrified. "*Sir*? Anyone? Is that a *yes*?"

I can't even hear him. The thought of the two of them in that building, it's just... it'd be my entire life.

Gone.

I love them.

I love each of them, and I love them together. Cate, Dylan, the both of them. They're my whole goddamn heart, every last bit of it. Hadn't they both tried to tell me, in different ways? Why hadn't I seen it?

Because on top of the crashing knowledge, I've got something else. This isn't new. I think I've always felt like this.

Why couldn't I ever give Cate a chance when we were kids?

Why did I explode on Dylan when I saw him with another guy?

If there's one sure bet in my life, it's that I push away the people that I love. Everyone except Sully, but that man just didn't take no for an answer, so I really had no choice on that one. But I did it with Cate and Dylan both, and I pushed so hard because... because I felt too much. I've *always* felt too much for them.

It's terrifying.

I take in a deep, deep breath, and shakily sigh it out as the force of my epiphany courses through my body. Not even close to as terrifying as the thought of them in that flaming building. No, I'm done being scared. Fuck that. They're not in there, and I'm in love with them.

I'm blessed.

Cate and Dylan, and the people they've grown into since the last time I saw them. I want to be with them forever. I can't imagine life without them.

"*Sir*," the officer shouts again, shaking my arm, and I turn to face him, grinning from ear to ear.

"No," I tell him, elated, and the officer looks confused. I continue, "Nothing I love is up there. Not a single damn thing. Just stuff. The people I love are far away, where it's safe."

The officer stares at me like I'm a crazy person, and I probably am, but I can barely hear what he's saying to me, because all of my attention immediately jolts at the sound of Cate's voice, and again with Dylan's right behind it.

"*Jack*." It's Cate, and I can hear it now in her voice. It's not just my imagination, and now that I'm not trying to talk myself out of it, it's plain as day. She cares about me, too. "Jack, are you all right?"

"*God*, Jack," Dylan's saying, talking over her as they both rush toward me. "We were worried sick about you."

I feel as though I've been struck by lightning. How could I have been so foolish? Of course those two want me. They've made it so crystal clear at every passing opportunity, and the only thing that keeps getting in my way is *me*.

Before I can say anything, the two of them plow into me, both wrapping their arms around me in a huge hug.

I laugh. Hard. Bending over, wheezing-for-breath hard, if they hadn't been holding me up. Because right now? Losing all the *things* I own? It might be the happiest I've ever been.

Nah, no "might" about it.

It is.

"Are you hurt?" Cate asks, her hands all over me as a look of concern grows on her face. She thinks I'm losing it.

"No, no, I'm fine," I say, still grinning like a fool.

"Thank God," Dylan says, his arms still tight around me from the other side. "I don't know what I'd do if anything happened to you."

I feel a shudder go through Cate's body, and she adds a heart-felt, "Me, neither."

The officer who'd stopped me earlier is waving at us to get back, clear the way, and this time, I don't put up a fight. The only place I want to be is wherever these two are. And then it hits me. They're *here*. Why? How? It's like they materialized out of thin air, just when I needed them most.

My life just doesn't work that way.

"What are you guys doing here?" I ask, stumbling to a standstill just outside the ring of gawkers. I look back and forth between them, dumbstruck. This just ain't the kind of luck I normally have.

Cate's eyes well up. "We were doing some painting at the townhouse—"

"Yeah, and the fire popped up on the news," Dylan interrupts. "We recognized your building right away."

Cate looks up at it, raging like an inferno. "We got here as fast as we could," she whispers, turning back to me. "I'm so sorry, Jack."

I grin. And then I'm laughing again. I don't even recognize myself right now, but that's okay. I see the moment they get it. These two, I tell you, they know me so well. I guess, in some ways, better than I do myself.

"Nothing I need is up there," I say, spelling it out as I tug them back against my sides, where they belong. "It's okay. What say we go home?"

Dylan's face splits into this heart-stopping smile. He's just... lit up, and hot on its heels, Cate's beaming at me, too.

Yeah, no two ways about it. Happiest day of my life.

# 21

## DYLAN

"*I* thought maybe we'd just skip right to dessert, if that's okay with you two," I say, carrying a tray of home-made pound cake and a carafe full of strawberry puree.

"Oh my God, Dylan," Cate exclaims, eyes rolling back in anticipation.

I grin. I love that she's stopped fighting good food and just lets herself enjoy it now.

"When the hell do you find time to do this stuff?" Jack asks. He looks comfortable, and I'm so happy for that. He's doing remarkably well for someone who just lost his home.

No.

Whose *house* just burned down.

And now I can feel my cheeks start to hurt, my grin's so big. Hearing him call this place, *our* place, "home" meant everything.

"I love watching the two of you eat my food," I tell them sincerely, setting the tray down along with the cake. "Serve yourselves. Whipped cream?"

"Please," Jack says, his eyes lighting up the way they used to when we were kids.

Cate just nods her head in excitement, and the look of anticipa-

261

tion on her face is sensual. Decadent. *God*, of course I like cooking for them. Their appreciation for it is like a drug I've become addicted to. I fetch the bowl of fresh whipped cream from the counter while they start prepping their own cakes, and put it down between us, taking the open seat between them at the head of the table.

It's quiet for a while as we all polish off the cakes. And not to put too fine of a point on it, but even I have to admit that I really knocked this one out of the park. Got the balance of sweet to sour just right with the puree.

"This was exactly the thing I needed," Jack says, putting his fork down after he's made sure to chase every crumb, every dollop of whipped cream off his plate. "Dylan, you're something else."

And I'm smiling again, loving the fact that I got to take care of him a little. That I put that look on his face.

"Jack, are you sure you're okay?" Cate asks, reaching for his hand. There's a note of concern in her voice, and I get it. That fire scared us both. Badly. "I mean, you just lost everything—"

He laughs again, squeezing her hand before dropping it so he can reach into the nearly empty bowl of whipped cream and scrape the sides, getting it all on his index finger. I relax, because there isn't a shade of concern in his voice.

"'Course I'm okay," he says, waggling his index finger across the table at her. "I'm here, ain't I? With you?"

He winks, then tries to smear some whipped cream on her.

"Stop that!" Cate squeaks, pushing her chair back, laughing. "I've had to get paint out of my clothes all week from the house painting, I don't need to add whipped cream to my collection of stains."

"Aw," Jack teases, "Duchess don't want even a little bitty taste?"

Cate narrows her eyes in good humor, then stands up, leaning over the table to take his finger in her mouth, sucking the cream right off. And *that* shuts Jack right up. Makes my pants suddenly feel a little tight, too, even though I can't help but laugh at the scene. It's so good to see them joking around so easily with each other.

Jack's happy.

They both are.

And what that does to me... it's all I need.

It's probably the first time I've ever seen them this completely casual and playful around each other outside of the bedroom. They're at peace and lighthearted, and it's the only thing I've ever wanted for the two of them. I have it all under one roof now, and I throw a smile up toward the ceiling. I think Sully would have been very, very happy with all of this.

"Jack!" Cate shrieks, as Jack rounds the table and grabs her up in his arms, spinning her around. The two of them laughing together is the happiest sound I've ever heard in my life.

"Alright, you two. It's late, and we have a very early day tomorrow if we want to get the house painting finished up," I remind them, my lips twitching.

"Aw, come on," Cate whines, pouting.

"Yeah, buzzkill," Jack says jokingly. "Don't you wanna have a little fun with us?"

"If we have any fun at all," I say, over-exaggerating the mock-stern tone of voice, "It's going to be from the comfort of that big fat bed of ours. I don't know about you two, but I'm fried."

And right on cue, I let out a big, stretchy yawn to prove it.

Jack's grin falters for a moment. "Hey, guys. I just want you to know how much I appreciate you opening the house up to me. I know I haven't made this very easy."

Cate shakes her head and gives him a gentle punch on the arm. "Don't you get it yet?" she asks with a smile, and looks over to me. "One of these days, we're really going to have to convince him that he belongs with us."

I step over to Jack and drape an arm lazily over his shoulder, smiling. "Yeah," I say to Cate, but keep looking at Jack. "We'll get through to him eventually."

Jack reaches up, and I think for a split second that he's going to push my hand away, but instead I feel his fingers wrapping gently around my wrist, guiding my arm over his shoulder like teenagers at a movie.

"Hey, I'm a smart guy," he says, and what I hear in his voice… *damn*. He winks at me. "I'll get it sooner or later."

And oh, shit. I'm thinking sooner might be *now*.

He grins, pointing upstairs with a cocky glint in his eye. "What do you two say: slumber party?"

Cate bites her lip, and I can see the telltale flush creeping over her cheekbones and the way her gorgeous breasts start rising and falling faster as she gets excited.

"Oh, can we please?" she asks, her voice coming out so breathy and eager that Jack and I groan as one.

Jack starts regaling Cate with stories about the two of us as we head up the stairs.

"Y'know, you missed out on a lot only being here during the summers, Duchess," he says. "Dylan and I spent a lot of time together, year-round. Sleepovers, campouts, you name it."

"Camping?" Cate says, laughing incredulously. "In Boston?"

"*Heck*, yeah," Jack says, his enthusiasm making him sound fifteen again. "You can put sleeping bags on the roof, can't you?"

And then he's off, cracking us both up and bringing up some memories that I'd all but forgotten. We all get ready for bed together, playfully nudging each other at the double-sink in the master bath and stealing little touches, soapy kisses.

It's heaven.

When we finally pull back the covers of the gigantic bed and slip right in, there's a moment of tangled covers and jostling as we figure out who wants to be where, but eventually we settle in, Jack on one side of me, Cate on the other. I think we all expected to come up and have another replay of some of the hot times we've had together between these sheets, but the day catches up with us and both of them crash out almost immediately, Cate with her head on my bicep, and Jack with his arms behind his head, his hip pressed against mine.

My cock swells at their nearness, but no matter. I'm content just like this. In fact, it's really nice how we all fit together, and my last thought before sleep takes me, too, is that I want to fall asleep just like this, with them, for the rest of my life.

## 22

## CATE

"It's just a hair too high on the right," Dylan says, holding onto my hips as I balance on a chair.

I'm trying my best not to be too distracted by the feel of his strong fingers, but I'm not doing so well.

The portrait of Grandpa Sully that we ordered finally arrived yesterday. Jack commissioned it right after the fire, about a month ago now. It's gorgeous work; whoever Jack found to paint it, they must've known the old guy personally, because they really captured him. His eyes practically twinkle with shrewd cleverness and good humor, and it makes me miss him all the more. I wasn't so sure it wouldn't clash with all the other changes we've made to the townhouse, but it seems to fit right in.

If only I can get the damn thing to hang straight.

"How about now?" I ask, hands spread wide as I tug on one of the bottom corners of the heavy, burled walnut frame.

It doesn't escape me that Jack chose a frame that matches the huge bed we all share. He really doesn't miss a thing; it's the kind of detail I'd choose myself, and it makes me smile. He's still not one to show he cares with a lot of words, but all the subtle things… oh, they get to me. They really do.

"Okay, I think we're good," Dylan says, slowly letting go of my hips. "Don't move."

"Dylan," I whine, up on my tippy toes. "Is it good?"

He doesn't answer, but finally, after what feels like an eternity, I feel his hands on my hips again. *Mmm.* His touch gives me happy shivers up my spine, even when we're nowhere near the bedroom.

Or the couch.

Or the dining room table.

Or… I shake my head, pressing my lips together as my racing imagination offers up a seemingly unlimited supply of eroticism. Dylan's saying something, and I come back to earth, determined to listen.

"What… um, what did you say?" I prompt him.

"I said, it's good, Cate." I can hear the smile in his voice. Oh, yeah. He knows all my tells, and I'm sure he figured out *exactly* what had me so distracted. "You can let go now."

"Thank God," I exclaim with a laugh, letting go of the frame.

He pulls me off the chair, and I squeal with joy as he spins me around in the air. He's so strong, both him and Jack; I love that they can twirl me around like I weigh nothing, can toss me around when we make love.

Dylan gently sets me down on my feet and I beam up at his beautiful face.

"Thank you for the help," I say, reaching up to gently cup his cheek. "This is going to mean so much to Jack. It means so much to me already."

"Of course," Dylan says, smiling. He wraps an arm around me and holds me close as we look at the painting.

It's the big centerpiece to the living room, a culmination to all the hard work we've been doing over the past month on the first floor. Jack has been wonderful about making sure we have the funds to really spruce this place up. Without his help, I'd be scrounging around thrift stores, committed to a decidedly "shabby chic" style.

But thanks to Jack, we can give this place the love it deserves.

I grin. It's not just that it's looking good, it's been fun. Definitely more fun than any of the decorating I did for MacMillan Designs. And sure, there's still a lot left to accomplish, and doing the kitchen alone is going to be *crazy*, but it's all really starting to come together.

"I'm glad we have a part of Sully here, looking out for us," Dylan says, and I couldn't agree more.

"I wish Jack were here to see this," I say, but then I furrow my brow. "Where is he, anyway? He snuck out of bed early this morning."

I'd been hoping he'd headed out to Dunk's to pick up donuts for us, but he's still not back, so it can't be that.

"I don't know," Dylan says, shrugging. "It's Saturday. I can't imagine he's at work."

As though on cue, we hear the door open, and both of us turn to see. It's Jack, and my heart trips at the sight of him, just like it always does. These two, it just never gets old.

He walks in all smiles, his hand outstretched and holding onto a manila envelope.

"It's official," he says, practically bouncing with excitement. "Clean as a whistle, lab-tested and science-approved!"

My mouth drops open, and then I squeal. Even better than donuts. I run over to him and jump into his arms. "Jack, that's fantastic news!"

"Whoa there, Duchess," Jack laughs, catching me easily and settling my legs around his hips.

"Damn, bud," Dylan says, approaching from behind, setting a hand on Jack's shoulder. "Then it's official. All of us are clean, and maybe we can stop buying stock in condom manufacturers."

"Thank God," I say, knowing I'm pink-cheeked. Not that I have any reason to be embarrassed around these two, I know for sure that they don't judge me for liking what we do, but still... sometimes I still feel brazen.

Well, okay, I kind of like that feeling, actually, but I'm still not sure how long it will take for it not to make me blush, too.

I unhook my legs from Jack and stand back on my own two feet as my men give me a bemused look.

"Not that every time we've been together hasn't been mind-blowing," I clarify. "But I've been dying to get to actually, um, *feel* you guys, instead of being separated by balloon material."

"I'll drink to that," Jack says, and leans in for a kiss. I arch up into him and marvel at how every kiss with the two men I adore still sends fireworks of delight bursting in my heart.

He takes his time, but once we step apart, his eyes shoot up to the fireplace.

"Oh, wow," he says, a gorgeous smile blooming across his face again. "That's really something, isn't it?"

"It is," Dylan says, reaching down and taking Jack's hand.

"It's perfect," I agree. "That's the only word I have for it." I look up at Jack and bite my lower lip in the way I know drives him crazy. That's right, I'm pulling out all the stops. "It took so long to get this just right. Any chance you've reconsidered selling the townhouse?"

I can see him wrestling between old Jack and new Jack. I'm so, so proud of all the growth he's gone through in the last month alone, but he has me just a little nervous. I want to trust him fully, completely, but the more memories I make in this house with the three of us, the less I think I can handle it if I have to say goodbye to the place.

"Yeah, about that," Jack finally says, sounding sheepish. "I think…" He pauses, looking a little pained, and I can't help it, I tense up.

"Out with it, buddy," Dylan says, and I see him give Jack's hand a reassuring squeeze. "It'll be okay, no matter what your answer is, right, Cate?"

I nod; it's all I can do. "Yes" would be a lie. If he still wants to sell the place, I'll be heartbroken. *Devastated.* But the last thing I want to do is hurt Jack, so I bite my tongue.

"I think... I want to reconsider selling," Jack finishes, his cheeks flushing.

I wait a beat to absorb his answer, and then, when I do—

*"Yes!"* Dylan and I shout in unison.

Dylan wraps his arms around both of us, squeezing tight.

Jack laughs. "Well, wait, I mean, this was always a temporary situation with my house going up in flames, I thought."

Dylan snorts. "Yeah, and?"

"And," Jack continues, "I guess I just figured that once the insurance closes on the investigation and cuts me a check, I'd be headed out again." He clears his throat. "I mean, what, we're not all just gonna live together forever, right?"

He laughs nervously, but it's easy to hear the longing in his voice.

"Jack," I say, raising my hand to cup his cheek. "It's okay."

"Yeah, Jack," Dylan says. "I think we'd both like that very much."

"Like?" I tease, beaming up at the two of them. "I'm over the moon for the idea. Please stay, Jack."

It takes him a second to join in, but finally he smiles, and I can feel his tension melt away.

"Yeah. Yeah, I think I really like it, too. But, y'know, what if this doesn't work out with the three of us? What if any of us changes our minds, rubs each other the wrong way... Hell, I don't know, gets outta bed on the wrong side or forgets to change the toilet paper roll? Are both of you really okay with this?"

*Are you really both okay with me?* That's what he really wants to know.

"Oh, you," I say, reaching out for both of their hands and leading them over to the couch.

We all sit down, Jack in the middle.

"I need you to listen to me very carefully, Jack," I start. "We've known each other forever. Those summers, years ago, were my only lifeline away from a place I couldn't stand, and from a person that I couldn't accept that I was turning into. I know we've had our issues, you and I, but even when we kept our distance from each other, I've always wanted to be here more than I wanted to be anywhere else."

"And now," Dylan jumps in, putting his hands on Jack's shoulders and rubbing slow circles that I know firsthand melt tension like it was butter, "We're all here. All three of us."

"Let's be real here," I say, grinning as I look back and forth between them. Goodbye, shy Cate. "I'm greedy. I've finally found the man of my dreams, and it's not just one, but *two*. You are the most beautiful, gorgeous men I've ever been with in my life. Not to mention, absolutely dynamite in bed. I would be a crazy woman if I didn't want to keep you both here with me."

"But it can't just be about us," Jack says. "You ain't no slouch out there. You don't deserve to just be all about us men, with as much talent as you have in your little finger."

"Of course!" I say, but blush all the same at the compliments. "Like I said a while ago, I'm not yours to take and trade. I choose who I belong to." I motion to the big bright windows, so different from Grandpa Sully's former decor. "Look at what we've done with the place in such a short time," I say. "I love it here. I love Boston. I love my job at the gym. And maybe, once we get the house together and settled the way we want it, I'll try to put out an interior decorating shingle of my own. If there's any one thing that the MacMillan name is good for, it's hooking a client or two once I'm on solid ground again."

"Honestly," Dylan says, "I thought you left New York because the job was killing you. But I've been so impressed with your work around here that I was kind of hoping that you were growing fond of it again. You know?"

"Yeah," Jack adds. "Finding the fun in it again, I guess?"

"Yes!" I exclaim, beaming. "I take genuine pleasure in it again, and it's because I'm doing it for *us*. I can be *myself* here, more than I ever have in my entire life. Now that I'm getting back into that headspace, why shouldn't I go for it?"

"Absolutely," Jack says. "You do amazing work. Shit, the interior designer I hired for my burnt-up condo was probably twice what you charge, and not gonna lie, he only did half the job you've done here."

"It's been uniquely lovely to watch you work," Dylan adds. "I'm proud of you, and impressed with you, at the same time."

And now I'm blushing again. The old me would have brushed aside the praise, but they're right. I *am* good at this. Even better, though, is knowing that they see me—the *real* me. Nothing could be sweeter, and as I thank them, I feel like I could burst with the amount of joy inside of me right now.

"I love you guys," I say, then freeze for a second. For all we've done, as close as I feel to these two, none of us have said *those* words.

Jack kind of grunts, like the wind's been knocked out of him, but Dylan just wraps an arm around him, pulling him close, and when I press against Jack's other side, Dylan leans around Jack for a moment, smiling, and plants a kiss on the top of my head.

"Cate, I've always loved you," he says, and I feel my heart leap into my throat. "And I've always loved you, too, Jack. Both of you, to the bottom of my heart. I can't imagine being with anyone else."

"I, uh…" Jack clears his throat, but then he does it. "Me too. You know, about loving you guys. I love you, too. And about this place, well, I don't want to go anywhere, either. Insurance'll clear soon, no doubt, and I think I just want to pour it all back into this house." He looks around a bit, and I can see the mist of memory in his eyes. "It's tough, the way it makes me miss Sully sometimes, and it might be a little rough for a while, but I love this place and I don't want it to be just another bad memory. I don't want to be that person anymore. You guys are my…"

He loses steam, but Dylan props him up.

"We're your family."

"Yeah," Jack says, leaning his head back and closing his eyes as a gorgeous smile spreads across his face. "That's right. I love you, and we're family."

My heart suddenly feels too big for my chest.

This?

This is… perfect.

## 23

### JACK

*B*oston in late June is fucking *sweltering*. I close the door of the townhouse and wipe my arm across my forehead. Would have been so much worse if I was still wearing the slate-blue linen suit I went to work in, but hitting the gym after work means I'm freshly showered and dressed in my post-workout clothes. My favorite worn t-shirt and a pair of thin basketball shorts are a lot more comfortable in this heat than a suit jacket and tie, both of which I dropped at the cleaners on my way here.

It's good to be out of that monkey suit.

Even better to be home.

I kick off my shoes at the door and drop my gym bag, smiling. Hell, best of all is *having* a place to call home.

I don't see any sign of Cate—she said she was going to the market in the North End this morning, might still be there—but I can hear sounds coming from the kitchen. My smile broadens. So Dylan's home, whipping up his latest work of art already.

I'm a lucky guy, maybe the luckiest, to have one of my best friends, my *partners*, be such an amazing chef. Keeps me sharp about going to the gym, too.

I'll have to thank him for that.

Sure enough, Dylan's at the stove, an apron thrown over his bare chest and jeans. I can't help it, my cock starts to swell. Damn. Should be used to it by now, and sometimes I am, but letting myself be this affected by another man still catches me off-guard sometimes.

*If you can't stand the heat, get outta the kitchen.*

I snort a soft laugh at the idea of anyone taking *Dylan* out of a kitchen, and when he turns and grins at me as I walk into the kitchen from the hallway, something turns over inside my chest. Definitely weird, these feelings I have for him. I mean, weird when looked at from the way I was raised.

They feel good, though.

He raises a hand in greeting before turning back to a steaming pot on a back burner. "Hey, Jack," he throws over his shoulder. "Good day?"

"Eh," I shrug. "Not too bad. What're you making?"

My day was a day, and whatever Dylan's doing is way more immediate and interesting. Whatever's in that pot smells incredible: rich and smooth and fresh in that herbal way. Mouth's watering already.

And, yeah, okay. Not just from the thought of food.

Dylan shrugs, a tiny motion of his massive shoulders. "It's not anything crazy, I'm just testing out a dill beurre blanc sauce for some swordfish I picked up this morning; figured I'd chargrill the fish and we could eat out on the patio tonight. Cate said she'd pick up wine; asked her to grab an oaky white if she could find a good one."

"Burr what?" I walk into the kitchen proper, leaning against the kitchen island for the best view.

Honestly, that all went right over my head, but I know it'll make my taste buds sit up and sing. I *am* catching on to some facts about what he prepares at the moment, actually, but right now?

MINE

A little distracted.

Dylan laughs. "Don't try that rube act with me—you go to fancy enough restaurants that you should know what butter sauce is." I shrug and he shakes his head, smiling. He holds out the wooden spoon. "Do you want to try it or not?"

"Yeah, of course I wanna try it," I say. "Give me that."

I'm a little too eager grabbing the spoon out of Dylan's hand, or else maybe I misjudge the speed with which he's passing it to me—instead of closing my fingers around the handle, I manage to overshoot it entirely. My fingers slip on sauce and the spoon goes flying out of Dylan's hand, clattering to the kitchen floor.

"Ah, fuck, I'm sorry about that," I say. "Here, lemme—" I move toward the paper towels, but Dylan's already grabbed the roll and is stooping to wipe up the spill.

Goddamn, I always forget how fast he moves.

Guess that's a chef thing, too many pots on the stove to be dicking around or something.

Gotta say, though, since I'm letting myself go there lately, it's sexy as fuck, the way he takes charge in here. Takes care of business. Kind of owns the place.

I know there's not actually much I can do to help, so I pop my sauce-covered fingertips into my mouth while I wait. Be a shame for it to go to waste just because I got clumsy. Dylan's right: I'm no stranger to a good restaurant, but this cream sauce is something else.

"Mmm, okay, that is delicious," I say, and fuck if it isn't. Actually pulls my mind out of my pants for a minute. Or, I guess, out of Dylan's pants. "Dylan, your sauce is fuckin' amazing," I tell him sincerely.

Dylan looks up from the floor and raises an eyebrow, and holy hell. Did I say my mind had gotten off sex? 'Cause the heat in that look sends it shooting right back down to my cock. Or to his. Christ... two guys. I'm still wrapping my head around that.

277

"Hell of a thing to say, Jack," Dylan says, winking up at me. "Given that you haven't had any of it yet."

His eyes are twinkling, but I guess I'm slow—or, again with the distractions—because I don't get what he's getting at.

"Huh?"

He stands, tossing the wooden spoon into the sink and turning on the tap. "So far," he says as he washes his hands, "The only person who's gotten to try my 'sauce' is Cate."

The innuendo hits me all of a sudden, and the way my body reacts to such a simple dirty joke makes me lean against the kitchen island for support. I reach down and adjust myself. Guess I'm not the only one whose mind went there.

"Shit," I say, my mouth suddenly dry. "I, uh, I walked right into that one, huh?"

Dylan snorts, grinning as he turns back to whatever he's making.

"I'm guessing you had one hell of a long day at work," he gives me. He takes a fresh spoon out of the drawer, stirs, tastes, grabs one of what seem like a hundred identical little jars on the spice rack and dumps some into the pot. He looks back at me, and oh yeah. There it is again. He's teasing me on purpose, isn't he? Bastard. "Hey, Jack, you okay? You look a little flushed. Did the heat get to you?"

My cock twitches again, but my heart does this little flip thing, too. He's joking, but... his comment *did* get to me. It just struck me hard all of a sudden; Dylan and I have been fucking Cate together all over this house, but there's never been a point where we've been alone together in a sexual way. Kissing, yeah, which... gotta say, I fucking love that. A bit of touching, some affection, like hugs and shit. But I guess it just...didn't occur to me that he might want to get me alone, spend time that way.

Do I want that?

Guess I've thought of it, especially after that first time he made it clear I could come over for sex with *him*, too. But then when it didn't quite go down that way, not gonna lie, part of me was a little relieved. And then... well, things are so great with the three of us—with *Cate*—that I guess I just didn't revisit the idea.

I mean, not too much.

Not, like, in the way that would bring it up in discussion or anything.

Truth is, in the privacy of my own mind, I've definitely thought about what it'd be like to take things with Dylan to the next level. What it'd be like to feel his skin under my hands. Have my mouth on him. Sometimes I still get a surge of guilt for those kinds of thoughts, but mostly?

*Dammmmmmmmmmm.*

I've had more than one fantasy of what it would be like to have his always-laughing mouth wrapped around my cock, how he'd look with my cum running down the flat expanse of his chest.

I hiss in a breath as my dick jerks hard at the thought, and I swear silently. *Fuck.* Basketball shorts are great for the heat, but they don't do fuck all to hide a cockstand. Dylan's looking at me, and he's got to know, right? I swallow, shake my head.

"I'm good, uh." I clear my throat. "Cream joke just caught me off-guard, must not be on my game."

I don't know why I'm trying to play it off. I mean, guess it's pretty obvious he's open to whatever I'd want to do. Habit, I guess. Old voices.

Dylan makes a *hmmmmm* sound that has my cock raring to go again, then he pulls the little pot off the burner, all slow and deliberate-like, turns off the stove, sets down the spoon, and takes off his apron before turning to face me again.

"Come here, Jack."

I let out a breath I hadn't realized I'd been holding. He's so damn good at just... getting me to do shit I want to do anyway. Like him being okay with it makes it okay in my head, too, somehow. I'm hard as a rock now, but despite that, or maybe because of it? It hits me: I'm really, really loved.

By him.

By Cate.

This isn't a game or some kinky sex thing. It's *real*.

I don't know if I'm ever going to get used to it.

My heart does that flip thing again, sweet and dizzying, and I think *now or never, Jack*. I cross the space between us, and when I reach him, I don't play it off like a bro thing. I reach out a hand to cup Dylan's cheek, run my thumb lightly over the stubble of his jaw. And then I take another deep breath—tell myself to stop being such a scared little wuss—and lean in to kiss the man I've been in love with maybe since we were kids.

Dylan makes this little growling noise in the back of his throat, like *finally*, and his hands come up to my head and sink into my hair. He tastes like fresh herbs and lemon and *Dylan*—delicious.

This still feels weird, kissing another dude, taking so much joy from something I spent so many years thinking was wrong, but I trust that that strangeness will fade with time. Because it's weird, but it's right, too. Down to my core.

Besides, this isn't just any dude, this is Dylan.

This is my oldest and best friend in the world next to Cate.

He tastes like home.

Well, I huff out a little breath, feeling his lips curve up next to mine, and yank him closer. Right now? He also tastes like pure sex.

His body presses into mine, the hard muscle of his bare chest against my shirt, and it's so different from Cate's body, strong and fit as she is. There'll always be a plushness to her, and it's always going to be spectacular. Dylan, on the other hand, he just feels *solid*, like a warm, slightly-yielding wall of power against me.

His cock, hard and huge, rocks against my leg, and my own swells even larger in response.

Weird is fading to just really fucking turned on, and when we break apart for a second—panting hard with our foreheads resting together—I realize I've got my thumbs hooked into Dylan's belt loops, my hands tight on his lean hips.

I don't want to let him go.

"Dylan," I groan, wanting more but not sure *what*. Not sure how to ask. My heart's beating like crazy, my cock throbbing desperately, and all I can think about is how *right* this all feels.

How good it is.

Why the fuck I waited so long.

Dylan palms me, cupping my aching cock through my shorts, and I groan—long and low and needy as shit—unable to help myself.

"You like it like this?" he asks, his lips twitching as he teases me and the heat in his eyes... fuck. *Me*.

I lick my lips, trying to clear my head, and I can't help from pushing into his hand.

"Yeah, yeah," I say, then insecurity twists me up inside. I *hate* being out of my depth. What if it isn't okay for him? Yeah, feels *great* to me... but what the fuck am I supposed to do for *him*?

"Jack," he says, going still. He reads me like a book, doesn't he? I know what he wants.

*Talk to me, Jack.*

*You can trust me, Jack.*

*I'm here for you.*

All true. All definitely true. Okay, I can do this.

"I mean, it's different, but it's good," I start. I look into Dylan's face, my voice nearly pleading. "I don't know what I like when it's another guy, Dylan," I admit. "I need you to... *shit*, I think I need you to take the reins on this one, yeah? Hand to God, anything you do is gonna be all right by me, I just have no fuckin' clue what I'm doing here."

Dylan grins at me, and it lights me up inside. Eases that pressure in my chest.

"So you're saying... don't ask you, just do it, huh?" he says, tightening his hand on my cock.

I groan.

"I'm going to take that as a yes," he says, laughing.

I almost sag against him with relief. Well, fuck. I guess "sag" isn't the right word, given that part of me—a very, very happy part—is pretty fucking firm right now. But Dylan gets me; always has.

It's why I love him.

He cups my face in his hands, kisses me slow and sweet. "I've got you," he says. And then he shoves me back against the kitchen island, *hard*, the edge of the tiled countertop a cold jolt at the small of my back.

Oh, *fuck* yeah.

It's a perfect counterpoint to the heat washing through me, pooling low in my belly as Dylan yanks off my t-shirt and drops it to the floor. I reach for him, trying to get at the fly of his jeans, and he slaps my hands away with a grin.

"You wanted me to take control, Jack, now you've got to let me do it," he teases.

I groan. "Fuck, that's gonna be hard to take," I mutter, even though my cock jerks at the reminder. So, yeah, maybe not so hard after all.

Or hella hard, if you want to look at it another way.

Dylan pats my cheek in mock sympathy before his hands go to the drawstring of my shorts. He's got the double knot undone faster than I ever could, the thin material slithering down my legs to the floor and leaving me bare in front of him. His eyes rake over my body, appreciation unmistakable in his expression.

"Damn, Jack," he says, then whistles low. "I wish you could see how hot you are to me."

Goddammit, I'm blushing, I can feel it, but there's nothing uncertain about the way my cock is twitching, straining toward him. Fucking leaking at the tip.

No doubts. I want this.

Dylan kisses me, hard, then sinks to his knees in front of me. A gust of air whooshes out of my lungs, hard and loud. This is really happening.

He leans into my groin and I give a silent prayer of thanks that I showered at the gym, because post-workout balls don't belong near *anybody's* face, and then Dylan spits into his palm and takes me in those strong, dexterous chef hands, and the last thing I want to do is *pray*. I don't know what to do with my hands, casting around for something to hold onto but not knowing if it's cool to touch him while he jacks me off.

I settle for lacing my fingers behind my head, that seems safe enough.

But oh damn, I can *not* look away.

"*Fuckkkkkkkk*," I hiss, almost tearing my hair out when Dylan swirls his tongue around the head of my cock, then takes me all the way down his throat like it's nothing. *Jesus H. Christ.* I grab at the edge of the kitchen island counter with one hand for support, biting down hard on my fist to keep from crying out and doing my goddamn best not to buck into his mouth.

He's doing things with his tongue that feel illegal, and I'm helpless against the brutal pleasure of it. It's like my bones are melting. My skin glowing with the raging fire he's stoking. My whole fucking *world* collapsing down to a single point.

That... *mouth.*

Dylan leans back on his heels and I make a little involuntary noise of loss as his mouth leaves my cock.

"You... uh, you done?" I manage, clenching my fists to keep from begging for more.

He looks up at me, lips red and wet and fucking decadent, and laughs. I swear to fucking God, I feel that laugh in my balls. It's low and throaty and dirty as fuck, and then he gives me a look that practically has my toes curling and sticks two fingers into his mouth.

Sucking them.

Soaking them.

I lick my lips, my wet cock jerking hard against my stomach. "Dylan?" I ask, needing... something.

*More.*

He slips his hand up between my thighs, and my eyes go wide as it hits me what he's doing. Where he's headed.

Sure enough, his fingertips start probing at my ass, circling the rim as that a-fucking-mazing mouth returns to sucking me off. A part of me wants to freak the fuck out at the ass play, but it feels so damn good and I'm so damn distracted by that mouth, I can't do anything other than make the kind of sounds that should probably be illegal.

I don't even realize my hands have left the counter—have buried themselves in his thick, dark hair like they belong there—until he pushes one of those fingers inside me and I clutch his head like a lifeline.

He moans, a sexy-as-fuck vibration that I feel all the way through me, and I gasp, lurching against him as I'm breached for the first time. That finger moves in and out, in and out, stroking me in a way I've never felt before. A way that makes what his mouth is doing to my cock so much *hotter.*

I feel like I should say something.

Thank him.

Worship him.

*Some*thing.

But before I can do anything more than make more of the dirty sounds that are already pouring out of me, he touches some spot inside me that makes my knees buckle.

"Holy shit. Holy... *shit.*" I would have collapsed if it wasn't for the too-tight grip I had on his head. "Dylan, what the fuck was *that?*"

He pops off, looking up at me with his pupils blown and his mouth wet from sucking my cock, and pushes that finger onto my spot again.

"Nnnnnngggghhhhhh."

I swear to fucking God, I see Jesus.

He pulls off my cock for a second. "That's what's going to make it feel so damn good when I finally fuck you," he says, and I shit you not. Those words? I almost come.

Dylan swallows me down again, and I don't even care how gay this is, I'm about to beg him for that second finger 'cause the first one feels so... damn... *good.* So good that I'm thinking it's all about to be over before I can bring myself to ask—over *fast*—but then, because apparently whoever's up there has a sense of humor, I hear the front door open and Cate's light steps walk into the room.

"*Shit,*" I say. Reflex.

My eyes pop open and I freeze.

Cate's right there, yep. She's frozen in place with her eyes wide, too, a big wicker grocery basket on one arm, just staring at us. I have a moment of sheer, all-consuming panic—panic that almost has me blurting out *this isn't what it looks like,* like some schlub in a bad romance movie. As though there's any misinterpreting the sight of Dylan down on his knees with his finger inside my ass and my cock so far down his throat I'm surprised the guy can *breathe.*

But then Cate lets out a low, soft moan that sends little arrows of raw need shooting through my entire body, and that beautiful blush she does floods her cheeks. She smiles, and it's wicked and loving and fucking *hot.*

"Shit shit *shit,*" I mutter, except I'm also panting. Kind of groaning. Not frozen anymore, but thrusting my hips forward into Dylan's mouth—and then back, fucking *Christ,* backward to fuck myself on that finger of his. Cock and ass, over and over, with Cate watching. Breathing hard and looking hotter than hell as the color rises in her face.

And Dylan? He hasn't slowed down at all. If anything, he's sucking me harder. Making some hot-as-fuck sounds of his own that leave me no doubt how *he* feels about Cate bursting in on our... moment.

My body wants this so bad, and my head... my head is doing a number on me. I'm trapped. Right on the edge of coming and so turned on I can't see straight, but also sort of... waiting for the other shoe to drop. A part of me screaming with all the voices of my past, telling me this can't be okay. Can't be *right*.

No matter how fucking perfect it feels.

Cate sucks in a shuddering breath, then gives me another hot smile and walks over to the kitchen island. She sets down her bag and pulls out a fat bottle of white wine, then reaches under the island to unhook a wine glass from the rack.

"Oh, don't mind me, boys," she says with a wink as she uncorks the wine and pours herself a generous glass. She sits down on one of the tall kitchen stools, resting her elbows on the counter and watching us as she sips her wine. "I wouldn't *dream* of inter-rupting this. You both know how hot it is to watch."

I groan and let my eyes drift closed. She's so right. And Dylan's mouth feels so damn good. And that finger is still fucking my ass, timed with that incredible suction on my cock... *fuck* those voices in my head. With these two? This is all kinds of right. So right that when it really hits me—I can have this; it's okay—I almost come on the spot.

But Cate's here, now, and yeah, watching is hot, but damn if I don't want her, too.

"Hey... Duchess," I pant, struggling to form the words with Dylan still doing his best to fucking wreck me. "This isn't a... a spectator sport, y'know." I reach for her, and she's just close enough that I'm able to tug at the thin strap of her sundress, sliding it off her shoulder. "Get in here, Wildcat."

That last comes out as a growl, but it's all I can do to hold myself together now. I want to, though. Wanna wait for her. Want it to be *all* of us.

Cate sucks in a sharp breath, biting her lip in that sexy way she has, and the hot little moan she lets loose with has my fingers tightening on Dylan's head again. For a second, I worry I'm being an ass. I don't want to force him to take more than he wants of me. But one look down at his face and I'm good again. For one thing, the man has no gag reflex. I'm not small, and he's got me buried so deep in his throat that his face is pressed against me.

And that is... *hot*.

But the clincher? It's the look he's giving me. Eyes hooded with lust and face kind of glowing, like he's enjoying this just as much as I am. And then I realize... he really is. Yeah, he's got one hand working me in back, but my cock? That's hands-free for him. His other one is occupied jerking himself off, and fuck... *me*.

Knowing he's getting off on this, too?

"Faster, Cate," I grit out, my balls tightening up so hard and fast that it's all I can do not to shoot. "Need you. Dylan... *more*. Please, *fuck*."

Dylan makes another one of those gonna-make-me-come sounds, and then he gives me that second finger. I don't want it for a hot second—fucking burns—then oh yeah. *Hell* yeah. I want it. So fucking good, my knees start shaking as he works my ass with the both of them.

"Oh, damn, boys," Cate says breathlessly, her voice trembling with lust. She's already off the stool, and now she rounds the corner of the island fast, loosening the straps of her dress as she stalks toward me like a lioness going in for the kill. When she stops right in front of me, the wicked smile on her plush lips widens, and she shrugs her shoulders, just a little... just enough to send her sundress fluttering to the floor.

She ain't wearing a bra underneath, and the white lace panties she's got on are so tiny they barely cover her.

I groan, and then her body presses against mine, hot soft skin like a brand as she wraps herself around me from the side, then goes up on her toes and kisses me.

My body tenses, and I'm not sure I can handle the intensity of both of them at once. That hot pressure is rising fast and fierce inside me, and I gasp against her parted lips, my hips jerking forward to thrust into Dylan's mouth.

It would be so damn easy to come right now... but if I do, it'll be just me. I need *us*.

I rip my mouth away from Cate's, wrapping one arm around her soft waist to hold her tight, and try to breathe.

"Wait... a second," I pant. "Dylan... hold up."

He groans, as if he's loath to let me go, too, but he rocks back on his heels, my cock sliding out of his mouth with a wet plop. He slides his fingers out of me, too, and then I'm the one groaning.

What, am I stupid?

I want them back. *Now*. But...

"I want you both so bad," I manage to get out, my chest tight with the desire and the pleasure and, fuck, the *love* I feel for them. "I want us to all be together like we were before, you know, all of us at once."

My cock is positively dripping, precum pooling from the tip and sliding down my wet shaft—wet from Dylan's mouth. Dylan's puffy, pink mouth that's quirking up in a grin as he leans in to kiss Cate.

"I just wanna be close to both of you," I say, 'cause as close as I am, that's more important right now. I *need* them. "I can't get enough of you, I need—"

I choke on it. I'm struggling, fighting with the feeling, words too difficult right now with all of this sensation, all this emotion, roaring through me. But my lovers, they've got me. Dylan tips my head back and kisses my throat—*damn*—and Cate reaches out, placing a finger to my lips.

"We know, Jack," she says softly, all her wickedness replaced by care, compassion for me.

She takes my hand and leads me upstairs, Dylan following with his hand on the small of my back. When we get to the bedroom, she pulls me down on the bed, wrapping her plush thighs around me. I move to lower my face to her beautiful pussy, to take off her panties at least, but she stops me, shakes her head.

"Dylan," she calls, and I feel his weight settle onto the bed behind me, his fingers running lightly down my back and across my ass.

"Oh, oh fuckin' God," I moan, looking between them desperately.

They're both so perfect, this is *perfect*, and I'm still afraid, but now the fear is that they'll *stop*.

"Where do you want me?" Dylan growls in my ear. "Fucking her ass, or yours?"

Cate moans, and shit, I can't say I don't do the same. There's something about a guy as sweet as Dylan talking like that, so utterly *filthy*; something about the contrast makes my dick jump and my balls tighten.

I take a deep breath, crane my neck toward him, and kiss him, short and deep and biting.

"Don't ask," I remind him, and my voice is raw with sheer animal lust. "Just fuckin' do the thing."

Cate laughs, then groans prettily as Dylan puts a hand on my back and shoves me down on top of her. She barely gives me any time to get her amazing ass situated against me before she's slipping her panties aside, pulling me forward and letting my cock slide into the blissful, liquid heat of her.

My eyes practically roll back in my head, she feels so good; I'll never get used to how it feels to sink into her, not in a billion years. I dig my fingertips into the softness of her thighs, hooking her legs up around my hips so she can really take me deep, and for a second, I forget about anything other than the heaven I find inside her, every fucking time.

"Oh, God," she moans, arching into me. "Oh, *fuck*, Jack. Watching you two together was so hot. I'm almost ready to come already."

And that reminder... the heat of Dylan's body is behind me,

possessive and sure, and I drive myself deep into our Cate and then go still, holding my throbbing cock as far inside her as I can as I force myself to stay still and wait for him.

Cate's eyes roll back, and I can tell by the pretty set to her lips that she's about to beg me to *move*, but then she sucks in a quick little breath and looks over my shoulder at Dylan.

"Oh, God. Oh, yes," she breathes out, her whole body trembling underneath me.

I hear the soft *snick* of the lube bottle, and then Dylan's slick fingers slide up and down the crack of my ass, start to tease me again, pushing past that initial resistance and giving me back that taste of heaven he'd been showing me in the kitchen.

I groan, my cock jerking inside Cate's tight heat, and push back against his fingers.

"So fucking sexy," he mutters against the back of my neck, his fingers moving faster inside me. "So tight, Jack. *Jesus.*"

I've been inside Cate's ass. I can imagine. And oh, fucking God, am I ever ready to be on the receiving end. Especially when he finds that spot again.

"*Fuck,*" I blurt, my balls almost bursting. "Hurry."

Dylan laughs, and then my ass suddenly starts to burn, and I get that he's pushed an extra finger into me. Stretching me the way we do Cate. And fuck if it doesn't ride the line right between pleasure and pain. I can't hold still. I'm fucking Cate before I can stop myself, pounding into her while he preps my ass, and if he doesn't hurry up and fuck me, too, it's going to be over for me before we get there.

"Dylan," I gasp. "*Dylan.*"

His fingers are making me see fucking stars, and I grit my teeth, feeling ten kinds of desperate. This is *torture.*

Cate's moaning underneath me. Already tightening around me. Her gorgeous body moving in all those ways that tell me how much she's enjoying this, and she looks over my shoulder at Dylan and licks her lips.

"You're being so *mean*, Dylan," she pants. "I want you to drive him into me."

"Not going... hard enough... for you... Wildcat?" I tease, every other word punctuated by a needy moan as Dylan's relentless fingering pushes me to heights I've *never* experienced before.

She smiles into my face, then bears down *hard*, squeezing my cock like a vise.

"Oh, *fuck*," I groan. "Oh *fuck*, fuck, you two are *killing me*. Dylan. Fuck me already. Jesus. H. Christ, man. My ass *needs* you."

He lets out a low growl, and then his fingers are gone. I gasp, but before I can react, they've been replaced by something hot and thick, pressing into me. Oh... *yeah.*

*This* is what I need.

"Jack," he growls, one hand on my hip and the other on my shoulder.

Leverage.

I try to brace myself, but it's impossible. There's no preparing for it when his cock finally pushes into me, driving me forward into Cate and then rocking us back together as he pulls out. I cry out, swearing; it feels like he's splitting me in two, like she's doing her level best to turn me inside out from the sheer perfect tightness of her own body.

It's too much.

Not enough.

It's fucking incredible.

They push and pull me between them, a duet of exquisite torture. I feel my eyes roll back as the three of us rock back and forth together, over and over again, faster and faster, until my entire body's fucking shaking with the white-hot bliss of it.

I can't think.

I can't do *any*thing.

I can only *feel.*

Feel, and hope like hell that I survive the feeling. They're tearing me apart. Tearing every bit of who I thought I was down and giving me something new in its place.

"*Jack*," Cate pants, her soft hands holding me tight as I pound into her.

"Jack." Dylan's voice, low and husky, rumbles through me as his thick cock slams into that magical spot he found in my ass, over and over, until I'm utterly wrecked.

It goes on for hours, or maybe for just minutes, I have no idea. I just know that my nerves are on fire, my skin is burning from their touch, and I've never been so perfectly, utterly ecstatic in my life.

"You feel so good."

I don't even know who says it, but suddenly Dylan's mouth is on me, his hand around my throat tipping my head back, and he's growling into my mouth like he owns me.

"I can't last," he mutters. "Too good. Wanted it too long."

He pulls his mouth away and grabs both my hips, driving into my ass so hard that I fall forward onto Cate. Cate, whose plush body catches me. Cradles me. Starts to tighten around me as I take her mouth and own it. Claim it. Revel in it as she suddenly bucks beneath me, crying out.

"Oh, fuckin' *yes*," I groan, held tight between the two people who mean everything to me. "I'm gonna come."

Cate's tight sheath clamps down on my cock, *hard*, and it's all I need to finally, *finally* let go.

Finally get the sweet release everything in my body is screaming for.

"Oh, fuck, oh *yeah*," Dylan cries behind me, the hard-driving rhythm of his hips, slamming into my ass, suddenly stuttering as he starts to come undone. As the hot rush of his release fills me from behind, I drive helplessly into Cate, my own body taking over as it starts to unload inside her. I push back against Dylan's wild thrusts, milking the bliss.

I give and take everything they have to offer, and I am utterly, entirely *theirs*.

And they're mine.

They're mine.

They're *mine!*

This is the only thing that's real. This is where I belong. And oh, fucking Christ, I am *never* giving this up.

## 24

## DYLAN

"*D*ylan Tater Smith!" comes my name from the speakers, followed by applause. I've been standing in this line, in the new suit that Jack helped me pick out, for what feels like forever. I almost don't react to my own name, dumbstruck.

How the hell did anyone find out about "Tater"?

"That's you, pal," the guy in line behind me says. "You okay?"

I shake it off and smile. "I'm amazing," I say, and walk across the stage to receive my handshake and my diploma.

It's been a hell of a year so far. On top of everything else going on with my newfound triad, I've been killing myself trying to get this degree, and now it's in my hand. It's finally mine.

"Yeah! Tater!" I hear from the crowd. It's Jack's voice, shouting over the applause. He must be so damn pleased with himself, and I can't help but grin from ear to ear.

"You deserve it, Dylan!" Cate shouts beside him.

I can't get any luckier than I already am. Not by a single bit.

About a half hour goes by as the ceremony wraps up, and I finally push through the crowd and find Cate and Jack waiting for me.

"Look at you, hot stuff," Cate teases, grabbing me gently by the lapels and giving me a quick kiss.

"You crushed it, bud," Jack says, standing next to Cate. "Proud of you."

"Yeah," I say, reaching out for his hand.

He hesitates for a second, but pushes it away quickly and grabs hold, pulling me in for a tight hug, and my smile gets impossibly bigger. I'm so proud of him for getting past his insecurities. It's been a couple of weeks now since we decided to keep the house, and it has been my pleasure to watch all of us grow together.

"So," I continue. "*Tater*, eh? How'd they figure that one out?"

Jack lets go of my hand and raises his own hands up, palms out and open. "Hey, don't look at me, pal, I didn't tell them anything."

"Much as I hate to agree with him," Cate says, playfully poking Jack in the stomach, "I didn't see him talk to anyone."

"My beautiful, beautiful baby boy!" another voice joins in the chorus.

I turn around, still smiling like I might never stop.

"Mom!" I shout, opening my arms. She's still up and about, still gorgeous, and she leans into my arms to return the hug. "I missed you so much. I'm so sorry I didn't call. It's been…" I look back at Jack and Cate, shrugging.

"Don't you worry about it, baby," she says, brushing my hair back and patting me on the cheek. "I wouldn't miss this for the world."

"But I forgot to call!" I say. "And I thought you went out to Florida after Sully's funeral. How'd you even know about this?"

My mother grins, holding up an invite card. "Hendricks was a clever, clever boy, you know."

"No way," Jack says, laughing.

I take the invite, and open it up, reading it aloud. *"You are cordially invited to the future graduation of our wonderful little Tater. You raised a hell of a son, and he's become a hell of a man, and it's my privilege to ensure that his skills as a chef are enjoyed the world over.*

*Sincerely..."* I can feel the heat hit my eyes, and I blink a few times, but there's no holding out on the hoarseness that has taken over my throat. *"Sincerely, Hendricks Sullivan, Esquire."*

"He loved you so dearly, you know," my mom says. She looks over my shoulder and smiles. "The two of you, too. Don't think I forgot your faces now."

"Hey, Mrs. S," Jack says.

"I hope you're doing well, Mrs. Smith," Cate says.

"Mom," I start, "Jack, Cate and I have all decided to live together in the townhouse. I don't think any of us could bear to sell it off anymore."

"That's good," my mom says. "I would have kicked all three of you in the pants if you'd done otherwise."

We all laugh at this, and I beam at how wonderful everything feels right now. It's all just so perfect, and I feel so full that I could burst.

"Listen, dear," my mom starts, "I'm in town a while, and I've been thinking about coming back up this way. I've got to go meet your Aunt Sylvia for drinks. You know how she gets."

I roll my eyes. "Yep. The classiest pickle in the North End."

She flicks my chest. "Watch it, young man. And don't be a stranger. Call me, we'll get together. I've been waiting for this day, you know."

"What do you mean?"

"I mean, if you think I hadn't been slowly building up my references list while I worked for Sullivan, you're crazy. I've cooked for people who have become very important these days. People that I think might really like to meet my professional chef of a son."

I laugh, and can hardly believe my good fortune. "Mom, you don't have to do that."

"Hey, let the lady do you a favor, eh?" Jack says.

"We've got your back, Mrs. Smith," Cate follows.

"You better!" my mom says. She looks back at me and smiles.

"I'd do anything for you, you know that. But this is the one gift that I've wanted to give you for years now. Ever since you picked up your first spatula in my kitchen. You call me, and we'll get those calls made, hear me?"

"I hear you, Mom," I say, and kiss her on the cheek. "I love you."

"I love you too, baby boy," she says, hugging me. "I gotta run. *Call* me."

"I promise!"

She scurries off, and I turn back to Jack and Cate, who are both grinning from ear to ear.

"I love that woman," Cate says. "She's always been the sweetest person in the world to me."

"She might be the only person whose cooking I enjoy more than yours," Jack says.

"Guess I got my answer on how they found out about Tater," I say.

"Hey," Jack says. "Sully always had our number. Right from the beginning."

"How about a little graduation afterparty?" Cate says, narrowing her eyes playfully as she slips her hand inside her purse, taking out a room keycard. "I took the liberty of booking us a room."

Wow. I didn't think this day could get any better. I've never been happier to be so wrong.

# 25

## CATE

"*O*f course, Dr. Salisbury," I say excitedly. "I can absolutely make those dates work out. I can send over my rate sheet so we can determine the best fit for you and your wife, and then we can move on to colors and themes and ensure that your office space integrates seamlessly with the rest of your home, while maintaining two distinct spaces."

I've been a busy little bee. We all have. Dylan's mother made good on her promise a couple of weeks ago, and Dylan was set up with a shot at one of the biggest hotels in Boston. If he succeeds there, and I know he will, he can write his ticket anywhere he wants. Maybe a year of good solid work, and who knows where he'll be? For now, he seems positively giddy about his new day job, and comes home in a great mood every day.

Jack has been good as well, as far as I can tell. We don't hear a lot about his cases, but he's been home earlier than usual these days. He apparently made a very good impression on the partners at his firm right around the time his condo caught fire, and seems to be really gunning for a partner spot of his own. It couldn't happen to a better guy; I really hope it comes through for him.

As for me, I'm just focused on my work. I still run kickboxing classes at the gym, and I decided to start reaching out to a few connections through there. I think I've just landed my first client, in fact. The thought of becoming an independent designer away from the tyranny of the MacMillan empire—out from under the thumb of my *mother*—fills me up with bubbles inside.

Before I can continue to speak, my phone vibrates. I pull it away from my face and see who it is.

Mother. Of course. Everything in my life was just too happy. Why *wouldn't* she choose now to call me up?

I hit the ignore button, and continue my conversation with Dr. Salisbury. "Yes, I think that's a perfectly reasonable idea. It sounds like Mrs. Salisbury has excellent taste."

And there it is again, buzzing against my face like an unwanted gnat. I sigh internally.

"Dr. Salisbury, I apologize, but I have a call that I need to take from a family member. Yes, I'm sure all's fine, but I promise you'll be the first to know. Sure thing, same time tomorrow. Take care."

I end the call and pick up Mother's. "Yes?"

"Three months, young lady," is how she decides to start.

I sigh. "Mother, if you called me to do this all over again, now's not a good time."

"Oh, going to run off to that class you teach?"

I narrow my eyes, but remain silent.

"Yes, I know all about it. At a gym, with no personal clients. It's like I told you, no one is ever going to bother hiring a chubby girl to tell them how to get fit. The idea is positively absurd."

I can feel my heart rate rising and my skin starting to flush, but I take a breath, determined not to let her get to me.

"Mother, you don't know what you're talking about."

"I know exactly what I'm talking about, Caitlin MacMillan. I'm talking about a spoiled little brat in the middle of an early midlife crisis, who walks off her job and deserts her family in order to… what? To teach truck drivers and waitresses how to tone up for summer?"

I open my mouth to speak, but feel my throat closing up tight.

I'm not going to cry on this call, though.

I'm not going to give her the satisfaction.

"Mother," I finally force myself to say. "For your information, I have an interior design client. I'm starting my own firm."

"Oh," she says sarcastically. "*Now* you want to do your job? After you abandoned us in the middle of our busiest season? The summer seasonal was a complete bust, young lady, thanks to the fact that we were shorthanded on a minute's notice. *You* did that, Caitlin. I hope you're proud of yourself."

"I am," I murmur.

"You *what?*" she shouts at me.

"I *am*, Mother!" I shout right back.

"That's it, Caitlin. You know, I called to be a good sport and offer you one last chance to have your old job back in time for fall. But if this is your attitude now, I fear you've done nothing but lower yourself to the standards of those classless Boston townies, just like your grandfather did."

Just then, I hear the front door shut. I look over.

Thank God, it's Jack.

I've never been happier to see him, especially looking the way he does. My emotions are high and fraught, and watching him smile at me while he takes off his tie is doing all sorts of good things for me. Mostly, though, I'm just completely relieved. The knot in my throat loosens up, and I feel like I'm able to deal with this now.

I'm not alone, and I feel like I can handle anything.

"Did you hear me, young lady?" my mother snaps, and I realize I've missed more of the venom she's been spewing.

She'd maligned Sully, though. I hadn't missed *that*.

"Yes," I respond coldly. "I heard you. You keep that man's name out of your mouth."

She sputters for a second, not used to me standing up to her in the slightest. Then snarls, "And if you don't straighten that attitude out, *you* can feel free to keep the MacMillan name off of your business cards. No more chances. Everyone who is anyone will know that Caitlin MacMillan is a flake, pure and simple. Just another faux-artistic modernist in a sea of mediocrity."

"You do whatever you think you have to do, Mother," I say, and hang up the phone before she can respond.

It feels good.

"So," Jack says, sitting down next to me on the couch. "That was ol' coal squeezer herself, eh?"

"You know it," I say, shaking my head with a sigh. "It's like she somehow monitors my happiness level, then calls me whenever she knows it's just too damn high."

"Believe me, I remember," Jack says, and we take a moment to laugh about the memory of that day in the kitchen.

I really had lost it when she'd called that time. But then again, it had definitely led to very good things.

"God," I start, tension easing out of me. "That feels like ages ago now."

"Yeah, that wasn't either of our finest days," he says, wrapping an arm around me.

I smile and snuggle in.

"I hate her," I say. It feels wrong to think that of one's own mother, but it's true, and it feels good to say out loud. "I just *hate* her. She's an evil, nasty woman, and always has been."

"Hell, I can relate to that," Jack says, squeezing me a little closer.

I can hear his heart beating through his chest, and it soothes my entire body.

"My old man makes my ma call me up just to ask for money," he adds, rubbing his hand up and down against my arm in a soothing rhythm. "Once a week, minimum, I gotta hear her go on and on about who pisses off who, who stabbed who in the back, who's in jail now, who just got outta jail, how much my old man lost at the track, oh and by the way could you send some money?

Least I can do because they raised me up so well, apparently." He shakes his head. "Pricks. The whole lot of 'em. At least we had Sully, I guess, right?"

"Agreed," I say. "Only the summers for me, though."

"Y'know," he starts, "I really used to think you were just some spoiled rich kid, way back then. Just another socialite's daughter, lookin' down your nose at me and my thrift store clothes."

"I was just shy."

I sigh. If only I'd learned to stand up for myself at a younger age, would my life have turned out differently? But then again, I really like where it's at now, so maybe everything had a purpose after all.

"I was shy and terrified," I go on, wanting Jack to understand. "Because you were so gorgeous and dangerous and everything that I'd never seen before in my life. And there I was, just a fat mess with too many pimples and no self-esteem. I couldn't have ever landed someone like you in a million years, as far as young me was concerned."

"Hey," Jack says, stroking my cheek. "That's all bullshit. You were gorgeous even back then. I just, y'know, thought that you didn't talk to me because of who I was and where I came from. I was so jealous of what you had. Money, Sully, this house."

"I guess that makes two of us," I say. "I was so jealous of your looks, the way you swung around like you could handle anything in the world. Sully loved you more than he loved me."

Jack laughs, shaking his head as he squeezes me close. "That's not true."

"I was just a little fat girl who didn't know what she wanted. I kept failing at everything I tried."

"Hey, now," he says, pulling my head back and kissing me on the forehead. "No more of that, okay?"

"But—"

"No buts," he cuts me off. "None of that is true, Cate. None of that was ever true. We all know better now. I know I do, Duchess. I'm sorry we lost so much time to it."

"Me too," I say, patting his arm. "It's okay. We have this now, and that's the important part."

"It's really too bad you can't just *choose* your family, isn't it?" he asks, grinning at me.

I laugh. "Definitely. *God*. I would divorce mine if I could."

"You ain't the only one," he says.

"Well hey, you two," comes a voice from the door.

Both of us crane our necks back to see Dylan, looking exhausted but elated, and so damn good in those jeans and that black v-neck. It clings to his body in all the right ways.

"Maybe we can, eh?" Dylan makes a gesture that encompasses all of us.

I smile, relaxing in Jack's arms. "You're right. Maybe we can. Maybe we already have?" I ask, looking up at Jack.

"Yeah," he says, and I can hear the relaxation soaking in his voice. "I think we already did. Get over here, Dylan, you're missing out on some prime-time snuggling here."

He does, and we end up wrapped up in each other on the couch, bodies touching one another in a perfect, safe pocket that's just our own and no one else's.

This is us.

This works.

And I'm safe here.

## 26

## JACK

"Mr. Kelly!" Gary exclaims as I walk into his office. He's put together, as always, perfect pocket square and all. If anyone did suits better than me or Sully, it was Gary for sure.

"Gary, how's it going with you?" I reach out and we shake hands.

"It's been a trying week," Gary says. "As they say in film, I'm getting too old for this shit."

I laugh and shake my head. "Y'know, that might be the first time I've ever heard you swear."

"Oh, well." He smiles and rounds back to his side of the desk. "I was in the Navy for a few years out of high school. You pick up one or two curses in the line of duty."

"I bet," I say, still grinning.

"So! I understand you want to discuss the terms of the contract for Mr. Sullivan's property," Gary says, flipping open a folder on his desk.

"I do," I say.

"Excellent. I'm certain we can find a buyer with no trouble at all, once everyone signs the appropriate paperwork."

"Actually," I start, "We've, uh, decided to keep the house."

"Oh!" Gary exclaims, looking puzzled. "Forgive my surprise, Mr. Kelly, you just seemed so adamant before about wanting to sell."

"Yeah, well, a lot's changed since then."

Christ, has it ever. So much. I know a ridiculous smile is stretching my cheeks, but can't stop it.

"Very well," Gary continues, nodding. "Then all I need to know is who we're transferring the deed to, and I can have this sealed and delivered by courier in no time at all."

"Perfect," I say. "It's going to be distributed equally between the three of us, so just let me know what I have to have all of us sign, and I can handle that on my end right away."

"Oh," Gary says, and I tense a little, because his tone of voice doesn't sound good.

"What's the problem, Gary?"

"Well, Mr. Kelly, per the terms and conditions of Mr. Sullivan's will, it's just not possible to put the house in everyone's name. You've read it over?"

I did. I mean, I skimmed it. Like I've said, estate law is not my area, and now it sounds like maybe I missed something that I should have looked a little deeper into. Unless Gary just doesn't get what I'm saying?

"No, see, we're looking at joint tenancy here," I explain. "We're all okay with owning equal portions. Want it that way, so that no one person has power over anyone else."

The slight tightening at the corners of his mouth tells me it ain't gonna be that simple.

*Shit.*

"That's just the problem, Mr. Kelly," he says, folding his hands on top of the desk in front of him. "Joint tenancy, amongst other forms of ownership, are not options per the will." He takes out a pair of small, round reading glasses, and flips through a couple of pages in the will. "Mr. Sullivan was quite thorough in his stipulations. He's set it up so that your only viable option is for one single entity to retain sole ownership of the property. If that doesn't happen by the specified deadline—" a couple of weeks, if I'm remembering it right, "—the property must be sold, and funds will be distributed equally amongst the three of you."

I can't believe what I'm hearing. Sully must've had a reason, but I don't get it. One thing I do know, though, was that he knew his stuff. Unusual or not, if that's the way he wanted it, the will is gonna be rock-solid. No loopholes available, and of course Gary will follow it to the letter.

I feel the office start to close in around me, and I shake my head, wanting him to tell me something different, even though I'm thinking that hope's probably in vain.

"That can't be right," I say. "Why would Sully do that?"

"Well, obviously, I cannot speak directly as to Mr. Sullivan's intentions," Gary starts, taking his reading glasses off. "But I can only imagine that he wanted to ensure that the three of you really take your time with this decision, and determine who the best caretaker shall be. He hated seeing any of you fight. Maybe this was his way of trying to ensure that peace was to be made, in one form or another."

"Alright, alright," I say, holding my hands up. Gary's got no more useful insight than I do, but the man is thorough. If this is the way it is, then this is the way it is, I just... "I just don't know what I'm going to tell the others. I don't think we're comfortable having this in just one of our names." I look Gary in the eye. "When do we have to make this decision by?"

Gary moves the folder aside to look at the large calendar blotter on his desk. "Today is Monday, July 17th, and it appears that the decision must be made in full by Tuesday, August 1st."

I sigh, pinching the bridge of my nose. "We want to make this our family home, here," I mumble.

Gary's eyebrows shoot up in surprise. "Your... family home? For the three of you?"

I grimace. Yeah, probably sounds weird.

"It's complicated," I say, shaking my head, but he doesn't press it. Doesn't even look judgmental, even, which is refreshing.

"I am most sincerely sorry for all of this," Gary says, looking genuinely sympathetic to how he sees me taking all of this. "For what it's worth, I am very glad that the three of you seemed to work out your differences. I think Mr. Sullivan would have been very pleased about that. And, if I may—he considered all of you family. I know this for a fact. Whatever your arrangement, I have no doubt that he'd approve."

"Goddamn, Gary, I just..." I shake my head. "I don't know what I'm gonna do here. How do we work it out?"

He looks pained, and I know he hates not having an answer. "Well, perhaps—"

"No, no," I say, cutting him off and standing up. It's not his problem to solve. He's doing what Sully asked of him. "It's alright. This isn't your fault, I know you're just executing the will. I just gotta figure out how we're going to deal with this."

Gary stands up and nods sadly, holding out his hand. "Very well, Mr. Kelly. Again, my sincerest apologies; it's not my intention to stand in the way of your wishes."

"I know, bud," I say, and shake his hand. "We'll figure it out and be in touch."

"Please take care," Gary says as I walk out the door.

By the time I'm back on the street, my mind is already racing for solutions. I have no idea how I'm going to break this to them. *Can* I break this to them? After all we've done to get this far in our relationship? Things have been so good, so damn good, and I'm just not willing to do anything that will jeopardize this peace that we've all found with each other.

I mean, I guess we could just figure out one of us to put on the deed. We're all pretty committed here. But all I can think about now is how much money I'm putting into the renovations, and how much work Cate has been doing to redecorate the entire house from the ground up. And Dylan, my God, he's the one that makes it our home, a safe ground for all of us to coexist together.

It just won't feel right unless it belongs to all of us. It wouldn't be fair to any of us, not now, not when we just figured out our triad. But that's not the kind of relationship—the kind of family— that gets recognized any way but in our hearts now, is it?

Shit.

Fucking *shit*.

I take a breath, pushing back my knee-jerk rage. No, I'll figure something out. Cate and Dylan have done more than enough to make sure that the townhouse is transformed into our home.

It's my turn to fix this.

# 27

## DYLAN

*G*od, this summer sure is gorgeous. I can't get enough of the sunshine. I know Cate and Jack chafe under the humidity, but I love it. I've always loved it. The more light, the better, as far as I'm concerned.

We spent the last week clearing out Sully's old patio together. It was the one place that he'd just genuinely never seemed all that interested in, back in the day. Or maybe, now that I think of it, he knew it was one of the places *we* loved, and left it for us. Cate, Jack and I used to treat it like our own personal jungle, weaving in and out of the overgrown plants and grass. Hours of imaginative play, or just a place to get away.

Of all the work we've done on the house so far, though, this might have been the roughest part of all. Not that it took us very long to clear out all of the old plants and clean up the leftover junk, but as we did, it became rapidly apparent that we were gonna have to sink a whole hell of a lot of cash into this venture. By the time that phase was done, we were left with just a big drab square of cracked cement.

At least, that's all *I* could see.

Cate, of course, saw what it *could* be with her designer's eye, and funding it? Well, Jack really came through. Boy, did he ever. We were able to get the cement redone in no time flat, and even got to add a platform area in the back. We surrounded it with very tasteful polished oak planters; Cate's idea. On top of that, Jack and I decided that we would build our very own brick barbecue together, something the two of us can do over beers.

Now, it still needs a whole lot of work and a whole lot of love, but I think we're all willing to put both into it. For now, I'm just happy to have ourselves an outdoor space for summer. We added some nice patio furniture, and it's become one of our favorite places to spend time together on nice days like this.

"Hey Dylan, where's that pizza?" Jack shouts at me.

I laugh. "It's coming, just hang on like two more seconds, okay?"

"I dunno. I'm an impatient man," he teases, throwing me a sexy wink.

"Oh, you'll get what you need," I promise, loving that he's okay with this kind of playful banter now.

"Hey, lovely," Cate calls out to me. "If you need a hand, let me know, otherwise I'm gonna mix us up another round of sangria."

Sangria sounds perfect right now. I slice up the homemade pizza on the stove, eager to get out there and join them, and then I hear the knock at the door.

Strange. We have a doorbell; only the delivery driver knocks, and it's Saturday.

"Want me to get it?"

That was Cate, but I'm closer. And I don't want to interrupt the important work she's doing. We definitely need those sangrias.

"No worries, it'll just be a sec," I call back to her, smiling. I wipe off my hands and dab at the sweat on my brow, throwing the towel over my shoulder as I walk for the door.

Before I can get there, it opens.

"Excuse me," I say, taken aback. "This is a private residence."

"Well, you certainly took long enough to open the door."

It's the voice that clicks, and I finally recognize this woman. It's Julianne MacMillan, Cate's mother.

"Oh, hello there," I say, going for a smile again. I know Cate isn't particularly fond of her mother, but I'm not going to be the one to add to the pressure. I can be pleasant to her. "It's Dylan, Ms. MacMillan."

I hold out my hand, and she stares at it like I'm offering her a strange and interesting bug. Then she stares up at my face. It takes her a moment before I see the clouds part. Recognition.

"Oh, right. Dylan *Smith*, is it? You're the chef's boy, right?"

"That's right." That's how she'd known me, I guess.

"Did Cate hire you to cook for her?" she asks.

I almost sputter, but do my best not to laugh. "I beg your pardon?"

"You know." She leans in conspiratorially. "Diet food and all."

I cross my arms, my good humor fading. It's amazing Cate has turned out as phenomenal as she is, with this woman as her mother.

"Let me just take you to your daughter," I tell her, reminding myself this isn't my fight.

But I'm damn sure going to jump in if needed.

"Yes, do lead the way," Ms. MacMillan says dismissively, as if speaking to a servant.

I turn around and roll my eyes when I'm certain she can't see, but lead her through to the back of the house. I'm sure Cate isn't expecting her.

"My God," the woman says behind me, and I tense at the utter cattiness in her voice. "Just *look* at this place. It's even uglier than I remember it. I assume Cate's behind all of... this?"

I see her flap her hand out of the corner of my eye, a gesture encompassing the entire interior of the townhouse, and I have to grit my teeth to hold in the comeback that springs to mind.

Normally, I like to pride myself on being calm and easygoing, but this woman is making it a challenge and a half.

"Excuse me," she says sharply. "I'm *talking* to you. What did you say your name was again? Smith?"

"Yes, Ms. MacMillan," I respond tightly, opening the sliding door onto the patio.

Jack and Cate both look in our direction, snapped out of their conversation at the sight of Cate's mother, and I wish I could have sent them some sort of psychic warning.

"Right," Ms. MacMillan says, brushing past me. "*Smith*. Such a common name. So… forgettable."

"Mother," Cate says, her eyes narrowing.

Cate's expression has me smiling a little, despite her mother's utter bitchiness. Not that I care what she thinks of my "common" name. That kind of thing has never meant much to me. But I really don't like the thought that her dismissive, condescending attitude toward me might hurt Cate.

Cate's definitely looking less put out than I'd have thought, though, and the shine in her eyes combined with the pitcher of sangria on the table make me think that she might be just a tiny bit buzzed.

Good for her.

Lord knows it will help dealing with *this* old bat.

"There you are, darling," Cate's mother says, swooping toward her, the flamboyancy of her greeting doing nothing to make up for the insincerity of its tone. Cate flinches just a little, and the sight immediately raises my hackles.

"Cate, are you sure this is okay?" I ask, frowning.

"It's fine, Dylan," Cate responds, sitting up straighter and waving me over. "Come and sit. I'm sure this won't take long."

I look between Cate, Jack, and Ms. MacMillan. Yeah. I doubt this will end well. Regardless, I honor Cate's request and move over to the patio table, taking my seat between her and Jack. I'm happy to offer her my support in whatever way she wants it.

Cate's mother eyes Jack and me with a sour look on her face. "So, you're eating with the help now, I see, dear."

Our Cate tenses a little, but replies calmly enough, "Dylan and Jack are my friends, Mother."

Jack and I exchange looks, and it's an unspoken agreement: If this woman does anything to hurt Cate, we're hauling her out of here in a heartbeat.

Ms. MacMillan gives a delicate snort. "The cook and the errand boy, right. I shouldn't expect anything less from you."

"Jesus, Mother, what the hell is the matter with you?" Cate bursts out, an angry flush creeping onto her cheeks. "Did you come all the way to Boston to show up unannounced just to lecture me? Belittle me? In my own home?"

"*Your* home? I beg your pardon, but this is only *your* home because no one would take this ratty old place off your hands in a million years." Ms. MacMillan gestures back toward the house. "Those colors... positively *garish*, and your drapes make the place look like filth. Like a common whore's boudoir."

I open my mouth, my blood beginning to boil, but Jack cuts in first.

"Hey, now," he says sharply, coming half out of his chair.

"Don't you *dare* interrupt me, young man," Cate's mother says sharply, cutting into Jack with her verbal razor.

I don't know if it's just ingrained respect for the fact that she's Sully's daughter, or what, but Jack backs down, jaw clenched tightly. I can see his muscles tensing up, too, and his fist clenching and unclenching.

I love this man; I'm so happy that he and I are on the same page right now.

If she tries to go too far, that's it.

"And *you*, Cate, just look at yourself," Ms. MacMillan continues, shaking her head as she dismisses Jack completely and turns right back on Cate. "The Smith boy must be feeding you the same garbage that comes from his old neighborhood, wherever it was he lived before your grandfather took his mother in."

Jack almost comes out of his chair again, but I put a hand on his arm as Cate's shoulders stiffen. Ms. MacMillan's insults to me and my mother roll right off me for my own sake. Her opinion means less than nothing to me. Besides, I can see that Cate needs to face this demon.

We've got her back, but it's her fight.

"Mother," she says after a couple of deep breaths, sounding almost bored. "Is that all you've come to say?"

I smile on the inside. Good for her. My own mother is wonderful, and it's hard to imagine what growing up must have been like for either her or Jack when it comes to having such awful family. I don't know what I'd do if my mother ever talked to me the way Cate's mother talks to her—it would never happen—but Cate's handling it well so far.

Not losing her cool.

Not yet, anyway.

Ms. MacMillan is on a roll, though. "You just keep gaining weight, Cate. Keep letting yourself go, and you're only getting older, you know. It's a miracle you haven't had a heart attack from all those gym classes you teach. Although maybe it'd be just as well; who in their right mind would date someone who looks like you do?"

*What?*

Who says that kind of thing to their own flesh and blood? To *anyone*? That's it for me. I'm on my feet at the same time as Jack, who looks as angry as I feel, face like a storm cloud and muscles rippling through his shirt as he clenches those brawler fists again.

"I don't *think* so, lady—" I start.

"That's about enough of *that* shit," from Jack.

"Boys," Cate says, her calm tone cutting us both off mid-rant.

Jack and I both freeze, because really, we'd do anything for her.

Anything to protect her from harm, verbal or otherwise. The three of us, always united, always having each other's backs.

"It's okay," she says to us, and I can see by her smile that it really *is*. "Sit down, please. I'll take care of my mother."

She rises from her chair and faces Julianne, and as riled up as I am, I can't help but think how sexy it is, watching her come into her own. She knows she's the queen of *this* domain, and even though I'm still outraged at her mother's over-the-top harshness, I can't help but grin.

I'm pretty sure Julianne MacMillan is about to be set in her place.

# 28

## CATE

*O*kay, I'm a little drunk, a little sun-touched, maybe, but *fuck... this.* I draw myself up to my full height, eyes locked on my mother's bitter face and fully aware that Jack and Dylan are sitting down only at my behest, still poised to leap to my defense if I give them the tiniest signal.

I love them so much, but this is my battle, one I should have fought a long time ago, but that my own hope of having an actually *decent* mother kept me from. But her coming *here*, being this cruel and callous in my own home? My mother just burned the last shreds of that hope like paper.

And somehow, shockingly, it doesn't hurt. It makes me feel... *free.*

There's truly nothing to be salvaged between us, nothing to preserve by holding back. The last ties of family that bind her and me might as well be ribbons of ash, blowing away in the wind.

Good riddance.

"Julianne."

Her eyes narrow at that, but she's not "Mother" to me anymore. Was she ever?

Or maybe it's my tone. I'm using the kind of slow, unbothered voice I used to hear from the few society women Grandpa Sully actually *liked*, the ones who had spent so many years handling their own business, fighting their own battles, that their reputations meant they rarely *had* to fight anymore.

This is the tone they'd use when someone new started to act up, the one that someone like my mother would instantly recognize. It told everyone within earshot that gauche rage and worked-up temper was utterly unnecessary. The calm was their due, and they were the most dangerous thing in the room.

That *here there be dragons,* and the dragon herself was right there in front of you, smiling all the while.

I'm faking the confidence right now—bolstered by the alcohol and my men and the time I've spent out from under her thumb these past months—but as my chin lifts, it starts to feel real. It truly doesn't matter what she thinks of me. I don't have to prove anything; the people who matter already know who I am.

She sucks in a breath as if she's about to launch another verbal attack, but this new confidence in me, this *surety,* makes me smile. It's a wide, sharklike grin, and as it spreads across my face, something flickers in my mother's eyes, something that might be surprise, might be fear.

Her eyes widen, and I suspect that for the first time ever, she's seeing who I truly am instead of who she tried to badger me into being.

And that flicker? *That* tells me she isn't prepared for who I've become, not one bit.

*Good.*

"You aren't welcome here, Julianne," I say, like I'm explaining something obvious, something that's inarguable fact. "You're behaving poorly, and I'd say it's beneath you, but you clearly have no lower depths to which you won't sink. It's *vile*, and it's unworthy of me, and I won't have it in my house."

She opens her mouth to spit more ugliness and I wave a hand sharply. I don't have any more patience to put up with whatever she might say. Her mouth snaps shut so fast, it's like she's a puppet whose strings I've just cut, and it's a heady feeling.

This is *my* home.

This is who I *am*.

She's insulted everything about me, including the men I love, and I'm done with it.

"You're casually cruel, and it's unacceptable," I tell her. "You can't see the truth of how things are, even when they're right in front of your face. I'm healthy, I'm happy, and I have a beautiful home shared with people who love me."

Dylan's hand brushes against my fingers, the barest ghost of a touch, and his steady support and love flows through me. Her eyes flick down to track the movement and then skitter away, a look of distaste on her face.

"My life is *good*, Julianne," I go on. "And I can see my happiness makes you just sick, but do you know how much your opinion matters to me now? How much all your bitter nonsense matters, all your pathetic attempts to hurt me because you can't stand how unhappy you are in your own life?" I slowly raise my fist up near my face, turning it palm-out toward her, then my fingers explode outward as though I'm flicking water into her face. "Not even *that* much."

My mother is practically vibrating with rage now, but that's all there is. There's no remorse in her expression. No apology. If I was still harboring any soft feelings for her, any thought that we might one day have a loving mother–daughter relationship, that fury in her face strangles it like a black vine strangles flowers.

"Now," I say, and I sound so *bored*, so regal, that it shocks even me. "*Get. The fuck. Out. Of my house.*"

I take a step toward her with each word, and, wonder of wonders—my mother, the infamous, monstrous bitch Julianne

MacMillan, the bane of my existence and terror of my heart since I was a little girl?—*she backs up*. She retreats as I advance, her face losing any semblance of composure as she realizes just how badly she misjudged me, how woefully unprepared she is for this confrontation. How much she's overstepped.

"If that's the way you want things to be, Caitlin," she sniffs, making a weak attempt to straighten her shoulders. Her voice is just a ghost of her usual commanding tones, though, thin and reedy, and we both know she's lost.

I flick a hand in her direction, dismissing her as I turn away.

"Don't ever come back to this house, Julianne. I *will* have the Boston police escort you off the property if you do." I glance back at her and give her the merest flicker of a smile, more a bared-teeth promise than an expression of mirth. *Try me,* my smile says. "And won't *that* be a diverting story for the New York City society pages—Julianne MacMillan arrested for trespassing in Boston, how *gauche*. How *common*. You'll be the talk of the town, for a season. And then?"

She flinches, and I name her worst nightmare.

"Then they'll all *forget you*."

The color drains from her face, and she clutches at her handbag with a white-knuckled grip. She sniffs, trying again to seem imperious, but the balance of power has shifted in my favor and she's never, ever going to get it back. Her mouth works like a fish's, opening and shutting on the air, but all she manages is a haughty-sounding, "Well!"

"Dylan, love, please show my mother out," I say, lightly running my fingers over his broad shoulder.

My mother flinches so hard at *love* that I can practically feel it. Good. Fuck... her.

Dylan looks up at me, pride and affection all over his gorgeous features. "It'd be my pleasure," he rumbles, beginning to stand.

*"I don't need your help!"* my mother shrieks at him. "I know the

way, I'll—" she licks her thin lips. "*Well.* I know when I'm not wanted."

"Oh, thank God," I can't help but drawl. "I was beginning to think I'd have to be *rude* about it."

Jack stifles a sudden bark of laughter with his fist, coughs into it, and my mother's face turns fire-engine red. She pivots on her heel and stalks off, not even bothering to close the patio doors behind her. A moment later, I hear a muffled *thunk-click* from the front door of the townhouse and I grin; from the sound of it, my mother just tried to slam the heavy new door we installed and utterly failed.

It's like the cherry on a perfect ice cream sundae—*delicious.*

And then it hits me. She's *gone.* Not just from the townhouse—although, thank God for that—but from my life.

I can breathe again.

I sink into my chair and take the glass of sangria Dylan presses into my hand. It tastes like victory. Okay, it tastes like strawberry and blackberry and peach and alcohol, but it might as well be the same thing.

"Oh, my God," I breathe, suddenly unable to stop giggling. "I thought she was never going to leave."

I feel giddy, balloon-light; I hadn't even realized how much pressure my mother held over me, even now, until I let it all go. The freedom is dizzying.

"Okay, so," Jack begins, "This might not be real appropriate right now?" I look over at him, and he's looking at me with what I can only describe as awe. "That was *hot as fuck,* Cate."

"I know, right?" Dylan mutters. "You see Coal-Squeezer's face? I thought I was gonna lose it."

I shake my head, laughing. "I can't believe I just did that."

"I can't believe you didn't do it sooner," Jack counters with a grin. He squeezes my bare shoulder. "You know none of the bullshit she was spouting was true, right? It's never been true."

I take a deep breath, and then another. In and out, willing my pounding heart to slow.

"I know." I *do*. "I just... she's been saying those things for my whole life, you know? It's really easy to forget that it isn't the truth, it's just *her* truth."

Dylan and Jack share a look I can't fathom, then Dylan says, "Are you saying you'd like some help remembering just how amazing you are, Cate?"

"I volunteer," Jack throws in, raising a hand and giving me a look hot enough to scorch. "Pretty sure Dylan and I both can fill those shoes, anytime."

I blush. It's one thing to be confident, it's quite another to accept the adoration in their eyes. I see it all the time, but I don't know that I'll ever get *used* to it. I open my mouth to joke around with them, but Dylan's finger covers my lips, shushing me.

"You were incredible, Cate."

"*Are* incredible," Jack adds, his hand kneading the back of my neck.

Heaven.

"Let us show you."

Before I can answer, Dylan is on his feet. He picks me right up out of my chair, holding me against his broad chest as Jack makes quick work of pushing the little table out of the way and rearranging our patio furniture.

My heart starts to race.

I'm not sure what they're intending, but it already feels naughty. *Decadent*. Something we should take inside, even though the sun feels so good and I don't really want to leave this space. This sweet patio that we've made our own. The place I finally came into my own and stood up for myself, once and for all.

Jack's got one of our plush, cushioned lounge chairs laid flat now, and I half-expect Dylan to set me down on it. I'm thrilled and a little titillated, a little scared, of getting intimate with them outdoors like this. Yes, our patio is walled and pretty private, but it's the middle of the day. We have neighbors. We have—

"Oooooh," I breathe out, a sound of pure pleasure as Dylan sets me not on the lounge, but back on my feet. He does it the way he does everything, though... *sensually*. His hands glide over every inch of my body as he lowers me down; he slides me against his body and steadies me once my feet touch the ground.

*God*, it's erotic.

"That's right, Duchess," Jack whispers, stepping in close and turning me to face him. Kissing me with a hunger that takes my breath away.

"You don't have to do anything but feel good right now," Dylan whispers from behind me, his hands skimming down my body, over my waist, down past my thighs to the hem of the sundress I'm wearing—and then back up. Lifting it off over my head as Jack obligingly breaks our kiss to let him pass.

I'm standing in the sun in nothing but a skimpy pair of lace panties and no bra—it wasn't that kind of dress—and I feel—

"Beautiful."

"*Gorgeous.*"

Jack goes to his knees in front of me as Dylan pushes my hair aside from behind, his mouth landing on the back of my neck. His large hands send shivers through me as they glide up my sides and cup my breasts, teasing my nipples.

"Jack, what... ?" I start to ask, but I'm already feeling drugged from the pleasure, from the sun, the sangria, the heady after-effects of the emotional high from standing up to my mother.

Jack doesn't answer me anyway, just shakes his head and grins up at me. I let out a sigh of surrender, my eyes fluttering closed as I lean back against Dylan's hard body, letting him support me.

Jack's hands slowly glide up my calves, up the insides of my thighs. His fingertips stroke the soft flesh of my inner thighs, sending little lightning bolts over the sensitive skin. It feels incredible, but I cringe in spite of myself—no matter how much I work out or diet, I've never been able to get rid of that plumpness at the top of my thighs, never been able to attain a thigh gap. It's one of the parts of my body I've always worked hardest to hide, and Jack makes a beeline right for it.

Now that I think about it, he *always* makes a point to touch this part of my body; the realization surprises me, shakes the foundations of what I think of as my Good and Bad physical features, and a wave of that confidence in who I am washes over me again.

I spread my legs wider, inviting him in.

"Your ma's wrong about everything," Jack says, the husky tone of his voice making me shiver. "Your body's strong, and healthy, and fuckin' *smoking hot.*"

He turns me in his grasp, his breath hot on the curve of my waist, and I wrap my arms around Dylan's neck, leaning into the devouring kiss he gives me as Jack's hands and words and love continue to move over me from behind.

"I fucking *love* this part of you," Jack whispers, kneading and squeezing the pillowy insides of my thighs. "Your thighs are so plush and sexy, so damn soft." I feel his teeth graze over my hip and I shiver. "I could stay between them all day. I love the way they cushion my face when I'm going down on you, my hips when I drive into you. I love the sound it makes when I'm fucking you and my hips smack into your skin."

Oh... *God.* His words make me whimper, and Dylan's hands tangle in my hair as he sucks the sound down like wine.

Jack's fingers hook into the edge of my panties, tugging them down, and Dylan's hot mouth trails across my jaw, down my throat, lower... lower... until he's kneeling, too. I step out of my panties, bracketed by these two men, and shock myself with how comfortable I am, naked and exposed like this.

Dylan's mouth stops at my belly, and he splays his fingers across it. It's always been another "problem area"—I've got a strong core, but abs are made in the kitchen, and I've certainly been spending more time in the kitchen these past months than my old usual of a grilled chicken breast and salad requires.

I let it go.

I have to.

The way Dylan is leaning in, kissing... caressing... loving my curvy flesh, it's positively *reverent*.

He smiles against my skin, the warmth spreading through me like a tiny sun. "You're perfect, Cate. Always have been, always will be."

"You're a fuckin' *goddess*, Cate," Jack agrees, his hands on my ass. Kneading. Stroking. Nipping at the sensitive spot at the top of my thighs. The hunger and adoration in his voice... in his touch... making me *believe*. "We could spend all day showing you just how perfect you are, go over every inch of you, make you really believe the truth about who you are to us. A goddess."

I twist enough to rest one hand on his head, the other on Dylan's, like I'm a priestess giving them a blessing. I smile down at my gorgeous, sexy partners, my loves, my men. I want this. Want them. Want to feel powerful and sexy and strong.

I take a deep breath, reveling in it. "Then *worship* me," I tell them. "Show me I'm yours."

Dylan's mouth is on me before the words finish leaving my mouth, and I gasp, feeling wanton as he lifts one of my thighs and drapes my leg over his shoulder, his tongue parting my folds and lapping at me with abandon. Jack's hands steady me from behind, keeping a firm grip on my hips and then, once he can see I've got my balance, caressing them. Sliding down the outside of my thighs and then circling back up, cupping the rounded bottoms of my cheeks.

Jack's thumbs dip into my crease, teasing my back entrance as a flood of naughty, loving words flows out of his mouth. I can tell that hearing him is getting to Dylan just as much as it is to me, and the groan he makes vibrates against my clit, making me gasp.

It's so right and so wrong, all at the same time, to be standing totally naked with the sun kissing my skin while these two amazing men prop me up, drive me crazy, *worship* me, just like I'd asked. And then Jack's hands become more insistent. He pushes me forward, until I'm leaning over Dylan, holding Dylan's shoulders for support as the position pushes my throbbing sex against his talented tongue.

And Jack... oh God. Oh... *God*.

He's parted my cheeks and is kissing... biting... licking his way toward the hidden part of me we've all come to love. When his tongue finally flicks over my little pink star, I cry out, the unexpected sensation sending a bolt of electricity to my clit. Jack doesn't wait to see if I'll like it, though; somehow, he *knows*.

He knows me so well.

He licks me with firm, steady strokes, circling... sucking... thrusting his tongue against my quivering entrance while Dylan does the same to my front. I'm mindless with it. Even when I've taken both of them at once, discovered the pleasure that anal play can bring, I've never felt anything like *this*.

My knees are useless, and I'm so wet that my juice runs down my thighs. The faint sound of traffic from the road and the splashing of a bird in the birdbath I know our neighbor installed last week feels surreal. I'm shaking, trembling as their mouths drive me toward a kind of bliss that I'm not sure I'll recover from. The kind that will tell me I'm theirs forever.

"Oh, God," I gasp, my fingers tightening in Dylan's hair.

Thank God they're holding me up, or I would have already melted into a puddle at their feet.

"Oh... *God*. Dylan," I pant, and then all I can do is try to breathe... let the hot, needy moans tumble from my mouth... hold on for dear life as they take me apart, lick by lick. Stroke by stroke.

Jack's tongue breaches me, pushing in and taking what's his, and I explode, grinding against Dylan's face as he sucks my clit with a quick, relentless, fluttering rhythm that pulls my orgasm out of me in endless waves.

"Jack."

And oh... oh... ohhhhhhhh... "Dylan."

Every cell in my body explodes in pleasure as my orgasm rushes through me, a chain reaction of ecstasy that goes on and on and *on*, that makes me come undone. I don't know if I've closed my eyes or if the power of it simply whited out my vision, but I can't see a thing. Can't move. Have gone boneless and turned into jelly. Am still in the throes of the aftershocks and only vaguely aware that their strong hands are still holding me up... lifting me... continuing to worship my body with firm strokes and gentle, teasing touches on my stomach... my breasts... my throat... my thighs.

"Duchess, you're amazing," Jack says reverently.

"Utterly perfect," Dylan whispers.

I open my eyes lazily, and realize they've laid me out on the chaise lounge, the way I'd expected at first. I feel decadent. Free. Naked in the sun. And somehow, they've managed to remove their clothes while I was being rocked by those waves of bliss.

My men are standing above me, towering over me, protecting me and worshipping me. And, better, they're both huge and hard and naked, and my body reacts. Knowing it's theirs... knowing they're *mine*. I'm still languid and replete with pleasure, but my legs fall open of their own accord, a frisson of excitement starting deep in my core.

I would be happy to watch them together. They're so amazingly hot that way. But I'm feeling greedy. Selfish. *Entitled*. I want them to fuck *me* right now. I want both of them.

"Wildcat," Jack whispers, the flare of heat in his eyes as he starts to stroke himself telling me I don't have to say it out loud. He can read me.

Dylan wraps an arm around Jack's neck, claiming a hot kiss that makes all three of us moan, and then he lets go and moves to my side. Lifts me like I weigh nothing at all and takes my place. He's on his back, and when he eases me down on top of him, positioning me so that we're both facing up—facing Jack—my back cradled by Dylan's big, hard body, I whimper.

This is another side of me, the one that knows that even though I don't *need* them to, these two men will always take care of me. That it's okay to put myself in their hands and let them have their way with me.

That their way will *always* have my pleasure in mind.

Without pausing, Dylan impales me on his cock, his thick girth sliding in to the hilt easily now that I'm so relaxed from my first orgasm. It still stretches me—always will—and I moan, sprawling back on top of him shamelessly as the sun warms my nipples.

Jack's hand starts to move faster on his cock as he stands above us, watching.

"Fuck her, Dylan," he whispers. "She's so relaxed. So beautiful. Get her ready to share."

I don't have to do a thing except let it happen, and Dylan's hands on my hips move me, sliding me up and down his body, letting his length stroke my slick channel and rekindle the passion they always inspire in me.

"Jack," I say… try to say. My mouth is dry and I still feel almost floaty with pleasure. I lick my lips and try again, thankful I don't have to do more than speak. "I want you, too."

"He's yours," Dylan whispers in my ear, his hot breath sending a cascade of erotic tingles racing through my body as he keeps slowly rocking in and out of me from below. "He's *ours*."

I moan.

*Yes.*

And I don't have to ask again. These men are so perfect. So perfect for *me*.

My thighs are draped over Dylan's, his hands on my hips and my ass cradled by his groin as he fucks me… as he moves my body on top of his like I weigh nothing—like I don't need to *do* anything. Like he'll take care of me.

And he will. They both will.

Dylan and Jack understand me—body, heart, and soul—and I let my head fall back against Dylan's shoulder and arch my breasts up as I watch Jack through hooded eyes.

"Fucking gorgeous," he whispers reverently, straddling my thighs and lowering himself down to kiss me.

His hands are braced on Dylan's shoulders, and he kisses my jaw… nips at the corner of my lips… plunders my mouth… presses against me so that I'm pinned between these two hot, hard bodies as they give me exactly what I'd asked for.

As they worship me.

Dylan is still fucking into me slowly, whispering sweet, wicked things to the both of us, and when Jack starts to *move*—his hard cock rubbing back and forth against my clit—I can't help it. I start to writhe between them, moaning. Begging with my body as Jack keeps control of my mouth and Dylan's hands take charge of my every move.

Every touch, every stroke, awakens more of that lovely, shuddering, electrified heat inside me that both these men inspire so easily. And they're drawing it out. Making sure I don't come yet. But oh God, oh *yesssssss*, the things they're doing to me… it's going to be so good when I do.

So, *so* good.

"Pull her legs up, Dylan," Jack says, releasing my mouth with a sexy groan. He pushes himself up to look down at us. "Christ, do you know how hot the two of you look?"

Dylan slides his large hands under my rear, down the backs of my thighs, slotting them in behind my knees and rolling me upward. He arches his hips so that his cock stays buried inside me and locks my bent knees over his arms, the hard muscles of his stomach flexing under my ass.

It feels amazing.

"Trust me, Duchess?" Jack asks, running an impossibly gentle hand down the side of my face.

There was a time when that question would have sounded ridiculous, but now? I can see in his face that he doesn't need an answer—he *knows*—but I give it to him anyway.

"Always."

"Hold still," he says, and I couldn't move if I wanted to, still wrung out and high on the pleasure they've already given me. That they're *still* giving me. But then I realize he's talking to Dylan.

"Kiss me," Dylan says, and Jack nips my shoulder as he dips low, claiming Dylan's mouth, too.

I'm pinned between them, and the urgent throbbing of Jack's cock against my folds—spread wide around Dylan's cock—feels like the beat of my own heart. These two *are* my heart.

Dylan goes still underneath me, holding me tightly, and Jack's hand slips between our bodies, stroking over my slick core, thumb teasing my clit, alternating between using his hand and his cock to press against me.

"Oh, fuck, Jack," Dylan groans. "You really... *God*... don't want me to... move? You're stroking me right through her."

Jack gives a throaty laugh that tells us both how much he enjoys driving us crazy, and then makes a slight shift in position that earns a desperate hiss from Dylan. I can feel the fat head of Jack's cock pressing into me, and I gasp, realizing what he intends.

Yes.

*Yes.*

Dylan groans, and the thought of what it must feel like to *him* —Jack's cock sliding against his—is so hot that it distracts me from the deep stretch as Jack pushes inside me, inch by inch, filling me in a way I'd never imagined.

I moan, and I can feel Dylan's strong body trembling underneath me as Jack's cock joins him inside me, stroking against his. I start to pant as my body surrenders, stretching to accommodate the impossible width of both of them at once, and it's such an overwhelming sensation that it blocks out everything else.

I don't even realize the words... sounds... need swirling around my head have tumbled out of my mouth until my men answer me.

"*Yes*, beautiful."

"Anything. *Always*."

My litany of *please... please... need you... love you...* both *of you...* is punctuated by ragged breaths from all three of us, soft moans, deep, shuddering sounds of satisfaction and need ramping up as Dylan holds my trembling body tightly between the two of them... as he throbs inside me, every muscle taut underneath me as he holds himself still and lets Jack fuck me... Jack's cock, thrusting in and out, slow and steady and pushing me toward a kind of orgasm I didn't know existed.

"So good... *fuck*... so, so good."

It's Dylan's voice, and I moan, because *yes*. I've never felt anything like it. Didn't know I could feel this full. The coil of pleasure tightening inside of me with every smooth, slow thrust is deeper than I've ever felt, all-consuming, overwhelming in the best possible way.

"Jesus, Wildcat," Jack says, his gorgeous face taut with pleasure. "So *tight*."

I imagine his cock sliding against Dylan's, every stroke stimulating that thick length I know so well, every thrust putting a deep, vibrating pressure against my G-spot. Jack's hard body rubs against my clit every time he moves and Dylan's mouth finds all the most sensitive spots on my neck.

They're making me crazy.

They're *amazing*.

They're going to wreck me.

The three of us ramp up, closer and closer, and I'm beyond thinking. I'm *begging*. Almost sobbing. Raw need tumbles out of my lips, and I can no more control my words than I could stop the glorious, erotic tide of pressure that's building in me... that's about to *burst.*

"Please, please, *more, God...*"

Their hot breath washes over me... strong hands hold me... the slick, sexy sound of our bodies moving together fills me... and I'm whimpering.

Pleading.

*I'm consumed.*

Jack groans. Or maybe it's Dylan. "Oh, *Christ...* oh... fucking *God...* can't hold out much longer..."

"Fucking amazing... fuck... *fuck.*" Their deep voices vibrate through me. *"Yes.* Oh *fuck* yes, so... damn... *good...*"

And then Jack's rhythm speeds up. His hips slap against mine and Dylan groans as Jack's cock thrusts deep.

I can't... I can't... I can't hold on.

"Oh, God... please... *please...*" I sob. "I'm going to sh-sh-*shatter.*"

And then I do.

I knew it was coming, but it's so overwhelming that it still catches me unaware, my body coming apart into a million perfect pieces with no warning.

A long, wailing cry escapes my throat, and the birds in the bird bath go silent.

I don't care.

*Can't.*

The rolling waves of my orgasm pour through me, blotting out everything else. I'm shaking. *Shuddering.* I'm pure bliss.

It's endless.

It's *everything.*

My body clenches tight around my men's cocks, and I'm so full with the two of them that every wave rocking through me spikes my climax even higher. It's a never-ending loop that has me trembling... panting... totally lost to everything but *this.*

And then Dylan cries out sharply, the sound almost drowned

out by Jack's hoarse shout. A hot rush of liquid heat fills me as they come together, filling me with everything they've got, until I'm overflowing.

And it's perfect.

It's exactly what they've done to my heart. I'm *theirs*, body, mind, and soul.

And Jack and Dylan... these two beautiful, amazing, *incredible* men... they're *mine*.

## 29

## JACK

"I really appreciate you both sitting down for this tonight," I say, nervous as Cate and Dylan join me at the dining room table.

"No worries, babe," Dylan says. "But I haven't prepped dinner yet, sorry, I didn't expect my shift to run so late."

"Oh, no," Cate jokes. "You mean the perfect chef didn't make us another perfect dinner, one night out of... *months* now?"

"What can I say," Dylan says, smiling at Cate. "I'm a sucker for the faces you two make when you eat my food."

I don't know about me, but he's right when it comes to Cate. Christ, half the time just watching her enjoy Dylan's food makes me hard. But right now, even that thought can't distract me.

I hope I'm hiding it well, but inside, I'm terrified.

It's July 31st, one day before our decision on the townhouse is due. Once we all agreed to go in equally on the house, the two of them put their faith in me to handle the legalese. I've been digging through that contract every single day for the last two weeks, ever since Gary dropped his bomb about the transfer requirements on me. I've been trying to figure out some sort of solution to the stipulation that it can only transfer to a single owner, and—thank fuck—I think I finally have one.

It was so simple that I'm just amazed that I didn't think of it sooner, although I'm still not a hundred percent they'll see it the way I do. Cate's right, though, I put myself through so much damn stress that it's easy to miss the small things. Gotta work on that still. That said, I still haven't told them about my conversation with Gary.

That's a big one, a huge lie of omission.

I could get off on a technicality, but what if the way I handled it—kept it from them for a bit—hurts them? They've both said they love me, together and separately, a whole bunch of times now, and I've said it back to both of them just the same. I know we all mean it, but there's no denying that this is still a new thing for all of us.

What if my lie—my *delay*, let's say—breaks us apart? Will that just prove that I didn't deserve this all along?

Christ, I'm spinning myself up so much. I swear, if I can just get through this, I'll never lie about anything again to either of them, so help me. I can't lose them now.

I *can't*.

They're both looking at me, and the teasing light has faded from their eyes, telling me they see right through me... as always.

"What is it, Jack?" Cate finally asks, looking downright concerned.

Do they even know how much they mean to me? I try to say it. Try to show it. But it's so big... I don't know if they can possibly understand that they're everything to me.

"Let us in on that secret," Dylan says, his tone calm and reassuring even though I can see the same concern in his eyes, too. His lips quirk up a bit, and he adds a teasing, "I promise it'll be okay."

Here goes nothing.

"Alright, so," I start briskly, pressing my palms against the table and going for a confidence I don't feel. "Got an update on the house for you."

They both look excited. I really hope I don't burn it out of them. I mean, my solution is pretty fucking perfect, if you ask me, but it's also sort of... a commitment. One I'm not sure they'd want to make, given that it's only been, what, three months? Insane. 'Course, we've all known each other half our lives, but crazy to think that all of this—*us*—has only been brewing since Cate came back to Boston in the spring.

I don't want it to end... did I come up with this answer just to try to tie them to me? Will they want it?

"Stop overthinking," Dylan says, reaching over to squeeze my hand. "Spill, Jack."

Right. Okay. I've got this.

"So, I spoke to Gary a couple weeks back," I start, swallowing past the lump in my throat. "And, uh, I let him know that we all decided to go in on the house in equal shares, joint tenancy. You know, like we talked about."

"Right," Cate says, the upward lilt she gives the word prompting me to continue.

"So, yeah. Uh, the thing is... there was a problem with that." The flash of apprehension that goes across both their faces just about kills me, but I rush on before they can interrupt. "The terms of the will state that only one entity can own the property. Gary's prohibited from transferring the title any other way, so joint tenancy is not an option for us. Given those parameters, we've got to decide how we want to handle this by tomorrow, or else the deed will be transferred back to the estate. And if we let that happen, well, Gary's gonna have no choice but to follow through with Sully's directive and put the house up for sale."

"*What?*" Cate looks horrified. "When were you going to tell us this, Jack?"

Oh, I've fucked it up now, haven't I? A heavy weight settles on my chest, and it's only when Dylan squeezes my hand again—

didn't realize he was still holding it, but glad he hasn't dropped me yet—that I start breathing again.

He reaches across the table and grabs Cate's hand, too.

"Hey, it's okay," he says to her, even though I can see the worry in his eyes, too. "Let's hear the rest of this, okay? Jack, please go on. We have to have alternatives, right?"

I nod, exhaling. "I've been digging into this for the past two weeks on my own, trying to find a solution. Didn't want to worry you guys, and figured there had to be something, right?" Isn't that what we attorneys did? Found ways to make the shit we wanted work? "I think... I think I finally found one."

"Well, what is it?" Cate presses me, leaning forward eagerly. "I can't lose this house, Jack. *We* can't. It's ours now. If we have to put it under one name, I don't care. I just want this, and I just want both of you."

"I agree," Dylan chimes in. "I know it's not what we talked about, but if we need to put just one of us on the title, we might as well just draw straws and get it done with. I know it's scary, but we'll learn how to adapt to it, just like we've been learning this relationship along the way."

"Well, I think we can avoid doing that," I say, suddenly feeling emboldened, feeling full and warm inside from their commitment to me, to *us*. I can do this. I can fix this. "That's why," I start, pulling a manila folder out of my briefcase and throwing it on the table, "I'm proposing this."

Cate reaches for it first, opening it up. Inside is a small pile of documentation, a good solid day's worth of write-up on my end. *"Transfer of Title from the Estate of Hendricks Sullivan, Esquire..."* Cate reads aloud. *"To the Smith Family Trust."*

Dylan looks confused. "So, we're putting it under my name?"

"Not exactly," I say, pulling out another folder, setting it in front of Cate. "This is paperwork that would allow Cate and me to legally change our last names. If it's alright by you..." I pause, feeling my face flush. Christ, I'm blushing like a schoolboy, but I mean, I'm kinda asking him—them—to, well, let's just say it's probably the closest the three of us will get to a *proposal*. I clear my throat, powering on. "We could both become Smiths as well. You know, all of us. If you... if you'll have us, Dylan. Cate, if *you* want—"

"*Yes*," she cuts me off, her whole face lighting up like the sun. "Oh my God, yes. *Please*. Can I just kill the MacMillan name forever?"

Believe me, I can relate to *that* feeling. I've carried the Kelly name for my whole life, and all it meant is that I just keep getting shit on for it, over and over. I'm the first one to make a name for myself out of all my family, and they just don't deserve it. This name doesn't deserve it. It hangs around my neck every day like a lead weight, and I'm just so tired of it. I know Cate being a MacMillan is kind of different—from the outside, probably looks worlds different—but now that I really know her? I can see that it's also the same.

*Exactly* the same.

"Yeah, Duchess," I say, "No more MacMillans under this roof."

She snort-laughs, and I'm grinning so hard it hurts, relief almost making me feel drunk.

"We do this," I go on, "And I'd be Jack Smith, you'd be Cate Smith, and, well..." I look at Dylan. "We can't legally marry into a triad, obviously, but that's where the trust comes in. Making the Smith Family Trust would tie us all together, equally, as partners, and we'd put the home in the name of the trust."

"Ours," Cate says, and she's fucking glowing.

"You know names have never meant as much to me as they do to your families," Dylan says, grinning from ear to ear. "But will I have you? You two are already mine. Sharing my name with you..."

He gets choked up, and that has *me* blinking hard. I fucking love this man. And Cate, *God*, Cate, too. I love her like I didn't know I could. Both of them. *Forever*.

And they *want* this. I'm on cloud fucking nine. They ain't just humoring me; I can see it. Hear it in their voices. *Feel* it. They really want it, too. The three of us, we're a forever thing, and never having rings—I mean, not unless the laws change a hell of a lot more than I expect them to in our lifetimes—that don't mean shit.

They're mine, and I'm theirs. And from now on?

We'll be the Smiths. The Smith Family.

# EPILOGUE

## DYLAN—ONE YEAR LATER

*I*'ve got the breakfast tray loaded up with eggs, bacon, toast—the staples—plus a carafe of orange juice and three glasses. I carefully make my way up the stairs, not spilling a drop, and I can't help the surge of satisfaction I get every time I walk through this house—this *home* we've made. It's everything we all wanted it to be; a memorial to Sully, the one who brought all of us together in the first place, but also uniquely our own, a new style, something that belongs to the three of us and no one else.

I push the bedroom door open with my hip, and a warmth fills my chest at the sight that greets me. It's early yet, and Cate and Jack are still in the early stages of being awake, still in a light doze, spooning with each other. It's adorable. I know it sounds like it belongs on a cereal box or a cat poster or something, but I really am truly blessed to have these two wonderful people in my life.

"Mmm," Cate moans, the first to stir. "Dylan? Is that you being perfect again?"

"Depends on if you want breakfast in bed or not," I toss back, winking at her.

She's gorgeous.

Jack stretches and grumbles, then scratches his chest, and my cock twitches at the sight of them, rumpled and warm and so damn inviting I'd consider skipping breakfast if I didn't know how much they both enjoyed me pampering them.

How much I enjoy it, too.

"You're gonna spoil us completely rotten," Jack says, giving me a lazy, loving smile.

"Been doing it for a year already, right?" I ask. "The two of you are already ruined. Besides, I'm guessing I'm the only one who remembers what today is."

"Oh, *shit*," Cate says, bolting upright in the bed. "*Brownstone Living*? Is that *today*?"

I laugh, can't help it. It means so much to her, and Jack and I are so proud of her. *Brownstone Living* is a home and garden magazine that's coming to do a professional photo shoot of the house and to interview Cate about her design choices. Not today, though, something that seems to click in her brain as that rush of adrenaline wears off.

"Cate Smith, *the* chic interior decorator of this season," Jack intones, going for an upper-crust accent and cracking us up. It's what they've been calling her, though, and it all started with this doctor she met in her kickboxing class and did some design work for last year. Turns out, he holds some kind of big annual soiree, and all sorts of power players just *had* to know who handled the remodel. Now she's writing her own ticket on her own name, and MacMillan Design is old news, so four seasons ago, as Cate might say.

Cate picks up a pillow like she's going to hit Jack with it, but then remembers the tray I'm still holding and seems to think better of it.

None of us want food spilled in the bed... at least, not by *accident*.

"Right, next week," she says, putting the pillow back down and fluffing it innocently, like she wasn't going to go after Jack for his incessant teasing.

It's so good to see her carefree. She works her own schedule now and keeps it light; money isn't a problem for her anymore, not with her choice of design clients, so why stress? She still makes time to teach her kickboxing class at the gym, and she's even roped the two of us into attending now and then.

No joke: our Wildcat is a bit of a badass.

"So what's today, then?" Jack asks, scooting back against the headboard and eyeing the bacon eagerly. He's just come off a big case, and now that he's a partner at his law firm—the youngest one in the firm's history, thank you very much—they work him too hard, in my opinion. He loves it, though, and even if his suits may have gotten more expensive, he's still the same old Jack that I know and love. Still rough around the edges, still dropping his streetwise wisdom wherever he can.

He frowns. "I told Marcus to keep me—"

Jack's mouth snaps closed as his face goes red, and I grin, seeing that he remembers. He actually got himself a driver a while ago, some townie kid named Marcus, who also doubles as Jack's memory and errand boy at times. Jack told me Marcus was the driver who took him to his old condo, back when it went up in smoke. Seems like Jack is turning more and more into Sully as time goes on, and it's been a beautiful sight to behold.

"Can't blame this one on Marcus," I say, winking. I don't care that it slipped their minds; that's kind of my place in the family, as I think of it. Holding us together with traditions, important dates, all the little things that weave through our daily lives and bind us tight.

And family... well, Cate's mother still isn't part of our lives, and good riddance, and with Jack's newfound level of wealth, he ended up setting up a trust for his former family—the Kellys—on the condition that they never contact him again. Far as I know, it's been months without a peep, and he looks like there's less weight on his shoulders than there ever has been before. He no longer has to carry around the burden of a name he didn't choose or want, just like Cate, and he still gets to feel like he's taking care of them.

I'll never quite understand it on the same level that the two of them do, but I'm just glad they're happy. The three of us—the Smith family—really seem to be enough for them. My own mother doesn't fully understand our triad, but that doesn't stop her from loving the both of them and accepting that we're happy. Which, in the end, is all that matters, right?

"Are you two going to keep me in suspense?" Cate asks, scooting over so she can tug me down on the bed and steal a piece of bacon. Then her eyes go wide. "Oh! Did *Boston Magazine* publish that review on you, Dylan?"

I shake my head, grinning. I'm not even entirely sure that the picky customer who was in my restaurant last week *was* a reviewer, but Cate and Jack are convinced she must have been. And yeah, that's right. *My* restaurant. After graduating, I paid my dues as quickly as I could. The kitchen can be a nightmare, but after everything that happened last year, it was a cakewalk by comparison. I got through it with no problem, no burnouts, not so much as a single bad egg.

After a while, I was getting noticed, and after a little bit more, I was getting my dishes featured on the menu. The head chef, my boss, knew I was ready for more, so she arranged a meeting between me and a good friend of hers in the restaurant business. That was a few months ago, and now I'm the head chef at one of the hottest restaurants down by the pier. It's a lot of work, and it's a little different than I expected it to be, but nothing makes me happier. It's what I was meant to do with my life, and I'll hold onto it forever.

Kind of like I plan on holding on to these two.

"Let's just say I'm not *just* trying to spoil you with breakfast in bed," I say, arranging the tray between us all. "But I wanted to make sure we started our anniversary off right."

"Oh my God," Cate says, closing her eyes and shaking her head. "How did I forget?"

"Yeah, sorry," Jake says, looking sheepish. "I'm so damn scatter-brained with dates as it is. Gotta get better at that."

"Don't sweat it, you two," I say, laughing. "I'm happy to be the master and commander of our family datebook. I'm the only one who gets up early enough to cook breakfast for us, anyway."

Jack's not a morning person by nature, although he does what he has to do on work days. Cate used to be pretty perky in the mornings, but lately? She's seemed to have a little less energy. Even caught her napping during the afternoon a time or two. It would have worried me if she didn't look so good. Not just her usual gorgeous, but positively glowing.

"Anyone told you how fucking beautiful you look lately, Duchess?" Jack says to her, as if he's suddenly taken up reading my mind.

She flushes, then grins at both of us with a light in her eyes that's something special.

Something different.

"Actually, I think there's a reason for that," she says, biting her lip as her whole body practically vibrates with excitement. "I wanted to be sure... and find a fun way to tell you... but maybe we'll call it my anniversary present?"

"Oh, we're supposed to do presents now, are we?" Jack teases, but I can tell she's got his attention.

Mine, too.

Not just my attention... as I look at her shining face, take in the sweetness of how Jack's gently stroking the back of her hand, feel my own heart swell with the depths of my love for these two... Cate's got my hopes up, too.

Does she mean—

"Boys, I'm pregnant," she says, sending a shot of joy straight to my heart. "You're going to be daddies."

"Holy shit," Jack says, breathing out the words and looking stunned.

I can't say anything for a second. We've never talked about it, but we've also been *extremely* sexually active. I start to laugh, just too filled with happiness to keep it in. "Oh, Cate," I say, pulling her to me and covering her stomach with a hand as I kiss her. *"Yes."*

"I'm going to get fat as a house," Cate says, but I can tell she's thrilled by the idea.

"Fuck, *yeah*, you are," Jack says, his shock wearing off as a cheek-splitting grin takes over. "And you're gonna be the hottest mom in the damn universe."

"If we're lucky, our baby will have your creativity, and your courage, and your strength," I say to Cate, and the picture of a miniature version of her running around the townhouse makes my heart swell so big I'm amazed it doesn't burst right out of my chest.

"Hopefully, he or she will get Jack's brains," Cate says, squeezing his hand and sending him a loving look before turning to me. "And your—"

"And Dylan's heart," Jack cuts in, eyes twinkling. "Ain't nothing better than that. But there's no *if*, Dylan."

"What?" I'm not sure what he means.

"You said *if we're lucky*," Jack says, his eyes looking suspiciously bright. "But you've gotta know..."

He stops for a second, and I can see his throat working like he's choked up.

"We're the luckiest people alive," Cate finishes for Jack, leaning against his chest and holding her arm out for me.

"Yeah," he says, his voice raw with emotion. "That we are, Wildcat. That we are."

I move the breakfast tray and wrap them both up in my arms, my heart overflowing. It's true, we really are, and it hits me that

Cate didn't mention a paternity test. Neither Jack nor I thought to bring it up, either. The baby is *ours*, and I think we all know it.

It will be the Smith baby. Loved. Wanted.

*Ours.*

Just like this love.

# ALSO BY CHLOE LYNN ELLIS

His: MMF Bisexual Holiday Romance

# ABOUT THE AUTHOR

Once upon a time, there were two authors who loved writing steamy love stories. Between them, they had published a fair number of books (*more than eighty, less than a hundred... but really, who's counting?*) in a variety of genres (*M/M contemporary romance, M/F paranormal romance, mpreg, and lots of hot and dirty erotica with all the "M" and "F" combinations a reader could wish for*) but, sadly, neither author felt that their writing accomplishments were complete.

Then, one day, fate smiled on these two.

They found each other, became fast friends, and eventually decided that trying their hand at MMF romance was an adventure best done balls out, feet first, and most of all... together.

And thus, the writing team that is Chloe Lynn Ellis was born.

Manufactured by Amazon.ca
Bolton, ON